THE CAPED COUNTESS

CLOAKS AND COUNTESSES BOOK ONE

JUDITH LYNNE

JUDITH LYNNE

BOOKS BY JUDITH LYNNE

<u>Lords and Undefeated Ladies</u>

Not Like a Lady

The Countess Invention

What a Duchess Does

Crown of Hearts

He Stole the Lady

No Titled Lady

<u>Maids Done Waiting</u>

The Lord Trap

The Lady Escape (Forthcoming)

<u>Cloaks and Countesses</u>

The Caped Countess

The Clandestine Countess

The Castaway Countess (Forthcoming)

<u>Ladies' Own Bakery</u>

The Regency romance comedy serial

DISCLAIMER AND GENTLE WARNINGS

This is a work of fiction and as such its characters, events, words, and places are the product of the author's imagination. (Even though the names of the Secretary of the Treasury and the Swedish ambassador of the time have been borrowed.)

It includes completely successful cross-dressing by our straight cisgendered heroine that tries to respect the history of transgendered and cross-dressing people in the Napoleonic wars; some violence; and the death of secondary characters (our heroine's mother, in brief flashbacks), or characters who completely deserve it. Readers of my books can rest assured that I am here to provide you with happy-ever-afters. So relax. This is probably the point at which we should start trusting each other.

PREFACE

My dear readers,

In the spring of 1813, gas lamps are just beginning to appear on London's streets. Better homes still provide an oil lamp in front, as they have done for decades. But most places remain dark, and often dangerous as well.

The wars and the collapse of textile industry in the north mean that people come to London from all over; and many fall victim to ruthless predators determined to make money.

The timber import questions that were a passing topic in *What a Duchess Does* turn deadly when someone decides to break all the rules.

Lady Donnatella thinks she is ready.

That will be for you to judge.

Your obedient servant,
Judith Lynne

CHAPTER ONE

*D*resses are a topic that can always disguise whatever is on a lady's mind that she does not wish to discuss. For instance, knife scars.

Dresses leaped to mind at Lady Julia's innocent question.

"Tella, whatever will you wear to Lord and Lady Tewksbury's crush tomorrow? The season is nearly over and I am exhausted. But you seem to have a never-ending supply of inventive ideas!"

Lady Donnatella, Tella to her friends, shook her head. "Not at all, not at all. It is my dressmaker who invents all these new combinations."

Lady Julia fanned herself in the warmth of a ballroom packed with people. "I must attend your dressmaker. Mine has given me no luck at all."

In Lady Julia's case, luck was a very specific word. This was her second season and she had not yet found a suitable husband. Her gown was a carefully calculated pale pink sateen, intended to make her look young and virginal, but with a sufficiently shallow neckline to make her look well-endowed. Which she was.

In Tella's case, luck meant something entirely different. This was her fourth season, and she had debuted younger than Julia. She had not yet found a suitable husband because she had no intention of finding a suitable husband. Her gown was exactly as she intended: a becoming shade of pale green, decorated with rosettes made of ribbons. Its rather clever angular neckline made the most of her assets there, which were considerably less generous than her friend's.

It also covered the knife scar that disappeared under her right arm.

It wouldn't do for her to look unattractive; on the contrary, it benefited Tella's plans to look as attractive as possible. She just didn't want to look particularly marriageable.

There was a young man approaching, no doubt to ask her to dance. She favored him with a smile.

He looked surprised. New to London, then. Not yet aware of her reputation as a flighty, flirty party ornament.

Well, she would acquaint him.

"I'm so glad you've come for the waltz! It's so wicked, I just know I shall be safe in your arms as we dance," she said, taking care to look down before fluttering her lashes at him.

She was, as in nearly every dance in every ballroom she had ever visited, three inches taller than the young man, at the very least. She wore flat slippers; it didn't help. Thus the coy glances and fluttering eyelashes.

It took some effort for Tella to appear helpless. She went to that effort.

As he slipped her hand into the crook of his arm to lead her on to the dance floor, she appealed to Julia, reclining on the chaise. "You aren't going to miss the entire dance, are you?"

"It is two in the morning and I am melting in this room.

Yes, I daresay I may miss it. Never you mind, dear, just run along and dance!"

As the dance began, Tella giggled into the collar of the young gentleman who held her in his arms. She'd already forgotten his name; it didn't matter, and it was easier to pretend to be silly if she didn't even try.

Throughout the dance the gentleman attempted to engage her in conversation on horses (she didn't ride), politics (she didn't care), and cards (she wasn't interested). Her carefully dull responses were designed to kill conversation and make her less appealing, and they did.

In truth, as the Duke of Gravenshire's daughter, Tella was not only fiercely interested in politics, she was better informed than many members of Parliament. She was also quite a good horsewoman, though she seldom left London for the countryside. And in fact, she was such a viciously successful card player that she made a point of losing more than winning these days just to avoid making enemies. It would not do for the Duke of Gravenshire's daughter to make enemies.

To all and sundry, the Duke of Gravenshire's daughter did not have enemies. She was lively and gossipy and pretty enough to dance with but too tall to marry.

In truth, this party was in a fair way to kill Tella with boredom.

Attending such parties and behaving exactly the Duke's daughter ought to behave was a strategy she had entered into years ago, however, and she had no intention of quitting now.

She did like dancing. But now this dance was over.

"Oh, look, whist! Are you a good player?" she said, looking through her eyelashes at Lord Dancing Whatever-hisnamewas.

"Rather," he said with a charming lack of modesty that

made Tella like him a bit better. She almost felt bad for leading him over to partner with Lady Winpole.

Not because he would become absorbed in the game and forget she was there—that was fine—but because Lady Winpole might not like it. And Lady Winpole owed Tella forty pounds.

Lady Winpole was fifty-five if she was a day, and therefore quite as invisible to society as Tella struggled to be. But she was also such a fine whist player that she would undoubtedly win the pot if this dancing fellow was as good a player as he claimed.

She did tend to win, her losses to Tella notwithstanding.

Perhaps gifting her with a good whist partner would remind her that ladies of the *ton* paid their gambling debts.

Or perhaps not. Tella didn't really care.

In truth, she needed to get home so she could get on with her real evening.

With a murmured farewell to the dancing lord—he didn't even look up—Tella crossed the room to find her melting friend Julia and suggest that they leave.

"Thank goodness that when you do get tired, you get completely tired," Julia said as Tella helped her limp out toward the carriage. "Thank you. These slippers have turned evil on me."

"Julia, don't slouch," said her mother, Lady Shoreton.

Lady Shoreton's idea of mothering was to criticize. The young ladies would have found it more tiresome if either had the least inclination to listen. Usually once she finished criticizing, Lady Shoreton could be relied upon for solid advice about accessories and intoxicating drinks and potential husbands. The fact that neither young lady had married was no reflection on Lady Shoreton.

The older woman also had an admirable amount of stamina, since she didn't look half as tired as Julia.

Nonetheless, as Lady Shoreton settled herself and her skirts in the carriage, the worthy lady let out a quiet sigh that made Tella feel a little guilty.

She was keeping her friends out to seem as she wished to seem: someone who loved parties but went home before the end, someone who followed the rules about chaperonage but had generous friends, and someone who was still looking for a husband.

Tella would do a great deal more, to keep up necessary appearances. But she did feel the guilt.

She distracted herself from the guilt by thinking over her equipment for this evening.

Julia and her mother ignored Tella's distracted look, assuming she was contemplating the possibilities of the new young man who had been brave enough to ask her to dance.

She was not.

* * *

THAT USEFUL DISTRACTED look stayed on her face all the way into her father's opulent townhouse, through the nod she gave the butler as he closed the front door after her, and up the richly carpeted hall.

"Are you still awake?" her uncle's voice called from the library.

She pushed open the door. Lord Preston was reclining in a broad, comfortable chair, a cut-glass tumbler of brandy at his side and a book open upon his knee.

Tella tip-toed over to settle herself on a footstool at his feet.

"Why are you awake, my favorite uncle?"

"I'm your only uncle."

"Still my favorite. Can you not sleep?"

"I am old, my dear. Sleep is for the wicked at my age."

"Then you ought to be able to sleep!"

His mock glare looked fierce. Tella ignored it. Albert Montague, Earl of Preston and Viscount Dunwick, loved her to distraction and she knew it. She had known it all her life, even before she had lost her mother at the age of eight.

Lord Preston had not tried to take the place of her beloved mother, but he had very much raised Tella, and she adored him for it. He was her great-uncle, in fact, her mother's uncle, and he would be living comfortably in the country if he weren't so determined to keep her company.

And to keep an eye on her.

"How can I sleep knowing that you'll be going out again tonight?" It was a statement, not a question.

"My lord! That happens nearly every night."

"You are what keeps me awake every night. Because you are an ill-behaved, ill-mannered girl."

Tella just smiled at him, a sparkling, wide, genuine smile. Almost no one got to see that smile but her Uncle Albert.

"I should not be letting you go out alone."

This was a familiar tune and a familiar dance. Tella was in a hurry tonight; she skipped to the end. "I know, you do not approve. But you are no longer young and your stiff legs would not admit you to keeping up with me. I am very careful and capable, and if you like I will look in on you before I retire. There, have we not fulfilled all the niceties of our usual back and forth?"

He scowled. "You will be getting no Christmas gift from me this year."

Tella stood and kissed his dry cheek. "You will be getting extra gifts from me, darling."

"Tella, truly." He caught her hand. "You ought not do this alone. You need not."

"As I keep telling you, sir, taking anyone with me would only slow me down."

"I've never slowed you down," he said with a fake scowl.

No, but in this, he would. "You are in a class by yourself. As you taught me yourself."

"True."

She didn't stay; he would only continue to spout objections. She knew he meant what he said. After all this time, she thought that he might have become used to her habits. He'd taught her nearly everything she knew, after all.

But he still worried.

He *was* darling, thought Tella as she ran up to her room, just as she ought to do, in case any servants saw her.

There was no danger of her father seeing her. His Grace kept rigorous hours at the Parliament house during the day as well as evenings, when it was in session, and slept the sleep of a man whose hours were full.

His apartment was also a floor below hers, and Tella had made sure, long ago, that it was not in a location where he could hear her steps crossing the floor.

Or moving down the wall.

Because in her room, Tella was able to slide her armoire away from the wall on rollers she had attached herself, opening the secret panel behind it.

Then she fit herself into the tiny winding staircase that led from her room down to the basement.

She'd discovered the passage as a child, and kept it a secret for years until she was old enough to decide what to do with it.

Which had been five years ago now.

It was almost five years since she had told the servants that they no longer needed the root cellar. Set it up as a closet in the basement with the things she needed for her after-midnight jaunts. Worked on the door so that it locked from the inside, although it appeared normal.

Since she had lined the wall with the curious appurtenances that she had fashioned, and acquired.

Lady Donnatella literally took a fashion plunge as she arrived in her basement closet. It was dark, and smelled of leather and wintergreen.

She no longer needed a lamp. She knew where everything was by touch. She would not emerge until she was ready.

Her fabulous draper not only created ensembles that were fresh in design and color, she also created ensembles that Tella could remove herself. And the clothes she put on next were even easier to manage.

When she let herself out through a basement door that looked from the street like an extra-large coal hod, she looked nothing like Lady Donnatella. In fact, she looked nothing like a lady.

The tricorn hat covered her hair, which was not only braided securely to her head but covered with a tightly wound dark linen scarf. A snug dark waistcoat, and her chest no longer looked feminine at all. And she wore the same fashionable black coat and fawn trousers worn by every other young gentleman in London.

Her gloves were sturdy riding gloves, unusual to see on a gentleman in the evening, as few rode horses in the city streets. But they were absolutely necessary, as their thicker leather not only provided protection in itself, it hid thin metal finger guards she had fashioned from steel boning picked out of her corsets. Their metal bars crossed her knuckles, and more importantly, her palms.

Most ruffians of the nighttime in London threatened with knives, and Lady Donnatella had learned quite a bit about defending herself from knives. The scar that slid under her arm was not her only one. And she had no intention of adding to her collection.

It was her deep blue cape that was the masterpiece of her

costume, for it held many small details that she had amassed over time either through painful trial and error, or through the skill of her own invention.

She could feel rather than hear the slight jingle of the chain encased in the cloak's hem as she walked; this bit of secret weaponry had many fascinating uses.

She'd muffled the sound by edging the thing with sable fur. Because she quite liked sable.

Tella cut a quick path through the small park of the square, putting distance between herself and her home as fast as she could, and then wound her way to her first perch of the evening, as she liked to think of it.

These quiet spots let her see into the streets, because that was the only way she could find where cutpurses, kidnappers, and panderers threatened the lives of London's unsuspecting citizens. She attended her spots, not in any particular order lest she be followed, but regularly.

London's unsuspecting citizens could be foolish, or new, or desperate, or criminal themselves; yet Tella was unshakably determined that they should be able to walk London's streets at night.

Truly, Tella thought as she slipped along alleyways, they were almost never unsuspecting. Londoners as a rule were not frail and they were not naive. But there were a lot of them, as people poured into London from all over, crowds of them, on some nights; and hapless nightwatchmen were few and far between.

Tella despised the night watch. Few watchmen would scrap with a cutpurse, and most turned a blind eye to anything if given a coin. They were more frequent in her little square mile of London than in many places, as it was full of Britain's titled families. They harassed people on the street after curfew... and that was about all. Tella did not subscribe to her father's plans for the city to fund more of them.

Still, she almost never left them tied up at the bottom of dark stairways.

And here was one now.

"Curfew, mister, stand to," said the night watchman, expecting Tella to stop and give an accounting of herself and why she was on the street at this hour—why *he* was on the street at this hour, in fact, as Tella knew that, to the watchman's eyes, she was a wayward young lord.

CHAPTER TWO

*T*ella had long practiced dressing and walking like an assertive young man, and she had learned to thrust forward her jaw when questioned. She looked no different from many of London's other young men. And few questioned her as long as she was loud and arrogant.

"Push off, there's a lad," she said, making her voice as low as she could and copying the speech of rude, rich men.

"You know t' rules, you know ye'll be up before the judge," said the night watch man carelessly. "I'll need yer name, young sir."

"Lord Morton, and I've no time for your tricks, man."

"Ain't no trick to keep to the law, m'lud, not as I do it, so hold up and let me find out a bit more about yer errand."

Inwardly, Tella sighed. One of the rarer ones who wouldn't be easily intimidated by an entitled attitude and an expensive cravat.

She felt in the pocket of her coat.

"Good man, keep up the work then," she said briefly, and dropped the guinea coin carelessly at his feet.

She'd learned that if she handed it to the man, she wound up engaged in some sort of discussion. If she dropped it at his feet, it was some sort of unspoken agreement: she pretended not to notice her lost coin, and he pretended not to notice his found bribe.

These types of watchmen were simply doing what they were told to do. If they flooded the court with rich young men who were out and about when they weren't supposed to be, they'd catch all types of hellfire from the judge himself.

Since their job wasn't to stop the rich and powerful from pursuing their nightlife, but to make sure drinking and brawling didn't get out of hand, they accepted this blind hole in the charge they were to execute with philosophical acceptance.

It was only a bonus for them when it came with a pecuniary reward.

As expected, the man picked up the coin quite quickly despite his gut. She continued on her way, and the fellow continued on his, for all the world as if the lordling he had just encountered were no more than a bubble of memory burst upon the evening breeze.

Tella restrained herself from rolling her eyes. The night watch was the least of her problems.

Not that she minded problems; at least they were interesting. Like London. She loved being out in London's night air, loved the cold damp of it, the smells of coal fires and candle wax. The stealthy miasmas that floated off the Thames, and from the squalid parts of the city itself, felt familiar. She loved the sound of her boots on the cobblestones and the raucous voices of people carrying on in inns and bawdy houses, and even the workhouses that she passed late at night.

Ballrooms and ball gowns were her keys to the outside, and much more interesting, world.

In the Duke of Gravenshire's circle, no one ever really looked at Tella and saw her. Nor would they have seen her alter ego. They seldom saw anything that they didn't wish to see.

On the streets, no one saw Tella either, but she did not mean for them to see her. They barely noticed the lordling she appeared to be. And of course, they did not see the Duke of Gravenshire's daughter.

Out here, life *felt* real. She'd take dead fish heads in the street any day over insincere compliments, and late at night, London's streets overflowed with reality.

The sellers, the swindlers, the streetwalkers, even the night watchmen, they all were living their lives as best they could far more openly than any members of the *ton*.

She felt real. She felt she could *do* something, not just wait for another disaster to befall another young mother, another child.

It had been several days since Tella had been able to make the rounds of her favorite spots.

As the night fog crept in, smudged with the dirt of London's candlelight and coal fires, Tella sorted familiar faces from new ones.

Sure enough, there they were, on the corner of the street with the druggists' shops. A young new cutpurse, accosting a family that was stupid enough to be taken unawares.

Tella tried not to think of them as stupid, she really did. It was uncharitable, and she had absorbed enough of lectures somewhere along the way to know that it was wrong to be uncharitable.

But they irritated her nonetheless, these country mice who didn't even know they weren't to be on the streets at this hour, or were perhaps simply so turned around that they didn't know what end was up.

Not as much as she was irritated by cutpurses.

This was an older lad with what had to be his mother, and a younger boy, too, clinging to her skirts. They were just visible in the smoke and fog of the street, all three of them clearly as shocked as they were frightened by the low, growled threats of the thief.

That made Tella walk quicker.

Children and mothers worried her most of all.

"What's all this then?" she said with the brusqueness she was careful to use on these occasions. Many a thief would flee at the mere appearance of someone who looked like a gentleman.

This one didn't. "Move along," he half-gargled, clearly having drunk more than his share of whatever grog was served nearby, and having lost what might have existed of his mind thereby.

"Move along yourself, you arse." Insults moved miscreants when authority didn't cow them.

Again, not this one. He must have a very high opinion of himself, or a very high proportion of alcohol in his body.

Tella suspected it was a bit of both when she caught the glint of the knife in his hand.

Like cards, this game was a game of percentages. Most roving wrongdoers were warned off by even the presence of a member of the upper class. Many of the rest skulked away from just a nudge, or if not, then perhaps an injury, if only to their pride.

There were only a few who had the self-importance, and perhaps the nerve, to try to attack a gentleman on the open street.

This was one.

She was ready for those, too.

The handful of ashes she tossed in the villain's eyes floated and glittered like demonic snow; it forced him to swear and fall back a step, two, pawing at his face, temporarily blinded.

While he swore and wiped at his eyes, Tella stepped in close to him, grabbing his knife-wielding arm, and spun *in* to his grip, hauling the arm around till it, and the knife he held, were in front of her. He tried to stab at her with the dingy thing, but she was too fast for him, bringing his wrist down in both hands to snap it over her upthrust knee.

She didn't think the wrist actually broke, but he howled as he dropped the knife, making the woman shriek with horror.

Brilliant. Now someone else might be coming.

Tella kicked the knife away from where it had fallen from his limp hand, and turned to face him again.

But the hubris of the fellow, or perhaps the alcohol in him, didn't let him give up. Instead, he grabbed at Tella's throat with his other hand, shoving her nearly sideways into the wall next to them with a mighty slamming force.

Tella felt the breath whoosh out of her as the wall struck her shoulder, her back. And she felt the man's fingernails digging into the skin of her neck as he squeezed, cutting off her supply of lifegiving air.

And when, as she choked, she looked into his eyes, Tella realized she had misjudged something.

He might be drunk, but he was very aware. And he fully intended to hurt someone—at the moment, her.

It was the look of someone who *wanted* to hurt. She would never forget it.

The half-grown lad next to his mother had eyes grown as big as plates. He looked about to charge rather than watch their rescuer murdered in front of him. But Tella managed to catch his eye and throw up a hand to signal *stop* before he threw himself into the fight. That would be all she needed.

Sweeping a hand back, she clutched the edge of her cloak

and, as black spots began to swim before her eyes, flicked it upwards so that the heavy chain in the hem wrapped itself around the miscreant's undamaged wrist.

When she yanked down, he yelped, from surprise at being restrained by a force much greater than he expected, as much as from the chain compressing and pulling on his flesh. He unwillingly released her.

Bracing a hand on the wall, Tella paused to catch a moment of breath.

She had no trouble making her voice angry, rough, and low. "Your life will be much more difficult if you do not choose to disappear immediately."

The man cast his red-rimmed eyes around at the silent street, then back at what must have once looked to him like easy prey: the mother and her two defenseless children.

Whatever he saw, he seemed to choose the wiser end of calculation this night, and with an appalling curse, turned and tried to make his leaving look unhurried.

She was not fooled. He was discouraged, not dissuaded. She watched him go, waiting till he well rounded the corner before turning to the woman behind her.

"Tell me where are you lodged, madame," Tella rasped.

When the woman stammered out the name of an inn not too far distant, Tella simply nodded, keeping her tricorn low over her face.

"Go now, go quickly, and do not stop," Tella said without any further ado, and the woman scrambled, a tight grip on each child.

She would see them to their destination, of course; she would not let them be further accosted. But it did not do to let them know that.

Almost no one knew that Lady Donnatella, beloved only daughter of the Duke of Gravenshire, kept her London streets as safe as she could make them. Not even the people she saved.

As Tella stayed in the shadows, trailing the little family to where they were supposed to be, she reflected that they, at least, had learned to stay indoors late at night. Even that little boy, she was sure, had learned a lesson. And his mother had learned far more.

And the ruffian whose thieving she had interrupted, he had doubtless learned something too.

* * *

THIS COUNTRY MOTHER WAS SMART. She went straight to the inn, just as Tella had said, and kept her children tight against her the whole way.

Tella bumped into the corner as she rounded it, keeping the family in sight, and winced. She had time to pause, and leaned against the building in whose shadow she hid.

She'd learned something too: how a man looked who no longer cared for any proprieties, and who was determined to do someone, anyone, harm. She wouldn't forget that look.

For now, she had the promise of a collection of multi-colored bruises, and scratches across her throat that it would be difficult to hide.

It was the warming part of spring, but Tella mused that it might be time for London to see a resurgence of interest in silk chiffon shawls. Particularly light ones that might be decoratively tossed around one's neck.

Once she saw the family safely indoors, her path circled around to some of her favorite hiding spots. She wanted to at least see them all before she arrived home.

She needed to be inside before the sun rose, and would welcome the hours of sleep she would finally get.

No fashionable lady would wake before noon, and the

party the night before would give Tella an excuse for lying abed well into the day.

Tella had a reputation for being a sound sleeper and a devoted one.

It was a reputation she carefully cultivated so that she could make forays like these while her friends were still leaving their parties. As the young gentlefolk of the *ton* staggered home to bed, she would also find her way home, and into the tiny cellar she kept locked at the bottom of her father's house.

Usually she exercised there, working the muscles of her body until she felt strong and contradicting every matron who advised against strenuous activity for young ladies, lest they overtax themselves.

Tella had learned the art of very selectively listening to those in authority.

Her great-uncle had taught her those exercises as a child, during storytelling evenings when he'd kept her transfixed with his experiences in battle. He'd told her everything about how soldiers might keep themselves fit in the battlefield, even when on long campaigns. And why not? It was what he knew, and since his wife and her mother were gone, they kept each other company, the little girl and the old soldier.

Most soldiers were never trained, and they fought and died as nearly nameless pawns in the wars of supposedly mightier men. Lord Preston told her those stories, too, perhaps thinking she didn't understand them. But she remembered.

The memory of all those lost soldiers haunted her uncle. If he'd had his way, he would have instituted far more instruction in the hand-to-hand combat the infantrymen would face, and far more in the way of physical conditioning in order to do it.

Tella had absorbed a great many lessons at her uncle's

knee, and he never realized how much the child Tella had practiced what he had shown her.

Not until he'd discovered what she had decided to do with her nights.

He'd argued, and threatened, and pleaded that she not put herself in danger. She had many clever arguments, honed and planned over years, that she had as much right to protect people as he had ever had.

He wasn't the type of person to try to jail someone in their own house, and she wasn't the type of person to be stopped.

She winced again. She wasn't foolish. She wouldn't be exercising tonight. The blow had been more of a shock to her system, and perhaps her mind, than she'd realized, she thought as she staggered a little. She would need to rest, not exercise, tonight.

Her uncle would be proud, though, of the way she'd kept her head and disarmed the thief. Tella made a habit of not waking her uncle at these hours, but looked forward to seeing him tomorrow.

They had a deal, she and her uncle. She would always see him for breakfast.

She wouldn't be able to tell this story over the breakfast table, but they could closet themselves together afterwards, and she would give him a blow by blow report.

Until she gave him the details, she never felt that she had a sure grip on how to improve for the next time.

She would wash as soon as she returned to her room, taking care not to be chilled as she slipped between the sheets. Her lady's maid knew never to disturb her room after she had gone off to "bed" after a party, but also, never to leave the bed without its warming pan of coals.

She knew the rhythms of her own house well. There was

no one about as she opened the low cellar door and slid inside.

Tella breathed deep. No exercise tonight, and she already felt the bruise on her ribs pulling at her breathing. But she was young and strong, and she was not afraid.

These streets were hers. She had done what she must. And tomorrow, she would do it again.

CHAPTER THREE

"Julia, you must be mad, no one pays a morning call in the morning," Tella moaned into her second cup of coffee.

She had slept well, but she was sore and stiff, and she didn't care for the way her day dress pulled at her upper arms.

But the gown was light enough for spring, the sleeves long enough to reach her elbow, and the collar a froth of lace that cupped her chin. And those were her primary criteria for dress selection today.

She'd had few moments to choose it when her maid awakened her at the unreasonable hour of half past ten, apologetically announcing Lady Julia's arrival.

Julia looked entirely recovered from the fatigue of the party the night before. Her face shone under her crown of golden-brown hair, and she smiled the smile of a young lady who'd had many, many hours of uninterrupted sleep.

At the moment, Tella hated her.

Julia was all unknowing of the hatred as she poked among the breakfast dishes arrayed upon the table. Tella always asked that the morning repast stay in the breakfast room until she and her uncle had eaten their morning fare, so they could keep their breakfast agreement.

"I don't want to have to wonder if you are lying dying in your bed," her uncle had harrumphed at her.

Tella suspected that injuries short of death would also persuade him to find a way to stop her, even when, she suspected, he was secretly proud of her ability to fight. It took effort to keep her injuries, large and small, out of sight. She went to that effort.

He could see little of her, after all. His eyes were too clouded now to see the thin knife scars on her palms, from before she'd devised her more protective gloves and clothing; he would certainly never see those on her ribs, particularly the one that wasn't thin. As long as everything in between wasn't visible, but Tella *was*, he assumed she was fine.

So she always came to the breakfast table, even when she didn't want to do it.

But today it was wasted effort; Lord Preston was not there to grace her with his presence. Neither was her father, though the House of Lords did not convene until evening.

Instead Julia *was* here, bubbling and happy, and Tella needed something more bracing than warm oats or cold toast for a morning like this.

Perhaps she would simply continue to drink coffee.

Julia knew better than to push Tella's temper before her morning fast was well and truly broken. But she looked so ready to burst that Tella felt she must have mercy upon her friend or watch her expire upon the carpet.

"What is it, dear? You look quite full of news."

"Tella, my very dear friend, I am going to be married!"

"Never tell me so!" Tella's spine straightened instantly in her chair.

"Well I like that! Is it so hard to believe?" But Julia was not angry; her dimple was coming and going as she fought down a smile.

"Of course not! The wonder is that you have not been married before this. Who is the man, do I know him? But I must know him, you look so happy!"

Julia's face became wreathed in unrestrained smiles. "I am happy, so happy! It is Lord Wendover, you know we met him before the season at that musicale. He has danced with me at every event this season but I did not dare hope, he is so dashing, and you know how many pounds he has a year."

"Is he dashing?" Tella mused. She was trying to picture Lord Wendover. Nothing was coming to mind. She tended to ignore things—and people—who were unimportant.

"I think he is very dashing, in a quiet way," said Julia, her excitement somewhat subdued by her friend's lack of same.

Immediately, Tella was contrite. "Oh darling, he must be dashing if he has caught your eye. And you have caught his, which does not surprise me in the least!"

"I think he is very handsome. And he has a lovely estate in the country, as well as a townhouse close by—not as grand as this, of course, but close by."

"But that is delightful! We shall be neighbors!"

"Will we?" Julia studied her friend curiously. "Do you truly not intend to marry at all, Tella? Would you not like a house of your own?"

"This house is very much my own," said Tella firmly. Then she remembered not to sound so sure. "Of course I should like to marry! But it must be a man I can love, you know that. Madly. No such man has presented himself. And my father is quite happy to have me as hostess, and to look after him, and this house, and my uncle."

"Is Lord Preston quite well?"

"I assume so." Tella's brow creased. "I have not yet seen him this morning, and I did expect it."

"His lordship is taking breakfast in his chambers," said a nearby footman whose name Tella thought she did know. Percival or something equally unlikely.

Her uncle breakfasting alone made Tella frown. That was not their agreement. She would have to go and check on her uncle directly.

After Julia's news. Of *marriage*.

"But why have you come at this unholy hour of the morning?"

"You are usually up by now." Julia shrugged. Tella made a mental note to cultivate a reputation for sleeping even later. "I had to tell you the news! And I am to have a trousseau, and I want you to accompany us to the draper's. Mama let me come by myself, since I am now safely affianced!"

"And your home is less than half a mile from here," Tella said with only a touch of sarcasm.

"Oh the news, the news, Tella, the news could not wait!"

"Of course not!" Tella wanted to jump up and run and hug her friend, but the bruises on her side were holding her somewhat cramped in her chair.

No, she had better do it or there might be suspicion. At worst, suspicion that she was not happy for Julia. And she was, she was! She loved Julia dearly, so dearly.

Attempting to keep her motion fluid, Tella rushed from her chair to lean over her friend and hug her soundly.

"I am so happy for you, darling, especially if you are happy! For that is all I want for you, ever, ever."

Julia squeezed her eyes shut in ecstasy, wrapping her arm around Tella's and squeezing it as well. Tella was grateful she had kept her body angled away.

"I am so happy. I have so longed for a house of my own, and a husband, and, you know, children."

"Why Julia! I had no idea you were pining so!"

"Pining? No, how can one pine for something one has

never had?" Julia looked more thoughtful, and older, Tella thought as she subsided into the chair next to her friend. "I wanted a place of my own. I have been ready for it, only waiting for the right man to offer it to me. I like Lord Wendover very much and we shall suit each other well."

"Only like him? My very dear!"

"Oh, don't lecture me, Tella. Not all of us have your exotically romantic plans."

"There is nothing exotic about wanting to marry for deep, passionate, abiding love!"

Julia asked practically, "How do you know if love is deep and abiding until many years have passed?"

"Well, I know how to tell if it is passionate!"

"Do you?" Julia's dimple had returned, but she looked appropriately scandalized. "Never tell me so! How did you come by this extraordinary knowledge?"

"Hush. You are taxing me this morning. What a flood of happiness and saucy behavior you are. I am quite overcome."

Julia just laughed. "Not all of us are a duke's daughter, able to put off marriage for this mythical love you claim to want. And I don't think you want it at all."

"Why, why ever not?" Tella was instantly on alert. She *didn't* want it, but it was in no way suitable for her plans for anyone to suspect that, even her dear childhood friend.

Julia studied her face. "I don't know," she said softly, "I just can't feel, somehow, that you really want it. Do you really feel you must have passionate and abiding love to have a happy life, Tella? Is that truly the thing you are seeking?"

Tella shifted uncomfortably in the chair. Her bruises hurt, dash it all. She ought to have put more wintergreen oil on them last night. "I know if I were to marry, I would not settle for less."

"Then I hope you find it, dear."

Her friend's soft kindness made Tella even more uncomfortable. She wanted nothing of the sort.

And anyway, she already had a place to belong. She belonged in London's streets.

"It is far more of the moment that you have found your own heart's desire. We must shop, you are quite right! Enormous, portentous shopping is upon us. Do you wish me to change?"

She knew her friend would say just what she said. "You are perfect just as you are; I had quite hoped we would start before the day is far along, and Mama is waiting at home with the carriage to accompany us both!"

It would be quite an adventure, Tella knew, for her friend to walk with her the entire half mile back to the Shoreton townhouse. It was much farther than Julia had ever walked in her life on London's streets, Tella knew, and here she was doing it twice in one day, once with only a footman!

"What a daredevil you are this morning. Marriage has turned you into an adventuress."

"I am only eager to acquire new gowns!"

"I do not think the acquisition of gowns is all that obsesses you today. Nonetheless. Let me check on my uncle, and I am all yours, my dear!"

* * *

She had half-expected to find Lord Preston sitting up in bed, its tapestry drapes pulled back to frame his silver hair and broad shoulders, perhaps in his regal purple banyan robe.

It was disconcerting, therefore, but hardly alarming, to find him dressed and seated at his small Eastern tiled table by the window, looking out into the sunlight and sipping a cup of tea.

"Why Uncle! Have you forgotten our engagement?" Tella cried half-teasingly as she swept into his private room.

It was not until he turned that Tella was really alarmed. Because his expression was so blank for a moment that Tella might have sworn he'd even forgotten *her*.

Then something in his eyes shifted, and he looked very slightly confused—Tella could certainly read that emotion in men's eyes—but then also very clearly recognized her.

"I am accustomed to take my morning tea here and read the paper, my dear, am I not?"

Rather than contradict him, Tella moved to take the seat opposite him.

She said as if it were of no particular moment, "I thought I had reason to expect you at the breakfast table."

That ghost of confusion veiled his eyes again for a moment, then he shrugged it off. "Nonsense, I always take my breakfast here."

He had indeed taken his breakfast at that very table for decades, whenever the family was in residence in London. He had lived in these apartments for decades, ever since his wife had died and he had joined Tella's household. He'd lived here even before her mother had died, which seemed a lifetime ago.

But for the last three years at least, she was sure, since he had discovered her binding a wound on her arm, he had insisted with the firmness of a giant oak tree that they breakfast together. Which they did. Downstairs.

"Is the tea quite to your liking?" Tella asked, casting about for a suitable topic of conversation, since she sensed that bringing up their breakfast bargain would not be the appropriate answer.

He shrugged and gave her a small smile. "It doesn't taste quite like it usually does. I assume the cook has tried some new merchant. Ask her to see if she can't send up some more of that quince jelly she so adores, tomorrow."

Tella froze.

Their previous cook had been wild about quince jelly, even though no one else in the house had a firm opinion about it. She had moved to the country to live with her daughter years ago. The current cook, Mrs. Brown, had no particular interest in quince jelly. Tella couldn't remember seeing it on the table since Mrs. Brown had arrived.

"Of course, uncle," she said distractedly.

His color was good, she thought as she examined him closely in the morning light. He seemed hale enough, and had consumed not only a cup of tea, but half the rack of toast as well.

Obeying an impulse, she jumped up and hugged him, as hard as she could, around the neck, as she used to do when she was very little.

"Oh ha, what has possessed you, child?" Lord Preston chuckled as her hair nearly smothered him. "You haven't hugged me like that since your mother died."

Tella squeezed her eyes shut. He very seldom mentioned her mother, much less her mother's death.

"I love you, darling, that's all," she said, half breathless from some emotion she could not name and half breathless from her sore ribs, and entirely frightened for a second, frightened in a way she had not been at all during the knife fight the night before.

"Well that's all very well, I love you too. Feel free to come in here and shower me with love at any time," her uncle said into her collar, unresisting to her sudden affection.

"I'm going to visit Dr. Burke and send him to see you, all right?" said Tella as she straightened.

"What for?" Seemingly unconcerned, her uncle picked up his paper again.

"It has been a while since he has seen you, and I am a silly flustered girl who wants her beloved great-uncle to live to a very ripe old age and so I am going to ask him to come."

Lord Preston shot her a look as pointed as ever. "Oh yes, you're very silly. Try that on someone who isn't me. You know I will do as you please, so do it."

"Thank you, sir." She smiled prettily at him even as she felt something sick in her gut. This was awful, far worse than her beloved Julia marrying.

Which had been far more unpleasant news than she had any reason to expect, she realized.

At least he wasn't arguing with her.

Though in fact, that also was a bit worrying.

So she kissed the side of his head and dashed out, determined to get to Dr. Burke's as quickly as her shopping errands would carry her.

CHAPTER FOUR

"Julia, honestly. An entire over-gown from this lace? It would be destroyed in moments."

Julia's eyebrows both raised before she put back the sample of the lovely handwoven lace. "Have you always disliked shopping this much, or is it only me you dislike?"

"I am so sorry. Ignore me, I am a lion of irritation today."

"More like an irritated lion. A lion with four sore paws. A trying lion."

Tella smiled her thanks. It was only Julia's good temper that was saving the day, and nothing to do with her.

She'd had no idea that her beloved friend was so desperately interested in being married. But here Julia was, selecting gowns and hair combs and toilet water, following her mother's advice in everything regarding what would be appropriate to her new station in life, and beaming with so much happiness that Tella was nearly ready to commit violence to make it stop.

She felt as if they were packing for a trip and that Julia was going far, far away. She would not, of course; she would be living, in fact, in the same neighborhood where she lived now.

Still, Tella couldn't shake the idea that Julia was leaving her; nor could she shake the near-panic she felt at the thought.

"Married ladies wear hats that are more restrained," said Lady Shoreton with her usual sense of conviction, arriving as Julia began to fondle a lace-edged cap that was decidedly not restrained.

Julia had been absorbing all her mother's advice about dressing for her new role as a married lady, like a sponge able to absorb the sea, but she was slow to put down the ruffled confection of a hat. Not everything about being married, it seemed, would be entirely to her taste.

"Married ladies also need practical gloves that may successfully be cleaned, more than they need *that*," Lady Shoreton went on, nodding at the carved fan Julia then picked up and began caressing with her fingers like fine jewelry.

Julia gasped. "Madame! Surely I am not to sit indoors all day and never venture forth to an evening ball again."

"Fewer," her mother said succinctly, and Tella saw a real tinge of regret as Julia put down the carved fan.

Her mother moved on.

Tella picked the fan up again and pressed it into her friend's hand.

She whispered, "I believe your mother is simply enjoying being authoritative on the topic of accessories for married ladies. Buy the fan."

Julia's conspiratorial smile and wink restored some more of Tella's equanimity.

Tella was in such charity with her friend by the time they crossed the corner that led to Dr. Burke's office, she was loath to disappear on her.

But disappear she would, because she must do it.

"I will be with you soon," she said quietly over Julia's shoulder from just a step behind. And then moved so quickly she never knew whether Julia turned to look or not.

* * *

IT WAS ONLY a few doors away that she found the stairs to Dr. Burke's quiet office.

Her hopes and dreams were answered; he was in.

"Lady Donnatella!" he cried, rising as she entered the little room above the druggist's. He offered her one of his two chairs.

"Doctor Burke." She nodded and sailed forward to take it.

The man of medicine sat, resting an elbow on the pile of journal papers and correspondence on his desk. "You look too well to visit me."

Given that her usual visits were late at night, and that the last time she'd had that awful wound that still made wide necklines impossible, perhaps he tended to associate her with bleeding. "Quite well. I do need your help, though."

Dr. Burke was an admirably good and admirably close-mouthed physician who had actually done surgery at the battle front. He claimed his practice consisted of holding the hands of older ladies, but she usually saw him with children who had needed his surgical hand, or men whose wounds had come from serving in the war as he had.

Tella sighed a little, inwardly. Dr. Burke was also, sadly and indisputably, terribly beautiful. There was no other way to describe his wide forehead and angular chin, or how they framed a pair of arresting eyes. Simply looking at him was a wonderful way to pass the time. He wore his hair unfashionably long, in a queue; to look older, Tella thought, or to hide the edge of his jaw. She very much wanted to tell him that it did not work.

"I must ask you to visit us immediately. Perhaps you'd be so good as to dine with us?"

"Is this a medically necessary dinner?"

"I worry that it is. Lord Preston, my uncle—my great-uncle—seems to have suffered a loss of memory this morning that is most troubling."

The small frown Dr. Burke always had between his brows deepened. "Tell me more."

When she had described all the morning's conversation with her uncle, the doctor's frown did not disappear, and Tella's spirits sank.

"I'm sorry to hear this, my lady. A bout of apoplexy has been known to bring on such conditions, and I have seen it in other patients his age."

"Apoplexy? But would that not have been visible, with... with convulsions or the like?"

He shook his head. "It can occur even in the sleep, and seems to convulse only the brain. He may have suffered some invisible damage. But you say he is moving well, and eating? And without undue anger, or sadness. It may have been a very gentle attack."

"A *gentle* attack? He did not appear to remember the last several years!"

Dr. Burke leaned forward to lay a reassuring hand over hers for a moment. "Would you rather that, or that he lost the ability to walk, or talk?"

Tella held herself still in her chair through force of habit. There was something roiling around in her and she was afraid it was a churning wave of fear that could drown her. But this was no time to attend to inner details like that.

"Please do dine with us, we will delight to have you, and

you can speak with him yourself. If you see the need, examine him. I told him you would."

Dr. Burke's smile seemed to clear away at least a few of the shadows crowding around her, and she inwardly promised herself to make sure the cook served some extra nice things to help repay him. "A small favor to do you, my lady, certainly."

* * *

When Tella caught up with Julia, she was just about to leave the corsetry shop.

"Where have you been? My mother has been considering becoming quite cross with you!"

Tella had to smile at this undoubtedly accurate description. Lady Shoreton would take no action, including becoming cross, without due consideration.

She had learned long ago that it was easier to tell the truth whenever possible, reserving her meager powers to lie in order to continue to conceal her larger untruths.

"I do apologize, I needed to visit a physician and ask him to the house. My uncle is unwell."

"Oh no! Why did you not tell me? And here I am dragging you all over half of London doing shopping!"

"Not at all! No no, dear, had it been urgent I would have said. He was not quite himself this morning and I am hoping that it is nothing. Or at least, nothing too serious."

"Tella," Julia said, taking her friend's hand in her own, "you always behave like the stoic captain of some ship at sea, keeping the course despite storms and mutinies and all manner of disasters. You know I would help you in any trouble, and so would my mother. You do have friends, you know."

"I know, I know." To her horror, Tella felt a warning prickle of tears coming to her eyes.

She would not burst out into sobs here among the corsetry. Instead, she grasped her friend's gloved hand gratefully with her own.

She was still glad to have missed Julia's corset shopping; it was not a topic Tella could pretend to discuss enthusiastically. She much preferred her corset bones in her fighting gloves.

But Julia was right. Tella had a good friend in Dr. Burke, a most necessary one. And she had Julia, and Lady Shoreton. And she still had her father and her beloved uncle, for whom she was most grateful, most.

She was a lucky lady indeed.

* * *

THREE NIGHTS LATER, somewhere past midnight, Tella reassessed her store of luck.

Dr. Burke had attended their dinner and had spoken with her uncle at some length afterward. Without observing any specific event, he then told her, his diagnosis of apoplexy stood; he expected her uncle to recover, but could not predict if any memory of the last few years would return. In fact, he warned her, her uncle was more likely to continue to lose memories of more recent events.

She still told Lord Preston every day that he was her very favorite uncle. And his eyes still twinkled. But there was a vagueness to them, some of the time, that disquieted her.

And their breakfast pact was broken.

Tella knew it didn't make any sense, but she felt as though she had lost the one person who had truly known her.

Which wasn't true; Julia knew her and loved her.

But Julia was definitely a part of the ballroom world, part

of her door into London's streets, not a part of the real world itself.

And if she told her friend, Tella could just imagine the endless corridor of *whys* she would be marched down, forthwith.

Why are you dressing that way?

Why are you sneaking out of your own house?

Why are you skulking through alleyways looking for trouble?

Why are you risking your life?

That was about where Tella put a stop to the inquisition, even in her own head.

Fortunately it *was* all in her own head, so she needn't devise absurd-sounding answers for anyone else's ears.

Because it is necessary.

Because I can.

Because someone must.

Because no one ought to be afraid.

Those were all the answers Tella had.

And they had better do. Because right now, her hand pressed to her still-bruised ribs as she skulked through the shadows, those answers brought her to the end of her luck.

She knew it, that man's face. Watched surreptitiously as he crossed the street and blended into the dark.

As he moved on, and passed through the beam of a window's light, she could see the rough knife scar at the edge of his jaw, and cursed herself for not noticing it before.

He'd survived plenty of knife fights.

And she knew the look in his eyes. She'd learned to see cruelty from meeting him before.

Tonight, he'd brought a friend.

They were following a cluster of light women making their way across the square.

Tella had seen those women before. They were wily, and far from helpless.

But as the mean-eyed man crept up on them now, Tella had a sick feeling that he was more than their usual trouble.

"'Ere, lad, are ye looking for a laidy to drink wit'?" said one of the women, stopping and pulling up the edge of her skirt to show her ankle in a supposedly alluring fashion.

But the woman's colleagues spread out on either side of her, both with hands in the pockets of their aprons, and Tella did not doubt that their pockets held home-made cudgels.

The mean-eyed man looked like he knew it too.

His thin colleague looked like he knew nothing and wished to know nothing. The mean-eyed man tugged him into position behind him as he spoke.

"Yer no laidy."

Tella was just close enough to catch the sound of his voice. He wasn't drunk tonight.

"I'll do till sompin better comes along, deary," tittered the woman, and her friends laughed with her. Being called not a lady was far from the worst treatment they'd had today.

Tella expected the men to threaten the women with knives, to force them to hand over their money. They'd do worse if they could, she knew, but not out here in the street.

She did *not* expect what the mean-eyed man said next, which was, "Yer workin' fer me now."

All three women scoffed and jeered. Tella slid into the shadows behind the trees that marched along the square. She was only a few yards away.

"'m dead serious. Yer new boss is me, an' I'll expec' a shillin' from each o' you before mornin'."

A second woman, in a stained overskirt, clearly thought very little of this yob and every other man in London. She spit in his direction. "We know where we work and we don't know you. Piss off."

"'Appy to show yer," said the mean-eyed man, with a glittering look in his eye that Tella did not like, and his knife appeared in his hand.

With a *whoosh* her thin, nearly invisible rope came whistling out of the darkness, thin and weighted on one end, and wrapped itself several times around the man's body, pinning his arm to his side.

Quickly Tella braced, and jerked the man off his feet.

When his knife fell from his tied-up hand and clattered on the ground, Tella stepped on it.

She glared down at him. "When I told you to disappear, I meant for good."

"Nah then, young mister, nuffin' but a bit o' tiff," said the third woman, a tiny, plump thing, giving Tella her best simpering smile.

"Oy, stupid," shouted the man from the ground.

This prompted his colleague to shake himself and realize his effort was now required. "*What?*" Even his *what* was without conviction.

Tella glared at him. "Silence yourself."

He silenced himself.

"Now what should I do with you?" Tella addressed her adversary on the ground. She was waiting for him to attempt to get up; that he did not, worried her. "You don't take good advice."

The man's unbound hand shot out from under him, grabbed Tella by the ankle, and yanked.

Not expecting an attack from that angle, Tella wobbled; before she could catch herself, the man yanked again.

She went down, letting out an *oof* of pain more from jarred hurt ribs than from landing.

But down on the ground with her assailant was not a place to be.

She heard Lord Preston's voice in her head, telling her stories of bayonet fights that might not have been appropriate for some little girls. *If you must fight a blade and you are in close, you may well get cut. Don't panic about it, control the weapon.*

Tella rolled over the half-bound body of the man toward his weapon before he could grab it. He let out an *oof* as her weight bounced his head to the paving stone; she grabbed the knife herself.

She dare not toss it away; his compatriot might retrieve it, or indeed one of the light women.

But as she grabbed it, the man beneath her made a roaring sound of pure anger and surged upwards, tumbling her back onto the ground.

Tella was shocked to hear another male voice, distant but coming close fast. "Hey! Stop there!"

As before, the mean-eyed man refused to stop for only words.

His compatriot, however, turned and ran away.

* * *

Wandering the streets at night was a stupid way to look for a story.

Fitz ought to have a better way.

But he was still trying to figure out what to write since he'd come home from the wars.

London had loads of stories, but they were too big, or too small. There were lords who bought their nephews House of Commons seats, and men executed for lying with one another. The government set the price of bread far too high, and tried to tax into silence the newspapers he needed to sell.

Fitz liked a story he could dive into, get to the bottom of, and tell in a way as vital and raw as his journal reports from the front.

This street fight looked pretty vital and raw.

The closer he got, the more odd it looked. A thickset man in rough clothes was flinging himself onto a slender, much younger man—flinging himself bodily, because one of his arms was bound to his side.

The younger man didn't seem much worried—indeed, his hat was still on—but he gripped a knife in one hand and tried to scrabble backward from the rougher man's weight on his legs.

Fitz yelled, "Hey! Stop there!" But neither one heeded. Nor did the ladies of the evening standing around watching.

* * *

THE THREE WOMEN fell back from where Tella struggled on the ground to keep control of the knife.

The villain lifted his knee, still struggling to land a sharp blow in the muscle of her thigh, trying to loosen her grip even as he could not reach. His unbound hand was clawing again, this time at her coat.

But the new voice wasn't giving up either.

"I—said—*stop*." The man's raised voice was punctuated by his grabbing and heaving back on her attacker's free arm.

Perfect. Another person close enough to get a good look at her. And one who'd probably fall on the knife before he was through.

Sure enough, the mean-eyed man managed to overbalance the new fellow; then all three of them mixed together on the ground. Tella wanted to roll her eyes.

But the new fellow wrapped his arm around the shoulders of the mean-eyed man, keeping him from repossessing his knife, and twisted.

With the help of a kick from Tella, the new fellow pulled her attacker off her and rolled him a few feet away.

Tella kept her eyes on the man whose knife she still held. She knew, this time, that he did not quit.

The new stranger stood, brushing himself off.

"Are you ladies all right?" he asked, and the fancy women tittered amongst themselves at the name coming from this swanky newcomer. Clearly so from his accent, and his boots, and the fine wool of his coat.

Tella's head swam in confusion for just a second, imagining herself so addressed. But no, the new man turned to her only once the night women were done tittering.

"Give you a hand?" he said, starting to bend over.

But Tella leaped up and charged past him.

"Oy! Stop!" It was now her turn to say it. The mean-eyed man had staggered to his feet, and was in a fair way to run off with her favorite rope.

Tella almost managed to catch the trailing end of it with her fingers as it whipped along past her, but she was too late. He was only two or three steps ahead of her, but apparently quite capable of some speed, and she felt her bruised ribs pulling already.

"Dash it," she had no trouble growling in a very manly fashion. It was difficult getting those ropes just so. It was difficult getting them at all.

In the distance, down the block, the dark figure of a night watchman took shape rounding the corner. Always when they weren't needed, never when they were.

"Here, you lot," he said, moving toward them without any real conviction.

Her father really was wrong about a shortage of watchmen.

More instantly than could almost be believed, the fancy women, who had watched the fight with deep interest, disappeared entirely, presumably, thought Tella with annoyance, into the ether, as their bodies left no trace they'd ever existed.

Leaving her with the man who had caused her to lose her favorite rope.

* * *

A PART OF FITZ' mind was already organizing these extraordinary events into a story. The attacker, the rope, the knife, the citizens accosted in the street; it was all pretty engrossing as it unfurled in his mind, right down to the young man posing right now in the street, hem of his blue velvet cape swinging dramatically as if a wind had just blown past him.

Fitz might actually get some dinner out of this story. Dinner for quite some time. He could write this.

It was gripping and dramatic without all the despair of his stories from the front. The editor of Bridle's Daily Gazette would love it.

* * *

"ARE YOU HURT?" The newcomer was catching his breath.

"No," snapped Tella. Catching her breath too. "Why, pray tell me why, would you throw yourself into a fight in the street?"

The question took him aback. "Wouldn't anyone?"

"No. For instance, those ladies of the evening, all of whom were armed, I assure you. Or anyone else with a mind to think about how they might get hurt."

The fellow was peering at her. "It looked like *you* might get hurt."

"I know what I am doing. You, sir," Tella said with conviction, "do not."

And she turned on her heel and marched off.

She was so irritated at the loss of one of her favorite devices that she began to march straight home.

She stopped herself. It wouldn't do. Instead, she turned so she could skirt the square along its eastern edge and still outdistance the night watchman, who was making no great effort to arrive in time to detain them.

The stranger followed her.

"He was really after you," the man said, his cheeks flushed and hair full of dirt and leaves. He was following her.

His fawn-colored trousers and dark coat, nearly a copy of Tella's own, showed signs of vehemently crushed earth and a bootprint on the thigh where the mean-eyed man had landed a kick.

He probably had a bruise there to match her own. Tella squashed the impulse to wince in sympathy. She hadn't asked for his help; indeed, it hadn't been much help.

And he was intent on asking questions. "What are you doing out here?"

She must get rid of him quickly. "What are *you* doing?" she rasped, as they turned a corner and put the greener square behind them.

"Asking what you are doing. You said you know what you are doing. What is it, then, sir, that you are doing? And how often do you do it?"

Tella just shook her head. "You should be at home."

"Good heavens, man, I must be ten years older than you—give me some credit for my ability to look out for myself. Are you not somewhat bruised as well?"

Tella did look at him again. How young a man did he think her? He couldn't be more than twenty-six, twenty-seven on the outside. Tall. He had sunny blue eyes and an expression to match, one that looked ready to smile at any moment. His tumble of light brown curls softened his rather raw-boned face, made him look quite young, but she was used to seeing men wearing the style, and she could tell how old he truly was.

She didn't know *who* he was, but that was of no import to her.

"You don't know what you're doing," Tella said in the deepest, gravelliest version of her voice she could muster, letting him see exactly what she thought of him. Nearly nothing.

He *did* smile. "Come on, I'll buy you a drink and you can tell me all about what I don't know. Particularly about you."

Behind them, a voice said, "Here, you. I said you." The stranger turned to see its source.

That night watchman had rounded the corner, puffing with his effort. He *had* been heading toward them, just slowly. Was he the same watchman Tella had paid off days before?

She was terrible with faces, and even worse with names.

The stranger started to turn back to Tella, no doubt to correlate with his erstwhile fight companion the stories they were about to tell the night watch.

But by the time he looked round, she was gone.

FORTUNATELY HE DIDN'T HAVE to run far; he didn't have the balance, with one arm tied to his side.

He just needed a quiet spot where he could get out of this rope.

He'd half-thought there was a trick to the rope, but no. Once he could relax, pull his arm in tight, and breathe out, the weight at the end shook loose. It pulled the thin little rope loose as well.

He drew back further into the shadows of the alleyway and rolled the rope in his fingers.

Sinew. Waxed. Slightly sticky to the touch, just enough to cling to him. A notched iron circle for the weight. Nothing particularly special; just nothing he had ever seen before.

He wasn't sure whether to keep it or toss it away. His instinct was to keep it. Keep things that were valuable, or strong, or both. Frighten people who could give him money, or power, or both. These were rules for living he had absorbed at a young age, and he believed in them wholeheartedly.

He kept it.

Minutes later, he was in a doorway along a different street, standing with his employer. Who issued orders...for now. Who had no special talent for knowing who to frighten or what to keep.

A man who dressed and talked above his station, and who didn't have the balls to use anger as a weapon. A man with the gall to give *him* a dirty look.

He swung the weight at the end of his new rope, and shrugged. "Them flash mollishers were ignorin' me."

"I trust you to handle a few Covent Garden nuns. You look more disheveled that I would expect from arguing with women."

"Bit of a fight."

"And what of your helper?"

"No help a'tall. I told you he wouldn't be. He may be useful aboard a ship, but he's no good on land."

"I'm very sorry to hear that."

Maybe; likely not. In his experience, men like this one, who so clearly wanted to be what they weren't, made a habit of running away from fights. They couldn't grasp the need for men who *liked* to shed a little blood. He didn't answer.

His employer went on. "We have goals, and we must meet

them to be paid ourselves; I leave you to sort the business out."

And then the man walked off.

Watching his employer go, he rubbed the iron weight against his lower lip.

Himself, he didn't want to be hoity-toity. He wanted the world tidy: people who listened to him, and people who didn't and got what they deserved.

He'd deal with the flash mollishers, and that useless weak deserter. And then he'd deal with that bastard in the blue cape.

CHAPTER FIVE

"*D*id you want more coffee, Lady Donnatella?"

Tella jumped, then just shook her head to the footman. "Oh no, thank you."

She should have had coffee and toast in her room. What had possessed her to come down this morning?

She'd hoped her uncle would be here, that was what she'd hoped. She knew that now.

But he wasn't here, and of course her father wasn't either, and today she didn't have Julia brimming with news.

No, this was the shape of her new life, breakfasting alone in a day dress that hid the parts of her scuffed and bruised in last night's fight.

What has become of my life? Tella thought to herself as she took another sip of the coffee.

Perhaps she should switch to chocolate.

"Would my lady like the papers?"

Tella took one up and looked inside it. Its first page was missing; her father must have taken it with him to the Lesser Hall where the Lords met.

They used to discuss the papers. She missed that.

But when she folded the gazette to replace it on the tray, perhaps for her uncle, her eye caught what was now the first page.

Caped Count Foils Attack Near Claremont Square

Tella had never fainted before. She considered doing it now. This might be the appropriate time and place.

What on earth? *How* on earth?

No, this was nothing to do with her.

Quickly she skimmed the story.

It had everything to do with her.

This was *not* luck, this was the *opposite* of luck. This was *bad* luck, that was what this was. So bad that it needed a different word.

There she was, in print in Bridle's Daily Gazette.

Well, not *her*, of course.

"The scuffle in the neighborhood of one of London's finest seems to illustrate the Duke of Gravenshire's point in Parliament: the night watch cannot keep safe a city rapidly filling with newcomers. In this attack on three young women, only the young Caped Count's determination prevented much more fearful violence."

What was the point of flattering ladies of the night? Tella would have bet money that it had been a long time since someone had called them *young*.

Still, it bespoke a certain gallantry.

Perhaps the type of gallantry that caused a young man to run toward a fight in the night instead of away from it.

She looked for the author of the piece. *Henry Fitzwilliam*, it said.

Henry Fitzwilliam was no doubt reporting from the position of an eye-witness. It just sounded like the name of the man with the blue eyes, a man who wanted to *talk*, no doubt about rainbows and puppy dogs. Who interrupted fights where he was not wanted.

The Caped Count?

This was disastrous.

She needed to see the first sheet of this newspaper.

"Percival, will you see that we receive an additional copy of Bridle's Daily Gazette from now on? Please do reserve it for me."

"Yes, my lady," said the footman as Tella rose to leave her lonely breakfast room.

Today's paper she needed to see today.

* * *

"Fitz, you're a swell who happened to be in t' way of a story last night and turned in some words. Some of us are actual reporters an' no amount of determination on your part will horn you in on my story."

Fitz looked evenly at the other writer.

He said, "I know you don't consider my dispatches from the front to be the equal of your writing here in London, Gerry, and I will tell you a secret. I don't either."

Gerry scowled and stuck his thumbs in the pocket of his stained coat. "Look here—"

"Gentlemen," interrupted the editor, "I don't care. Fitz, tell me why you're so determined to find out more about Gerry's story."

"Because *he* wrote about a man who was murdered last night, and I want to know what else he knows about it. I went to see the body in the morgue, and I'd seen that fellow before."

"Saw him, maybe, at this fistfight you turned into rubbish for my morning edition?" asked the editor.

"If you call the truth rubbish, Clement." Fitz shrugged.

He knew how he appeared to them: a sunny young swell

in a fashionable coat, a poor match for the grubby ink-stained offices of Bridle's Gazette.

But he also knew that both of them had read his work from the front. They knew what he'd seen, and more than anyone, they knew what it had taken him to turn what he'd seen into words.

Fitz couldn't do anything about his birth, or his accent; he couldn't fix that they rubbed Gerry the wrong way. Therefore, he ignored it. "What's the point of the paper, if not to tell people the truth?"

"Money," the editor said promptly.

Fitz gave him a level look that said *stop joking*, and the editor, Clement Bridle, gave him a look right back that said *I'm not joking at all.*

At the Gazette, only Clement knew that Fitz was a marquess' third son, peer by name and breeding but without any other living to his name.

Clement knew that Fitz needed this position.

And Clement knew that Fitz ought to share something of his reverence for coin in the publishing business.

Fitz did care. He had gone looking for a story to please the Gazette's readers, and he'd found one. He couldn't be bothered justifying it much more; he didn't have the time.

The sole proprietor of Bridle's Daily Gazette was shaking his head. "The chap's dead, Fitz. That's usually the end of anything he might do that's interesting enough to report in a newspaper."

"If he were a common thief, Clement—and I thought he was—there'd be no reason for him to turn up later with a slit throat. Someone wanted his mouth permanently shut, and I'd lay a wager that it was the ugly fellow with him. I'm the only one who saw them together, and I have a vested interest in finding out more."

"You're not the only one. This Caped Count must have

seen him too," sneered Gerry, and Fitz felt a little sour when he saw Clement smile.

It had been very late, and he had composed the story too quickly.

He'd practically written it as he'd typeset it, helping the typesetters rip out a section of the page with something stupid in it about a new carriage line. It wasn't the way it was done, but this couldn't have waited two days for the next edition.

Gerry had been right there with him the whole night; in fact he'd helped.

Fitz knew the editor saw the point. Bridle's Gazette needed to be something other papers were not. Timely, for one thing.

"The Caped Count disappeared. I'm saying *I* saw the murderer last night. That's of no interest to the readers of Bridle's Gazette?"

Clement rubbed his knuckle across his nose.

"Look, Gerry," the editor said, "what's the harm of letting Fitz in on any details? He's doing his job, there's no mistake about that."

"It's my story!"

"And that's why I'm *asking* you," his editor said patiently. "If you have more to say, I respect that. If you're done with it, it couldn't hurt to give Fitz a tip or two if you have it."

Gerry looked like he was fighting with himself. "I've got nowt more to say about it," he mumbled grudgingly.

"Brilliant!" Fitz cried. "And look, fair's fair, if you want to subscribe both our names under any further stories, I'm all for it." Fitz was prepared to be big about this, primarily because he had to. He needed Gerry's information and there wasn't much he wouldn't do to get it.

Clement counted on him to chase down big stories. And Clement paid for those stories.

Which Gerry knew too. "And the money?"

Fitz swore inwardly at himself. Again, he'd been in too much of a hurry. He needed the money, and splitting it with Gerry, when he quite fairly suspected Gerry would be doing absolutely no work on this from here on out, would be a bitter pill. Nonetheless he'd said it, so he stuck by it.

"Split with you, of course," said Fitz with a careless shrug. He grinned.

"Fine," said Gerry, still a bit grudgingly but with the wind taken out of his sails. "I can tell you where they found him, and who found him. That's all I've got, but it ought to be something, for you."

* * *

"LADY SHORETON! I am so pleased to see you."

"Lady Donnatella!"

Lady Shoreton did look genuinely surprised, Tella thought, and not particularly pleased.

Tella could not recall another occasion when she had arrived, unaccompanied and unexpected, in the Shoreton house. In the *morning.* It was completely inappropriate, and it had to be the third or fourth entirely inappropriate thing she had done publicly just this week.

Not the way to stay unseen.

She hurried to reassure Lady Shoreton. "I have a rather urgent errand that could not wait; I knew you would have the morning papers, and I need to see them. My father, of course, avails himself of all the front pages."

"You had an urgent need. To see the papers."

Belatedly Tella realized she should simply have sent someone out to acquire another set. She so habitually did nothing to draw her father's attention in the house, that it had not occurred to her. But how would he notice? Who would tell him? A footman? Not her uncle.

The wave of sadness she felt as she realized her uncle was drawing away from her, through no fault of his own, threatened to choke Tella with very real tears that would in no way match the desire simply to look at the papers.

"Yes, my lady." Tella smiled. "And of course to see Lady Julia. I know she is deeply absorbed in wedding preparations and I miss the time I have spent with her during the social season."

"Yes." Lady Shoreton seated herself on one of the embroidered sofas. "Please take a seat for a moment. I am glad for this opportunity to speak with you."

As there were no bonnets here on which to pass judgment, Tella sensed this was a conversation she ought to avoid. "I believe Julia expected me to—"

"This will only be a moment, child."

Reluctantly, Tella sat.

"I am sure you have realized that Lady Julia's change in state will of course necessarily also change the relationship between us."

Tella had to think. "You mean, between you and me?"

"Yes, naturally. Julia no longer need attend so many social functions, now that she has found a suitable match."

Tella suppressed a shudder. The way Lady Shoreton said *suitable match* just made Tella think *iron trap*.

"I see," she said cautiously.

"We have both been glad of your company, dear, very glad," Lady Shoreton said with uncharacteristic softness. "I know your mother would have wanted me to do no less."

"Thank you, Lady Shoreton."

"But you must realize that I am no longer young myself, and the entertainment I take from attending balls till all hours of the morning is not what it was when I was your age."

"Oh." Tella felt as though she had been slapped, though Lady Shoreton was being very gentle, especially for Lady Shoreton. "I did think you enjoyed them as well, my lady."

"I do. I have friends, of course, and conversation will be so much more pleasant, now that Julia's prospects are settled."

Meaning that she no longer had to face barbs about her daughter's unwed state, Tella translated for herself.

"But I don't care for dancing, myself, as you know, or drinking, or cards. I have been attending to provide you girls with the appropriate chaperonage. But I would like to spend some of my evenings with his lordship, whom you understand is no longer up to very late evenings."

"Oh, of course!" Tella had new appreciation for the fleetingness of time.

Lady Shoreton now waited, hands folded in her lap, for Tella to say more.

Oh. *Oh.* Lady Shoreton expected Tella to say that she understood how her social life was about to be curtailed.

"Surely Lady Julia will still have a social calendar, and I would be happy to attend with her," said Tella carefully.

"I believe your father will not find that to be chaperonage appropriate for your station, *not*—" she raised her hand before Tella could argue, "—not that you have been *in*appropriate, and not that you are bothersome at social functions in any way. Surely you know you are the opposite. You are a delightful companion, and I know Julia will not part with you. But she will be a young married woman, and her interests must necessarily change."

"Of course," Tella said, a little more quietly.

"I will chat with your father, of course, at the earliest opportunity. I know you will forgive a curtailment of your social calendar given that, as I have heard you say to Julia many times, you do not wish to marry for yourself."

But I don't wish to stay indoors *all the time*, Tella restrained herself from shouting.

"This will be a wonderful new time for you, too, to develop new interests." Lady Shoreton was clearly unaware of the sinking sensation in Tella's stomach. "And of course Lady Julia may well want your help in planning affairs she must host as a lady of standing in her own right."

"Wonderful!" *I will become the planner of my best friend's parties!* Tella thought a little wildly.

"You do understand, don't you, that this is not because we don't love you?"

Lady Shoreton truly did look sorry, and despite her roiling insides, Tella mustered a smile.

"Of course! You have been wonderful to me, Lady Shoreton. No mother could have done more."

The lady's eyes teared up slightly, which both astonished and appalled Tella. She counted on Lady Shoreton to be a pillar of strength. Pillars of strength did not cry.

"I have wanted to do for you what any mother would, Donnatella. You deserve it."

She *deserved* it?

No one had ever said anything like that to Tella in her life. What would make Lady Shoreton think she deserved anything?

Before she was truly overcome, Tella rose, and kissed Lady Shoreton's cheek. "I must find Julia," she murmured, setting off down the familiar hallways.

First the papers. She had come for the papers. She must remember them. Then her friend.

* * *

"THERE'S NOTHING HERE."

"'At's what I tol' ya."

"No, I mean, there is literally nothing around here. Look." Fitz gestured an arm in a wide circle. Due to the buildings' odd organization, no doors opened on or even near the corner. Though it was a tight-turning, tiny London street, one could stand at this corner and see into nothing.

And not be seen.

"What's yer point, Fizzie?"

Fitz ignored the nickname. "This is not accidental."

"Nowt accidental 'bout 'avin' yer throat slit. 'At's what I always say."

"I mean, this is a carefully chosen spot in which to kill someone in plain sight. And you said the fellow's throat was slit. Cleanly?"

Gerry rubbed his gray-stubbled chin again. He didn't like Fitz, but surely he knew Fitz could write. That he had a good eye for detail. Fitz held his breath.

"Aye," the older man finally said. "It were clean. Didn't look like 'e were fightin' it."

"So someone perhaps came up behind him and just slit his throat. Someone he knew was there, or he would have been alarmed when his attacker drew close."

"Someone 'e would have joked wit'. A friend?" Gerry looked around. "Or someone 'e din't want to look in th' eye."

Fitz nodded. "A colleague he'd accompanied last night. To do something. Be somewhere."

"A to-do like yer fisticuffs, I wouldn't be surprised."

Fitz was staring off into his memory. "The useless friend is alive for that fight, sees me, sees… the Caped Count, takes off, and then later someone slits his throat. Not much later, for he was here to be found at dawn. So who was the likely killer, other than the fellow in that fight?"

"Not yer Caped Count?"

"Perhaps." Fitz scratched his jaw. "I don't think he was the type. He didn't start that fight. I really don't think so. Didn't look eager to kill either. And his attacker had blood in his eye."

Gerry nodded. "At the very least 'e'd know who done it, wouldn't 'e."

"Thanks for this, Gerry. I won't forget it." Fitz clapped a hand on the other reporter's shoulder.

"Oh aye, I can always use a favor from a nob," said Gerry, but there was no heat in it.

They both knew that their visit, right here, right now, was the closest anyone had come to the identity of the killer.

* * *

"WHAT ARE you going to do for your evening, Tella?" Julia was happily packing away her new purchases.

"What evening? And why are you packing?" Tella asked absently, running her eyes over the front pages of the news-papers that had finally been found for her. She had them spread all over Julia's bed.

"We're going away after the wedding. A wedding trip."

When Tella looked up, her friend was blushing.

"You didn't tell me! How long will you be gone?"

"We expect to do some walking on the Isle of Wight. Lord Wendover has been there, and says I will enjoy it too."

"I will miss you horribly." Tella couldn't help the catch in her voice. It was only true, and it was choking her a bit, that she missed Julia already.

"Oh no! No, you must..." Julia caught herself, Tella could tell, right before she invited her friend along. As she had done all her life.

"No, I mustn't trail along on your wedding trip," Tella said softly, smiling at Julia's look of concern over the question.

57

"At least it is a few weeks away. And you never told me, what you are planning for the evening entertainment you are hosting. That will be before I go."

"I don't have one!"

"You do. The Duke of Gravenshire is most definitely on the social calendar. Everyone has invitations from you, but they're maddeningly vague. A celebration of spring. Really, Tella, how could you? How can one decide how to dress when you don't provide any details?"

It came back to Tella in a rush, flashing before her eyes like the moment before drowning was said to do. "Oh no!"

"Oh yes."

Tella recalled herself sending out the invitations, receiving the responses... and then forgetting about the entire thing because she had more pressing issues with which to deal.

"Julia, you must help me."

"Gladly, darling, but what is there to do?"

Only everything, thought Tella grimly before her eye fell on the words *murder most foul* in Bridle's Gazette.

The same newspaper as the report of the Caped Count.

She skimmed it quickly. This wasn't about the Caped Count. This was a front-page story about a murder not too far from here.

Julia came and read over Tella's shoulder.

"Dreadful, isn't it? My mother will not let me walk abroad without a squad of footmen."

"It is dreadful."

It was dreadfully close to her encounter with the mean-eyed man. Had he turned on the compatriot who'd abandoned him?

Tella looked up to see Julia's woebegone expression. Poor Julia had only had freedom to walk alone out of doors for a few days, after all.

Tella could feel cage walls closing in, herself.

"You must help me with this dreadful party, is what I intended to say." No need to draw Julia's attention to her interest in the murder.

It was true that the idea of organizing parties had seemed unbearably constraining to Tella not a quarter of an hour before. But that had been the idea of planning them alone. Julia enjoyed planning for such social affairs, and she was good at it.

"I can devise decorations for a ball at the drop of a hat," Julia said with pardonable pride, because it was certainly true; Tella had seen her do it. "But it must be something for which people can dress without warning, that fits your invitation for a celebration of spring. So no fancy costume balls for you."

"Of course," Tella answered, as if she cared the least bit.

She needed a look around the scene of the murder herself. And Lady Donnatella, the Duke of Gravenshire's daughter, could not venture abroad alone any more than Lady Julia.

Therefore Lady Donnatella couldn't go.

She must change and go out earlier than she ever had before. She couldn't let it wait for the dead of night.

Apparently, she was the Caped Count, and the Caped Count must look more into this murder.

CHAPTER SIX

*H*enry Fitzwilliam planned his evening far in advance.

The more he replayed last night in his mind, the more it seemed the Caped Count and the man he'd been brawling with had known each other. Fitz had no reason to think it, really; it was only a feeling he had.

There was no guarantee that this Caped Count took the newspapers, especially not with the current sky-high tax upon them.

But Fitz guessed that the Count *had* seen the papers, and would be just as interested as Fitz in the nearby brutal murder.

He stayed in the neighborhood of Claremont Square as the sun went down, the lengthening days fending off the dark for some time, the sun finally succumbing.

As the lamplighters came, making glowing pools of light on the walkways, the hatters and glovers closed up shops, the flower-sellers and street musicians disappeared, and the thoroughfare filled with men and women of every class going somewhere: home, or to an evening's entertainment, or to chase other personal missions that Fitz couldn't guess.

He'd have liked to know them all. Learn their stories. Write a few. He'd rather meet a thousand flower-sellers than one duke, and he'd have more to show for it, too.

The trees in the square cast uneven shadows, and Fitz studied each one. If he knew anything, it was that the Caped Count, as he'd quickly gotten into the habit of thinking of him, preferred to stay in the shadows.

Fitz lounged against the wall, wishing he'd worn a thicker coat against the chill creeping up the stonework, and watched until every flicker of leaf, every darting rodent, looked to him like a young man skulking in the shadows of the square.

There! Wasn't that him?

No, just a peddler, carrying his pack of goods away home.

No—there, he almost missed it. The fawn breeches and black coat could have easily escaped his eye in the shuffle of evening walkers and the passing hacks and carriages. Every gentleman in London wore them.

But Fitz was sure of that deep blue, fur-edged cloak. It was odd, in spring (as he immediately forgot he'd just been wishing for a thicker coat), and definitely odd for the hood to be pulled up over the man's tricorn in only the thinnest evening mist.

He fell in a few steps behind the wiry lad, and stayed with him for half a block before his quarry dashed across the street, just ahead of a four-horse carriage. The carriage blocked Fitz' view.

When the carriage had passed, the Caped Count was gone.

Cursing silently to himself, Fitz ducked through the traffic and made it to the other side alive, a few drivers shouting imprecations at his back.

Where had he gone?

Fitz continued on as fast as he could, trying not to shove the dozens of women and men going his way. The cobblestones sank a little and turned to his right. The other side of the street was just as busy. No Caped Count.

Had the man ducked down a side street?

There was nothing for it but for Fitz to follow, taking one side street after another and searching each one for a slender young man hiding in a fur-edged cloak.

* * *

TELLA WATCHED the man searching the alleyways, undoubtedly for her.

Those who fell into trouble in London because they were new were one thing. Someone actively searching for trouble in London was by far the most annoyingly ridiculous person she'd ever seen.

She left him to it.

* * *

HER ALTER EGO, whom she had never named in her head despite his aliases (because after all, it was *her*), did not have friends or even acquaintances.

She didn't wish to start thinking of him, or herself, as the Caped Count.

Nonetheless, there were people here and there who owed the Caped Count a favor or two. A person who'd been spared a beating, or a robbery, or worse.

A few rasped questions in the right place, and she had some answers.

Her voice would be sore tomorrow, but Tella pretty quickly arrived the spot she'd come out to find.

It wasn't hard to confirm it was the right place. The dark stain of blood splashed the cobblestones and trickled between them. It would stay there, she imagined, until the rain truly came and washed it away.

This evening drizzle would not do it.

Tella looked around. There were people all about, of course, but the shape of the corner and the lack of doors was such that it created a bit of an empty space, a pocket of silence right here.

It was eerie and, Tella suspected, it was why the blood-stain was here.

"I thought the same thing," said a voice behind her.

Tella whirled and drew her dagger, facing the threat.

Damn it, it was the same swanky idiot she'd slipped away from earlier.

"I thought the same," he said again, nodding and waving a hand at the space around them. "A quiet spot in which to kill someone and then slip away pretty much unnoticed."

He looked straight at Tella. "Was it you?"

He was good-looking, Tella realized with a jolt. She hadn't had time to properly look at him in the middle of a brawl. The raw bones of his face fit together in a way that was handsome; and the nose was regal enough to match that aristocratic voice. It contrasted with his blue eyes, and the grooves from frequent smiling at their corners.

Good-looking didn't make her answer questions.

"You..." Tella's irritation might give something about her away. "You're here to make up stories to sell to the papers."

"No," said the young man. "And yes, in a way."

"What's the no and what's the yes?"

"They're both sides of the same coin. I don't need to make up anything. I'd like to find out why he was killed, and yes, if I do, I'll write a story in the paper about it."

"Why?" Tella resisted the urge to poke at the bloodstain with the toe of her boot. "He's dead."

"Even more reason since he's dead." The man was grim, even bitter, as he regarded the bloodstain too. He looked as though he were rarely grim. "Dead people deserve to have their stories told. They deserve justice."

"Justice isn't the same as selling papers."

"Sometimes it feels like it is at least in the right direction."

"You'll be safer somewhere else," Tella rasped at him. As she stepped back from the street, she felt tired for a moment imagining how much effort it was going to be to lose him. "I have to go."

"Did you kill him?"

Tella kept her eyes shadowed. But she met his look.

"I don't do that." She did not *want* to talk to him. People ought to fear her when they saw her in the street. Not chat.

For some reason, her answer bothered him. "You sound as though I'd accused you of using the wrong spoon."

"Killing is for the clumsy, and the cruel people who enjoy it."

"People who use the wrong spoon?"

Tella didn't have time for this. "If there's anything that will get a man killed, it's rushing in where he isn't wanted."

And instead of taking the answer just as it was, the man's eyes narrowed. "A man could be killed practically anywhere."

What sort of conversation was this? Tella turned on her heel and walked away.

The annoying man followed. "You're looking for the same man I am."

"But I am going to succeed, and you should be..." she waved a hand at him. "Wherever swanky young men spend an evening. Don't try to follow me."

"I followed you here."

"No you didn't. You knew where I was going."

The young man looked like he intended to hold his serious expression, but then he grinned. "Well spotted. I'm Fitz, by the way."

"I know," said Tella, stalking around the corner and back into the foot traffic.

* * *

"I DON'T SUPPOSE you know where you're going," Fitz asked as he stayed right with her, step for step.

"To the docks." Tella considered hitting him in the head with something heavy just to get him to stop following her. In fact the only thing preventing her was that she didn't have anything heavy.

"Why?"

"He smelled of fish. Look, just push off, will you? I didn't ask you to tag along."

"You don't think you can use a hand?"

Tella felt her throat tighten. "A fellow gets used to that sort of thing and he'll wish he hadn't."

"Look." He tugged on her arm; Tella yanked it away. They faced each other in the dim dark. "I'm a good man to have at your side in a fight. I was in Wellesley's army, fought in Spain and managed to come back. Might as well let me go with you."

Tella refused to be intimidated by the way the man cast a huge shadow. "Surprised you didn't buy someone to go to the wars for you." A man with an accent like that had been educated, by a family with money. Was he the son of some nabob who had made his fortune in India?

She was terrible with names and faces, but surely this man moved in the same circles she did; so why didn't she already know him?

A half-smile twisted his face into the least sunny look he'd had yet. "Oh believe me, I'm expendable."

Tella looked left. Then right. Occasionally late at night, people saw her. She wanted them to see her, wanted them to behave when they saw her coming.

But she didn't talk to them for any length of time. If someone discovered who she was, her life, as far as she was concerned, was over.

And she was *not* prepared to lose anything else just now.

Still, he was damn determined. And another pair of hands *might* be useful.

"Have you got enough to pay for a hansom cab?"

"I'll ask again. Do you know where you're going? The docklands are miles away, and how would you know where to look for him?"

Tella folded her arms across her chest. "He's not coming from that far away. He's here all the time."

They looked at each other for a moment.

"He's *here* all the time," Tella said again.

"Why's a man like that skulking around Mayfair?"

"Meeting someone."

"So." Fitz folded his arms to match. "Do we wait till he comes back and then learn what his business is here?"

This was a nightmare. Tella had no intention of spending hours in the company of this tall, annoyingly persistent man waiting for their target to return. There might be an appeal to it, but not one she intended to indulge.

No. No appeal to it.

"Fine. We will wait to see if he appears. But don't expect conversational entertainment."

* * *

"Do you care for riding?"

"No." They were leaning on opposite sides of the building's corner, keeping watch in two directions. Tella had insisted there be no conversation, but of course her companion paid that no mind.

She was not about to converse with him about horses. Or anything.

Fitz seemed ready to carry on a conversation by himself. "I quite enjoyed riding."

"Gave it up?" Tella had leaned upon one side of the building's corner, leaving Fitz the other side. She liked having the sturdy stone between them.

"No horse. And no money," he said cheerfully.

Must be a close-fisted nabob, Tella thought. Didn't most of them set up their sons in government positions? Since she had no intention of marrying anyone's son, she had never paid it any mind. Julia's thrice-bedamned Lord Wendover had probably been well-set-up by his father, Tella thought gloomily.

Then her eye caught something. "Isn't that our man?" Something about the way the figure moved felt all too familiar.

For such a big fellow, Fitz moved quite quickly. He craned his head her way. "Can you tell from here?"

"Looks like him to me."

"Good enough for me. Now can we stay with him?"

"*I* can. You will simply have to try to be a little smaller and keep up."

"What a bitter child you are. This won't be easy. I suspect given the hour, he has only recently arrived, and has business to conduct." Fitz laid his hand on his companion's shoulder, did not look surprised when it was shrugged off; still he added, "Can you let him be while he does it?"

She chewed on it in silence. "To find out his source, yes."

"Then let us see what we see."

* * *

THOUGH LACKING IN CHARM, his companion was stealthy, Fitz had to admit. It was more on him than his Caped Count to stay out of sight; that dark blue velvet cape was more useful than he might have guessed. It was a far cry from the British infantry uniform.

Fitz had worn that uniform for years, and all during the long siege at Cadiz. He'd picked up Spanish and Portuguese words and learned to talk to villagers, and soldiers, that weren't British at all. The officers sometimes had speeches about stopping Napoleon from taking over the world. Fitz thought they'd memorized them to help them get through all this.

But for himself, under those stars, Fitz had felt just as forgotten by Britain as he had been by his own father. He doubted the *ton* had given up anything for the defeat of Napoleon, while he and his fellow soldiers had given up everything.

This young man was the most positive picture of London society Fitz had seen in a long time. If there were London gentlemen, even very young ones, with this much grit and determination, perhaps they were the equal of Britain's soldiers after all.

And the two of them made a good team following their quarry. They could drift quite far apart and still stay within sight of each other. When the mean-eyed man made a turn, one of them followed, letting the other trail behind; when their quarry ducked into a building, they did not close ranks but stayed some distance apart, waiting for the man to exit.

They didn't discuss it, just did it.

Had the mean-eyed man known he was being followed, he could have all too easily slipped through some back door and been lost. But he seemed oblivious. Clearly his talents lay more in pure violence than subterfuge.

He had a length of rope shoved into the waist of his trousers; it dangled over one hip, making it very easy to see him as he went in and out on no doubt repellent business.

Their path took them through the Covent Garden area, as Fitz expected given the man's interest in ladies of the night. They witnessed no bloodshed, which was fortunate for many reasons, only one of which was that Fitz strongly doubted his Caped Count would ignore it.

Fitz began to worry a little when he realized their quarry was drifting farther and farther south.

He caught up to his companion to discuss it. "He's heading for the river."

"I *told* you, he smells of bilgewater."

"Do you have a boat under that cape?"

That seemed to give his newfound friend pause. "Perhaps he is simply lodging nearby."

"Or perhaps he *is* traveling the several miles back and forth to the docklands every evening."

There was a blue velvet shoulder shrug. "If he engages a boat, so can we."

"Unless he has a compatriot taking him back and forth."

The boy thought that over too. "He doesn't strike me as someone to have friends." Then he added under his breath, "And frankly I'm due for a bit of luck."

Fitz shrugged. "You cannot go alone, and I have an interest in finding out if the man wants me dead. You likely have the same interest."

He got no answer, and that was enough.

* * *

THEY HAD to hang back or risk being seen when their quarry crossed the Strand on his way to the water.

Tella could see shadowy figures on the grounds of the houses, here and there; no doubt guarding the private residences from any encroachment by river. Some of those houses contained friends of hers.

The idea that she might have to explain herself to some card-playing acquaintance if she were caught trespassing nauseated her. She was far afield from her usual haunts and her very life felt stretched too thin.

But then what support lines had she? Her uncle did not remember that she went out at night, and dear Julia had never known. In a short time Julia would be married and on her way into a new life, and Tella would be alone to watch her beloved uncle sink farther into his old age, and eventually leave her too. Her father was for all intents and purposes already gone.

If she disappeared, it would be some time before anyone in London society missed the Duke's too-tall daughter.

At least this impulsive fellow was an additional pair of hands. He was *someone*.

Why *not* climb into a smelly boat with a strange man to sail down the Thames in the middle of the night?

* * *

TELLA LET Fitz climb down to the wherry boat first, in case the silly giant overturned it.

It rocked as she boarded, but the handful of dark-clad figures hunched over the oars simply swayed with the motion.

Only the wherryman in the bow spoke, and the voice surprised her. It was a wherrywoman. "Show yer coin first."

Tella just looked at Fitz.

"Have you *no* money at all?" Fitz grumped as he fished out a coin and showed it to the girl.

The girl looked unimpressed. "Where d'yer want to go?"

"We want to follow that boat just ahead, and there will be additional for you if you can manage to look like you're *not* following."

The girl looked up and down the water. The boat they wanted to follow was clear enough; but that meant, so were they. "Show me two more o' them and I'll consider it."

Making some grumbling noises, Fitz produced two more.

The girl promptly grabbed all three coins. "We'll do our best. Stay low yerselves."

* * *

FITZ SHOVED himself down a bit on his bench. The Caped Count was taller than all the rowers too, but Fitz didn't want to be blamed if they were noticed.

As the low voices traded back and forth in the dark— "Steady on, Cam,"—"Watch that oar, Will"—Fitz realized most, if not all, the voices were girls. Children.

It didn't sit well with him to let a boat full of children row him down the Thames.

"Where are the men?" he asked a bit gruffly.

The girl who'd taken his coin just laughed, a short bitter bark of a laugh. "Pressed into the Navy, where'dya think?"

Of course.

He'd have to come back and get more of that story.

He wanted to question the Caped Count more, but if the lad wouldn't talk while they were alone, it seemed unlikely he would open up on a boat full of girls. He didn't think young men in British society were *that* different from young men in the British army, or Spanish ones either, for that matter.

Fitz had plenty of time to feel the seat plank imprinting itself into his backside, and to question his choices in life. He dare not even ask his companion's name again.

He wondered if the younger fellow knew anyone in Fitz' family. In seven years in the Army, he had not heard from his father or brothers once. His mother's letters said only that she thought everyone was well. If his family didn't even talk to him, they certainly wouldn't tell him any of the Caped Count's secrets.

Fitz would just have to show him, as he had his fellow soldiers, that he could keep secrets.

A principle rather opposite to his employment of finding out news and printing it in the papers, he mused.

"There he goes," muttered his companion.

Fitz jerked upright, then reminded himself to slouch.

There *was* a shadowy figure climbing out of the wherry ahead, on to one of the old wharves on the south side.

That, he had not expected.

"I hate to be accused of planning ahead, but have you considered how we will get home once this is over?" he muttered under his breath towards his blue-caped new friend.

"Give her another coin."

"I don't *have* another coin."

With a look of great disgust, the lad produced a coin from the depths of the blue velvet cloak.

A gold half-guinea.

Fitz could practically feel their pilot's attention fixated on that coin.

His companion told her, "If you wait here for our return I'll give you another like it."

"Oh, for that we'd wait as long as you need, my lord," the girl said fervently, snatching up the gold coin as quickly as his companion let her.

"You bloody sneak," Fitz hissed under his breath as the rough worn boards of the small old dock appeared off their starboard side.

"I never said I didn't have any money," the blue-caped lad said with perfect calm as he climbed, in two steps, out of the boat.

CHAPTER SEVEN

"You ought to stay in the boat," said Tella.

Predictably, he climbed out.

"I cannot creep all over the London wharves and never call you by a name," Fitz said as though it were reasonable to say, as he followed Tella down the wooden wharf.

"Of course you can." They hadn't lost sight of their man yet. The length of rope at his hip was still visible; she could see it swing a little, a lighter smudge in the dark.

Tella stopped and tried to look as though she were standing carelessly, then moved a few steps forward and did the same again, leading them through the shadows after their quarry.

"But it is awkward. I bet a fellow like you picked up a nickname at school that I could use that would still keep your secrecy for you. Twitchy, perhaps."

Tella looked back at Fitz over her shoulder. "Do you realize how many weapons I have?"

"Thorny. Fred? I'll bet it's Fred."

"I didn't go to school." Tella had no intention of telling

Fitz anything at all, but the man just did keep pressing, and he was so disarmingly cheerful about it, too.

The mean-eyed man disappeared into a warehouse right on the water.

"Ah, I see. So, brothers who nicknamed you, then. Scrawny, or—I know! Runty."

"Not everyone can be built like a bridge pier," Tella said absently as she drew a metal claw out of an inner cloak pocket.

"What is that?"

Instead of answering the question Tella kept pulling. A length of her beloved thin rope came coiled after. "This is my way into the building, as our quarry has gone inside."

Fitz looked up. "You're not thinking of climbing all the way to the roof." They both stopped near the warehouse, which was several stories high.

"Not unless I must, no." Truthfully, she did not have that much rope.

But she did have hopes, hopes set on an open window she could see on the story above. Its sill was up, to catch air from the river which, fetid as it was, was probably still fresher than that inside.

Twice, three times, four times she let the clever, strong little hook loop around her head in a circle, then, changing the angle of its arc, let it fly as gently as a small bird to travel silently through the open window.

"I say, you're good at that," Fitz said without a trace of sarcasm.

Tella just flashed him a smile. "You should see me throw a knife."

Holding her breath, Tella drew the line closer to her. If the hook did not catch on something sturdy, her skills would be for nought.

She felt it catch, tugged a little and felt it hook in securely. Nodding to herself in satisfaction, she pulled the line tight.

And started walking up the outside of the building.

"Oy, Fred. We were talking. I think I actually saw you smile. What the—what if you fall?" Fitz's vehement whisper was almost lost in the noise of the river's water, sluggish though it was.

He'd taken off his hat and was watching her climb.

"You can break my fall if you like." Tella kept moving.

"What about *me*?"

"I said, break my fall. Oh, you mean to get in. No idea. You could wait here."

She peeked over the windowsill to make sure no one with a poor temper was waiting for her. The room beyond the open window was empty, but the door on its other side was ajar, and through it she saw a glow of lantern light. Faintly, she heard voices.

Landing on her feet as lightly as a cat, Tella made her way toward the light.

* * *

IT WAS a relief to leave Fitz behind. He never stopped talking.

The mean-eyed man had entered on the ground floor, and Tella was now on the floor above. If she wished to cross paths with him, she would have to go down.

And she did want to cross paths with him. She needed to find out if he'd done that murder. It was exactly what she wouldn't allow, killing people in her neighborhood. And there was no way the fellow had deserved it.

One reason why she didn't do it. It was impossible for her to know if someone deserved it.

Fitz might get to know someone well enough to know if they deserved it. Tella found herself looking for him. Why?

When she'd been so glad for the quiet not ten seconds ago? A space of hours was too short a time to be comfortable around someone, much less get to know them.

Frowning at herself, she got back to work.

Carefully, and silently, she examined all sides of the little workroom to see if she could locate an exit other than the one that led towards the lantern's glow. The sounds that way seemed to be of guffawing men.

Staying low to keep from being silhouetted in the window, Tella tiptoed toward the door. She heard wagering, and the sound of dice.

It would be hellish to creep back down the outside wall the way she'd just come. But it also sounded like there were more than three of them, and Tella didn't favor her chances.

She was standing in the darkened room, looking toward the light but half-leaning back toward the window, when she heard the hullabaloo.

Concerned shouts mixed with cries of dismay and the men picked up money, dice, and lantern, taking no time to argue about which belonged to whom, and ran, tripped, and stumbled out of sight.

Leaving Tella plenty of opportunity to slink after them.

Moving with care, she crept past where they had gamed and found herself on a walkway. It spanned the length of the building, with ladders down to the main floor. She could see into the gaping cavern of the warehouse, and it was full of trimmed trunks of trees. Rough logs.

And between the stacks of logs staggered a remarkable-looking figure.

"Got to find my 'orse, 'ave you seen him?" shouted a tall man who clutched an oilcloth cape around himself and could not keep upright on his feet.

Tella was disinclined to swear but realized in a flash why soldiers took up the habit.

Stealthy, her paper-writing companion.

Hoping no one looked up, she scurried down a ladder as fast as she could go, trusting her cape to hide her as well as she could be hid in the shadows.

Underneath the loft where she'd just been, Tella saw stacks and stacks of flax straw, tied in bales. She ought to have noticed the slight scent of hay. She let the shadows around the straw bales swallow her up.

Bales up to the ceiling, she realized; they stuffed the end of the building, everything that wasn't full of the timber logs.

"Fantastic 'orse, if you'd seen him you'd know it," bellowed Fitz, drawing the workmen around him closer. Tella wondered what on earth he'd found to put on his head. Something draped down his scalp to his shoulders, making it look almost as if he had seaweed for hair.

"It's a ghost," one of the men shouted, pulling out his pistol.

Tella stopped.

"Ghosts don't stagger, you arse," yelled another and Fitz entered into the argument with gusto, encouraging them to shout at one another.

Tella had *no* idea how they would manage to exit this building when the time came, but since Fitz clearly wanted her to have the chance to search the place for the mean-eyed man, she took it.

And she smelled him before she came upon him, a mix of river bilge and… coal oil.

She rounded the last heap of straw bales.

He was there.

And he saw her.

Their eyes locked together and she knew he recognized her—not her, but the Caped Count who had already run afoul of him twice.

And if she'd thought he looked cruel before, now she knew that hatred looked worse.

She dove at him. Her dagger was already out, and he looked to have none. But before she could close with him and take him down, she saw one hand toss something away, and the other hand appear, clutching a knife.

She twisted as she met him, away from the blade, missing its fall. Well, most of its fall. The tip caught in the blue velvet of her cape, the thick fabric saving her from most of the downward thrust.

Her own knife sliced through his shirt… then tangled in more. The man was wearing multiple shirts of thick linen under his street clothing. Effective poor man's armor.

Tella recovered from her lunge and yanked her knife out of the trap of his clothing. In the next instant, balanced again and able to look, she found that the man had disappeared.

That she had not expected.

Fitz was still shouting something about a truly sagacious horse, smarter than any ten judges put together. As long as he was shouting, she supposed he was alive.

Tiptoeing forward, dagger drawn, Tella came closer and closer to the spot where the mean-eyed man had disappeared.

When she looked down between the bales of flax straw, she saw nothing but leaping orange and yellow.

It was aflame.

And the smell of coal oil, strong enough to make her retch, filled the air.

He had set the stuff ablaze.

Tella started shouting. And running. "We have to go. *Now!*"

As she shouted, she crashed her way through the circle of dock workers to shout it to Fitz, ignoring their yells of "'ere now!" and "Bloody 'ell!"

"Where d'you think you're going?" The man with the lantern swung it in front of them.

Tella just pointed behind her.

The flames were already licking over the tops of the farther bales, a wall of flame advancing like engulfing soldiers. Above, one of the timbers of the warehouse had started to smoke.

The men's shouts immediately became frantic, and they charged for the large double doors through which they'd come.

Which refused to open.

Eight, ten men were left pounding on the door, words dissolving into cries of anger that were beginning to be touched with fear.

Tella reached up to pull down on Fitz' shoulder to get him close enough to hear her over the din. "That rope in his pocket. He's tied the door shut."

He muttered something she couldn't quite hear over the din. Tossing off the components of his disguise Fitz shouted the type of shout a man learned in the Army. "You lot! Help me get this log!"

A couple men turned and looked.

No longer shuffling around pretending to be drunk, Fitz had grasped the bole of a small tree trunk and had lifted it, heedless of the bark gouging his hands.

His muscles bulged, and it was clear both that he could lift the tree, and that it would not move further unless someone helped.

Smarter even than very smart fictitious horses, the docksmen clambered over themselves to get back to Fitz and pick up a share of the log. Tella took the narrowest end; Fitz was by the door.

With the sort of organization that can happen in a disaster, the men heaved the log forward, then forward again, synchronized by Fitz' shout. "Heave! There we go, heave it again! We've got her, lads, heave one more time!"

Yielding to so much abuse, the doors, not designed to repel battering rams, finally shattered.

As the dockworkers scattered, Fitz and Tella staggered along with them. Both steadied on their feet as Fitz grabbed Tella's hand, and they ran with all they had in them away from the dock, across the road and up the alley on the other side.

When it was finally clear no one was following them, when it was finally clear they were alone, they stopped with a good solid brick wall at their backs.

Their hands parted. They looked back at the fire. Both of them were breathing hard.

"You saw my erstwhile cape?" Fitz at least still had his wits about him, speaking of the oilcloth he'd had draped around him.

She nodded. "Swedish arms. And *what* was that thing on your head?"

"I don't know, I found it in the water, and I am *not* happy about it."

"That fire moved so fast!" Tella couldn't help betraying her shock. She had never seen anything like it.

"Straw, and all that wood. It may go slowly, but it will all burn. Unless they put it out."

"Look, they're trying."

Silhouettes barely visible in the fog and the dark, lit by starlight and a wan moon, had pulled a fire engine from somewhere nearby and were using the machine to pump water on the blaze, which had reached the outside wall.

"See that." Fitz pointed at an insignia painted on the warehouse's wall. "Insured. Their fire brigade will come, sure as you're born. They can't be far away."

But no one did come. Flame started to crawl out the windows, its fingers clawing toward the roof.

"Why don't they—why?" Fitz just couldn't believe what he was seeing.

Tella's eyes were seeing back inside the fire. "So fast! He poured coal oil, Fitz, he did it deliberately." Reaching over to grab Fitz' lapel, Tella hauled him around to look at her. "Did he mean to kill all those men? *Did he do it because he saw me?*"

"Don't think that. You cannot help what a man like that does." Seeing his blue-caped friend looked stunned, Fitz grabbed his upper arms and shook him a little, trying to get color back in his face.

Tella hissed and jerked.

Which made Fitz toss back the blue cape and look more closely.

"Not too much blood—nicked you, did he?"

"It's nothing." Tella clamped the arm close and drew back.

But Fitz wasn't having it. "You look like every man I've ever seen who was surprised to find he'd been shot. Once your energy fails you—"

Fitz' big hands were moving over her back, her chest, her hips, her belly, making sure she didn't have another wound on her he couldn't see.

"Get *off* me, you great walking mop—"

He passed a line.

She felt him know.

Jerking back his hands and keeping them in the air, Fitz' jaw fell open.

Then he closed it and just looked at her.

"What should I call you, Fred?" he asked quietly.

"Don't tell anyone."

"I won't."

"I mean it, I'll—" Gasping for air, Tella's mind fought to decide what she could do to him if he revealed her secret.

"I've kept other soldiers' secrets," and those blue eyes looked right into her. "I'll do the same for you."

Nodding slowly, Tella felt herself unclench, her fingers loosen from the hilt of a dagger she had grabbed in reflex.

"Are you Fred all the time, or just in battle?" Fitz asked her, just as softly.

Seeing him stand there, hands wide, eyes soft, Tella felt something inside her start to shake, something at her core. He could see her. He could *see her*, and instead of telling her who she was, he was the first person in her life who had *asked*.

It came out of her as a laugh, choked and startled. She clapped a hand on his shoulder, squeezed and shook it. He chuckled a little in return, perhaps in relief at her relief.

Tella had suppressed her instinct to fight or flee many years ago, ruthlessly determined to keep her head in a fight. But the events of the last hour, the last few days, chopped up her interior defenses and as she laughed, everything tumbled together inside her.

She felt like she had things she had to say, but nothing came out right.

"You—we might have—it was—"

She clutched at his other shoulder, letting his bulk support her even as she tried to shake him. The blue-caped nighttime adventurer never would have, but she was Tella. She was Tella and he could *see her*.

"That fire—"

"Easy on." Fitz nodded as his hands came up under her arms. "We made it out just fine, old chap. We're not dead yet."

She wasn't dead yet, he could *see* her, and he was beautiful.

When she found herself kissing him, she was just as shocked as he was.

She tore herself away. "I'm sorry, I didn't intend—"

Fitz also looked about as confused as one could expect, but all he said was, "Don't stop on my account."

Oh no, she *had* intended.

And she intended again.

This time she noticed that when she threw herself at him, he caught her.

His mouth was so warm, the softness of his lips an extraordinary contrast to the hardness of the muscles under her hands.

Neither the duke's daughter nor the caped adventurer had ever done anything like this.

This was Tella doing it.

And Fitz, who did it rather beautifully.

Amidst the smells of sweat and smoke and nameless river trash, the taste of him was rich and sweet and intoxicating. His mouth slanted a little to fit hers and the way they tasted each other was effortless and perfect.

Her arms slid up to wind around his neck, and his came around her and crushed her close.

He was so hard, so hot against her, Tella felt herself involuntarily melt into him. He made her soft.

He made her forget who she was.

"Wait."

She didn't just pull away from his kiss, she pulled away from his arms. She pulled away from *him*.

Fitz handled confusion very well. Again he kept his hands spread, open, not threatening, though his eyes...

"What?" he asked her softly.

Instead of answering him, she turned and ran.

CHAPTER EIGHT

The Caped Count could run far faster than Fitz, apparently.

By the time Fitz realized Fred wasn't coming back, and arrived, puffing and choking on smoke, back at the edge of the water, the wherry boat was gone.

He stood several landings away from their original wharf, as close as he could get to the fire and still see, and peered across the water in every direction. No sign of the boat, no sign of the Caped Count.

Fitz had to walk away. No fire brigade had come. The smoke was thick and black, and there would be nothing around these docks that did not smell of it. Fitz smelled of it himself.

And somewhere in those flames, he'd lost his hat.

Taking care to stay out of sight of the dockhands, who were still trying to put out the fire with their single, hand-pumped, fire machine, he started walking.

* * *

IT WAS A LONG, cold, tiring walk for a man already shaking with reaction from being nearly trapped in a fire, then kissed, then abandoned.

Fitz was only able to flag down a hansom cab when he approached the bridge, where there was still the odd late vehicle clop-clopping by with tired horses.

He winced as he stretched his legs, trying to get comfortable.

Fred must have bruises all over from the other night's fight, and from tonight. Yet he'd climbed up that wall as though it were nothing, tried to stop the mean-eyed man, and helped them all break out of the burning building. For a young man, he had stamina.

For a young man, he could also kiss.

The *clop-clopping* of the horse's hooves started a counter-point thudding in the back of Fitz' skull, the headache just adding to his confusion.

Fitz had known several soldiers at the front whose trouser contents differed from his. One of those soldiers intended to go home, if he lived, and find what was left of his former family. The other two intended to muster out of the army just as they were; one said it with a smile and a wink, the other with a look that was deadly serious.

He'd also known several soldiers whose trouser contents were exactly the same as his, whose relationships with each other had taken a serious turn during the long sieges, the heat, the loneliness, and the fear. He'd seen soldiers kissing late at night once. Never thought it would happen to him.

Would he have kissed Fred back the way he did if he hadn't known the contents of his trousers?

Maybe, he had to admit. He liked the lad. He was brave, and moved quick, and Fred liked his sense of humor. There was a shocking thought for a man his age. New.

Tight-fisted lad, though.

Confusing as the whole experience was, Fitz knew a few things, and those he would act upon. His comrade-in-arms had been hurt. And had run away. If he was bleeding to death somewhere, Fitz ought to find him. Those were habits left over from the war, and he hoped they never left him.

Best place to look was right back where the wherry boat had found them.

* * *

TIRED ALL THE way through to his bones, Fitz surveyed the area as closely as he could. It was really just steps leading down to the water.

No dead Fred, so that was a good start. No drops of blood. No wherry boat either; it would have been nice to question those rowers, but he wasn't to have that sort of luck today.

The sun's glow crept up over the tilted roofs as Fitz walked away from the river, and wondered if he'd have any luck at all.

Probably not much. He'd needed that hat.

Fitz didn't doubt the mean-eyed man was a killer as well as an arsonist, but he still had nothing with which to identify the man. No way to pin any of it on him when he'd disappeared again.

And where had the Caped Count gone? Hard to write stories for the newspaper, Fitz thought with some bitterness, when he didn't know much more than he had the night before.

Well, he knew a great deal more. But nothing that he would tell.

* * *

Fitz retraced their steps back through Covent Garden and back toward the site of the first knife fight he'd seen the Caped Count have.

He was filthy, tired, and very confused about kisses. Surely if there were no fallen comrade along the track, he ought to return to camp—home, it would be, and rest?

When he kept walking because he was too tired to stop, he found himself in Claremont Square.

The daylight was creeping into the square, too, shedding daylight on the places underneath the trees that had previously been too dark to see.

He was too tired even to walk around the square, he admitted to himself as he leaned against a trunk and sighed.

There were perhaps a dozen grand homes here, the richest of London's elite, houses staring at each other with fat satisfaction across the green as if nothing bad would ever be allowed to happen, as if a knife fight hadn't taken place just a few yards away.

Fitz' eyes popped open. Just a few yards away—

He looked around. With the dawn came a bustling wave of maids and footmen, dusting carpets, emptying chamberpots, wrapped in bonnets and hats and off to various markets.

Any one of these houses could easily shelter a young man with the money for a blue velvet cloak.

Or—and this just barely seemed possible, but could also be true—a young woman.

In war, Fitz had seen wives, mistresses, and camp followers put on their men's clothing as coolly as you please and ride onto the battlefield. Some of them tended to men's wounds, some of them rifled the pockets of the dead, some of them took up bayonets and gutted the enemy. And there was no predicting what a woman might do from where she started.

That was all besides those men whose trouser contents differed from his own.

As Fitz stood musing, he realized that one of the footmen outside the tiny gate of the largest house was eyeing Fitz, and with some suspicion. But the man turned away to tip his hat to a bouncy little maid walking up the stairs from the kitchen below. "Off to market, Allie?"

"Cook says his lordship wants quince jelly, what a notion. I'll be back in plenty of time for his breakfast, never mind her ladyship's."

"Oh aye, the way she sleeps you're safe enough for sure." The footman helped her to the street, then gave Fitz one more good glare, just to make sure he stayed where he was, Fitz thought, as the maid bustled away.

Fitz kept his face looking straight ahead but rolled his eyes to take in the house from top to bottom. It was enormous, easily the largest house he'd ever seen in town proper. He'd have to find out who lived there. It couldn't be that easy, could it?

Probably not. But a lady who slept late might well be a lady who stayed out late, *very* late, doing goodness knows what.

CHAPTER NINE

*T*ella didn't know what to do with her clothes, her cloak, any of herself. It all smelled of smoke, and fear, and the sweat of running away.

She had *run away.* She couldn't have stayed next to him another minute.

Tella had never kissed any of the men who paid court to her, not in all the years she'd been part of the London social season. She had never once *wanted* to. They were all so easy to fool, and so put off by her height and her laughter and her skill at cards and the fact that she couldn't be bothered to remember their names.

Then she'd gone and kissed that great galumphing tree trunk of a man. She had definitely kissed *him,* no matter how much she wished, in the safe dark of her hideaway, that it had been the other way round.

What a sad sack of desperation she was, so rattled by losing her uncle, and Julia, that she grabbed the first man who met her eyes and didn't think of her as someone else.

What must he think of her now? What must he think of *him,* the Caped Count? Because for all that Tella had never felt so seen, it had been the Caped Count Fitz had written about for the papers.

Oh no—and what would he *write* now?

This was far worse than any discovery of her secret she'd ever imagined. This wasn't her father learning about her nighttime jaunts, though that would have been horrifying; this wasn't Julia. This wasn't even Lady Shoreton. This could be all of London, if Fitz chose to hang her out to dry.

How desperate was he to sell papers?

If he'd once been rich, and missed riding, wouldn't he tell the juicy tale of the night-time woman with a knife and cloak and bag of clever tricks who'd led him to the scene of a *fire?*

The woman who had *kissed him?*

Tella wrapped her arms around her waist, unable to stop her own shivering. She must force herself to wash, change her clothing, climb the hidden stairs to her room, and try to sleep. But fear seized her, a more convulsing fear than she had felt since the night her mother died.

And then she remembered that she could sleep as late as she liked because her uncle wouldn't expect her at breakfast. Tella sat down against the rough wooden wall, and cried and cried and cried.

* * *

THE HENRY FITZWILLIAM who broke in on Gerry Hirst's breakfast table looked like he had clawed his way out of the grave.

"What *ails* you, man?" Gerry jerked Fitz' coat, drawing him into the tiny flat. "Have you been run over in a carriage accident?"

"Might be the only thing that hasn't happened to me tonight," murmured Fitz.

Then he caught sight of the plump little woman standing, mouth gaping, by the table, a steaming teapot in her hand.

"Oh bollocks," he said under his breath. "Of course you're married."

"And how does *that* offend *you*?"

"No, no, I mean, I'm sorry. I'll just—"

"Yer here first thing and you haven't slept and you smell like someone dunked you in the river and *then* set you on fire. Come in and have a sleep at least."

Fitz doffed his hat to the still-astonished wife. "No, I mustn't. My apologies."

Instead of accepting his apologies, that woman shook herself all over, then reached for another teacup. "You look like you've had an uncomfortable adventure. Sit down and have a bite and we'll see about putting you to rights."

Fitz looked at Gerry. That man just raised both hands as if he was out of it. "I listen to her. You should too."

"Thank you, Mrs.—it's Mrs. Hirst, isn't it?"

"What the hell else would it be?" muttered Gerry, but the little woman just bustled about, carving a thick slab of bread, spreading it thickly with butter, and putting it next to the tea.

Which, truthfully, looked better than any feast, to Fitz.

"Just a few moments, then." He slid into the chair.

"We're gonna hafta scrub that chair. What are you *doing* here?" Reluctantly, and with a slight curl to his lip, Gerry sat back down before his own breakfast.

"If I tell you about the night I've had, and then pass out, if you write anything about any of this, you have to split the money with me too, you know," said Fitz around a big mouthful of bread and butter.

"That story?"

"*That* story."

* * *

"Your Grace, Lord Preston isn't quite well."

Tella simply could not keep everything she was hiding inside her. *Something* had to come out. She'd picked this.

The Duke of Gravenshire looked up in astonishment from his toast.

"Lady Donnatella, *you* do not look quite well. You haven't made yourself ill waking so early just to see me, have you?"

"No, Papa, of course not," and with the informal name, Tella swept up to the chair beside him.

She wanted to hug him.

The Duke would have permitted it, but he wouldn't have liked it. Change in London, in England, in the United Kingdom did not upset him; in fact he pushed for it. His eagerness for the world to change was balanced by his desire for everything at home to stay predictable.

Or perhaps it was simply the effect of losing his wife.

Leaning towards her father, Tella put her hand on his sleeve. That would have to do. "Dr. Burke has been to visit, sir. He believes Lord Preston may have suffered some sort of apoplexy."

"Really?" Now the Duke put down both his toast and his paper. "He seemed fine yesterday. Did we not have sherry together last night?" His brows pulled together. "Was that last night?"

Tella had no way of knowing and didn't want to point out that with her father's schedule, it could easily have been days ago.

All the time blurred together when he woke, went to the houses of Parliament, returned, ate, and slept. He'd mentioned once that he preferred it that way.

"He does not remember the last... year or so. Perhaps two." Tella was proud that her voice did not waver.

"Not really. Extraordinary. Odd that I hadn't noticed that quicker."

Tella had noticed immediately. But she did not bring that up, either.

"I think...I think he might need a nursemaid, perhaps? To look in on him once in a while. Or just—" Should it be her?

Should it be her, staying here while Julia went off to the Isle of Wight, a married lady? Should it be Tella, making sure her father's toast wasn't burnt and checking on her uncle multiple times a day?

It should, shouldn't it?

If she could still go out at night, wouldn't she be glad to do it?

It ought to make her glad, a future calendar of days spent caring for the men she loved best and nights spent caring for her beloved London streets and all the people in them.

It ought to.

But instead, it almost choked her.

"Never mind, Papa," she said in a rush. "I will do it. It ought to be me."

"He does adore you, child, but oughtn't you keep some of your time free for the social scene? Isn't this your third round of looking for a husband? If you don't make that effort, it won't happen." He looked back toward the paper, shaking it out. "It doesn't happen by accident."

No. It didn't happen by accident. Her father's father, Tella knew, had suggested that his son dance with Tella's mother at a ball with the theme of the countryside. She'd been dressed as a shepherdess. She had a hook and everything. By the end of the dance, her father had asked her to use it to pull him a little closer, please.

Not *exactly* an accident.

"It's my fourth season," Tella said quietly.

"Is it?" Now her father's astonishment exceeded the ability of his eyebrows to climb high. "Really, Tella, you ought to find some eligible man this season."

He did not add aloud that it was spring and the season would be over soon. He didn't have to.

"Is that a greater or lesser crisis than Uncle Albert having an illness and losing his memory?" Her voice was climbing, too. Why didn't the Duke ever grasp what truly worried her?

"It is certainly getting to be a serious matter, wouldn't you say?" He peered at her. "*Wouldn't* you say?"

"Would you?"

The Duke looked around the breakfasting room. At the porcelain vases filled with flowers, the silver-rimmed bowls, the blue damask wallpaper, the chairs upholstered in needlepoint. "There's nothing wrong with you staying here, well, always. I just assumed you would not wish to do so. Your mother...of course your mother was always interested in the larger world."

She had been.

Tella's mother, who like Julia had been allowed to walk perhaps a whole half mile the day she became engaged. Who, like Tella, had enjoyed riding in all weather, but had never had anywhere to go.

Tella's mother, who always described London as a whole world right outside their door, if only they could open it and look.

"Mama loved London, and she loved you. So do I." The waver was creeping, all unwanted, into Tella's voice.

The Duke of Gravenshire wasn't reading the paper, but he wasn't looking at his daughter either. His jaw thrust forward, as it did when he was thinking over something he intended to say. "Some families have many daughters just so one or two stay home to take care of the parents when they are older. I've never cared for that idea. And I have only one child, one beautiful, delightful daughter, and there is no one to take care of but me. I know, and his lordship. I have made provision for you in my will, Donnatella, and the cousin who is my heir will not gainsay it. I mustn't be the reason that you miss having a home of your own. A husband. If you like."

"Thank you, sir." And Tella meant it. It was more than her father had ever said before on the subject. She'd never cared before, but today, it felt important. "But for Lord Preston...?"

"By all means, engage a nursemaid. Your problem isn't finding a nursemaid, it's that he will turn her out as soon as he learns he's got a nursemaid."

"Well, I'll tell him she's only a new maid for the upper floors."

His Grace gave Tella an appraising look over the top of the papers. "I haven't noticed him so ill that *he* won't notice you manufacturing stories."

Well, there was ill and there was ill. She wished her darling uncle were well enough to tell about last night.

But then she might have to tell him about the kiss, and she still didn't know what to say about that. Because she still didn't know what to *think* about that.

Later. Right now she had a chance to ask her father, "Will I see you at the Woolacre ball tonight?"

His eyes were already back on the news. Tella wished he would stay with her a little longer. But this entire conversation was more than she'd had in weeks. She could not expect more now, especially if she wanted him to join her this evening.

But he surprised her, and looked up again. "Yes. I apologize, Donnatella, for not taking more of an interest in your social affairs. Too much confidence in Lady Shoreton, perhaps."

"Oh, you can have infinite confidence in Lady Shoreton, Papa, I assure you!"

"Very well, no criticism intended. But I ought to come see what this social scene is about, if no one has snatched up my daughter yet."

He rather made it sound as if she were a cake on a plate that ought to have been eaten by now through simple hunger of the masses.

All right.

"I would love to be there with you, sir. Will you dance with me?"

"We've established that the point is for you to dance with eligible young men, surely," said her father, turning back to his paper.

He loved her, she knew that. Without disturbing him further, Tella rose and kissed him gently on the temple, patted his arm. He made some sort of noise, some sort of approval noise, and that was about as much response as she could expect.

He loved her but he thought she should get married and leave him. And if she didn't, she would be the spinster daughter of a duke until she died. She'd still have the freedom of the night. Hardly anything to cry over.

She'd go back upstairs and cry in private.

* * *

LADY JULIA ARRIVED at the Gravenshire house in a four-horse carriage her family usually used only outside of London. She understood why her mother did not want her to walk. But seeing Tella couldn't wait.

Just before she knocked, some movement caught the corner of her eye and she turned, and looked across the street.

Just there, at the edge of the square, several disreputable looking characters lurked underneath one of the trees. And in the middle of the day.

She squinted hard at them. If they rushed her, she'd have a good description of them, at any rate.

It was a good thing she'd brought the carriage.

* * *

"Where did you two meet, exactly?"

"'S not a dinner party, Fizzie, you said you needed information." Gerry shuffled his feet back and forth.

"I am simply fascinated by your colleague here."

The slight man in patched clothes, gray from many washings, narrowed his eyes. "I'm not fascinating."

But he was. For one thing, this was London, where you could practically tell who someone was by the way they spoke.

Not this fellow. Gerry's informant, who said his name was Dan Fox, spoke like a clerk and dressed like a chimney sweep.

"Oh but you are," Fitz insisted. "Where are you from, again?"

"Where are *you* from?" Fox jerked his chin at the massive house that took up the entire side of the square. "Duke of Gravenshire—you don't mean you don't at least know that?"

"Fine, fine, the Duke of Gravenshire." Gerry was gruff. "You know any of these people, Fitz?"

"How on earth would I know them?"

"Listen to yer accent, man! I assumed you went to school with them, or rode to hounds, or something."

He might have gone to school with some of them. "I don't ride to hounds." Not while serving in the Army for seven years. "Gerry, I'm a *third son*. I'm entirely expendable. My father would have to lose two entire other sons before he would give one damn about me."

Gerry gave him a sideways look. "I wondered why he let you go off to war, when so many other rich lads bought their way out of it."

"I doubt he knows I went. I'm certain he doesn't know I'm back."

In fact, looking around these grand houses, with their sweeping mullioned glass windows and people all bustling in and out as though what happened here was so, so important, Fitz could put the feeling straight into words. "I've never set foot in any of these houses and I'd be happy never to do it. Of all the people on the face of the earth these are the least… human."

That set Gerry back on his heels a bit. Even their informing street rat looked taken aback by Fitz' vehemence.

"I thought once you'd had your fill of playing with the paper, you'd take yourself off to Dad's house by the river somewhere," Gerry admitted.

"I'd rather be hanged. I work for my money, same as you, and we need another taste of this story or we won't get paid."

"*I* will," put in Fox, patting his pocket. Not the one holding Fitz' coin, of course. He was a professional. Professional *what*, Fitz didn't know, but he was definitely a professional one.

"You got plenty of news last night."

Fitz had informed Gerry of his adventures with the Caped Count—leaving out the kiss and all the feelings that had gone with it. "If I print an account of the fire with any sort of detail, everyone will know I was there. I'd be lucky to stay out of jail."

"What fire?" asked the informer, with evident interest.

Fitz looked back toward Fox. It was like the magnetic pull of a compass; the second he looked at the man, he wanted to know more. "I don't suppose you'd let me ask you a few questions. Strictly to get to know you."

Fox drew back. "I don't need to get to know you."

The Bridle's Gazette readers would devour this man's story; Fitz could just feel it. "Look here, if you—"

Just then, the closed draperies behind a window on an upper floor of the Duke of Gravenshire's townhouse were pulled back.

The window framed a dark-haired young lady, one with a turn to her jawline that made her look opinionated.

Fitz imagined it under a tricorn hat.

Gerry saw him looking. "You don't mean that's the—"

"You're not needed any longer," Fitz said bluntly to Fox. The readers of Bridle's Gazette would just have to do without.

"I will be. If I'm not mistaken, you want to see inside a few of these houses. You may need me."

"I'm not going to break into houses in Claremont Square!" In the middle of his bluster, a thought struck him, and he looked at the street rat again. "Though I might need some other information—if you can find it out?"

"Such as?"

"Whether the Duke of Gravenshire has a daughter? Or a son?"

"Phew, you *have* left society! That's the Duke's daughter right there, as you ought well to know. Even a third son must occasionally hear the society news."

Fitz was too wise to look down on society news. It paid well. But he didn't think it would ever suit him. "Very well, what if I wanted to know what was on her calendar this evening?"

"Oh, that would cost you. More than a shilling. Have you *got* more than a shilling?" The fellow looked Fitz up and down. "Or a different suit?"

"I *have* got a different suit, and I'll thank you to keep your insinuations to yourself." Fitz had one additional suit. He had better get into it, as even with Mrs. Hirst's strong efforts, this one still looked the worse for wear after last night. "And I'll get you three shillings for the information."

"Five."

"Three."

"Four."

"Three."

Fox glowered. He had a dark complexion and black eyes, and managed to make the glower quite something despite being slight. "Three and a half and don't get so smart you do yourself out of a deal."

"Three and a half." Fitz nodded. "And at some point you let me ask you a few questions about yourself."

The man hesitated. "All right," he finally said, with the air of someone who expected his bargainer never to collect.

"See, I told you Dan Fox could find out anything you needed to know about the gentry." Gerry rubbed his hands, anticipating further story sales.

"Yes, he's marvellous. Look, Gerry, you had better get to writing something we can print—the murder, that's what we've got, that there's a witness to the murder who connects it to a fight near Claremont Square."

"Ye're cracked. He'll come straight for ya."

"Not unless Dan Fox tells him where I live."

"I don't know where you live," put in Dan.

"Nor will you. Later, Gerry, I've got an engagement to go to. Fox, I'll meet you here in three hours, and by then I expect to know where the Duke's daughter is being entertained tonight."

* * *

"Julia, you ought to have sent just a card. I am no fit company today."

"But my dear! We have the Woolacre ball tonight, and not many days remaining before your own affair. We must discuss it." Julia folded away her reticule with a pleased smile.

"It is so easy to decorate in spring, I've simply ordered wall after wall of flowers. But it will need a bit more to it."

Tella sat deep in the corner of the settee, with her arms wrapped around herself. She felt frail. She had a place in London society, a place that allowed her to do what must be done, what she'd longed to do ever since she'd lost her mother.

A place in London society that depended on her entertaining the guests that she had invited to her father's house. No matter how frivolous it seemed.

Even when she felt it impossible. "I cannot do this, I simply cannot."

"You're ill!" Julia jumped out of her chair.

No doubt to throw her arms around Tella. Which would hurt. Tella put up a warding hand to stop her. Which also hurt, but differently.

Slowly, Julia sat back down.

Julia was the one person who would be interested to hear all of Tella's tangled feelings about that kiss.

But it had to do with the Caped Count, and anything to do with that was dangerous. And she could not bring any danger near her beloved Julia, she could not.

She would retreat to the same position she had taken with her father.

"Not I. My uncle." Tella had to swallow. "My *great*-uncle. He can't remember things, Julia, he can't remember what happened a fortnight ago. My—" Her head sagged.

"Oh, but...you said it wasn't serious?" Slowly, Julia sank back down.

Tella hadn't wanted it to be serious. "I didn't want to burden you."

"Tella. We're friends." Julia didn't try to come closer now. "Good friends. I thought we were. Why would you not tell me?"

When Tella looked up, at her sweet friend's sad, serious face, she had to pinch the inside of her arm to keep the tears from beginning again. There were so many things she'd never told Julia. Most of them, she *never* could. "Julia, your life will be wonderful. Our paths are parting, aren't they? I couldn't, I didn't want to burden you."

"Our paths needn't part that much. Unless you wish it."

I don't wish for any of this! But Tella forced herself to sit upright. She could pretend that all was normal. Normal enough. Normal enough would be good, for Julia.

Slowly, she said, "I think you'll find that the paths of a married lady and a spinster don't cross all that often."

"Tella." Julia's hands clasped each other tightly. "If my company won't suit you any more, you may simply say it. You are so stylish and exciting, and you have let me follow along in your wake for years. I would certainly understand if you don't wish to socialize with a boring married lady."

"No! No, no no no!" At that Tella launched herself across the small space between them, winding her arms around Julia and squeezing her tight. "Never. Never at all. Never say so."

"Well then why... Oh, you poor thing. You look so very tired. And is that a bruise?" She lifted a curl to look underneath; Tella ducked away. "What have you been doing to yourself? Do not worry another second about this party. Just tell me what you plan to wear. In fact, let us go put together your outfit for this evening, shall we?"

She could do it. She could do it, if Julia was with her. Be the silly daughter of the Duke, too tall to marry, madly in love with... dancing and cards.

It had never sounded so lonely before.

Tella never realized how closely loneliness had stalked her since her mother's death until it threatened to become total.

"Let us stop in and greet Lord Preston." Julia's voice was soft as she helped Tella to her feet, all unknowing of Tella's bruises and sore parts. "Have you told him of your worries?"

"What good would it do? He cannot help it."

"He must know something is wrong, dear." Julia's soft, firm voice persisted. "Perhaps he is waiting for you to say something. Perhaps it is he who is afraid you will notice."

That sounded terrible. "I don't want that for him, of course I don't."

"Bring his lordship some tea, would you please?" Julia addressed a footman as she led Tella out of the room by the hand like a little girl. "And something with jam on it for him. Don't I remember that he likes sweet things?"

"He does." Tella stopped her friend to hug her around the waist. "Almost as sweet as you."

Perhaps she wouldn't lose her friend entirely.

At least, not until she was married.

* * *

But when she faced her beloved uncle, she couldn't make the words come.

Julia had to start that, too.

"Lord Preston. Lady Donnatella tells me she worries that you aren't feeling well."

"Well enough, well enough." His eyes, usually so sharp, clouded as if the thoughts behind them had gone vague. "Well enough—" But then he looked up at Julia's soft smile, and at Tella. "I'm not *quite* well, Donnatella, but I didn't want you to worry."

She knelt at his feet. "It never worries me for you to tell me how you are." And then, even with Julia hovering nearby, Tella felt she had to risk the question. "Do you not remember, our pact to tell each other how we were every morning?"

"A pact? No." The straight, strong lines of his face crumpled for a moment. He must be so frightened too, frightened of what he'd lost, thought Tella. "What a thing to forget."

"Never mind it, sir. You are still my favorite uncle. I'll bring my breakfast in here with you each morning, shall I?"

He looked around, the blue curlicued patterns on the small tile table bright in the afternoon light. "Did we do that? No, I don't think we did."

It was encouraging, just that small denial. "We did not, we breakfasted together downstairs. I don't remember why we started." Talking meant lying, Tella realized; that was why she'd given it up.

"Well, I don't either," and he laughed, and Tella felt a little better.

If only things could stay like this, just like this. She could forget kissing Fitz, and the terror and the dark and the smoke and the fire, and the mean-eyed man who liked to hurt people. She could stay in here and be Lady Donnatella all night as well as all day.

It wouldn't be too lonely, if only time would stop now.

CHAPTER TEN

*N*ew gloves were always a pleasure, and Julia insisted Tella borrow the new fan.

Tella suspected that Julia was hiding from Lady Shoreton that she had bought the fan after all.

It was another London ballroom, another swirl of people she'd known since birth who didn't know her at all.

So many people, that they warmed the night air and filled the room with color and motion.

One of the many positive features of being the duke's daughter was that Tella set fashion more than followed it. The chiffon shawl wrapped around her throat suited her, and it would be reported in the publications that followed such things. She could expect dozens of ladies to be wearing similar shawls within the week.

The Duke of Gravenshire, on the other hand, seemed a little out of place, with his outthrust jaw and gruff questions. Tella half expected him to start interrogating young men about why they hadn't yet married her.

Well, she and her father were related.

And Lord Preston looked handsome and hearty in a purple coat. Though sadly, if there was one thing he definitely remembered, it was that Tella was not married.

And his eyesight at a distance wasn't as bad as she'd thought.

"I say. Haven't seen that fellow before. Strapping young lad, isn't he?"

Rolling her eyes and laughing gaily, waving her borrowed fan, Tella turned to look.

And stopped.

Strapping was a word for Fitz. Also looming. Towering, certainly. Men's fashions these days were stark and plain, and they certainly didn't make him look smaller. His clothes hugged every inch of him and outlined all his long limbs exactly.

He should not be here.

He could change everything she didn't want changed.

She'd stay away from him. Far away from him. The tiny part of her that was relieved to see him was only glad she needn't feel guilty about leaving him on that dock.

Where she'd kissed him. Then run away.

Why was he *here?*

And why was he *moving her way?*

He didn't even *know* her. He knew the Caped Count.

Lady Shoreton noticed him too. Of course she did, she was primed to notice available young men. "I am not acquainted with that gentleman; have you met him?"

"No," said Tella feeling perfectly honest, since they'd never been introduced.

He seemed to give her statement the lie anyway. Though he did stop to nod and smile to a few others in the room, his path was quite straight, and it led straight to her.

Just as he had made straight for her in that street fight.

Tension wrapped her tighter. These two worlds mustn't get any closer.

And there was something else. She didn't want him to see her here, where she had to be soft.

She'd been fully armed and armored before, and she'd *kissed him*. And she had spent days fighting off horrible things like tears. She didn't want to see him now. Certainly not without weapons.

Tella didn't know why she cared what he thought. He looked like any other young boor who spent his time in clubs and gaming halls, his hair a little shaggier, his boots a little more scuffed. His careless grin reinforced the impression she had of him as someone too rakehell and foolish to avoid a fight.

But even as he drew closer, the light showed her new things. Sparks of gold in his curly hair, as if he spent time outdoors; yet his face didn't have the leathery look of someone who rode or hunted. He lacked the reddish flush or sleepy eyes of many a habitual drinker. His clothes had been expensive when new, but they were not new.

Sadly, he was an idiot, but attractive.

Her eyes traveled up the length of him, from his boots to his face. He was quite near now.

"Would my lady like to dance?" he said, seeming to find her examination amusing.

He extended his hand.

The next dance was a waltz.

Tella considered giving him her usual little speech about how, doubtless, she would feel safe in his arms.

She decided not to say it.

While it had always been a lie, as Fitz drew her, first to the dancing floor, then into his arms, she didn't feel safe at all.

He recognized her. He must. That was why he had that

look in his eyes—and why he had to go. "You should not *be* here."

"You shouldn't stick me with the cab fare, Fred, nor kiss me and run off—with *our* boat."

His voice was soft enough to keep others from hearing the words, but he spoke to her exactly as he had that night on the pier.

He knew exactly who she was—*he knew exactly who she was,* and treated her just the same. He kept talking. "Nor should you leave me behind when invading an enemy stronghold. Nor should you invade, for that matter. I could go on." He leaned just an inch closer. "Did you want to discuss this now? Here?"

"We're not going to discuss it."

"Oh, we will discuss at least part of it," and he smiled as he moved even closer, looking out over the room as if he were pleased to have a dance with the duke's daughter, but making no great meal of it.

She hoped it would be the invading they would discuss, and not the kiss.

He truly was tall, not just gangly; so tall that she even had to look up, just a little, to meet his eyes.

It was a new sensation, but not what Tella found dangerous.

It was the way his arm went around her, the way his hand closed around hers. She'd had dance partners whose hands roamed alarmingly into inappropriate places; his stayed entirely appropriately placed.

Yet she had never before so clearly felt the sensation of being *held* in a man's arms.

"I would wager that you are quite a good dancer," he said, which also sent a tremor through her. He seemed to *know* her. Not just her alter ego; all of her. *Did* he?

And then the music started, and they had to dance.

Tella thought that she had danced. She had been out for so many seasons, had attended a dizzying number of parties.

But now, swept away in his certain arms, she realized that she had been wrong. This was her first dance.

His confidence moved her with him. Not as if they followed the rhythm of the music, but as if it happened because of him.

She could feel the music how he must feel it. They were inside it, and she floated on it, following his lead because it would be unthinkable to do anything else.

Tella wasn't conscious of her feet or if her heart were pounding, or even beating. She was enveloped in the experience. She moved and spun and it didn't even feel like dancing. It felt like breathing.

When the music slowed, Tella felt his arm against her back, pulling her a little closer to him so that she could feel the warmth of his chest brushing against hers. As they slowly twirled the last twirl, she could feel him take in a sudden breath, and she realized that they were very close, much too close, deliciously close.

And then he was looking at her in the golden bubble in which they had danced, and he murmured, "The music has finished."

"Has it?"

She wanted to move closer.

But some tiny part of her brain responsible for telling her these things reminded her that they were in a public place, in fact a ballroom.

As she took a deeper breath, hoping it would make her feel a little less light-headed, she realized too that the room was so quiet because no one else was on the dance floor.

Only them.

They had displayed themselves like street performers, dancing across the entire floor so entirely wrapped up in themselves that they had not noticed when the other dancers retired to simply watch them.

Tella's feeling of floating in a golden bubble popped.

Her father would be angry. *She* would be angry. She didn't do *this*. She didn't draw attention to herself, not this way.

London mustn't see her *now*.

When she looked back at the man's face she expected him to be leering, or smug, or anything she could dislike and then she would not regret walking off this dance floor and closing as many doors between them as it took to keep him at arm's length, keep away his questions and his smiling eyes and his dangerous dancing. Away from her.

Instead, he looked as astonished as she felt.

His lips were slightly parted, as if he was just stopping himself from leaning over to kiss her, and his eyes were as surprised as she felt her whole body to be.

And that, she realized in a sudden flash, was even more dangerous.

"Thank you, for the dance," and if Tella sounded a little breathless, well, she couldn't help that. She curtsied to him, deeply, and then forced herself to walk, slowly, off the floor.

* * *

IT HAD BEEN easy to slip into the party on the heels of an old acquaintance, even an exclusive affair in the heart of London society. Fitz knew the rituals, the language; he probably knew some of the people.

He thought he'd feel like a snake in the grass, sneaking in. Instead he felt disoriented, as if he'd walked into a field tent and found himself in his father's drawing room. It was all here, the life he'd left behind. Somehow he'd thought that if he left, it would change.

Plenty of young ladies milled about, in pallid gowns, looking as if lifting a cup of tea might overtax them.

Also, they were short.

If he hadn't known her, he still would have headed straight for Tella to ask her to dance. She was always in sparkling motion, her fluttering fan, the rise and fall of her voice creating a whirlwind of temptation that drew him towards her. He thought it would draw any man.

And he didn't like to waste time.

He might have rushed a bit too quickly, though. There were people whispering all around. All these people, who likely knew nothing of the wars raging all around the world but were dying to know about Lady Donnatella's dance partner.

Well, her dance partner was sure of it now. Even without the blue velvet cloak, Fitz recognized the Caped Count's eyes, and jaw, and that particularly displeased expression that he—or she—wore when looking at him very, very closely.

He was desperately interested in *why* the Duke of Gravenshire's only daughter spent her nights thwarting street vultures; but in his writing he'd found that *what* had to come before the *why*. She was here, she looked quite recovered from their narrow escape, and she clearly recognized him, too.

Fitz wondered if she'd recovered from the kiss as well. It was having a delayed effect on him.

He needed a much more in-depth interview with the Caped Count, and had no idea how to achieve it in public.

* * *

TELLA KNEW Julia would be on her within moments, and no amount of hiding behind vases of lemon branches would prevent it.

Indeed it was less than two minutes by her time estimation before Julia found her.

"Who *is* he?"

"Don't squeak, Julia. It makes you sound like a mouse."

"Don't you bite at me, young lady. I know when you are rattled. And you are nearly never rattled. Is this something else you're not telling me? Who *is* he?"

Tella snapped open her fan. Julia's fan. She felt in dire need of it. So, so many things she wasn't telling Julia. "I don't know the gentleman."

Julia looked back to the dance floor. Couples were once again forming patterns, the sound of chatter in the room ticking upwards to a more normal volume.

Julia said, "If you didn't know him before, you do now."

"I agree," put in an obviously male voice, and Tella whirled.

He was standing right there.

"Please forgive me, my lady, I should have introduced myself before I asked for the favor of a dance."

At least he hadn't said the *pleasure* of a dance, thought Tella. That would have been entirely too accurate.

"I am Lord Henry Fitzwilliam, sadly out of society, I'm afraid." Fitz didn't sound sad at all. For anything, much less improperly introducing himself.

She would have to speak. "My apologies, sir, I feel I ought to be familiar with your family—is it...?"

He rescued her from the lack of a handy copy of Debrett's list of peers. "No need for deference, I assure you. My father has other, far more satisfactory sons. Just Lord Henry. At your service."

There was something about the intentional way he said *at your service* that continued to get under her skin, warming her up from the inside.

"It's lovely to make your acquaintance," said Julia, curtseying when Tella didn't. "I am Lady Julia Harrell, daughter of Lord and Lady Shoreton. Perhaps you know them."

"I do not know many people here tonight," said so-called Lord Henry Fitzwilliam. "I don't attend many such evenings. But I'm very glad I came," and the smile crept back into his eyes, and Tella wanted to smack him with that fan.

Would have, had it not been borrowed.

Julia kept going. Apparently she could not hear Tella loudly thinking *stop*. "Allow me to introduce my friend, Lady Donnatella Fairchild. You must at least know of her father, the Duke."

"I do. I have been following His Grace's proposals for improvements to London with great interest, Lady Donnatella. And I have wanted to meet you."

The man bowed over her hand, which distracted her more than even the touch of his lips to her glove. Because she knew the strength of his body, had felt it under her hands. It had been entirely different, the way he'd held her and moved her while dancing, than when they had collided in the middle of a brawl or escaped from the fire.

It was so incredibly intimate, knowing how he *felt*.

"It is so nice to meet you," said Tella briefly. "I must visit my father, and ensure that my uncle is quite well. Please do excuse me."

"Of course," and he withdrew so smoothly, it was almost as if she had not rudely rebuffed him at all.

"Well!" Julia turned wide eyes to her friend. "You really do not want to get married, do you?"

"Julia, please. The man is obviously a rake. Who would want to further their association with a rake?"

"*Many* women would want to associate with a rake like that. My goodness, I am considering it myself and I am very happy with Lord Wendover."

Tella squeezed her eyes shut very tightly. Perhaps if she did so this evening would disappear like a bad dream.

Unfortunately when she opened them, there was Julia in her flawless cream-colored gown, looking at Tella with open astonishment, and the rest of the room still filled with milling members of the *ton*, many of them casting glances her way as if wondering what she would do next.

Perhaps I could perform a circus act, Tella thought a little wildly to herself.

"Truly, I must see to my uncle. I do not want him over-taxing himself at his age."

* * *

HER UNCLE WASN'T OVERTAXED, he was delighted.

And Tella was sure he would be interrogating her smartly, except that he was quite enjoying watching her father do it instead.

"Who is that young man? Where did you meet him? Why have you not mentioned him to me before?"

"Your Grace, it is not as though we see each other often enough for me to convey every detail of my social life."

Her father drew himself up to his full height as if he'd been slapped.

"Forgive me, that was not what I meant to say." She truly did feel contrite. She missed him, and hadn't expected to feel so angry with him, not here and now.

"It was clear enough." The Duke of Gravenshire became suddenly very interested in the ceiling fixtures. He had never been a demonstrative father, and clearly he wondered how much of one to be, in public, at this time.

"I do apologize."

"I'm sure it is only true. I have been absent much of late.

But you cannot know what your performance looked like. All eyes were upon you."

I didn't even notice, she thought to herself. But she said, "Obviously his lordship is an excellent dancer, sir, and I was simply swept away."

"His lordship. I must find out more about him."

So must I. "I cannot say I know him well, but he has impressed me."

"Obviously," and Lord Preston's dry sarcasm rubbed Tella the wrong way too.

"Are you both enjoying yourselves?" she asked them, apparently addressing them both but shooting a pointed look towards her uncle.

"Immensely," that gentleman answered, and this time sounded so pleased with himself that Tella wanted to step on his foot. She had to remind herself that he had been ill.

At least she could imagine how he wouldn't be so saucy if she replaced his champagne with cabbage juice.

* * *

TELLA ACCEPTED TWO MORE DANCES, and was almost succeeding at putting her bad mood behind her when she ran into him again.

Well, when he *cornered* her.

It was nearly literally in a corner. Tella had wanted quiet for a few moments to collect herself, but suddenly he was there.

"I hope I have not made such an unfavorable impression upon you that you are avoiding me, my lady."

Just the sound of his voice was enough to start her palms itching. She wanted to dance like that again. She wanted to dance like that forever.

Which was a problem, because she really did need him to *go away.*

"You cannot be in the habit of unfavorably impressing young ladies with your skill at dancing, Lord Henry."

He shrugged. "To be honest, I have never danced like that before."

"No?"

He moved closer and his eyes lost their amused sparkle just for a moment and she saw something darker and deeper in them. "Not like that."

She felt something leap inside her. It soothed her somehow to think she had not been the only one so affected. That he too might have felt… whatever that was.

Instead she said, "There are any number of other ladies with whom you may practice."

"I came to meet you."

"So you said."

"I didn't say."

"I cannot imagine," she went on as if he had not interrupted, "*that* is sufficient entertainment for a party. Not when there is dancing, and card-playing, and other competing amusements."

"But I did," he finished also as though she had not interrupted. "Attend expressly in order to meet you."

"Lady Agatha is lovely, and very good at the quadrille which I believe they're about to play."

Fitz stepped closer. It was Fitz, he was here, and he was coming closer. It was disconcerting to have someone taller than she so close.

He said quietly, "If you would stop moving around so much, we might be able to accomplish something."

* * *

TELLA PRIDED herself on her quick reflexes. She did not stand there gawping at him. Instead she smiled sweetly as if he had just complimented her, and put her hand through his arm.

The motion disguised that she had a grip of steel on him and was steering him inexorably toward the French doors that led into the garden.

"If you take me outside after a dance like that, we will have to be married," Fitz said with his perpetual tone of amusement, and Tella wished her borrowed fan had a sharper edge.

"*You* are taking *me* outside," she said, and closed her fan so she could poke him with it if he stopped moving in the direction in which she wished him to go.

He didn't stop moving. "Then I'm going to have to propose very soon after," he mused, and Tella pinched his arm even as she smiled through her lashes at him.

"My father is a duke. He is already looking into you, and will dispose of you as necessary afterwards, I'm sure."

Fitz shrugged. She liked the way his shoulders filled out that coat, damn it all.

He said, "He will find me in Debrett's. I am exactly who I say I am, my lady."

"No, you're not." Tella hissed at him but kept her voice low; the garden had other walkers, though far enough away for privacy. Walkers obviously seeking private moments in order to share personal feelings. She just wanted a quiet place in which to interrogate this ruffian. "You follow me around and get in my way."

"You make that sound delightful."

She pinched him again.

"Ow," he said peaceably. "Look, the person who is following you around and getting in your way, as you put it, is me, and I am indeed Lord Henry Fitzwilliam."

"You are not. You are that horrible newspaper writer,

Henry Fitzwilliam. I saw your name, I saw your pieces in the paper."

"The pieces about you?" He looked delighted. "Did you find them flattering? I do apologize for the name. It was late, and I was in a hurry."

"You're going to ruin everything!"

"I won't. At least, not if you tell me what not to ruin."

He would ruin *her*, but she couldn't say that; she didn't mean that quite as it would sound. Not quite. "You will put me in your writing and tell everyone what they *must not* know about me."

"I know the difference between a good yarn and people's lives. I sell one, not the other."

Ugh. He was so believable. "Please *be quiet now*."

The inexplicable irritation she felt at his sunny smile and the concern she felt over her father's agitation washed away in a wave of feelings too complicated to name. *She had already lost; he knew her secret.*

It was freeing, in a way, but also terrifying. He could use it against her. He could take away all she had left.

She really could not bear losing more than she was already losing.

"My lady," he began again, softly, "I am Henry Fitzwilliam, Lord Henry, exactly as I said. I am the third son of the Marquess of Ashbury. I am indeed in Debrett's. I am also an author, fallen into the trade of writing reports for the papers, and it was more in that capacity you and I came across each other."

She looked at him out of the corner of her eye.

"*Truly.* I have not been in society since I returned from the war; I never cared for it much, and I despise it now, I don't mind telling you. Though I'd go through far worse to speak with you more."

They stared at one another.

"Well, what am I supposed to do with you now?" Tella sounded half irritated and half genuinely at a loss.

Several ideas occurred to Fitz, none of them appropriate to the situation. "As Lord Henry, or as Henry Fitzwilliam, journal writer?"

"I don't want either of you!"

The sting of that clearly heartfelt declaration made him draw a little closer. "I don't think that is entirely true, my lady. You might want at least one of us for something."

* * *

THE COLOR FLUSHED in her cheeks and Fitz marveled again. She was very clearly the lad he knew from the street. She was also a striking young woman, with flashing dark eyes and a wide smile, and the feel of her in his arms just now, dancing rather than fighting, had been softer than he had imagined. Unlike most ladies, she had a strength he could feel, her muscles moving as they danced, as well as softer parts, and if he thought about the combination too much right now, he would become indecent in public.

Society parties were more interesting than he remembered.

Tella glanced around to ensure that no one was close enough to hear them. She smiled again, prettily, in case anyone was watching, but her eyes shot darts. "That mean-eyed man doesn't think twice before murdering."

"Indeed."

"I've seen him before, and he no doubt recognized… me. Which is a danger."

"Quite."

"And he purposefully set the fire at the warehouse that you and I both so disastrously attended," Tella went on through gritted teeth.

"I think so too."

"But I have no way to bring him to the law's attention."

"Neither do I."

She fluttered her eyelashes. "While it is delightful to find a man with whom I am in so much agreement, this is a useless conversation."

"Not at all, my lady." Fitz bent close as if bewitched by her thick dark eyelashes, and indeed he was. But what he said was, "There is a murderer and arsonist in the London streets. Do you not believe people should know? Perhaps with many eyes looking for him, he will be brought to justice."

"I believe I should find him and deal with him," Tella said through her teeth while pretending to smile.

"Alone? One person, far less willing to kill than he?"

She did not answer.

Fitz went on. "After you… retreated, I found an informer able to tell me quite a lot. Where I might find you, for instance. And where our friend tends to appear, of an evening. I thought you would be interested in that."

Tella *was* interested in that.

"So tell me the name of your informer, and I will find out more."

Gently, Fitz wrapped a large warm hand around her upper arm.

The one with the shallow slash on it.

Even bound as it was, Tella hissed involuntarily at the sting.

He said, "You are not going alone."

His blue eyes looked clear of guile, and determined.

Tella just shook her head a little, her irritation leaking away and leaving her deflated. "Why did you tell me? I would imagine a man would simply go on without me."

"I wanted to meet you. I wanted to talk to you. I wanted to understand you."

"So? And you have done it," she said, frowning to cover the urge to return his smile.

"I have at least begun," said Fitz, tucking her hand back into the crook of his arm to escort her back inside before her father might take offense. "Please don't pinch me."

* * *

THEY HAD NOT MADE it two yards into the ballroom before her father was there.

The Duke of Gravenshire was a tall man, which of course Tella knew but forgot in her familiarity with him. Right now he did not look like the father she might see over a breakfast table. He looked every inch the Duke, still leanly muscled at his age and with broad shoulders, and Lord Preston, even taller, standing behind him, looked more like the colonel who had won battles abroad for Britain than her dear great-uncle.

The Duke said, "My lord, I hesitate to meet you under the cloud of a reprimand, but your behavior is unbecoming."

Tella expected to feel Fitz tense, or even cringe. Many men would.

Instead he stayed exactly where he was.

When she looked at him, she saw a man with his feet planted like a tree. His amiable expression and sunny blue eyes drew the eye, but his gangly limbs had settled and he looked immovably in place, as if resolutely defending a position in battle.

Something about it tugged at a place inside Tella that was new to her. She wanted to dance with him, *and* she wanted that solidity, that certainty.

That certainty… could lead to dangerous possibilities.

Fitz bowed to her father with the appropriate amount of deference for a man confronted by a duke. But his words were not deferential. "Your Grace. I cannot apologize for taking the opportunity to speak with the Lady Donnatella and press my suit for her hand."

Tella did not show the way she was reeling, and possibly screaming, inside.

Her father's brow was truly clouding up as he turned to glare at her. "Lady Donnatella, just moments ago I understood you to say you did not know this man."

Tella was nothing if not good in a crisis.

She didn't often try to dissemble in front of her father; he knew her too well. But *she* knew when she could persuade him of a particular truth.

She cast her eyes down a bit and then looked up as if reluctant to elaborate. "Of course we have met here and there, Your Grace, it is the social season. I told you I cannot say I know him well. But a man like Lord Henry necessarily stays in one's mind."

Stays in one's *mind?* She certainly wouldn't forget the man who'd come uninvited to a party just to talk with her, and then told her father he'd proposed.

He had definitely *not* proposed. She would have remembered *that*.

This was far too much for just the chance to talk.

The Duke returned his glare to Fitz. "You should have spoken with me first, of course."

"Again, Your Grace, I should apologize, but it would be insincere. Lady Donnatella deserves a better man in every respect than I could claim to be. But I am nonetheless hopeful that she will accept my proposal to marry me."

The words went through Tella rather like a lightning shock. She did not expect them, but the surprise of his words was only part of it. He sounded certain. He sounded *real*.

But he didn't sound mollifying, and the Duke wasn't mollified. His glare had not diminished. "This is not an appropriate discussion for this place or this time. Lady Donnatella, if you will accompany me."

Invisibly, Tella took a deep breath. Her father was going to treat this proposal seriously: as a seriously bad joke. And that would keep her and Fitz apart.

She would not get another chance to speak with this man again soon. And she needed that, at this moment more than she needed just about anything.

"I understand, Your Grace," she said softly. "But I have accepted his proposal. I am sure that after all these years of expectation of my marriage, you will not give the lie to my acceptance."

She was extremely aware that there were enough people nearby, listening very closely, to save her reputation should it be necessary to do so. Lord Henry had offered for her most appropriately, and she had accepted. What could be more acceptable to the *ton* than that?

Except that they did not know Fitz, and once they realized who he was, the tide of opinion would turn firmly against the idea of a third son marrying the daughter of a duke.

Would it be so bad if, instead of remaining in her father's house and taking care of him into her old age, she pretended to be engaged for a little while? Engaged to a tall, dashing young man, even if he was a social nobody?

It would suit the picture people had of her. And while this had never been a dream of hers, she found that now she was in it, she didn't want to throw it away before examining it much, much more thoroughly.

Her father, who was no fool, would want to know why she had gone from claiming not to know the gentleman to accepting his proposal in less than half an hour.

Even if she spurned him later, even if they could not have another private moment at this party, Tella looked down at the wear on Fitz' shoes and wanted to speak with him more so very, very badly that she would publicly agree to just about anything.

"I am grateful," said Fitz, and when he looked at her, she could tell he meant it. "I do wish to show His Grace that I am as protective of your reputation as a betrothed should be. But I cannot resist asking for yet one more dance. Would you do me the honor of a dance, my lady?"

"Of course," and she put her hand in his, not giving her father a chance to stop her.

CHAPTER ELEVEN

A sudden and public betrothal was a high price to pay for the dozen more words they could exchange, as this dance was one of many couples moving in patterns.

Many of the young ladies met Tella's eyes with envious smiles, or tittering giggles. She supposed the story of her betrothal was sweeping the room like wildfire. Young ladies would remember this evening for years as a cautionary tale about what not to do.

Well, the Duke's dizzy daughter had never been engaged before. It was bound to happen sometime.

She tried to look as if all her dreams had come true, and calculated her comments to Fitz for those moments in the dance when they were together.

"We are going to have to stay in the public eye for the rest of the evening," she told him.

"Perfect. I've just discovered that I love to dance."

Despite herself she felt the corners of her eyes draw up in a genuine smile.

Then later, "I can meet you at the square to talk more freely. After midnight."

Some heat came into his eyes and he said with what again seemed perfect sincerity, "I live in anticipation."

A part of her must also be living in anticipation, because before Tella knew it, the dance was over. All she remembered of it was those few words.

"My profound thanks, Lady Donnatella."

Fitz swept low over her hand. Everyone could see him.

No one could see his lips against the back of her hand, but she could feel their heat even through her nice new glove.

She tried to glare as he stood. "You'll have my uncle after you with a pistol if you keep this up."

Fitz just grinned and winked—*winked?*—and was gone.

She felt pulled to follow him around the party. But that wouldn't do, any more than it would do for him to keep kissing her, *any* part of her, in public.

Funny how the private kissing now seemed so much more believable.

So. She just had to get through the rest of this party. Even though for once she felt dizzy, truly as dizzy, as if she'd been knocked off her feet into a somersault.

Get your bearings. Find the enemy. Find your weapons. They're both more important than having your feet under you. Lord Preston's voice, in her head.

Tella turned. There was her uncle himself, discussing something intently with her father. No doubt her.

Even if he didn't remember giving her that advice, it was good advice. As in a knock-down fight, she needed to get her bearings. Perhaps breathe for a few moments.

No one had ever told her how death-defying it felt to get engaged.

At the card tables their hosts had crammed in between the dance floor and the lady's retiring lounge, Lady Winpole and Lady Agatha were playing whist.

When Tella looked over, Lady Agatha waved. She must have been watching, wondering if Tella and Fitz would do anything else exciting. Lady Winpole only glanced her way, and nodded.

Feeling seen, and obvious, and foolish as well as dizzy, Tella wandered over and settled in to watch.

She sat near Lady Winpole through several rubbers. That lady sometimes enjoyed some good gossip, but she was serious about her game, and Tella let her be. It wasn't truly diverting, as Tella's mind was still spinning too much to follow much of the game.

Of course she noticed Fitz' progress around the room. He wasn't lying, apparently, as several men his age greeted him with loud cries of delight and claps on the back. He knew some of these people.

But for the moment, he let her be, and she tried not to be annoyed by that.

Surely he was *more* annoying when he was near. Surely.

Should she be following him? What would they talk about in public that wouldn't sound stupid? *What was the best way to maintain her disguise?*

She really ought to have sorted out many things, including how she felt about kissing Fitz, before she accepted his proposal.

The bidding went round and round the whist game until it almost made her sleepy. All the voices of the players blended into the same pleasant mush of sound.

Mush caused by a sleepless night chasing a murderer, followed by a glass of Lady Woolacre's claret punch.

Tella shook herself as if to wake herself from a dream. Had someone just played a *second* queen of spades?

Usually she was better at remembering cards than people.

She looked around the table. Lady Winpole bent her dark and silver head over her cards, as did Lady Agatha her blonde curls, and two gentleman Tella did not know. No one seemed to notice the second queen of spades.

No, of course there hadn't been one. The very thought showed how little Tella had paid attention to the cards. She was all tangled up in kisses and fires and boats and proposals; her mind had no space in it for a game.

Thank goodness she hadn't bet.

If she stayed, she'd jar Lady Winpole's attention on her playing. It would only be fair treatment of her friend to leave her to it.

Tella patted Lady Winpole's embroidered sleeve and went looking for Julia.

* * *

THE MOMENT SHE FOUND JULIA, Tella wished she'd looked for someone else. Her friend was frankly staring at her as she approached.

Julia did not mince words. "Oh, now we can talk? What on earth are you doing? I know you do not know that man you danced with earlier."

"Julia." Tella grabbed her friends hands in both of her own. "You must trust me. I do know Lord Henry, better than you might think."

"Obviously! If you have just agreed to marry him!" Her eyes narrowed. "We must have a very long talk."

"Please, darling. Don't be angry with me. My father has—I am driven to distraction."

Julia's expression softened. "My goodness, dear. Is this really what it appears to be? Have you found your wild notion about true romantic love?"

Of course not, Tella wanted to shout. But she knew Julia would accept no other answer.

"It is amazing, is it not?"

"This is stunning! But when will you be wed? Should we not plan together? I am so happy for you, Tella, if this is truly what you have waited for all these years. If he will make you happy."

I have no idea what he will do. But I like the way he plants his feet. "We have no plans yet, truly, he surprised me with his proposal tonight." *That at least was entirely true.*

"I am beside myself. We have so much to do. And all those shopping trips, and you never said a word! Why I have not even met him before?!"

"Listen to me, Julia. He is not... He is not highly placed. My father may not accept him. Please, oh please, if you have any sway over your mother and she has any sway over the duke, please plead my case."

That was not what she ought to have said. Why ask for Lady Shoreton's help? The less notice of Fitz the better. She would find a way to rid herself of this troublesome betrothal, as soon as she learned if he'd discovered anything else about the mean-eyed man and the fire.

Fitz ought to have the sense to know that the Caped Count couldn't get married.

And now she'd gone and given Julia stars in her eyes over this supposed passionate love affair. Hours after promising to tell Julia more of the truth.

She was a terrible friend.

Julia, however, was a perfect friend. "Of course I will! When you have waited so patiently for a love that would sweep you off your feet? If this man is the man for you, you must have him!"

When Julia gave Tella a reassuring hug, Tella was shocked to find she had real tears standing in her own eyes.

This had been quite an evening.

Perhaps she should have *more* claret punch.

* * *

As Tella said goodbye to their hosts, Julia found a way to float casually past her best friend's surprise fiancé.

"Lady Julia," he greeted her most seriously as she was about to pass him, apparently unaware.

"Oh!" She smiled and looked surprised to find him in her path. "We must get to know one another better, Lord Henry. You know I am incredibly fond of Lady Donnatella. We have been friends since childhood."

"I would enjoy that, my lady."

Julia closely studied the sincerity in his eyes. "Would you? I suppose that remains to be seen. Because you see, I have very good eyesight, and I am not lacking in intellect. I saw you in Claremont Square earlier today with two men I am quite sure I would not find in Debrett's Peerage. I wonder what you and your associates were doing watching, but not entering, the Gravenshire house?"

* * *

Fitz nodded. "Of course you must wonder, my lady."

But he said nothing further about it.

Julia was only of average height, as rounded and soft as Tella was long and lean. Her eyes, however, could be as hard as agate, as Fitz discovered as she stood there, looking at him, waiting for his explanation.

And when he still did not give it, she said, "As you may recall from days when you were more often in company, a great deal of privilege attends a duke's only daughter. A very cared-for daughter. What you might not know, is that her security also comes from the care of her steadfast friends."

"That is very reassuring to know." Fitz bowed with all deference. "Truly. I would wish for nothing else."

"We'll see," said Julia, the shortness of her words belied by her small curtsey and even smaller smile before she left him there.

* * *

FITZ LEFT the party soon after Tella did. He saw no reason to try to keep up the pretense that he had attended for anything other than to see her, especially when all of London knew exactly what he had done.

He had surprised himself as much as anyone with his proposal. But then again, he *had* tried to warn her. He knew what was required for a gentleman; his father had seen to that through tutors, even though his father had also never said a word on the subject himself.

In fact, Fitz could probably count the number of words that he remembered his father saying, on any subject, to be less than a dozen.

So it was odd that he dashed off a note to his father first thing upon returning to his rooms, and it was further evidence that, despite what one part of his mind might be thinking, another part of his mind was deadly serious about this proposal.

It was easy, in fact, to consider all the reasons why his proposal had been a *brilliant* idea.

He could easily remember the feel of her in his arms, simultaneously strong and soft, and tall enough to kiss comfortably. If she held still long enough.

So much for his hesitation about Fred. He *did* like Fred. He hadn't taken offense at a kiss from Fred. But Lady Donnatella Fairchild bewitched him.

He wanted to see the way her dark curls fell over her shoulders when they were bare, and he wanted to see her eyes overcome with passion, and he wanted to be there when she needed someone at her back.

Because she definitely needed someone at her back.

* * *

THE LATE NIGHT meeting was a first for both of them in that it did not center on violence.

Perhaps that was why it felt so awkward, standing on the empty square in the wee hours of the night.

Or perhaps it was because he had proposed, Fitz thought.

Watching the Caped Count come toward him through the trees made his pulse race. This time, it wasn't just imminent danger; this time, he knew who it was.

And he had asked her to marry him.

Though really, he'd simply announced to her father that he'd asked her. Which hadn't been strictly true.

For once he, or she, had left off the usual scarf, and he could just see the glint of her hair. Most of it must be tucked up under her hat.

It would be practically impossible to kiss her in that hat.

She looked more uncertain too, more uncertain than he had ever seen her.

"Are you well?" he called softly as she approached.

"If you meant what you said about keeping my secrets."

"You know I did."

The evening was warmer tonight, and the rain that had fallen earlier in the day was gone. The smell of street lamps and horse carriages and damp earth was everywhere.

"What will you call me now?" she asked as she met him under the shadowed tree, and he knew that he would forever associate this smell of spring in London with this leaping of his heart.

"If it is what you prefer, I could call you my lady, but only very softly," he said with that always-teasing sparkle in his eye. "Unless it is not correct because in your heart you are the Caped Count, not a Countess. Are you?"

"I have never thought of myself as anything but Donnatella, and I am she. You are the one who came up with that ridiculous name."

"It was late."

"Hmph. And what should I call you?"

"Call me Fitz. Everyone does." Though it would sound different, in her voice, in his ear.

"Everyone?"

He could see his dancing partner in the caped young man, just as he saw the experienced knife fighter in the lady he'd danced with. It was all Donnatella. Tella.

But she'd asked him a question. Who called him Fitz? "The men at the gazette. Men of business," he clarified.

"And your father? I suppose he calls you Lord Henry, if he is as formal as mine."

Fitz felt barely even a twinge of pain at the mention of his father. Perhaps his disinterest in his father, and all his society world, had finally grown to match his father's disinterest in him.

"I don't recall my father ever referring to me in any way at all."

"Oh."

Tella looked unusually uncomfortable at that one.

Fitz decided to help her out of the conversational pit. "My mother called me Henry."

"I like that," said Tella, and something inside him raced again. That couldn't be his heart, could it?

"I should... I should tell her about my proposal."

Tella shifted and studied the ground at her feet. "I know you... did not mean it. I could... I will jilt you after a little while, I promise. Just tell me how long."

"You want me to tell you when to throw over my suit for your hand?"

"Surely that would be easier for you."

"Can't you imagine that it might be easier for me to match my actions to my words?"

She gave a little shake *no*. "My father will inspect every aspect of your history, your life. I don't know what I can say to get his agreement if he doesn't approve of what he finds. And he will find everything. It could be very uncomfortable."

"Well, then if you feel the need, you may jilt me, but for my money, I'd prefer to stay betrothed."

"Why?"

She had pulled closer, apparently without knowing it. He could see the flush in her lips, on her cheeks, even deep in the shadows here.

That hat was simply going to have to go.

When Fitz tilted it gently off the back of her head, her hair in its thick braid fell across her shoulder.

But now he could see her eyes.

"You are flirting with me," he said, leaning down say it very quietly in her ear.

He was so close he felt the shiver go through her as his breath brushed her there.

"Am I? I do not believe I have ever flirted sincerely before. Do tell me if I am doing it poorly."

"We are going to be arrested under this tree, but I think you are doing it extremely well."

And at that he settled one arm around her waist and the other around her shoulders, not so differently from when they had danced, and he kissed her.

Tella had always expected that if anyone *would* make so bold as to kiss her, she would need to keep her eyes open, as it was sure to be a trap.

If this was a trap, it worked.

Because she closed her eyes and melted against him the way she had wanted to on the dance floor.

The warmth of him radiated through his clothes and hers, and made it seem as all those layers of cloth were not even there. She could feel him, solid and warm, against every inch of her, and it made her press against him before she had another coherent thought.

And she closed her eyes because it was impossible to keep them open while his mouth was so gently and so enticingly opening hers.

It did not go on forever, which might have been almost long enough.

When he pulled away, his absence felt like an ache.

"Tella," he said against her cheek, "I would very much like to stay betrothed. To you."

"Mm," she said, rubbing her cheek against his. Why had no one ever mentioned how lusciously intimate it was, feeling his cheek against hers? His slightly masculine stubble, the line of his jaw, and knowing that his delightful mouth was just an inch away?

"But if you do not wish to marry me..."

At that, Tella drew in a breath, and stepped slightly away. She *couldn't* wish to marry him. An accident was one thing; actually intending to marry him would be quite another.

She felt the racing of her heartbeat and the heat in her hands, in her body, even as she examined him at close range.

She did not really know him. Though perhaps she knew him better than many young ladies knew their husbands.

But that didn't matter. Something in her wanted to rush out a *yes*, but something else, something hard and sore and very deeply buried in her, said *no, of course no*.

Well, her family needed her. It was also true that if she intended to keep doing what she did, she needed to stay in her father's house. All of her arrangements, from shipments of equipment to her hidden closet, were set. She could not up and leave her father's house without leaving the work that was her absolute determination.

Nor could she just disappear from London society. No one would connect the Duke's party-loving daughter with the Caped Count, and it had to stay that way.

Besides all that, despite her father's encouragement that she hurry up and wed, she didn't think he had pictured Fitz as his son-in-law.

She drew in a breath. Then another, so she could talk. "I agree there might be tactical reasons for me to marry you."

Something seemed to be choking Fitz, and he stepped back. "*Tactical reasons.*"

"Someone should know if I am out and about at the very least." That *was* a safer plan.

"To call a surgeon, if you get yourself sliced open again?"

"That would be better than bleeding to death alone in the street, yes."

"Tella. If you don't wish to marry me, you have only to say so. But you must say so."

She sighed her momentary lapse of judgment away. Surely he could see how impossible that was. They'd met in a *knife fight.*

She was who she was, and marriage wouldn't fit into her life. "Marriage is supposed to be what little girls dream about. I never have."

"Truly?" He didn't smile; he was taking her utterly seriously.

It felt far more intimate than the way his slightly rough cheek had brushed hers when they'd danced. Almost too intimate. He went on, "What do you wish for when you dream, my lady?"

Tella had spent her life looking into the eyes of political

schemers and petty thieves. Such men's eyes tended to be distant at best, coldly calculating at worst.

This man's eyes could cut her open. And show the world far too much.

Desperate to turn his attention away from herself even for a moment, she said, "What do *you* wish for?"

He could have let her evade his question, could have laughed off hers, but that wasn't Fitz.

He said, "If it were anyone else asking me that, at any other time or in any other place, I would have said that I wanted to tell people how truly vile war is so that we never have another."

She had forgotten to breathe. "But here?"

"Looking at you, I feel compelled to confess that I wish that just once my father would notice me."

Drawing in a ragged breath, Tella felt as though some invisible part of her insides were reaching out to entwine with the part of his soul he was sharing.

She said, "If anyone else asked me what I wished for, in any other place or at any other time, I would have said that I wanted my father to notice me."

"But no?"

She shook her head again, *no*. "All I really want is to have one more day with my mother."

Perhaps he felt it, whatever it was that tied them together.

He nodded, and he didn't move away.

* * *

SHE WAS LOOKING at him again, with that penetrating dark gaze that did not discomfit him at all.

In fact, he liked it.

She was so much more than simply direct, and incisive, and good in a knife fight.

"You can't..." Why did she keep stopping herself from talking? "You mustn't call me Tella out here, not in these clothes," she finally said, slipping her braid back up under her hat and stepping clear of the tree's shadow.

"If I call you Fred and we get caught doing what we were just doing, it will be even more trouble for us."

"Why?"

Fitz grinned at her. "If night watchmen think I am kissing a man?"

"Yes? Do tell me more."

"*That* is what you want to discuss in more depth?"

Laughing, Tella walked away from the square altogether and Fitz followed her across the street.

It was good to see her laugh. "Should I call you Donnatella?"

"Not like this." She didn't gesture to her clothes; he knew what she meant.

"But do people generally call you so?"

She shrugged. "People do. My mother had a romantic streak and an enormous fondness for Italian opera. There's nothing about me that matches the name."

"Of course. You are the opposite of dramatic." That kiss had been very dramatic, at least for him. If he continued thinking in that vein, he would at the very least need to drag her back under that tree, so he said instead, "I'll call you Dante then, shall I?"

She grunted her assent in a way he had never heard a lady of the *ton* do, and he realized that she understood better than he how to behave like a man on the streets of London and not arouse suspicion. "I suppose."

Fitz stretched his legs to keep up with her. She could move very fast in breeches. "Would it make you uncomfortable? You don't sound as if you like the idea."

There was a bit more silence than was easy before she

said, "It sounds like something my mother would have called me."

"She died, then?" he asked softly. He knew she had; he knew the Duke of Gravenshire was a widower, never remarried. Society talked of it.

He'd never heard anyone say that the Duke's daughter also still mourned the loss of her mother.

"Right over there." Tella jerked her head; she knew exactly the direction.

"You were there."

Tella nodded. "She had taken me out into the street. She and I were together."

Fitz' boots thudded against the cobblestone; she did not look up to see his face.

He said, "Why had she taken you into the street at night?"

Tella half-snarled, "Why should she not be able to take me out of the house? Why should not anyone be able to walk abroad when they please?"

That gave him a moment's pause, which was unlucky; Tella almost left him behind as she stepped around a drunkard lying in the street.

Tella kicked the man's shoe as she passed, and the reclining man snorted. "Get out before the watch gets you, Tommy," she told the vagrant in her gruff voice without breaking stride.

Then she turned left, crossing the street, and Fitz again had to stretch his legs to keep up with her.

He thought she was still thinking of their conversation as she stayed silent while following the twists and turns of the old street.

But then suddenly she stopped, and reached into a doorway. She pulled out a ragged old man, his collar tightened around his throat.

"Here now." Fitz jumped back, almost as if he expected Tella to produce a toad out of her pocket next.

But she ignored him.

"There's a mean-looking fellow out on the streets just lately, you've seen him," she told, not asked, the man whose shirtfront she was gripping.

"I ain't seen a fing," said the hapless fellow, his hands and arms flopping at his sides as if to emphasize his helplessness.

That made Fitz step back and keep a wary eye out. People who tried to look harmless usually weren't.

"You've seen him and you know who I mean. You likely know he slit his friend's throat, not too far off. What I want to know is, have you seen who commands him?"

The old man whined and made a sad face, and Fitz wanted to feel badly for him, almost did, till Tella reached in to the man's pocket and pulled out a snuffbox. A silver enamelled snuffbox.

"Arnold, I will make the effort to find a night watchman and turn you in if you have suddenly become uncooperative. And if I do that, you'll hang."

"Ain't seen a fing."

Tella's eyes narrowed. "Because you were told you ain't seen a thing."

Arnold laid a finger aside of his nose and winked at her. "I ain't seen 'at guy yer talkin' about, I ain't seen 'im at Wiggins' warehouse."

"If Wiggins is across the Thames, we've seen that warehouse. When it was still a warehouse." Tella didn't let him go.

"An' I ain't seen 'im at the Bottle an' Bird, oh, I fink it were last night. A man can't go 'round seein' fings 'ese days, like to get 'imself killed seein' people who don't care to be seen."

"And I haven't seen you either, Arnold," Tella said gruffly, letting the man fall back into the dark space of the doorway.

* * *

"Bottle and Bird? Is that what your informant said?" Tella was already on her way there.

Perhaps Fitz' question about her mother shouldn't have turned her mood so dark. But when she remembered that night, she remembered most not the fear, but the overwhelming fury.

A fury that drove her to this day. Why shouldn't *anyone* walk about as they pleased?

"My informant didn't have much. Always the same man, and a description that could have been half the men you just saw at the Woolacre ball. Average, nothing standing out about him."

"Except to look rich enough to be at the Woolacre ball. *Was* he ton, do you think?"

Fitz shrugged. "No one heard him speak, as far as I know."

"Wonderful informant."

Fitz didn't say anything to that.

* * *

As they approached the Bottle and Bird, a young woman pushed the door open to come out.

As she came through, a man leaning against the wall outside grabbed her bottom and laughed.

Before the young woman could protest on her own behalf, Tella had shoved between them, making the grabber thump heavily into the wall as she knocked him backwards.

He looked ready to complain, but Fitz just gave the man a glare and followed Tella inside.

They went straight to a dark corner.

"Why should anyone be afraid?" Tella muttered to herself

as if Fitz weren't even there. "Why should anyone *have* to be afraid?"

Fitz took the place in. There were respectable-enough men here and there, an early evening crowd, along with night folks settling in.

"These kinds of folks like to drink and talk, and they're far better company than you'd find at the Woolacre ball," Fitz told his caped companion. "Let me see what I can find out. You stay out of sight."

* * *

Fitz half-staggered into the center of the room.

"I need some ale. And some company." He crooked his finger at a passing serving-maid.

One who came so quickly that she seemed quite willing to provide both. Or anything he might want.

He managed her falling into him so that he just ended up with his rear in the chair, and the maid's rear on his lap.

He laughed as if he'd made a fantastic joke, and the maid laughed too.

"Drinks first, laddie, company later, at least while I'm working," she said, patting his hair as she slid off his lap.

As Tella watched from the shadows, Fitz made a spectacle of himself in an extraordinarily short period of time.

This surely couldn't be who threatened to upend her life. A man, just like all the rest here, ready for wine, women, and song, and ready to do it all again tomorrow.

He laughed, he clapped men on the back, he bought all of them ale, and he talked to anyone and everyone who walked by him and many who didn't.

He looked like a young lordling, not too deep in the pockets but deep enough not to care, out for a good time and ready to greet everyone he met as a good fellow.

He downed an extraordinary amount of ale while making all these new friends, and Tella was about to leave him there and find her way back out into the streets in search of more information about the mean-eyed man. Fitz must be three sheets to the wind by now; how much use could he be?

When he finally came back to her corner from glad-handing around the room, he was, to her surprise, utterly sober.

His back to the room, he let his omnipresent smile finally fade.

"My face hurts."

"Not surprising." Tella sipped from her own tankard. "Have you ever met anyone you didn't like?"

"Not in a tavern."

"You can talk for hours."

Fitz grinned that wide, easy grin. "Everyone here has a story, Fred; you just don't know what it is."

"I'm only interested in the story of one man."

"Well, no one likes our stabby friend, I can tell you that. *Your* friend was right, he comes here." Fitz kept his eyes on her, trusting her to keep a lookout over his back.

That, she liked.

"They've seen him?"

"Often. They saw him with the dead man, which no one really wants to discuss. And they've seen him talking to a swell in a velvet coat. Not me," he pointed out in exaggerated fashion, as if she might mistake him for a member of the criminal enterprise. "A green coat."

"Anyone know where he's from?"

"The docks."

"The new ones?"

"As it happens, the old ones."

"The Greenland dock?" Tella frowned. "Where whaling ships used to go?"

"Yes indeed." Fitz looked pleased with himself. "It's all timber shipping now, I think. Well, the bulk of it."

"Charming. Shall we away, then?"

"You're not thinking of going there!"

"Yes indeed." The look she gave him was level.

"See here, a young lady can't—"

"You and I aren't here with any young ladies." She leaned closer over the sticky, splintery table. "And if you cannot treat me as your friend, best tell me now. Because then I will regret trusting you. And I do not wish to regret trusting you."

Fitz searched her dark eyes under the brim of her hat. "I don't wish that either."

* * *

"NOT THAT I'M eager to hare all the way to the Greenland docks." She sank a little in her chair.

Tella clearly had no intention of discussing their kisses— several kisses, now—and Fitz had the feeling that unless he found the right way into the subject, she would never discuss it. The Greenland docks were five miles away at least, over city roads that would not be quick. She might talk more in a cab.

But the downside was, it would not be quick. A trip to those docks tonight, after last night, would wipe them out.

She must be thinking the same thing. She was more battered than he, and had a knife wound.

"Do you have a physician who can attend to your wounds when you get them?" Like so many of the gentry, Fitz thought with an uncharacteristic touch of bitterness, she was surrounded by people, none of them seeing to what she actually needed.

"Yes." That was her entire speech about physicians. "I suppose we should get started?"

The very fact that she asked it as a question told him all he needed to know. "You're knackered, as they say around here, and I am exhausted myself. It's a shame we cannot simply drive down there tomorrow."

Tella's eyes were looking around, behind him, above them, and Fitz wondered for a second if she had seen something, but then he realized she was thinking.

Then she moaned.

"Honestly, I can think of a way to do it. It will be awful of me." She looked unhappy. Reluctant. "But you, you will have to go through with this marriage façade for a little while longer." She winced. "*Are* you willing?"

Fitz couldn't tell from these conversations if she wanted to be engaged to him or not. Because he was bright, it also occurred to him that maybe she didn't know either. That seemed likely to work in his favor; his best bet seemed to be to simply play along. The benefits of betrothal ought to become apparent to her, given time.

Hopefully he wasn't putting too much faith in his kisses.

He needed to think more about this betrothal business, too. As far as London knew, he was now in a contract. "I can stand it if you can."

"Then we'll do this. I will arrive there tomorrow during the day, never you mind how. Let us meet at the southeast corner of the docks—do you know the place?"

"Not at all."

"Nor I. We'll have to find each other. Will you trust me to be there?"

Knowing who she was didn't change Fitz's view of her at all. The jaw was hard and set, the eyes dark and dead serious. The Caped Count would be at those docks to find the man in the green coat one way or the other, and surely Fitz ought to be there.

"Yes. And while you are traveling, think up some things

for me to print about the Caped Count." He was serious about *that*. "The offices of the gazette are taking in a dozen requests an hour for more news about him."

"Don't push me," she said, just as serious still. "Murder is an easy way out of an engagement."

CHAPTER TWELVE

The next morning, it was Tella for once who surprised Julia with an unexpected call.

"Seed cake for breakfast! How luxurious. I have too austere a lifestyle, living with two bachelors."

Julia closed one eye and resentfully peered at Tella stuffing bite after bite of seed cake into her mouth. Delicately, as suited a duke's daughter. But the seed cake was disappearing fast.

"Lady Shoreton says that it is in poor taste for a bride to gain much weight between the betrothal and the wedding. Why are you here? Oh! To tell me more about this engagement of yours, I hope!"

"I am sure your lady mother was in no way criticizing your exquisite figure. Gracious, Julia, if I had your looks I would have been married years ago."

"You don't mean that! Has someone been telling you that you are not beautiful?" Julia's eyes narrowed. "What sort of engagement is this?"

Julia was far too quick. And no, no one had ever said Tella wasn't beautiful.

No one had ever said she was, either.

Why had she even said that? She would *not* have married years ago. She wouldn't marry now, either.

And if she did marry, it wouldn't be to a man who gushed about things. She much preferred the idea that Fitz trusted her to meet him tonight as planned; and that he trusted her to watch his back.

These weren't things that factored into Julia's marriage considerations. Or Lady Shoreton's.

Tella looked about for coffee. "We can discuss the engagement on the way! We must make a little trip today, and it cannot wait."

"A trip? Where?" Suspiciously, Julia stole a piece of the seed cake that legally belonged to her.

"Did you not suggest something of a classical theme for our party?"

"I did, yes. Not to include sailing off to Greece, though."

"Lady Agatha's mother lives in that stunning house in Greenwich, darling, and she has invited us to visit sometime. You remember, she has that terrible gout. Well, I've recalled her telling us to tour the Queen's House there, it has that wonderful classical architecture, don't you remember? Simply loads of columns."

Julia was blinking. "Columns."

"Oh yes. Columns everywhere."

"Isn't there anyone in residence in the Queen's House?"

"Someone must be; hardly the point. It's just what I need, to get out of this neighborhood for a little while. Lady Dunsby, Agatha's mother, will be so glad to see company."

"This simply isn't done, Tella." Julia looked about to dig in her heels. "I don't care how betrothed you are. Unannounced calls in our neighborhood is one thing. One does not simply arrive on another's doorstep, in Greenwich of all places, and announce that one is there for a visit."

"Only for one night, darling!"

"Not even the Queen would do it. And we are going to see the Queen's House."

"Pheh, but she doesn't live there. Julia, I am telling you, Agatha will be thrilled to have us. And who would say no to a duke's daughter?"

"My mother will not go with us."

"She needn't. You *are* very safely betrothed. Extremely betrothed." Tella made a walking motion with her fingers. "We will just go."

She did not clarify whether she was *also* safely betrothed, or not.

"And what will we tell her when we return?"

"We will give her Lady Dunsby's regards."

"This isn't like you at *all*."

All the swirling worries about to overflow inside Tella went into making her face as bleak as could be. "This party may kill me, Julia. I have no skill for entertaining, and even with you doing all the real work, I have absolutely nothing to offer London, nothing special. If I wish to marry Lord Henry, who has no title in his own right, I need *something* to set this affair apart. And if I refuse him—"

She didn't have to say it. Her social desirability would plummet. Her first proposal would be her last.

There, for once she'd taken her own party seriously.

And hopefully Julia would overlook that in fact, Tella *had* accepted him. Publicly.

Julia was suspicious. "Something to make your *party* a success. Something in Greenwich."

Tella took the last bite of seed cake. "In, as you say, Greenwich."

* * *

FITZ WAS NOT LIVELY in the mornings, but he staggered from bed with a head full of plans.

He must get to Gerry and find out what he was doing with this story. He hadn't even seen the latest issue of Bridle's Gazette.

He must also ask Clement Bridle for a small advance on his earnings. If he must travel to Greenwich, he'd need more coin than he had on hand.

Somewhere in there, he must figure out how to convince Lady Donnatella of the benefits of his proposal.

Because with every passing minute, he was feeling more serious about it.

But just as he was about to leave, settling his coat on his shoulders and eating a last bite of apple, a letter slid under his door, *swoosh*.

An experienced soldier shouldn't have a stomach that flip-flopped so easily.

Heavy paper, with a textured laid finish. He slid his finger under the wax seal, unfolded it.

He recognized the writing. It was the hand of his father's secretary. One of them.

The Most Honorable the Marquess of Ashbury wishes to meet with you at two o'clock today.

That was it, no reason, just a summons from the father he hadn't seen for more than seven years.

Fitz had no interest, and he had no time.

But wait. His father had never summoned him before, not since Fitz had gone to the Army instead of paying a man to go in his place. A decision his father had thought worse than stupid.

Fitz hadn't understood how a marquess of Great Britain wouldn't send his sons to defend her; his father didn't understand why a man from a titled family would put himself in danger when other, lesser people could be sent in his stead.

At least, that was how the secretary had explained it.

So why now? Why this thick imposing piece of paper with a dozen words on it?

It had to be something to do with Tella, with the stories Fitz was writing of the Caped Count, or his nosing around London looking for answers.

If his father knew anything about any of those—especially Tella—Fitz wanted to know. *Needed* to know.

Mentally, he revised his schedule. He must still visit the offices of Bridle's Gazette. He needed money, and his father had never helped him before; it seemed unlikely that he would start now.

* * *

"This is madness."

The way their carriage bounced over the City's street's, Tella felt inclined to agree with her friend.

But since she was using this trip as subterfuge for something else entirely, and since she had dragged Julia along on the errand, she ought at least to be entertaining.

"It is an *adventure*, darling. And as much as you long to keep house for your Lord Wendover, you can't object that I wish to fit in a tiny adventure for us before you go."

"I am coming *back*, you know." Julia had braced a hand against the carriage's door frame. She didn't care for travel. "Not only is the Isle of Wight quite near, geographically speaking, but I will be returning to keep Lord Wendover's house not half a mile from where you live."

Then she covered her mouth with both hands, startled. A carriage wheel thumped into a paving stone, and the resulting thump rocked them both. "Or—will *you* be going away? When you are married? I haven't even asked where Lord Henry resides!"

Nor had Tella the faintest idea. Not that it mattered, since she wasn't going to marry him. But again, her mouth had some different plan, because she said, "Do you think he would live in the Gravenshire house? Do you think it would be awful?"

"No." Julia's brows wrinkled prettily. "If he has no estate of his own. Why not? Does he object to living in your father's house?"

She hadn't asked him, because she *could not* marry him, though the prospect of having those kisses whenever she wanted them was mouthwateringly appealing when she let herself think about it.

It didn't matter if she really married him or not. This was the only proposal she had ever had, and she must make a meal of it, ensure London remembered it, if only to make it seem...

Perhaps, to make it seem as if she had once been truly wanted.

"I told you, I don't know if my father will raise any large barriers or not. I am hoping he wishes to see me wed." He hadn't even changed his schedule to see her the morning after her supposed betrothal. "And if he does, I will have to choose between living there or living...well, with nearly nothing, I suppose."

As she spoke, Tella realized that all this was entirely true, and had been stirring in the back of her mind. It wasn't just that she couldn't leave her father's basement, and still do the work she needed to do. It was that the work she needed to do took money.

Some part of her still wanted to have everything—her house and status and money and... and Fitz.

"I cannot leave my father and of course I cannot leave

Lord Preston. He and I—I feel as though we are all we have, one another."

"Ah, I see." Julia's brow cleared. "So then, you *do* intend to marry?"

"It's very complicated!"

"Aha." Julia went on as if Tella were making sense. "And, if you will forgive the question, you do like this Lord Henry, don't you?"

"For pity's sake, no one should go around marrying people they don't like."

"Tella." Julia looked up, then at the floor, then somewhere around Tella's ear. "I mean, your... your deep, passionate, abiding love. You feel... that way, about him, do you not? As in, it might be awkward to be a newly wedded couple in your father's house?"

Oh. *Oh.*

Tella hadn't thought about it at all.

Or thought she hadn't. Because when Julia brought it up, the problem was immediately apparent to Tella. All she had to do was close her eyes, and she could easily see the shape of Fitz' long, gangly body, the complicated movement of muscles in his neck, in his arms, in the thighs that gave his breeches such an appealing shape. Just imagining it all, plus that grin, and the way those eyes seemed to see every inch of her with one glance—

Yes, it would be extremely awkward to be newlyweds in her father's house.

"You put it very well." Then Tella looked again. Her friend was blushing. "*Julia!* You cannot possibly think that way about Lord Wendover!"

"Why ever not?" Her dimple was showing. "And what a tone! What were you thinking about, not two seconds ago?"

"Oh, I—not Lord Wendover, I assure you!"

Julia laughed, and while she kept one hand braced against

the door frame, she seized Tella's hand with the other. "Oh my dear! How else should you think of your beloved? Wasn't that what you always said you wanted? You have found your deep, passionate, abiding love after all. Oh, I'm so glad. That was what worried me most, that you had taken a fright somehow and wished to marry for some other reason." Her eyes sparkled as she squeezed Tella's hand. "I can see *that*, you know, in the way he looks at you. If you feel the same way, he simply must measure up to be the man you deserve."

"It's not—" Tella couldn't seem to finish a sentence today. What was she stopping herself from saying out loud?

If Julia thought she saw something in Fitz' eyes, why should Tella convince her otherwise?

In fact, she should let *Julia* talk. Julia was a good judge of character, her uninspired fascination with Lord Wendover notwithstanding.

Tella was only wronging Julia more and more every minute. She couldn't tell her the whole truth about Fitz, because she couldn't tell her about the Caped Count.

Why couldn't she? She told Julia everything. She'd just told Julia Fitz was appealing, in a newlywed sort of way, and she hadn't even realized that she thought so until she said it. Why not tell Julia about her work?

Because Julia would want to do something to help. Her loyal, sweet Julia would *insist* on helping. And that was a good way for her to get hurt. Tella didn't even know how. But without a sharp barrier between her day life and her nights, something could happen to someone she loved. And it could not be Julia, it simply could not.

"I don't speak of him as my beloved," Tella said slowly, "but I am glad to know you feel the same way about Lord Wendover."

"Oh yes, not just that we shall want to make love all over the house once we're married, but that we will be together forever." Julia made this astonishing statement with a plump, feminine satisfaction that spun Tella's head around more surely than a solid punch to the jaw.

"My *word!* Should I cover my eyes? You will make me blush!"

"Why?" Julia's smile was coming and going with a new slyness. "You are just as betrothed a lady as I am. We cannot shock each other, surely."

"I have no guarantees that my father will accept his suit."

"But I hope he does, if Lord Henry is the man for whom you have waited!"

"So do I." And as with other thoughts, once she said it, Tella realized she meant it. It was an appealing prospect, as unlikely as it was, being married to Fitz; or at least, having free access to those shoulders. "So do I."

* * *

JULIA WAS NOT USED to Tella giving more than one answer, or such a brief one, to any important question.

Her answers to questions about this Lord Henry seemed to change by the second.

This sudden trip *was* exciting, and Julia was glad to take advantage of Tella's odd whim. It would do no harm, and they could both see a little of London too.

But she watched Tella watch the view change outside their window, and thought that she was still waiting to see if Lord Henry Fitzwilliam were good enough for her very best friend.

* * *

"HAVE you seen this item in this newspaper?"

His employer had the paper tucked, folded, under his

arm; he wasn't offering it. Perhaps he thought his muscle man couldn't read.

"At the prices they go for, the rich can keep the papers."

His employer, who fancied himself upper crust, probably thought he fell into that category. He didn't.

"The item reports that there is a witness to a fight that involved you and… our departed friend."

It was customary not to use names, and neither of them wanted anyone to hear them discussing the dead ship's mate.

"Me?"

"A description that rather matches you."

"Are you gonna show me?"

"I wasn't sure that you read."

The paper's owner, however, surrendered it at the sound of the other man's growl.

When he'd skimmed it, he shrugged. "This could be half the men in London."

"Not every man in London starts brawls as he's collecting light women cutting through Mayfair neighborhoods."

"Not e'rry man thinks he's better'n e'rryone else because he can do sums and write a banker's draft."

His employer's eyebrows went up. He absolutely was the sort of man who felt he was better than everyone else because he could write a banker's draft.

And the more money he could call upon, the better he thought he was.

Well, they'd see. In a fight between a banker's draft and a knife, the knife was always going to win.

"Are you going to find him?"

The paper slammed back into its owner's chest; his employer stepped back before the ink made a mark on his green coat.

"You don' need to ask me that, you know it a'ready."

* * *

"LORD HENRY, SIR."

The butler still knew Fitz' name. Fitz knew his, too, but didn't use it. He knew the stiff old fellow had no interest in reminiscing about his childhood; and indeed, the man didn't try.

He showed Fitz in to his father, and withdrew.

And there sat Lord Ashbury, right where Fitz had left him more than seven years before. At a table reading correspondence, to which he would later dictate replies to one of the two waiting secretaries.

Two secretaries who had worked there as long as Fitz could remember, and Fitz had never heard his father say anything to them that wasn't about a letter he wanted written, and immediately.

All business, no heart.

Just the same way his father spoke to him now.

"Lord Henry."

He rose, his old-fashioned embroidered coat settling around him as he came to… well, greet wasn't the right word, there was nothing in it of feeling that would betray how he felt seeing his son after so many years.

Well, maybe there was nothing to betray; maybe he felt nothing.

"Sir."

They looked at each other for a moment, neither moving. Fitz was sorry to see that he still had his father's eyes.

Now that he was a betrothed man himself, Fitz was even sorrier that his mother had, for some reason, married this man. Tella wouldn't get a title or money by marrying him, but she'd never have to wonder how Fitz felt.

In fact, there were thousands of people in Britain right

now, mostly readers of Bridle's Daily Gazette, who knew Fitz better than this man did.

Knowing that anything he said would only draw this appointment out, Fitz kept silent, a skill he'd learned from the man before him. And he hoped his father would say something to him, actually to *him*, and he hated himself for that hope.

His father quit his silence first. "I have letters from the Duke of Gravenshire which surprise me. From His Grace, and from his solicitors."

"Indeed."

Ask me about the war, sir, Fitz wanted to say. *Ask me how I felt about being shot at, being stabbed, or visiting the edge of death. Or tell me you've read my dispatches. Or even the stories I write for Bridle's Daily Gazette.*

Ask me about the woman I wish to marry.

His father asked him nothing.

Finally, Fitz broke the continued silence to say, "I have not heard from my mother lately." *Perhaps you remember your wife. She lives in Northumbria. I've never heard you say a word about it.*

"She is well. The Duke tells me that you have offered for the hand of Lady Donnatella. This puts me in an awkward position, Lord Henry."

That hardly counted as asking Fitz about Tella.

If his father thought Fitz' proposal to Tella inconvenienced him more than losing his own wife inconvenienced him, he hadn't changed a bit.

So Fitz shrugged. "I would say that I'm sorry to hear it, sir, but that might imply I regret offering for the lady, and I do not. I do offer a little sympathy for your trouble."

"As well you should. If you had discussed this with me beforehand, we'd have established what might or might not occur." Meaning he'd have told Fitz not to do it. "As it is, hearing this news from the Duke himself, I am put in the awkward position of finding a way to tell a duke he is mistaken, which would be disastrous, or that I do not want his daughter to marry into my family, which would be worse."

If Fitz wanted Tella to marry him, it wasn't to please his father. "What a shame."

"You don't mean that." There was no heat to his father's words; just the constant exhaustion of disappointment in a son who fell short. "Nonetheless, I am the one in the awkward position."

He continued to stand there, looking at Fitz with those eyes so like his own that Fitz couldn't even entertain the idea that he'd been sired by someone else. Not that his mother's honor would allow that.

When Fitz still said nothing, and said nothing, Lord Ashbury finally turned on his heel and went back to his desk.

"I am deeding you the Mercywall house, off Grosvenor Square. You will receive a sizeable income annually, as I am also deeding you the following farms, and money invested in the three per cents." He took another sheet of that thick creamy paper and handed it to Fitz, who almost dropped it, his fingers were so frozen.

"What?" Fitz just stared at the man he'd known his whole life, with whom he'd never once had a deep conversation. "*Why?*"

"It is a singular honor for this family to be joined to the line of the Duke of Gravenshire." He made it sound like chalk marks on a wall instead of a marriage. "I will not have it said that I dishonored the honor done to Ashbury by Gravenshire. There must be a suitable acknowledgement."

A suitable acknowledgement. A fortune to live on every year, and a London townhouse.

"What have you provided for my brothers?"

"Not your affair."

Fitz didn't even know if they'd married. "Obviously what's entailed will go to your heir—"

"Not your affair, sir. The Ashbury line will continue. You seem..." At this the older man's eyes seemed to actually move a little, in the corners. "You seem to have arranged something splendid for yourself. Or perhaps you had some plans to arrange it and then smash it; I do not know, but that seems like something you would do. If you manage to undo what you have done, it will not be because of my money or my name."

He got his tendency to tell blunt truths from his father, Fitz realized. He wondered if it was just as unpleasant a trait in him.

"Always such a pleasure to speak with you, Lord Ashbury." Fitz waved the paper a little. "You are joking, surely. You have never done anything for me. You wouldn't do this."

"Not for you, no." His lordship turned on his heel again, back to his table. "For the name of Ashbury, of course I would. Good day."

* * *

"I AM SO EXHAUSTED." Tella's hand hid her theatrical yawn. "We must to bed early."

"Yes of course! You will find the Greenwich air *so* reviving." Lady Agatha, who was truly a sweet thing with her blonde curls and china shepherdess smile, was darting around the room bringing Tella and Julia plates of dates, and cushions, and footstools, and a platter of tea.

The arrival of visitors had made her swoon with excitement, and as predicted, her mother was also delighted, and immediately closeted herself in with the housekeeper to plot entertainments for their guests.

All in all, Tella was a horrible person, and felt more horrible every second. Because she did not want the entertainments, the cushions, or the tea. She wanted the time to speed forward till she could meet Fitz.

Or rather, till she and Fitz could discover the name of the man in the green coat, and find out some solid facts to pass along to…

Well, that *was* the next problem.

The night watchmen only kept order, and barely that. The owner of the warehouse that had burned, and likely the owners of its contents, no doubt had offered a reward for whoever burned it down.

If Tella could make a convincing argument against some miscreant for the fire, plenty of thief-takers would be willing to capture that miscreant, and present the case to a constable, for that reward.

But for the vicious murder of an innocent man, there was no one to offer a reward for an arrest.

Tella wanted the mean-eyed man brought to justice for both.

That meant she'd have to swear a statement against the mean-eyed man—or the Caped Count would. She didn't like attaching the story any closer to Fitz than he'd already done himself, writing for the paper. She needed a name.

And the mean-eyed man wasn't working by himself. Someone had arranged for the fire brigade not to come. That couldn't have been coincidence, and it seemed a bit subtle for a fellow who slit throats and burned things down.

Perhaps she should put the fire brigade men into the Bottle and Bird with Fitz and a barrel of ale, and see if he came out with any answers.

"Do you like sugar in your tea?"

Lady Agatha's voice brought Tella back to the present, to stare at an inlaid metal platter. Agatha had arranged little glasses of tea upon it, each in a metal ring. "What a clever contraption! Yes, I'll happily have sugar, but is that jam?"

"Oh yes! My grandmother came from Russia, and could never be persuaded to give up tea in glasses, with jam. It is so good."

Tella watched with fascination as Lady Agatha prepared a glass for her, then one for Julia.

"Why do we not see more of you, Lady Agatha?" Julia asked as Tella sipped her tea, which lived up to its reputation.

"I try to get in to the City as often as I can, but my mother often doesn't feel well enough. No matter!" The girl's curls bounced as she shook her head with the kind of determined smile that became real halfway through. "I do not mind keeping Lady Dunsby company. And if I am to marry, the right man will find me, even if he must come all the way to Greenwich!"

"I must see what I can do." Julia was looking at Agatha with a thoughtful expression.

Tella *tsked*. "You needn't become a matchmaker, Julia, just because you are to be married."

"It is required, actually. You will do it too, see if you don't."

"Girls!" Lady Dunsby hobbled in. "What would you say to a jellied fish?"

Tella nearly spit out her tea. *What is a jellied fish like you doing in Greenwich?* sprang to mind, and she must make sure she didn't say it.

Fortunately Lady Agatha had presence of mind as well as lovely golden curls. "A jellied fish would take the kitchen hours, surely, madame. I believe Lady Donnatella and Lady Julia have come more for the company than the supper."

Inwardly Tella cursed at herself for the horrible person she was.

"That is exactly right, Lady Dunsby," Julia answered for both of them with her sweet smile.

Surely there was no point to asking what kind of jellied fish they were turning down. "Truly, madame. Please do not take any great trouble; we deserve only bread and water for imposing on you this way."

Lady Dunsby just beamed, balanced there on her two dark canes, and in that moment Tella resolved that she would visit this family once a month or die trying. Murder chopped a whole life short, but wasn't Tella chipping away at her own, calculating every interaction based on how it appeared to others?

There had to be more to life than defensive weaponry.

"Do you play dominoes, Lady Agatha?" Tella had some vague memory of the game. It would be fun to play it again, something frivolous.

"Why, no! But perhaps I should learn. There is a rumor the new Duchess of Talbourne is mad for some game called nim. I have never played that, either, but I intend to learn."

"Do you know the Duchess of Talbourne, Lady Donnatella?" Lady Dunsby was practically trembling with excitement at the idea that she might.

Reflecting again that she was a horrible person, Tella turned to Julia. "*Do* I know the Duchess of Talbourne?"

Julia just rolled her eyes. "You know perfectly well that you don't. She was only just married—*only* just. A shock to London. She ought to be at your party in a few days, you know. The Duke will be there."

That… was actually perfect. Tella pushed away her horror that she must entertain a duchess and realized how perfect it was. Having the brand-new Duchess at her affair would practically be a social success in itself.

No wonder Julia had looked at her funny when she suggested that they needed to see columns.

"You two will surely attend," Tella told her hostesses.

"Oh!" Eagerness to meet an actual duchess brought Lady Dunsby low; she plumped down into her chair. "What a lovely, beautiful idea! But I couldn't, not really. Agatha, you ought to go—but you need a chaperone." The good woman's face went from lit with smiles to drooping with regret in moments.

"Not at all. It is perfectly possible. I will send you a note, we must arrange it." Ugh. She would try harder, but Tella wasn't good at this. She had plenty of problems on her plate with a mean-eyed man, one in a green coat, a warehouse fire, and a dead man. The party was just the last straw, and now she must get her friends *to* the party. Clearly, Lady Dunsby did not have a carriage.

But Tella was a duke's daughter, she had Julia's help, at least for a little while longer, and maybe, if she let herself hope, Fitz's.

She must find an exit for the Caped Count for this evening, and thanks to Lady Agatha's enthusiasm for entertaining her guests, Tella even had an idea of the docks' direction.

Maybe a great deal was possible.

* * *

FITZ SPENT much of the advance he'd wheedled out of Clement on the drive to the old docks. He wondered who had paid for Tella's ride, or if for once she had paid herself.

He'd never have expected a lady to pay for things before. Clearly, the way in which he'd met Lady Donnatella had put him in a new frame of mind.

He had never expected any financial support from his father, either, certainly not after seven years of silence.

His first inclination was to burn both the note his father had written him, and paper detailing what his father claimed were his new holdings.

But why? Among titled families, providing a living to a third son would have been a cause for grateful joy, never repudiated. Every young man waiting to dance with Tella that he'd seen at the ball had a living provided by his father, or wished to have. Merchants, even tradesmen did the same, if they could.

So why did this feel different?

Was it the nature of his relationship with his father? Or his family in general? Knowing he would never have the title, he had never wanted it; and for some reason, he'd never expected anything from the Ashbury holdings. Possibly because he'd never known his father to *give* anything to anyone. Vastly wealthy, he thought of himself first, his title and money tied for second, and there was no third. The reputation he could attach to the Ashbury name never seemed intended for *any* of his sons, only himself.

And why now was Fitz' first thought whether he was taking something one of his brothers needed? Was he feeling guilty he'd spoken to his father before speaking to them, since returning from war?

Or just guilty that he didn't even know where they were?

His wasn't a close family.

Did it matter more, now Fitz felt deeply inclined to take his betrothal to Lady Donnatella more and more seriously?

He left the papers in his coat be. It couldn't *hurt* to have a house in his pocket, nor an income suitable for supporting a duke's daughter. Perhaps he would find a use for them. He needed to see how things were going with Tella first.

And perhaps find out the situation of his brothers.

CHAPTER THIRTEEN

Any other man waiting a long while would be leaning against a wall.

At first Tella saw Fitz just as a distant shape among shadows, but she knew it was him. Fitz didn't lean. He had his two feet planted solidly on the ground. He would never be moved.

Her heart started pounding. It made her wonder if she was being followed. Tella trusted her senses; they often warned her of someone's approach before her mind caught up to what they already knew. She looked behind her.

There was no one behind her.

No one near at all, but Fitz.

The pounding of her heart made her face warm, and for some reason, she wanted to smile.

When she drew closer, she saw the side of his face, lit by the moon, the angle of his cheekbone and his jaw. And she saw him looking right at her.

The thump her heart gave then woke her. It was Fitz. It was all Fitz. He was the danger, and the excitement.

* * *

THERE WAS THE CAPED COUNT, swinging along the walk without a care in the world, blue velvet cape billowing. Fitz ought to have told him—her—to leave it at home.

She wasn't smiling, and that just made it more clear it was her. The Duke's daughter might smile at social affairs, but Tella didn't; and neither did the Caped Count. As he was coming to think of her, Tella had more in common with her caped alter-ego than she did with the Duke's daughter. Though all were her—the chap who'd stiffed him on boat fare, the man who'd fought by his side, the woman who'd danced with him—all her. He could easily spend a lifetime learning all there was to learn about all of them. About Tella.

He knew it with a certainty that went right down to his bones. It wasn't about anything his father did, and it wouldn't be about her father either. It was about the two of them. If he could convince her to take his proposal seriously.

He'd never have offered for anyone else, and that was the truth.

He checked again to see that no one was near before greeting his caped companion. "I don't want to know what you had to do to get here."

"No one was harmed." Tella winced a little. "Well, the truth was bent. Do you know which ship?"

"I believe I do."

* * *

IN TELLA'S EXPERIENCE, staying out of sight in deserted places was nearly impossible.

She hated the dark old docks, the stale smell of dead whales in the air and the bilgey water. She especially hated that there was practically nowhere she and Fitz could loiter out of sight.

Especially Fitz.

There weren't many people about, and where they did gather, the business being transacted also made those few seek the shadows.

"People will think us here to find some of those night women," Tella muttered, as she and Fitz leaned against a warehouse corner.

"No, they won't. They will think we are exactly what it looks like we are. Exactly what some of those sailors are."

"What's that?"

He looked over, apparently trying not to look too amused. "Two young men finding each other."

"Never tell me so!" Tella looked around. She could just see a couple of sailors ambling along the dock boards in the distance, and a few knots of men closer to the ships. "Are we doing what we should to maintain our disguise?"

Fitz smothered a laugh. "First, I'll admit I don't exactly know. Second, if we are staying out here in the moonlight, I don't think we can do much more without danger of being taken up for crimes way too serious to play with. And third, you are at least ten times more interested in men engaging each other than you are in feminine birds of paradise. Why the fascination?"

"Apparently, I am one. And I never heard of such a thing before."

"Of course not. You're a lady."

She looked up at him. "Henry, if I were only that, I'd go mad." What an odd thing for him to say, and not accurate at all.

"You're not going to start calling me Henry. Only my mother calls me that." He turned a shoulder to shade her even further from the street. "There's a fellow who matches the description they gave me at the Bottle and Bird."

Fitz was either jittery or simply unable to stay still; he seemed determined to block her view from every angle—or block the world's view of her. Tella took care to keep her face shaded when he finally let her have a view of their quarry. In, yes, a coat the color of new grass.

The man strode quickly along the dock, clearly feeling important. But then he leaped lightly upon one of the gangways and disappeared onto a ship bobbing in the water. A heavily loaded ship.

And Fitz's first guess as to the correct ship.

* * *

A FEW MOMENTS LATER, a faint light appeared below deck, as though someone had lit a lamp.

Tella's and Fitz' eyes met.

Tella was doubtful. "Surely that isn't the only green coat in London."

Fitz was undeterred. "Green velvet coat, at *this* timber dock, half-silver hair. That's our man."

"Then you'll need to keep an eye out for the mean-eyed man. I don't like him."

"I bet his own mother doesn't like him." Fitz made the joke without thinking, as if he were back in the lines with his fellow soldiers. Then he winced. Surely Tella wouldn't appreciate jokes about mothers.

But Tella didn't take it amiss; she even managed a small twist of a smile. "I bet you're right."

Carelessly, they strolled down the dock, trying not to betray how they peered at each ship looking for the shapes of crew on deck.

"I won't melt if you mention mothers, you know," Tella told him, keeping up conversation.

"Understood."

"You've just mentioned yours. Though only barely."

"Not much to tell." He dropped a step back so as not to outpace her with his longer legs. "She lives in an Ashbury house in the north. Gave up on living with the rest of us quite a while ago."

Tella considered. "Do you remember her at all?"

"Oh yes! We were all quite grown and at school when she left. Well, I was, as the youngest."

"She provided the family with three sons?"

"She did."

"And how did your father show his appreciation?" They paused again, half-hidden behind the post anchoring the gangway of the ship next to their target.

"I believe she's still waiting." Fitz looked over their goal again. "It might not be easy to follow him onto that ship."

* * *

TELLA LOOKED AROUND to ensure no one was looking before she felt under the collar of her cloak and pulled a thin string.

A fine billow of linen, black, rolled down and settled over the blue velvet of her cloak. Another pull, and the string contracted just under the cape's edge, enclosing it in a sort of outer sack. A sack made of black linen that reflected little light.

She pulled up a thin hood of the same material, draping it over her hat.

She wanted to wink, looking at Fitz' expression. "What? Your coat doesn't do that?"

"You're not proposing we walk on to that ship."

"I'm not?"

"Fred, what are we doing?"

That made Tella frown. "Tonight, following that man. Tomorrow—I am promised to visit the Queen's House with Lady Julia, I won't bore you with the details but trust me, I shall go."

"That's not what I meant."

"Apparently you and I are men engaged in illicit—"

"*Fred.*"

She subsided.

"What are we doing, going on that ship? If this were war, I'd call this a sortie with no purpose. We need to tell more people what we know, not walk into enemy hands."

Tella wasn't ready to risk involving the law and exposing herself. Not until she knew she must. "Not at all. If this were war, the sortie would be necessary reconnaissance. We need to know who that man is."

"I know he's not a nice man, and I know he has at least one friend who is not nice either."

"I mean—"

"I know what you mean. Listen, let us find the name of the ship. Find a way to learn its owner. See why it's here. There are other ways to move forward than going aboard that ship."

Without moving, Tella's eyes measured the length of the ship, the depth of her draft. She was heavy, low in the water; yes, loaded. "I do think you needn't go with me."

"*What?*"

"Alone, I am quicker, lighter. I can be on that ship and back within half an hour."

"You cannot imagine I would let you venture on to that ship alone."

"Gallant, sir?"

"Tactics. One doesn't go into enemy territory alone."

"You must weigh fifteen stone. You're like a walking oak

tree. There is no way you can cross that deck silently, and those boards *will* creak."

"Very well. We will not go aboard."

She felt the usual nerves, and quite rightly, at the idea of going somewhere she should not go; but they were mixed with a cold terror, somehow both a familiar and an unfamiliar feeling.

He *shouldn't* go. He mustn't. Someone should; therefore, she would go.

"The night is wasting. You should stay here." Tella started across the street. She preferred that difficult discussions end immediately.

"You've clearly never served in the military," Fitz muttered, falling in next to her.

That stung. She'd treasured everything her uncle had ever told her about the soldier's life. "You needn't be insulting."

"Sorry, I suppose. It's just that we're walking into the enemy camp on a sea-faring vessel, and I've only known you a couple of days but we don't have a marvellous history with boats."

No one would question two men boarding a ship openly in the middle of the night—why would they go there if they shouldn't? Once aboard, however, they risked meeting crew who knew differently.

"Nonsense." Tella looked around to confirm no one was close enough to see their faces. "We have had marvellous luck with boats, aside from you having to pay for them."

* * *

Fitz followed Tella as she stepped on to the deck, in his mind trying to imagine the story he would tell if they were challenged.

It occurred to him, a bit too late, that Tella had come to have too much faith in his ability to improvise.

Then it occurred to him that he put too much faith in it himself.

Nearly silently, they followed the deck's edge, trying to stay shadowed from eyes that might look their way from the dock.

They crept closer to an open hatch glowing with yellow light from below.

As they drew near, men's dim voices became clear.

"You hafta give me some more men to do somethin' about it."

"You had one."

"He was stupid. And gutless. I need someone tougher."

Slowly, very slowly, Tella reached into a pocket deep in her blue velvet cloak and pulled out a very, very polished little circle made of silver.

It was slightly domed—a mirror, Fitz realized as she carefully reached out to position it so that she might see inside. And the mirror's shape let her see much.

Fitz squeezed Tella's shoulder. One of the fellows sounded like the mean-eyed man.

And the other wore a green coat.

"You don't need to make decisions. Especially not like that. The men don't want to go into the city with you. They know why Jim didn't come back."

Jim. That must be the murdered man. Could there be a less helpful name?

"Jim didn't come back because he was gutless and useless. If they ain't gutless, or useless, nothin' to fear from *me*."

"You did a job with some fire. I did mine with a fire brigade. Our patron asked us to do a thing, and it is done. Do you not grasp the purpose of actually doing what the person with the money wants done? If you don't keep this situation clean and tidy, it will only cause trouble for her."

Her? The word shook Fitz so, he thought the men below might hear his bones rattle.

"I'm *doin'* what ya told me to do."

"I told you we could use this time waiting for word on the timber loads to set up a side business with whores in Covent Garden. That is what I do. I make time into money, and I am paid for it. I didn't tell you to puff up your pride over some child in a blue cape."

"He was no child." The mean-eyed man sounded sullen and thoughtful. "No baby fights like that. Skinny, but well-fed. Something odd there."

Fitz didn't move, but he wondered what Tella's face looked like now.

It made his blood run cold, to think how close that man had come to ending her.

"You might make yourself useful by mending bridges with the sailors nearby. I'd like them to warn us if someone boards this boat."

Fitz saw Tella stiffen.

"I've got two big men with muskets abaft right now."

Marvellous.

"Probably sleeping off whatever you paid them in ale. Your choices in company aren't good, Burgiss."

Neither of them moved, but Fitz felt the air crackle. A name.

"Want more guards, give me more money. This ship is bloody huge, and only two men to guard it is stupid."

"Seven-eighths of the crew have left because of you. If we start bristling with guns, people will start wondering about our cargo."

"Who cares? It's wood. What's suspicious about wood?"

What *was* suspicious about wood?

He and Tella both balanced on the balls of their feet, the slow rolling rock of the ship beneath them in the dark.

"It's timber, you imbecile. Money can also be made from *things*." Then his tone changed. "Perhaps I should pay you and we part ways now. I need a man with more of a head on his shoulders."

"You won't find anyone tougher than me and you know it."

Both their voices stopped as the wood under Fitz creaked, somehow out of rhythm with the sounds made by the rocking of the boat.

Fitz was good at staying still, from years doing patrols. He knew how to shift his weight silently from foot to foot to stay still without hurting.

What he was not familiar with, was dry rot.

And he *was* heavy.

The next gentle pitch of the ship sent the floor up under him as he pressed his weight down, just on that foot.

The crunching, groaning noise as a board gave way under his foot seemed as loud as a gunshot.

"Who the devil is that?"

Fitz didn't wait. He whirled toward the gangplank and looked for Tella. She was already ahead of him, shadowy shape light on her feet, running.

Was it important to be quiet now?

He figured not.

His boots pounded heavily on the deck as he followed her.

And that was when he saw the men ahead. Coming from abaft. Two big men with muskets.

Right about to run into Tella.

Fitz paused, looking for a weapon. The deck was clean. He had to think of something, anything, to keep them from seeing her, stopping her, killing her.

They had a story, the two of them, and this wasn't how their story would end.

* * *

"Hey!" The two stalwarts with muskets popped into view ahead, running around open hatches. Unless they tripped, they'd be here in a second.

And Fitz was right behind her.

Time stretched. Tella looked around carefully during the long, long time between heartbeats.

Two men in front of them, two men behind, and soon, one would see Fitz' face.

He was too tall, too gangly, too noticeable.

And too handsome. If one of them saw his face, he'd be far too easy to identify. No one else had those eyes.

She could see his face. And in that moment, all her answers became one answer.

Right here, right now, she could lose yet one more person. Fitz.

That couldn't happen. All her tactical thinking focused on that point. In this order of battle, Fitz must maneuver first. Off the field.

Above Tella, a loading boom jutted out from the mast. She could see the line that kept the boom from swiveling, a faint black line against the brighter sky. She could see the path it traced through pulleys, and its tension at the mast.

Behind them, she heard yelling, getting closer. The vicious Mr. Burgiss, no doubt.

Fitz was looking about wildly for some sort of weapon. It was a clean deck; there was none.

"Stop!" she hissed to Fitz—

—and in the same instant drew a knife from within the folds of her heavy cloak, threw it at that one taut line.

It was yards and yards away, the rope no thicker than her thumb.

Tella was *very* good at throwing knives.

The knife sliced the line, all but one tiny strand; that too snapped as the boom swung, pulled by its weight.

And, freed, careened across the deck.

It had taken no more than two heartbeats.

In one smooth motion, she jumped and caught the boom as it swept over her, and used her weight to keep it swinging, aiming her feet straight into Fitz's chest.

She slammed him over the railing into the water.

* * *

SURELY IF FITZ couldn't swim, he'd have mentioned it the other night on the river.

He was just too big and heavy. She couldn't defend him, and he couldn't run fast. Nor was there anywhere to run, on a ship.

She pulled up her feet and hooked them over the boom, swinging the weight of her body to get the boom to swing back.

The boom slowed, stopped, then swept back across the deck.

It carried her over the ship's railing so she could drop, cat-like, to land and roll a little on the boards of the dock.

As a gun went off.

It didn't seem to be anywhere near her. Had they shot Fitz? Her heart, her guts all clenched.

No. They were looking at her. As long as they looked at her, they weren't looking at him. If he was smart, he'd swim alongside the ship till he could hide under the dock, work his way toward a place to climb out.

And he was smart.

Tella's heart was pounding far harder from the fear that Fitz was shot than from swinging off the ship.

It was also true what she'd told him. Alone, she was lighter and faster. And she could *run*.

Sailors on the dock looked up as she ran, but none came after her. The green-coated man was right; this ship didn't have friends.

Behind her, she heard the thuds of heavy footsteps on the gangplank. She stole a glance. Burgiss' two hired men were following her; one, without his musket. Slightly more brains than the other, perhaps.

Or maybe he'd already emptied into Fitz. That last gunshot. No, she couldn't think that.

Tella felt inside the lining of her cloak for a small strip of cloth sewed inside.

When she pulled on it, a hidden pocket opened, and from the bottom of the cape, handfuls of clay marbles pattered onto the dock, scattering behind her.

Unpolished, earth-colored marbles, too dark to be seen at night.

As she expected, when her pursuers hit the patch of marbles, they went down.

Blam went the musket as its stock hit the dock in exactly the wrong way. Of course he had been carrying the musket primed and cocked. Even half waiting for it as she was, it made Tella duck.

But she still ran.

As she approached the warehouses stacked along the water's edge, she ought to have kept going. She'd be safe, she'd be hidden.

She didn't. She couldn't. She had to know he was all right.

Tella ducked behind a piling wrapped with rope, trying to become one with its shape in the dark.

Two more strips inside were pulled tight, and the cloak

fitted itself to her body, contracting around her waist and hips, the fabric gathering and bunching. She became smaller.

An unfashionable look, but it made crawling easier. And crouching.

She could keep out of sight of Burgiss' men until she knew Fitz had reached land.

In a pause in combat, she should do what she could that was useful. Her uncle had always said that. What useful thing could she do while she waited for Fitz to paddle ashore? Besides breathe. She must keep breathing, slowly, quietly, deeply.

That conversation they'd just heard. Practice made her able to force herself to repeat it over and over in her head, to remember its every detail rather than worry.

With tiny movements, she slipped a thumb-sized bundle from another pocket: a soft British pencil, wrapped with a few slips of good, plain paper. Nothing that could identify her.

Just like the earthenware marbles could not identify her. She must remember that pocket was empty.

Her knife could identify her, but it too was gone; she'd aimed it towards water, and it wouldn't be found. It was Huntsman steel, Britain's finest, sold nowhere else in the world since the Continent had cut off trade with Britain. The blade-smith who served her knew the properties of the metal well.

Was that Fitz? No, just a fish in the water. She could force herself to wait a little longer. She just had to concentrate. On what? Yes, her lost knife.

Not that the bladesmith knew she was his customer. He sent his packages to a merchant, who sent them to another with questionable habits, who sent them to a tradesman in London. The tradesman did a great deal of business with Tella, though not under that name. He was glad to receive parcels and send them on to the Gravenshire townhouse, in fresh wrappings that bore his company's mark.

The knife could be traced to her, though not easily; just as well it was at the bottom of the Thames.

The shapes of Burgiss' men finally pounded past, their boots echoing on the wood. They must have stopped at other ships. One still waved his musket; she'd bet a shilling he still hurt himself with it, even unloaded.

They passed her by.

Her breathing slowed. After what seemed like hours, *years*, quiet descended and the only sound was water lapping at the pilings below.

Where *was* Fitz?

She'd endanger him if she looked for him.

Forcing herself to stay still, Tella wrote down on a slip of the paper, as plainly as she could, everything she could remember of the conversation they'd heard. Not just Burgiss, the name they now had for the mean-eyed man, but all they'd said, as much as fit on both sides.

Which she slipped into a waxed leather pouch before hiding it, and the pencil, back into the depths of her cloak.

There was nothing left to do. She wasn't capable of staying still all *night*.

Surely that great ox could swim?

Finally, what seemed like lifetimes later, she heard someone splashing in the water, under the dock.

Someone who swung himself up into a dinghy, which rocked heavily under his weight. Someone who lay there, spitting curses and river water.

He was alive.

She ought to speak to him. She'd never felt cowardly before in her life. She felt cowardly now.

But if she reached down, and he came up here...

If he did that, she couldn't hide anything from him. She felt like he could see her anywhere. Even in the dark.

She willed her heart to slow, slow down, listening to Fitz stumbling in the boat. There was a rope ladder alongside; she knew how hard those were to use.

After swearing at it repeatedly, so did Fitz.

By the time he reached the dock, Tella had slid yards away, behind another piling. She saw his square shoulders blocking out the sky, saw him snap his head to the side, tossing his wet hair. At least he'd stopped swearing.

If she could have been sure he'd only talk about their mission, she'd have gone to him. She suspected his conversation would stray to other, more personal topics.

Hers would.

It was precisely because she wanted to go to him so badly that she stayed where she was.

Stayed silent, and motionless, hunched under the flat black of her cloak and hood. And he walked right past. That was what she wanted. She didn't want to get too close.

It was too dangerous.

CHAPTER FOURTEEN

*H*e'd never get all the garbage out of his hair.

Hours of searching had not found him Tella, or answers.

He couldn't wander the city till dawn again looking for her. His head said she must be safe; the rest of him just wasn't following.

Fitz dunked said head, as best he could, in the bucket of cold water from his landlady. She claimed there was soap, but with head and hands numb from the cold, he couldn't feel any.

He could only use the icy nubs of his fingers to try to prod everything free from his hair that didn't belong there. Algae. Or barnacles. Whatever it was, he didn't want it.

The cheap bed he'd rented in a sailor's inn smelled of it too.

Fitz fell into it and decided he could be angry just as well tomorrow.

* * *

IN THE MORNING, Fitz paid extra for a tub of cold water to wash again. The landlady, house stacked full of sailors paying for beds that didn't rock, was happy to take more of his money. She also found the soap.

His clothes needed more than he could do for them. Between smoke and seaweed, he wouldn't have many clothes left.

Fitz finally took out the trusty razor he'd taken to the Continent and back, and suppressed a snarl so he could scrape it over his cheek and jaw.

Last night had damaged his disposition, and the few hours' smelly sleep hadn't healed it.

What ailed the woman? She *must* have escaped. If they'd had her, they wouldn't have run after her; and he'd heard their boots on the dock.

Among buildings, it was a guarantee that she had eluded their capture.

But why had she left him? Pushed him *overboard*, and left him.

Lady Donnatella was rapidly becoming the largest topic in his mind. Larger than the news story he ought to be writing with Gerry, far larger than the problems of his family. Larger even than the problems presented by his proposal to her, which were many.

She was far more than his proposal.

She was close to becoming everything.

Her dark, determined eyes were all he could see. And he saw them, achingly clearly, fixed and hard as she had pushed him over that railing.

It hurt, far more than her boots meeting his chest.

Surely he'd proven that he was handy to have around? She needn't like him at all to admit that. And he trusted his instincts about people. She liked him. He was positive. Mostly positive.

So what ailed the woman?

Some tiny part of his mind wondered if she might be the employer of the man in the green coat.

But that idea was rubbish. Burning a load of Swedish timber in order to sell timber of one's own was simple, selfish, risky, and, Fitz would bet, traitorous. Britain had forbidden imports of timber from America; they were at war, too. Fitz didn't know trees by sight, but only Sweden and America had timber that was plentiful and large like that.

Tella didn't fear risk and liked things simple, but he did not think her selfish. She'd sought nothing in the knife fight where they'd originally met but the saving of innocent people.

Nor could he imagine her traitorous.

He'd thought of Tella simply because she was all-encompassing right now. Clearly, some other woman had arranged all this. Someone very clever and far more unscrupulous.

Though Tella had been quite unscrupulous enough to push him overboard.

Something ailed her, he decided as he wiped away the last soap on his face. Not because she had run from him. But because she was a good companion, a good fighter, and he thought he'd been the same. For some reason, there was a line between them that they kept tipping over, and she kept running away.

He had one clean suit of clothes left, and it was in his pack. He'd need it.

Because he knew that Lady Donnatella was visiting the Queen's House today, and he would be damned if he was going to miss seeing her there.

* * *

"Oh my!"

Julia was so delighted by the colonnade that she ran for a better look before they even had Lady Dunsby settled.

Fortunately, it was a sunny day, and the brougham's top allowed it to be pushed back. "I shall sit here in the sun and enjoy it, girls, and you must take in the vistas. Look, Lady Julia is showing you just how to do it."

Lady Agatha did not look pleased at the idea of leaving her mother alone, and not just because she was their supposed chaperone.

Her mother seemed used to her tucking and re-tucking in the lap robe. "Go on, Agatha, do enjoy, and when you return, you will tell me what the other side looks like."

"We won't make a long visit, Lady Dunsby, Lady Agatha," Tella assured them both, her eyes scanning for Julia's pale pink dress. "We will take in the vistas and return straightaway."

In the distance, she saw Julia, waving her hand.

"Well, Lady Julia seems to have found an interesting vista."

Lady Agatha giggled. "She is so energetic! You must take your exercise trying to keep up with her."

"A bit." Tella kept on her careless expression.

"Oh. Is she—she's not near that gentleman?" Lady Agatha's nerves flipped direction again.

Because among the columns Julia had already passed, a shadow detached itself from shadows among them, and they could see it was the outline of a man.

Fitz.

Tella's heart began to pound so hard Agatha must hear it. What was he doing here? Julia thought him her betrothed, and now Agatha would hear the same story.

Lies dug one in so inconveniently deep.

Even, or especially, when they were partly true.

"Lord Henry! What a surprise," Tella called as she and Agatha approached. She did not offer her hand.

He did, however, bow. "Lady Donnatella. Not a surprise at all."

"Is it not?"

Julia had returned behind him, her usually sweet gaze measuring him from top to bottom and back up to the top. "How is it you come to see us here today, Lord Henry? It cannot be by accident, surely."

Tella thought she saw him pause for the slightest second, before he opened his coat and half-withdrew a folded letter, seal broken. "No accident. Her ladyship let me know of her visit, and I thought it an opportune moment to see her."

"An opportune moment to impose herself on you, you mean." Julia bristled.

"No no, Lady Julia, please. I just thought it might be nice to see Lord Henry away from crowds. And of course my father." The lie made Tella's face flame in a way no lie had ever done before.

Julia was turning that measuring look on her.

"Did you?"

"Well of course she did!" From alarm, Agatha had flipped again just as quickly to delight. Her blonde curls swung; she couldn't stop looking back and forth between Tella and Fitz. "Of course she wants a few minutes alone with her courtier, as what lady would not?"

"Yes," and for the first time Fitz met Tella's eyes as he said directly to her, "what lady would not?"

Was this knowledge between them what happened to soldiers who fought side by side? Because she felt that she knew exactly what he was thinking.

"Of course!" Agatha's imagination was providing all the information anyone needed. "Lord Henry wished to walk along the colonnade with her ladyship, and take in the views in peace. Didn't you, Lord Henry?"

He was still looking straight at Tella. One corner of his mouth tipped up, just slightly. "That would be nice. If you wished to walk with me, Lady Donnatella."

She wished him at the bottom of the ocean. She did. She'd kicked him to send him there.

"Lady Julia," Agatha said, since Tella didn't answer, "do walk with me. Do you draw? We ought to have brought pencils."

Agatha seized the arm of the still suspicious-looking Julia and they walked ahead, remarking on the open view from the colonnades.

Tella stepped back from Fitz.

"Am I so alarming to you?" His voice was low, puzzled. "I've seen you fight with a knife, you know; aren't you armed? Regardless. You are safe with me, in many ways."

"You ought to have gone home."

"Why? Walk with me. Fred, please." He put out his hand.

He was as solidly planted as a tree. His shoulders seemed to block out the bright sun.

She wanted to take that strong, square hand.

So much that she could not.

Head bowed, she walked past him. He fell into step next to her.

"What went wrong last night?" Fitz kept his voice low, ensuring it wouldn't travel. Ten paces ahead, only the light sound of Lady Agatha's chatter reached them; they couldn't make out her words.

"Nothing went wrong."

"You shoved me over a railing into the water. That was wrong."

"They were going to *see* you."

"So? They've seen you."

"No." She whirled on him; he stopped. "They've never *seen* me. No one sees me. They see the gowns, or the cape, or the hat, or the knife. They never see me."

"They've seen the Caped Count, and they are after him."

"Not the same." Her mouth was twisting; she couldn't stop it.

Unheeding of their nearby companions, Fitz stopped in the shade of the colonnade. His thumb stroked her chin, but she wouldn't let him lift it so he could meet her eyes.

"Donnatella," and she'd never heard that note in his voice before, "it worries *me* that those men have seen you. It would only be reasonable if it worried you that they have seen me."

She looked down again. She couldn't explain that it wasn't the same, it wasn't the same at all.

He did not stop touching her. "Were you so worried for me, then?"

When she didn't answer, he tried a smile. "Reasonable, surely, to worry about your betrothed. Just a little. Don't you think?" The smile went out of his voice, slid away from his face. "Don't you remember, we are betrothed?"

Tella couldn't laugh. She'd made light to him of the betrothal, pleaded for it with Julia, and avoided saying what she must say now.

"I cannot accept your proposal," she choked out.

He moved, a startled movement, before he stopped himself, hand dropped. Had he been about to put his arms around her? She wished he would. But was grateful that he didn't. That would make all this so much harder.

"You *did* accept my proposal. Before your father. And half of London."

"You must allow me to withdraw my acceptance, sir." She still felt as though her throat were thick and dry. Did he not understand?

"I don't understand. Tella. Won't you look at me? Tell me

what you are thinking. As betrothals go, I know it was a surprise, but I don't wish to take it back. Do you hear me? Why..." Again he reached out, and finally succeeded in tilting her chin up so her eyes met his. "Why would I want to let you go?"

"You don't understand?" The treacherous swell of tears she could feel rising had no reason, there was no reason, but Tella could barely hold it back. "Don't you see? *You're just someone else to lose.*"

The angle of his head, the way his mouth fell open, made her think he understood. That he was about to say something to make it all different, make it all better.

And as they stood there in the shade on a spring afternoon, somewhere not far away, in a structure at one end of the long colonnade, three bells sounded, *gong, gong, gong*, the ring of a ship's bell stranded on dry land, mysterious and beautiful and out of place in the wide expanse of green all around them.

And his hand dropped from her face just as both of them turned to see a churning, teeming flood of children roll out the doors of the building where the toll of the bell had sounded.

"What the..." Fitz pulled her to the side of the walkway, between the columns, as a veritable river of children came running past, some waving to them, some gawking, most too busy shouting and laughing to each other to pay Tella and Fitz any attention.

"I see," Fitz finally said, as a few taller adults came in view at the back of the pack. "It appears to be a school."

Tella shook herself. She ought to have known the building was a school. Of course, her hosts hadn't mentioned it either.

They probably presumed she knew.

Two small children, brown-haired and a bit dusty, peeled

themselves off of the surging flood and stopped before them. "Who are you?" the little girl asked baldly.

"Yeh, who?" piped up the little boy with her.

"May I present the Lady Donnatella?" Fitz said just as if it were the Duke's drawing room.

The girl nodded. The boy just stared.

A teacher approached and laughed. "Using your weather eye, Kenneth? Don't stare."

"No sir," both children said, in unison, staring.

"Is it a day school?" Tella recovered her wits enough to look around at the children. There were hundreds.

"No indeed. The Royal Naval Asylum, miss," said the teacher with great pride. "Since His Majesty deeded us the building six years ago."

* * *

TELLA PALED.

The Royal Naval Asylum. Of course, for the children of the Navy men lost in war.

Orphans.

Children who'd lost their fathers. And then their mothers.

She dropped to her knees. A few dark locks of hair slid forward as her head bent. She genuinely had trouble talking now, the words rasping as she said, "Would you like a shilling?"

"Would I!" Then the girl remembered her companion and pulled the little boy close. "We both would, miss!"

She dispensed with some coins, and gave the little girl her handkerchief, too. She didn't know why. Would a child need a linen handkerchief embroidered with the Gravenshire arms? She might.

Need or not, the little girl's face, thin like Tella's, with determined dark eyes that looked familiar too, nodded. "Thank you, miss, thank you many times!"

"You are too kind, madame; we did not know we were to have visitors today. Shall I show you to the offices?" To the students he said, "Get along, now; you don't want to be late for your next watch."

Fitz waved to the children as they skipped off, the boy still looking back over his shoulder at them.

"No," she said faintly, almost too faintly to hear.

It took the men a moment to realize she'd answered the teacher's offer to show her the offices.

The teacher, surprised, looked at Fitz, who shrugged. There was no problem, no problem here.

The teacher's tiny answering shrug was almost invisible. "Have a good day, sir, madame." And followed quickly behind the receding wave of children, in good position to catch stragglers.

"Tella." Fitz reached down for her hand; she didn't move. "Donnatella."

She was still fixed in place. Only looked up at him with that white face, papery against the blue of her gown.

Just as papery and dry as her voice. "Orphans. All orphans."

Oh, no.

He didn't wait any longer for her to take his hand.

Checking to see that Julia and Agatha were still looking away, Fitz slid his hands under her arms, lifting her swiftly to her feet.

"Tella. They are all well and happy as can be. Tella. Do you hear me? Did you see?"

"Orphans, Fitz. I hope they don't feel guilty every time they smile."

Her eyes were killing him.

Just as swiftly, he pulled her to him, laying her head on his shoulder, folding her in his arms.

He focused on warming her, holding her tight. He couldn't feel her breath or her heartbeat.

He couldn't tell her that children recovered quickly from the blows of life. She knew they didn't.

CHAPTER FIFTEEN

*I*n his arms was the warmest, safest, *quietest* place that Tella had ever been.

All she could hear was the distant rush of wind over the grass, the distant sounds of children shouting and laughing in the school, and the very near pounding of Fitz's heart, just under her ear.

She'd like it, to stay here.

"Lord *Henry*." Sweet, quiet Julia managed to get a world of disapproval into her tone.

Tella closed her eyes. She wasn't ready to move yet. She wasn't ready to keep lying yet. She wasn't ready to keep hurting. Because she hurt, though not from a blade or a bullet, and she didn't even know why.

And then a miracle occurred.

Fitz didn't move.

"Just a moment, Lady Julia. I'm afraid Lady Donnatella is a bit overcome."

"What? By what? What have you done? I swear, if you—"

"Lady Julia." And his voice was just like the rest of him. Solid. Unmoving. And real. "Just a moment, please."

Tella heard Julia's shoes tapping on the paving stones, Lady Agatha whispering at her elbow. Agatha must be leading Julia away again. It wouldn't last.

But it was heaven, pure heaven not to worry that anyone was watching for a whole minute more.

She pulled in her hands to tuck them between their bodies, flattened against Fitz' wall of a chest.

Pure heaven.

But heaven wasn't for her.

"Of course she is right, we are making a spectacle of ourselves. Not for the first time. I cannot do it, sir, not like you can."

She didn't look up at him as she stepped back.

"Because you are a lady? Because you would be compromised?"

Tella still didn't look at him, her eyes following the rolling green grass beyond the colonnade instead. "I would be so much more than compromised. I would be trapped, all my work ended. No one left to watch over my streets. *My* streets."

It was vital that she be lonely.

"What if I could arrange not to compromise *or* trap you?"

His words forced her to meet his eyes.

Clear blue eyes full of conviction. "What if I could *swear* it to you?"

Tella shook her head, just a little, with a small smile she didn't mean. "I would say, you have never lied to me. Don't begin now."

A flicker of pink caught her attention in the corner of her eye. Julia was marching towards her, towing an unwilling Agatha along behind.

And Julia said, "Lord Henry, I am sure you must necessarily understand why we must go. This visit is entirely inappropriate."

* * *

FITZ WANTED to take Tella's hand. She still looked hurt, and sad, and Fitz wanted to be the one to comfort her.

Vehemently, he reminded himself that a wise gentleman did not anger a lady's best friend.

But if he could not keep Tella to himself, he could still speak.

"I'm afraid Lady Donnatella has had a fit of sadness, ladies, a circumstance with which I'm sure you are familiar. I will gladly leave her to your care if you promise to ensure that she eats and drinks and rests. Will you?"

That set Julia back on her heels a little. "We intend to return to Lady Dunsby's home, and then make our return trip. It is not so long, but we will do it today."

Fitz reached out to brush Tella's check with his fingertips. "Will you do it today?"

"Must you keep fussing over me in a schoolyard?" She pushed his hand down. "I am perfectly fine."

"Not in a schoolyard, but I would like the chance to keep fussing, as you say. May I walk with you to your carriage, ladies?"

Agatha was perfectly happy to take one of his arms, and Fitz did not give Tella a choice about taking the other one, leaving an unusually scowly Julia to follow along behind.

* * *

"TALK TO ME." Tella wanted easy conversation on their trip back from Greenwich. She couldn't just watch the scenery roll by in silence; she'd lose her wits. "Tell me all the rumors of the new Duchess. I ought to know, if she will be attending my party, oughtn't I? Will it be her first evening out as Duchess?"

"Why do I have the feeling that man is doing you no good?"

Tella looked out the window and risked the scenery. "I don't know, why do you?"

"Tella." Julia reached out and tugged on her hand. Tella sighed and let her have it, met her eyes. "Do you love him? I mean, are you really in love with him?"

"I don't know what that means, Julia." About this, Tella could be entirely honest. "If love strikes one out of the blue, filling one with the certainty of their feelings, then no. I have never felt like that. Perhaps I never will."

"But you have always wanted love. You have always wanted that forever passion of a love. You've always said so."

"I know what I've said."

The further they drove away from Greenwich and the awful tangle of feelings she'd felt there, the clearer Tella's thoughts became. She'd tried to always tell Julia only one lie: that she was waiting for that passionate, abiding love.

Now she'd told Julia so many lies, she realized the first one was no lie.

How could she begin to tell Julia it had been true all along, when she also knew now it was the one thing she could never have? She did not have it in her, to love and lose one more person.

"I don't think—please forgive me, darling, if this sounds awful—I don't think I am as uncomplicated as you are. You have found your Lord Wendover and the two of you fit together like peas in a pod, and you are happy. Did you ever really imagine it would happen that way for me?"

"Well..." Julia's lips folded as she thought. "Truly dear, I have never found that easy to imagine."

"Then let me puzzle this out. Whatever it is, it is my affair."

"No."

Astonished, Tella whirled and stared at her friend.

"I mean it. I do. You never seem to realize that you *have* a friend, Tella. A friend for life. A *good* one." Julia seized Tella's hand in both of hers. "Real friends share your problems *and* your joys. Real friends are there for you when you need a friend, and that may be the only true definition."

"Oh my dear." Tella threw an arm around Julia's shoulders and squeezed. "And you are a very good friend, by that very definition."

"Then you ought to tell me what is going on between you and that Henry Fitzwilliam."

"I ought, and as soon as I am sure, I will tell you. Is that not fair?"

Tella even smiled a bit, looking into Julia's eyes, stern where they were usually soft.

"I suppose I must trust you," Julia finally said, "but I wish you would tell me more. There seem to be any number of things between the two of you that I ought to know about, and I don't even know for sure what makes me think so."

"You are very discerning." Tella leaned closer. "I kissed him."

Julia gasped. "He *kissed* you? *When?*"

"*I* kissed *him.*" Tella still wasn't sure whether she was proud of it or mortified, but at least she was telling Julia the truth. Well, he *had* kissed her... but she'd kissed him first.

"Never tell me so! I had no idea you could be so forward."

Tella's face screwed up somewhere between a grin and a grimace. "Neither did I!"

And both ladies laughed at themselves as the carriage rolled through the London streets.

* * *

NEITHER WAS LAUGHING, however, when Lady Shoreton herself came to meet them at Julia's door.

And marched them right in to the ballroom, the first available room, and shut the door.

"I would be sad for Lord Shoreton to hear what I have to say to you, both of you. Lady Julia. Gentlemen do not find it admirable for young ladies to fly all over the city at a whim just because they are safely betrothed. That is a very quick way for them to become *un*betrothed.

"And you, Lady Donnatella. What a sad betrayal of the Duke's faith in me. Not only have you set an extremely bad example for other young ladies, accepting a proposal in *public* from a young man *no* one knows, now you have dragged Lady Julia across the entire city for an ill-advised visit. Alone."

"Lady Julia was only being the true friend she is, Lady Shoreton. The responsibility is all mine. I would not be dissuaded."

"Oh, I believe you." Lady Shoreton's hands clasped each other calmly, but her hair was shivering with anger. "Yet I believe a daughter of mine ought to be *able* to dissuade you; you are not that threatening a person. Had she the mind to do so."

"Really, madame, I—"

"Lady Donnatella. I do believe your presence is awaited at home. Please do use the Shoreton carriage; I have asked them to stay at the door for your use. Lady Julia, if you will come with me please."

Julia followed her mother down the hall, turning to wave as Tella walked back toward the front door. Her little smile said for Tella not to worry; it was just another one of Lady Shoreton's fits of pique.

But Tella felt truly awful. She had not expected Lady Shoreton to blame Julia.

Yet another example of why she should be glad she and Julia were parting ways. Ladies simply couldn't gallivant through the city at their own wish. And Tella had *needed* to get to Greenwich. Involving someone else, anyone else, was only asking for more notice to be taken of Tella's movements, and would cause anyone who helped her more trouble.

The Caped Count had always traveled alone, and needed to do so again.

* * *

"Mr. Burgiss." His employer's face was in shadow, as the sunlight streamed in from the porthole behind him. "Is it a correct statement that once again, you've failed to eliminate this threat to our business?"

Burgiss squirmed. He didn't like it when the swell got stiff and holier-than-thou. It made his fists itch.

"It's a fact, governor, that boy in the cape is still causing us trouble."

"Trouble even for the men you hired, who are big, and have muskets. Another failure. What will be your next move? As I expect it to be a *different* one."

"All right, there's no point rubbing my nose in it. My men ain't hounds. They lost 'im just as you'd expect as soon as there were buildings to hide around in. We ought to trap him somewhere, somehow he can't get loose."

"Yes, you ought to. Or you ought to kill him. I thought you were so keen on killing people."

The man's face, backed by shadow, had a regal profile, with waves of silver and black hair brushed back all around.

"It's not that it's fun killin' people. It's just that it makes things better. Tidier, as it were. They're better off, I'm better off—everyone gets somethin' out of it."

"Now that's the first interesting thing I've heard you say, Mr. Burgiss." The man stepped away from the porthole, and walked around the captain's table to sit, never taking his eyes off Burgiss. "I admire a penchant for keeping work tidy. Let's see you do it. There were two intruders last night, not just one; quit focusing on the man in the cape and forgetting the other. And start tidying." He tapped a fingernail thoughtfully on the wood of the table. "It can't be that hard to find a man that big."

"No problem at all," and Burgiss was whistling as he climbed out the hatch.

Had Fitz or Tella seen him, they would have recognized the swagger in his walk as the one he had just before he'd set fire to the warehouse and tied its doors shut.

His employer watched him go thoughtfully. Burgiss was probably the wrong tool for the job. He was blunt, clumsy. This job required delicacy.

Delicacy was a word Burgiss would never use, or think.

Leaning back in his chair, the man tugged down the sleeves of his green coat. He had better start devising another plan, just in case Burgiss failed again.

But hopefully, he wouldn't.

CHAPTER SIXTEEN

*E*verything sparkled with candlelight and glowed with the soft colors of spring flowers.

Flowers that sprung from every type of container, stacked on every type of surface. They were in porcelain and crystal vases on the tables, shaped onto fascinating sculptures for the floor, and hung from wall sconces in baskets.

There were even two huge arrangements, lilacs and camellias bursting from buckets covered with découpage of butterflies and branches, sitting atop the stone Egyptian plinths that had been gifted to her father last year.

And it was all because of Julia.

Tella wanted a party like her old ones, when she had far fewer cares, and Julia and her uncle on whom to rely. Tonight, she would do her best. Julia was already doing hers, despite Lady Shoreton's disapproval of their jaunt to Greenwich.

Lady Shoreton would hardly stop her daughter from helping to arrange a social evening hosted by the Duke of Gravenshire.

When Tella swept in, the gold-embroidered blue silk of

her shawl sailing behind her, it was Julia she looked for first. And Julia she hugged.

"You have done glorious things, just glorious!" Her grin was wide as she looked around. "Look what a beautiful party you have given us all!"

"Not at all, my lady, it is the Lady Donnatella and the Duke of Gravenshire who provide us with hospitality tonight." But Julia's eyes twinkled as she made a little curtsey that wasn't at all sincere.

"Your mercy shines from the heavens, my darling." Tella hugged her again. Hard. "What will I ever do without you?"

"What is this obsession you have developed about doing without me?"

But there was no time for Julia's frown, as here was the Duke himself.

Tella curtsied. "I hope it all pleases you, Your Grace. Lady Julia is to be praised for all of it. The Duke and Duchess of Talbourne are coming, and the Prince Regent is not! It should be a happy evening all round."

A lively flute, accompanied by a sweet piano, began to play a bouncy little tune. The music floated over the room.

"I'm sure it will," was all her father said.

* * *

TELLA HEARD RATHER than saw when the Duke and Duchess of Talbourne arrived; the crowd parted for them.

The Duke of Talbourne reminded Tella of flint: gray, stony, in danger of producing unexpected fire. Most of London considered him icy and stiff; she had a feeling they were wrong.

His lady seemed quite the opposite of icy and stiff. The new Duchess was quite pretty, with great quantities of golden-brown hair that shone in the candlelight, though not, in Tella's opinion, as richly as Fitz'.

The Duchess had some companions with her, but she didn't look like the sort to have them fussing over her hems all night. She looked like the sort who would happily tear a hem for a good dance.

And she was blind.

Tella *tsked*. Why did no one ever tell her these things?

She took a deep breath and greeted her guests as the Duke's dizzy daughter who played at cards. A bit rudely since, as she managed to mention, the Duchess could not play them.

"No card games for me tonight," said the Duke, "I am still recovering from a very bad loss at chess."

That was surprising both because the stony Duke was famous for not having fun—he never played games—and because no other duke in the realm would have publicly mentioned a loss.

Curious.

"Oh! Truly?" It wasn't hard to sound a little confused. "My father has been so hoping you would attend. You never add your presence to these social occasions."

"Her Grace of course causes me to be a more social animal."

Had the Duchess just snorted?

Tella could certainly imitate the shrewd look of a young lady gauging the marriage prospects of a wealthy and titled man. "Had you come to more social events, Your Grace, you might have married sooner."

"No," the Duke said, tucking the Duchess' hand possessively into the crook of his arm, "I would not have. Good evening, Lady Donnatella."

Well.

He seemed more attractive since he'd married. Still

appallingly brusque. And if he wasn't besotted with his wife, Tella would eat this shawl.

Oh no. Had Julia been right? Was she becoming a matchmaker?

No, of course not. She couldn't match a man with his wife.

* * *

HAD Tella ever thought parties like this were harmless fun? Parties were *awful* when they were hers. All the pointless talk, plus the horror of wondering if one's guests were happy.

"Are you quite well, Lord Preston?"

He was standing, looking steadier on his feet than his conversation companion, in fact.

"For the third time, yes," her uncle said with some forgivable shortness. "I am *enjoying* my conversation with Lord Halworth, Donnatella; is there no one here with whom you can do the same?"

"I'm the hostess, darling, I must make sure everyone is happy."

"We're quite happy, Lady Donnatella, and thank you," said the gentleman with whom Lord Preston had been talking.

A gentleman with kind eyes. Clearly was not one of the parties spreading rumors about the new Duchess.

Because this party was full of rumors about the Duchess. Tella had already heard that she'd been the Duke's mistress before they wed, that she was with child, and that she could not get with child; and there was one odd story that she was secretly the daughter of Catherine the Great.

That was *exactly* what Tella liked in a party: everyone talking, and not about her.

It was tiring, though, enjoying the gossip without letting

it run tastelessly rampant. The new Duchess seemed charming. No need to destroy her reputation at her first affair. A duchess needed a reputation.

A Caped Count just needed to be able to survive a fight.

"Will you dance, Lady Donnatella?"

She whirled. The invitation had come from a good-looking fellow, whose smile went all the way to his eyes. He looked familiar.

"Have we met? Oh yes, we danced, didn't we?"

His smile faltered a little, but he put it back on. "Yes. You said you felt safe in my arms. It might have been a week ago?"

"Oh yes, my lord—" She stopped.

"No idea what my name is, have you? Never fear. I'll happily tell it to you again if you will dance with me. You do enjoy a waltz, do you not?"

Then, just behind him, she saw a tall man with long arms folded across his chest, feet solidly planted.

"What are you doing here?" It was out before Tella could stop it.

Fitz inclined his head, returning her greeting. "Learning things."

The second she saw him, she wanted to go to him. Wanted to be folded up in those arms and feel safe and quiet.

That was exactly why she must not.

Why was he here, distracting her, making awkward and public advances? He ought to know she needed her place in society to do what she did. And he ought to know he was endangering that.

"Do go away. I must attend to my guests."

The young man between them—Tella *must* find out his name—just looked back and forth from Tella to Fitz.

"Your guests look entertained, my lady." From his height, Fitz could look round the room and see almost everyone. "London's new duchess apparently wishes to meet every member of the House of Lords with a vote, and every member's wife wishes to discuss her. It's extremely diverting."

"Have you seen her companion, Miss Díaz? You might find her diverting."

It was hard to believe that he was still standing here, in fact, if he *had* seen Miss Díaz. The young lady was beautiful, and she stood at the center of a knot of men that had formed around her and not moved.

She too was an object of Tella's gratitude. No one was looking at the Duke of Gravenshire's tall, silly daughter with Miss Díaz around.

The gentleman who'd asked her to dance was not so easily put off. "I believe our waltz is beginning, my lady."

"If only it were." She favored him with a bright smile. "Would you be willing to collect me for the next one, after you've kindly reminded me of your name?"

"Lord John Harman, and I will be delighted to return." He looked up at Fitz. "I'll see you later."

"Confident fellow, isn't he?" Fitz observed as Harman departed.

"About dancing and card playing, and justly so. You must leave."

"I needn't do anything of the sort. I am your betrothed, you know."

"Just go before anyone—" Tella stopped.

"What? Before anyone realizes that I am *not* your betrothed? Or even a friend?"

"No, don't—don't say that." She met his eyes. "Don't ever say that."

"You told him you were safe in his arms? Is it something you say often?" Fitz seemed to be wandering somewhere between truly curious and a bit bitter. "Weren't you safe in my arms, too?"

Much safer.

Much too safe.

"You did not listen to a word I said, did you?" She didn't wish to *discuss* this. Discussion was exactly why she avoided relationships, with *anyone,* in the *ton* or on the street.

"I heard it."

"But you didn't listen. What a charming quality in a man. And how did your commanding officers find this quality in you?"

"They were against it." Fitz stood straight as a tree and just as immovable. "Tella, we do need to talk, much more."

"Well, we can't."

And she sailed away, blue shawl trailing, to see why the Duke of Talbourne had backed in between the Egyptian plinths and was shredding the lilacs.

* * *

FITZ HAD A SHRED OF GALLANTRY, he did. It must have come from his mother, early in life, when he was malleable.

Tella was right; he hadn't been very malleable since. He did fix on a destination, and then he went there. Admirable quality when charging a line of French soldiers; less admirable in a drawing room.

Just another reason to avoid drawing rooms.

What could she possibly see in all this? There were layers upon layers of discussion happening, none of it interesting to Fitz; he couldn't imagine any of it being interesting to Tella either.

He ought to try to eavesdrop on some of the lords, see if there were any stories worth printing. But that was shallow. The readers of Bridle's Daily Gazette did *not* care who was or was not voting according to the wishes of the Duke *or* the Duchess of Talbourne.

Perhaps they ought, but that wasn't the sort of story Fitz had it in him to write.

There were no deep dives here. Everything was embroidery and cuffs, and all-too-obvious maneuvers to get or protect either money or rank.

Some Gazette readers might care if the Duchess had been the Duke's mistress. Fitz would lose all respect for himself if he tried to write of it. Nor could he adequately describe what she was wearing.

Perhaps Lord Preston knew something about the Duke of Talbourne, his wife, or her gown.

Or why Tella was now determined not to marry him.

But before Fitz could reach Tella's great-uncle, he realized two things: the pretty young Duchess of Talbourne was dancing with someone who was not her husband.

And her husband, with whom she was not dancing, was talking to Tella.

If Fitz had learned one thing about relationships as a child, it was that British peers had marriages, not relationships.

If this Duke didn't care to spend his time dancing with his wife, Fitz would be damned if he'd turn his attentions to Tella.

Not because Fitz was jealous; he wasn't. He was privy to secrets of Tella's that no one else would ever know.

He just didn't want her feeling safe in yet another man's arms when he was *standing right here*.

* * *

TRULY, Tella had never seen the like before. There was the Duke of Talbourne, all flinty silence, backed in between the Egyptian plinths and creating a small heap of flower petals by ripping apart her lilacs.

And watching his wife dance with someone else.

She had to take a good, hard look as she approached. It wouldn't do to ask if he had a green coat. But she needed to look twice to make sure he wasn't the man she'd seen by lamplight in her mirror, down in the ship's hold, sitting on a load of mysterious timber.

He wasn't. The silver in his hair was scattered throughout, like light veins in dark marble. The one she sought had hair that was only silver on the sides.

This Duke hadn't hired Burgiss. He was most likely exactly what he appeared to be—a duke slightly in distress.

It wouldn't take much effort to get him to go dance with his wife as he wished.

Tella would make that effort.

* * *

"I've heard a dozen rumors about your wife in the last week," Tella said to the Duke by way of greeting, "but I hadn't heard this one."

"What's that?"

"That you are in love with her."

Why else would he look at the Duchess so longingly? He couldn't seem to take his eyes off her; indeed, he looked as if he wished he could.

Perhaps she had turned matchmaker, from her brush with betrothal. Or perhaps she just wanted others to have what she couldn't.

Loneliness was dreadful.

"Lady Donnatella—"

"Never fear, I'm actually quite good at keeping secrets. Why, Lady Winpole owes me forty pounds from losses at cards and I've never told that to anyone. Except that I've just told you. Oh well."

"My lady—"

Tella did not let him make silly excuses; instead, she recited the rumors flying around the room. Even the one about Catherine the Great.

A bit grudgingly, he said, "That last one is quite good. I thought Catherine hated the French. Also, she was nearly sixty when my wife was born, was she not?"

"What I did not expect to learn is that you love her."

"I'm afraid your instincts for drama have led you astray, Lady Donnatella."

"You are not the first man I've seen standing in a corner shredding flowers." In truth, she thought he *was*. But it was her policy never to be surprised. The Lady Donnatella the world was supposed to see was too careless to be surprised, and took nothing particularly seriously.

Regardless, he didn't look like he believed her. "Mm hmm. Speaking of men. Is that someone from your uncle's former military brigade coming to toss me out for my violence to your flowers?"

She knew who it was without looking. She looked anyway. "That walking tree trunk. I will leave you to your flower murder, sir, and advise you that you may yet have time to claim the next dance with your wife. If you don't dawdle."

Tella didn't dawdle either. If she moved quickly, she'd reach the card tables, and could check on the whist before Fitz caught up with her.

If he did, she had no idea what to say. With Fitz, it would be impossible to keep appearing careless.

* * *

THERE, she'd slipped away again, between the throngs of people.

This was ridiculous. This was the definition of chasing after a woman, and one who said she didn't wish to be chased.

Fitz didn't do this. He'd never done this. He'd had a few flirtations, a few lucky encounters, and a few brushes with the type of female companionship that followed soldiers into war.

It was far easier dealing with the Caped Count.

* * *

LORD PRESTON RAISED a glass of punch to greet Fitz as he joined them. "Lord Henry, do meet Lord Halworth. You both have a military background, unless I am much mistaken."

Jolly. So Tella had been right; her father had no doubt been learning everything there was to know about him. Fitz felt a flash of sympathy for the people he questioned for his work.

"Nothing like as distinguished as yours, sir," he said with all honesty, Lord Preston's long career being well known to everyone in London.

"It's a funny thing about military life, it stays with you whether it was long or short. Don't you think so, sir?" Lord Preston gestured to Lord Halworth.

Lord Halworth looked a little sleepy, generally well-disposed toward the world; he'd undoubtedly had several glasses of the punch already. Fitz wondered what on earth they had so much in common.

"Just as we have been discussing, sir," said Halworth, "surely it is a matter of perspective. In wartime especially, everything one sees and hears is so vivid. It impresses itself upon the mind so sharply. What else can possibly compare?"

Fitz looked hard at the man. It was so nearly what he had been thinking himself since he returned to London. At least, until he'd stopped a brawl with the Caped Count in the middle of the night. "It is a strong argument that military life is the genuine kind, then."

"Not at all." Lord Halworth had tired lines around his mouth and eyes, but he looked over the swirling mass of people, dancing and talking and laughing and drinking, with evident pleasure. "Every day that you breathe is genuine life, Lord Henry; the question is what you will do with it."

"A sound philosophy." Lord Preston toasted this.

"A bit too sweet an outlook for sour realities, though, surely?" Fitz had no idea he thought such things until his words came out. "London is full of people suffering, in pain, desperately trying to get through one more day. You are misled, perhaps, by too much exposure to people like these. They do nothing, and they have everything."

Lord Preston narrowed his eyes, but Lord Halworth only nodded. Slowly, thoughtfully. "It is my conjecture that nearly every life has complications, only we do not know them."

"I doubt it, sir. Not if you think these lives complicated." Fitz shook his head. "Not one of these dancing people has ever walked anywhere without shoes. None has ever gone three days on two mouthfuls of water. Nor have they ever watched good men die by hundreds, wondering what it was all for."

"See here," Lord Preston began, but Lord Halworth waved him off.

"Lord Preston has, and you just said you knew it well," said Lord Halworth in a mild way. "But I believe people still suffer, here, everywhere. You and I might not know how, but they do. You have met so many more people than most of us in this room, you must have had the same experience. Life comes with so much pain. Yet life is still a gift, and we must do what we can with it, and I daresay for it."

"You sound free of most disappointments, sir, if at your age you still feel that way."

"It is exactly because I have reached my age that I do feel that way, sir. I am dying more quickly than so many people, and yet still have the gift of time."

Fitz looked more closely at Lord Halworth's face, seeing now not the daze of someone who'd imbibed, but the thin lines of someone in pain.

Who nodded. "Yes, more slowly than soldiers on the field, I dare hope, and with the blessed mercy of laudanum. Lucky, in my own way. How many soldiers would trade places with me? Many, perhaps most. Perhaps not; a slow painful death isn't to everyone's taste."

He was *smiling*. How could the man be smiling, in his situation?

Puzzled, Fitz looked to Lord Preston, who understandably looked disgusted at Fitz' blundering, then back at Halworth. Fitz' first instinct was somehow that Lord Halworth ought to be lying down somewhere.

Perhaps everyone gave Lord Halworth that look. "No need to lie down just yet."

Lord Preston toasted his guest. "Just how I feel, and as you've freed me from the need to hide that I sometimes don't feel well, you've freed me to enjoy the time I have left. It is in some ways sad to be an old soldier, and in other ways, the greatest grace one could possibly desire."

Their sentiments rocked Fitz back on his heels as a blow never could.

These men were so little like his father, coldly calculating how to get what he wanted from the world and ignoring everything else.

They'd put words to feelings that had dogged him since his return from the front.

And he thought himself a writer.

His eyes drifted over the crowd, rested on Tella, his tall, beautiful Tella. Her midnight-blue gown, quite daring for an unmarried young lady, twisted gently over her body and fell in great sweeps to the floor. The sleeves didn't quite suit the design; no doubt added to cover her current knife wound. And perhaps some old scars.

She wasn't the only woman in the world like him, who had scars from battle and still wanted the sharp, clear taste of a life lived in the present.

But she was the one he wanted.

"At least, sir," he responded to Lord Preston without even realizing he spoke, "you have lived your life for your fellow soldiers, and for Britain." Tella must have learned it quite naturally at her uncle's knee.

"For things I hope were just." Lord Preston's face sagged a little; he looked his age again, and indeed, a little unwell. "The older I grow, the more I worry that I have been wrong there, too."

Fitz just nodded. Soldiers followed orders.

Tella followed her conscience.

Even if for some godforsaken reason Tella wanted to stay in society, perhaps she already knew what Fitz had just learned. He couldn't be interested in everyone's stories and still hate the *ton*. Battle wasn't the only news worth printing. And there were men here entirely unlike his father.

Like Lord Preston. "Lord Henry."

Startled out of staring at Tella, Fitz met the old colonel's eyes.

"I may have done only one thing absolutely right, and that was caring for my niece's daughter. I won't stop now. I won't stop until I am dead. And I am not dead. I also have several well-made pistols, two rifles, a bayonet I keep quite sharp, and more types of knife than you can count. I hope that is clear enough."

"Very clear, sir." And even under threat of all those weapons, Fitz' eyes returned to Tella. She was laughing. "There's a type of immediate clarity, too, one finds in Lady Donnatella's company. That, too, is very welcome to me. I won't pretend to know what I ought to be doing with my life, but I do suspect I know with whom I should be doing it."

"Aha. Well, I'd have to know you better, sir, before I can encourage that."

"I'd understand if you thought an ex-soldier a poor match for the Duke of Gravenshire's daughter."

"Eh." Lord Preston shrugged at that. "These people should have seen Lady Donnatella at twelve, charging up a hill with a wooden bayonet."

* * *

LADY WINPOLE WAS DOING RATHER WELL at the card tables. Tella was glad.

Not that she strictly needed the forty pounds, but still, there was the spirit of the thing. She'd like to see them again someday.

Lady Winpole's graying hair was twisted into a simple knot on the back of her head, and her bombazine gown was one Tella had seen before. She looked plain, and boring. Almost excessively so.

Where had that thought come from? Lady Winpole was modest and predictable, and Tella had known her all her life. That was partly why she hadn't minded the missing forty pounds.

Tella must try to remember what she had ever found entertaining at parties.

Lord John Harman sat across from Lady Winpole, and they had formed a pretty deadly pair at whist.

Lady Dunsby sat between them, and silently Tella sent

out another wave of gratitude to Julia. Julia, who had remembered to send a carriage for her and Agatha. Bless her. She was too good, Tella didn't deserve her.

But Tella needed her. It wasn't that getting shot at on a ship took precedence; it only left no room for such social details.

And then feet approached the fourth chair. "May I make your party's fourth hand? Or is this young lady planning to play?"

Tella looked up to assure the man that she did not plan to play, but forgot.

Because he wore a green coat—corduroy, it was easy to see close up, not velvet, so much more practical, her mind raced—and had silvering hair brushed back from his temples.

She'd seen his face before, dimly. By lamplight, reflected in a mirror.

And she'd heard that voice before.

CHAPTER SEVENTEEN

"*N*o. No, I wasn't planning to play. Only fascinated by Lord John's..." Tella couldn't think of anything about him that would fascinate her. "Strategy."

"Sit down, Mr. Storey, and be our fourth." Lady Winpole was deeply absorbed in the task of shuffling the cards; apparently Lady Dunsby on her right would deal the game.

"Thank you, Lady—Winpole, isn't it?"

Her ladyship simply nodded, not looking up from her cards.

Tella settled in slightly behind Lord John, on the far side of Lady Dunsby.

It was an effort to look bored by the game.

Tella went to that effort.

She yawned and pretended not to notice when Lady Dunsby went to pass the shuffled deck to Lord John to cut, and winced.

"Gout bothering you again, Hortense? Never mind, I'll do it." And with a curt sort of solicitude, Lady Winpole reached most indecorously across the entire table, passing the cards to Lord John herself.

Tella felt a bit sad, wondering a moment if Lord John were involved in something nefarious. He seemed harmless. She wanted to believe that the world had harmless people in it.

She watched his every move. He simply cut the cards.

"Thank you," said Lady Winpole, reaching across the table to pick them back up, her shawl brushing the table and, along with her hand, obscuring the cards from view.

"There you are, Hortense," and Lady Winpole put the cards down on Lady Dunsby's left just as she ought.

Tella was certain those were the cards Lady Winpole had so definitively shuffled, but not the cards Lord John had just cut.

Lady Dunsby, worried by nothing but the pain of her gout, chattered away as she picked up the cards and dealt them. "I have never liked the sound of trumps. We should call them party cards. Or squares of surrender." She giggled.

Meanwhile, just as the rules required, this Mr. Storey, he of the green corduroy coat, was shuffling the next deck of cards for play. He put them just to Lady Winpole's left, ready for her to deal when Lady Dunsby had dealt all her cards.

Lady Dunsby turned over a ten of spades for trumps.

"We shall see how much strategy I have, Lady Donnatella," said Lord John with a self-deprecating little laugh. She could see why; from where she sat, she could clearly see his hand full of high cards in the suit of spades. Not much strategy necessary, though scoring could depend on what his partner played.

His partner, the Lady Winpole, whom Tella had known literally as long as she had known anyone in her life. Who had just stacked the deck.

And who proceeded to play, with the same calm focus with which she always played. And, of course, won.

Tella didn't think Lord John an accomplice. He seemed

disappointed, if anything, by his hand, and his eyes glittered a little when a chance came next round to bid a particularly high trump.

Or party card, as Lady Dunsby styled it.

Mr. Storey, whoever he was, played quite calmly, just as Lady Winpole did. But he lost. It was Lady Winpole who kept winning.

She and Lord John were far better players than Lady Dunsby with her haphazard play, and a casual observer might have thought it reasonable that the pair of them continued to win three out of four tricks.

Tella felt absolutely positive, however, that Lady Winpole and Mr. Storey between them were stacking most of the decks.

Something clicked in the back of her mind and Tella remembered. She'd seen Storey before. Before the ship.

She'd seen him at the Woolacre ball. *He'd produced a second queen of spades*, and without truly thinking about it, her mind had noticed it and tried to bring it to her attention. She remembered. It was Lady Winpole and Lady Agatha, that time, and two gentlemen at the table.

She hadn't particularly noticed that one wore a green corduroy coat, but then why would she? Men's fashions were so boring.

This was a task for Fitz. Tella stopped herself from looking around for him. He needed to ask this Mr. Storey questions. Perhaps end up his close personal friend after five minutes or so.

She shook herself. She was the one who didn't want Fitz near this whole affair. She was the one who wanted him out of the way, so he'd stay safe.

She was the one who'd have to ask the questions.

Tella smiled at a footman, relieved him of two glasses of punch and served one to Lord John.

"Gracious, Mister—Storey, is it? How *do* you keep track of the points? The play is moving so quickly I can barely remember how many games have been played!"

"Practice, your ladyship."

"No need to be so formal, surely!" He wasn't of the peerage; Tella felt sure of that. And didn't he know her name?

Frankly, *everyone* knew her name.

"A great deal of practice, surely. Why, your partner must work to keep up with your speed! Should I fetch you an ice, Lady Dunsby?"

"Oh no, dear, that's not necessary, it's… what type of ice is there?"

Tella hadn't the least idea. She also did not intend to go look; she'd only said it to be friendly. "Raspberry, I think?"

"Never mind, it is not my favorite. I thought it might be lemon."

Unless she draped herself over Lord John in a scandalous way, Tella was not going to be able to see Lady Winpole's hands clearly when she next passed the cards.

She decided to drape herself over Lord John in a scandalous way.

She felt him jump with a bit of surprise as her chin came to rest on his shoulder. Then he sounded amused. "Will you be consulting with me on my bids?" he asked her quietly.

"Not at all—you do not need *my* help," she assured him under her breath.

He huffed out a suppressed laugh. "Perhaps, but I might enjoy it."

Perfect. He was actually charming as well as a good dancer and a good card player.

This evening was terrible.

She needed a way to get more information. *When I saw you at the Woolacre's ball, were you sitting next to Lady Winpole then? I can't remember,* was probably not the way to go about this.

Fitz always seemed to get information by being everyone's friend, but being friendly was only getting her deeper into flirtation with Lord John, and that was not her goal.

"Lady Donnatella, if I may?"

That was Julia, appearing at her elbow, and—well, and tugging on it. Tella felt as if they were five again.

With so many more problems.

"Please excuse me," she said to the table. "Lady Julia. You are quite right. I must circulate among my guests."

Julia gave her a most uncharacteristic rolling of the eyes. If anything, they were Julia's guests, and both of them knew it. "I am not interrupting you for that—and we will speak later about how close you sat by Lord John, I definitely noticed and so did everyone else and your supposed betrothed or not-betrothed probably saw it from across the room, he is tall enough to look over everyone's heads. That isn't why I fetched you."

Was something wrong with Fitz? "Why, what is it?"

"The Duchess of Talbourne went into the ladies' retiring lounge, and everyone else in there came out. Then her ladies' companions came out too. She is in there. Alone."

"My ladies' lounge isn't dangerous, Julia." Tella considered. "At least I don't think it is."

"Tella. For once think of other people. Your most highly ranked guest—feminine guest, at least—is hiding in the lounge. At your party. And won't let anyone else in." Julia was looking around. "This isn't good."

The remark stung. If anything, Tella thought of other people far too much. She wasn't getting into knife fights at night for her own benefit.

But when her mind finally left the whist game, she understood Julia's point. "Is she well?"

"Who knows? You would not *believe* the rumors that are circulating about her at this party. And you didn't see her dancing with her husband—her husband, of all people. It nearly put your dancing with Lord Henry in the shade. And he is her *husband*."

"How many rooms did you say you and Lord Wendover would want to yourselves?"

Julia flushed a bright red, but she did not relent. "I am making no personal judgment, you understand. Only saying how it appeared." She leaned a little closer. "I think they were *kissing*, Tella. Behind a *curtain*."

Tella could only imagine what sort of gossip kissing could cause between married people. Truly, she could only imagine it. She had never heard anything like this before. Was this what the young ladies talked about, while she was dancing and playing cards and telling young men whom she would instantly forget that she felt safe in their arms?

"I am going to see if the Duchess is quite well."

"I think you had better."

* * *

THE CONVERSATION FITZ was having with this Lady Fawcett he had just met was difficult for two reasons: one, she was half his height, and he had to bend down to hear her delicate little voice. And two, she was so practiced at *not* answering questions that he was beginning to wonder if she worked in the King's service. Or Napoleon's.

But it was better than following Tella around asking what she was doing. He could see the pattern. She was having a close personal conversation with a Duke among her flower arrangements. She was draped over a young man at the card table. This was clearly how she interacted with men at every party—shallowly, with no intent to remember them or even really talk to them.

No wonder she was not married.

When Julia went to talk to Tella, Fitz kept his eyes on them. Anything involving the two of *them* would be serious.

And just a few moments later, Tella disappeared into the ladies' lounge.

As politely as he could, he interrupted the not-answer Lady Fawcett was giving him (he'd asked about her family; she was telling him a story about pie). "This may seem very awkward, Lady Fawcett, but I'm going to impose on you and ask if you would be willing to visit the ladies' lounge."

"Why?"

Reasonable question. He hadn't thought that far ahead. "I believe I just saw the Lady Donnatella disappear into that room and I am hoping she is not feeling faint."

"The ladies' lounge is where ladies go in order to feel faint, young man," Lady Fawcett said with more than a touch of disapproval to her bird-like voice. "In any event, the Duchess of Talbourne is also there, and I do not think I should interrupt Her Grace's rest."

Fitz filed that thought away for later—Lady Fawcett was not close enough with the Duchess of Talbourne to ascertain her welfare. Regardless, his interest was in Tella. "You understand I cannot check on her wellbeing myself."

"Do *you* understand that you cannot check on her wellbeing yourself?" If he was hearing her right from several feet below his head, Lady Fawcett was clicking her tongue in a very disapproving way. "You have a great deal to learn about ladies, young man."

He could not argue with that.

* * *

WHEN TELLA WALKED INTO THE LADIES' lounge, she snapped into a different version of herself instantly.

The settee in the middle of the room had been turned over somehow. Someone was struggling behind it.

In two long steps, she could see exactly who was behind it. The Duchess of Talbourne, wiggling on the floor, her hands tied behind her and cloth stuffed in her mouth.

And someone in a dress kneeling on her back.

This was a situation where, oddly enough, Tella felt *entirely* comfortable.

Hiking up her skirts so they wouldn't rip, she leaned down as she kicked to keep her balance and knock the other person off theirs, and off the back of the Duchess of Talbourne.

Being who she was, Tella no longer assumed who other people were. And of course it didn't matter if this attacker was a woman or a man. The person had solidly muscled arms, and didn't sprawl when kicked; they tumbled, rolled, and came up reaching for Tella.

This close, Tella would have called the person a man, if she were forced. The chin might have been very closely shaved, but the hair or two left were coarse. There was more than one dowager in town with quite a fuzzy chin, but Tella thought someone genuinely interested in dressing this way would know better how to do it. The reddish-brown gown was bland.

Or perhaps she only imagined herself in the same position.

The attacker grabbed Tella's cut arm, and Tella smothered a yelp, clasping her hands and shoving upward to break the hold.

If she could get a hand on the other person's wrist, she might be able to get them down on the floor without going down herself.

Thump. Tella's head whirled around.

The Duchess hadn't fallen limply to the floor; she was kicking the bottom of the settee, perhaps unaware that her rescue was at hand.

But if she kept doing that, other people would come.

Tella's reputation might survive a duchess being attacked in the ladies' lounge at her party.

It would not survive all her guests rushing into the ladies' lounge and seeing a duchess bound and gagged on the floor of the ladies' lounge at her party.

She grabbed the Duchess' ankle.

The Duchess, pluckier than Tella would have guessed, sucked air in through her nose, clearly preparing to scream even if the fabric in her mouth gagged her.

Tella snatched out the gag.

"Please don't scream, and don't kick any more either. I don't want you to ruin this party."

The Duchess, thankfully, did not scream.

But when Tella turned back, the attacker wasn't there.

* * *

It was the ladies' lounge, so there was some cool water Tella used to wash the scrapes on the Duchess' wrists. "I would be so grateful if you kept this little problem to yourself."

"I am sorry I distracted you and the attacker escaped. It is as though she was never here. How am I to explain these to my husband?"

The clearly painful cuts and scrapes of the rough rope marred her smooth skin. Tella winced. "Um. I suppose he will notice?"

The Duchess felt around her gown, which was miraculously undamaged, and her hair, which was not. "He is already worried that I was threatened by my maid. I had not taken it seriously, myself."

That stopped Tella's thoughts cold. She'd already been cataloging all her questions: who had that attacker been? It hadn't been Burgiss. Had he hired them?

But if the attack had really been meant for the Duchess of Talbourne, perhaps this had nothing to do with murder, arson, or a ship full of timber at all.

"Truly? Madame, you had better tell me about your problems, quickly. I had thought this was one of mine, but I might have been mistaken."

* * *

THE DUCHESS' companions clucked and exclaimed over her when they returned, just a few minutes too late to be useful guards *or* witnesses.

Or just in time, if Tella focused on the fact that least the general party wasn't aware of the attack.

Its aftermath was bad enough.

But the Duchess secured herself an everlasting place in Tella's heart when she convinced both of them to wait for her outside and give them just two more minutes of privacy.

She wasn't just pretty, she was smart, this Duchess, and Tella decided she liked her.

Which was good, because if the Duke was fond of his wife at all—and Tella believed he was—Tella had probably just lost any chance of making friends with *him*.

"I cannot tell if this attack was meant for you or to cause problems for me. You had better tell the Duke everything, and I must hope that he can forgive me for allowing you to be so hurt in my home."

"The Duke has no reason to blame others right now." The Duchess wasn't merely irritated; as soon as Tella mentioned the Duke, the Duchess turned coldly angry. Tella was glad that she herself was not on the Duchess' bad side. "But was it my old maid, do you think?"

Tella thought over the tale the Duchess had shared of her own problems. "I think it was a larger woman than you describe, or even a man, but I could be wrong."

"Would others not have noticed a man entering this room?"

"When one makes an effort, madame, it is quite possible to appear as either. Trust me."

The Duchess had a very pretty little frown, too. "Who *are* you?"

Tella stood and helped her new friend to her feet. "My friends call me Tella. Come. Let us repair your hair a bit, then I must let the servants know to tidy this room. There must be other ladies, too, in dire need of a place to nearly faint."

* * *

YEARS OF PRACTICE dressing her hair in dark closets had given Tella the ability to tighten a few combs, smooth the curls that tumbled down her shoulder, and look as if she had not just been engaged in a wrestling match. She picked up the silk shawl and wound it again around her throat.

But she couldn't do much for the Duchess' hair. There was just... too much of it somehow, and it did the wrong things.

She left the Duchess to her companions and slipped out the door.

She had that feeling she had, after a fight had started, when she knew she was going to keep getting hit.

She'd found the man in the green coat, and instead of making things better it only made them worse. Somehow now Lady Winpole had also moved from longtime acquaintance to probable criminal and possible danger.

Tella's world was getting tinier by the second.

She glanced around the room. All the ladies and gentlemen were smiling, talking, flirting, playing. All gentle games with no place in them for her.

And there he was, standing out in the crowd, not for fashion or title, but because he was looking at her. Only at her.

Seeing her, again.

Seeing every tiny detail of her. Probably that her hair was quite smooth, but that it had been disheveled; that one of the loops of ribbon on her skirt had been nearly torn off; that she was a bit flushed. He probably knew she had just been in a fight, and he knew she had come through just fine because she knew how to do it. He saw her, and trusted her to be exactly who she was.

He would never try to lock her up, or hold her back.

And Tella also realized that only she really saw *him*. Not how many pounds he had a year, or the manner of styling of his hair. She saw him, the man who would talk to anyone, the man willing to throw himself into a knife fight, or a fire, or a wig made of seaweed if it would help her.

The man who, just like her mother, ventured into every corner of London, unafraid, ready to make a friend wherever he went. All unheeding of what danger he was in just from being near her.

The man in whose arms she truly *did* feel safe.

The man coming her way.

CHAPTER EIGHTEEN

itz could see something in the way Tella walked when she came back out of the ladies' lounge; there was something brittle in her movements, and in the false smile on her face as she whispered to a footman.

He'd heard her when she'd told him to go away; he'd heard her when she said she couldn't marry him.

But she needed someone now, and *he* needed it to be him.

Though Fitz was tall, people did not part for him, and he had to dodge and weave a little to reach her side.

"Is everything all right, Lady Donnatella?"

She whirled and showed him a glittering and very false smile.

"Why, Lord Henry. Are you still here? Yes, everything is fine. Too much of the punch, perhaps. The Duchess felt the same way. Do you think it too strong?"

Over her shoulder, Fitz saw the Duchess finally emerged from the lounge with her hair somewhat askew and both her ladies' companions following right behind her. Punch could be blamed.

The Duke, who was standing with some young man Fitz

didn't know, saw his wife emerge too. He said something short to the nearest footman and made straight for the Duchess.

The people parted for *him*.

Fitz leaned close enough that only Tella would hear him. "Is the Duchess hurt?"

"A little. She will be fine. Her attacker got away."

Fitz felt a muscle jump in his jaw. "Her attacker, or yours?"

"I'm not positive, but likely hers." Tella was sweeping eyes over everyone in the crowd now, so Fitz did the same.

Heads were turning and whispering; only one man's attention was on the Duchess, besides the Duke's. "Who is that with the satin cuffs that the Duke just abruptly abandoned?"

Tella's eyes flicked over the man in question but immediately flicked away again. "Oh, that's Lord Callendar. He loves politics too. He must be friends with the Duke."

"No, I think it's the Duchess."

Clearly Tella didn't care. "He didn't attack the Duchess, I'm sure of that."

Tella seemed sure of many things Fitz wasn't sure of at all. And Fitz wasn't friends with the Duke or the Duchess. "Hm. Who would chance such an attack on such a highly placed lady? Is the Duchess a mastermind of crime?"

Tella's eyes went a little wild. "Don't repeat that!"

Fitz wanted to tease her, make her smile more real. "My readers might find it delicious. You're sure she has nothing to do with importing timber?"

"Positive."

This was a Caped Countess, unsmiling and flushed with what must have been a fight.

"As long as you're sure you're all right, Fred, it's all right with me," Fitz said under his breath.

* * *

TELLA DIDN'T KNOW how Fitz always made her feel like they were having the first real conversation they'd ever had.

She knew no one else made her feel that way.

"You surely are not worrying about me, Lord Henry." She swept her curls forward over her shoulder and dipped her eyelashes as if she were flirting, as if this were every other ball for the last four years, as if she were the dizzy daughter of a duke.

But when she looked up at him, none of that was true.

He saw her, and she saw him.

It didn't matter that he probably made everyone feel this way, special and real. If the London streets felt more real to Tella than society ballrooms, the way Fitz smiled at her felt even more real than that.

And she could not let any more danger near that smile.

Fitz made a *hmph* noise. "Not precisely worry."

"It is all an accident. Nothing to do with—" Tella cut herself off.

"What?"

"Of course I must wonder if the Duchess was attacked because of me. Because she was here."

Fitz was clearly working to keep the frown off his face. "You just said it had nothing to do with you."

"Surely it is too much coincidence—"

"You just said she was already facing difficult problems at Talbourne House. There *is* such a thing as coincidence, you know."

Slowly she shook her head, unable to take her eyes away from his face. What if something happened to *him*? Because he was near her? That was the whole reason he was in danger already. Because he'd tried to save her in that first fight with the mean-eyed man. Because he didn't want her to go alone into that warehouse, or on that ship.

He was in danger because of her.

And he wasn't just a new person to lose.

He was her everything to lose.

* * *

THROUGH THE CROWD, Fitz saw the glossy head of Lady Julia approaching.

That was never good news for him. "I don't think Lady Julia is pleading my case with your father."

When he looked back at Tella, she looked different. Her dark eyes were softer, and she was taking in every detail of him.

"No," Tella said quietly, firmly, and so utterly seriously that it made Fitz's smile fade. "I don't believe she is. As I told you, Henry—" She had a look in her eye that was tender and hard at the same time, and Fitz felt cold all over when she said his given name, "I cannot accept your proposal."

Fitz realized he was shaking his head *no*. He stopped.

"Because you do not wish to marry me?"

"No, I cannot."

"Cannot is not the same thing, my lady." He said *cannot* like swearing.

Now it was Tella shaking her head. "No, it isn't." She did not meet his eyes. "I am losing everything. I cannot lose you too."

Fitz didn't have time, he didn't have time to find out what she meant, because that made no *sense* and Lady Julia was descending upon them with an avenging look in her eye. It made no sense at all. And Tella was sensible.

Or a type of sensible, since after all she did go out at night in a disguise and rescue people.

Fitz felt an irrational urge to take her by the chin and shake her, or kiss her.

"If you don't want me for a husband, I accept your decision. But I won't let you get rid of me at your back. I am still with you to find out more about the murderer who likely wants us both dead, and whoever employs him. I am still with *you*. You, Tella."

* * *

"I AM SO glad that we can be sensible about the end of this whole affair, sir; it has been melodramatic of both of us. Here my father has not even completed the contracts, and I have come to my senses."

She didn't even believe herself.

"Lady Julia. You remember Lord Henry."

Julia took a deep breath as if about to begin a speech.

Tella shook her head a little, and Julia let out the breath, deflated.

"Julia," Tella said in the same soft but steady way, "Lord Henry has been a good friend to me. I know that for my sake you will befriend him too, though he and I have parted ways. That is what I wish." She moved closer. "I do wish it, darling."

"What a civilized end to a passionate, forever love," Julia said, looking straight into Tella's eyes.

"*What?*" The word escaped Fitz at greater volume than usually used in a ballroom.

Tella ignored Fitz' outburst. "As you said to me, Lady Julia. There are things one doesn't know for years and years. And I cannot take this risk."

Tella turned and started to offer Fitz her hand in parting, then thought better of it and curtsied instead.

"You cannot seriously end... all our conversation this way." Fitz was clearly struggling to find a way to describe their interlocked lives in a way that would not reveal too much to Lady Julia.

"Watch me." Tella arranged her scarf one more time and sailed away without another look at either of them.

* * *

HE DID WATCH her tall figure, draped in blue, disappear into the crowd.

"Can you not even be polite enough not to stare after her?"

Fitz looked down to see soft, round Lady Julia bristling at him like a bulldog.

Three hours earlier, all he'd have seen was her rank and her money and her comfortable exchange of the luxurious house of her parents for the luxurious house of her husband.

Now he heard Lord Preston's and Lord Halworth's voices, and reminded himself that sometimes peers also suffered.

She wasn't a soldier, but there were so many emotions fighting in her eyes—worry for her friend, and protectiveness, and anger, anger at Fitz.

Fitz smiled at her.

"Lady Julia, I hear that you are recently betrothed yourself. I have not had a chance to congratulate you. Lord Wendover, is it not?"

Surprised, Julia blinked. "Well, thank you."

"A much more civilized gentleman than I am. Let me tell you something he likely has not. If he truly wishes to marry you—"

"I beg your pardon!"

"—if he truly wishes to marry you, there must have been a moment when something tumbled into place inside him, a moment when he thought *that woman is spectacular and I need to be with her*. And a man in that moment has to decide to go with that feeling, or risk knowing that he was within reach of exactly what he needed, and let it go."

Julia did not budge. "I imagine every man who has followed a woman until she is frightened has justified it to himself with some such story, Lord Henry. And it doesn't make it true, and it doesn't make it right. From anyone, much less a man with nothing to offer."

Fitz had to nod. "You are very right, of course. I can only agree. It is a greedy feeling. And I cannot force Lady Donnatella into—well, anything at all. Just trust me when I say I'm quite chagrined that you two seem to have had some conversation about mad, passionate love, for she had no such conversations with me. I am only left to wonder why she didn't. I would have been interested."

He bowed. "If you will excuse me, Lady Julia."

* * *

TELLA DIDN'T REMEMBER any more of the party after that.

Her mind was quite occupied now with the problem of how to take action against the man in the green coat, and if there was a related way to bring justice, not only to Storey and Burgiss but also to Lady Winpole.

What did Lady Winpole have to do with any of this, anyway?

That was what concerned her now.

And definitely not the look on Fitz' face when she had walked away.

She was so determined not to think about that look, in fact, that when the last guest, even Julia, had left, and Tella was alone with her father and uncle, she didn't bother to hide that she needed information.

"Is Lady Winpole quite rich, Your Grace?"

Whatever topic of conversation her father had been expecting amongst the empty chairs and scattered crystalware of their party, that wasn't it. "I have no idea. I understand that you were overheard breaking off your engagement with Lord Henry Fitzwilliam."

"How would one find out about the state of her financial affairs?"

"Through a solicitor or a less scrupulous investigator, I suppose. *Did* you break off your engagement with Lord Henry?"

"Yes. Do you have a solicitor you use for such investigations, or do you not use a solicitor, yourself?"

"May I ask why you broke off the engagement?"

Tella didn't answer.

"May I ask why you wish to find out about Lady Winpole's financial affairs?"

Tella didn't answer that either.

Lord Preston looked back and forth between the two of them.

"Very well," the Duke of Gravenshire finally said, "you ought to know that I have received letters from his father discussing property and financial settlements upon him if you two were to wed. You look surprised. He did not mention that?"

"No," said Tella in a far-away voice, "he did not mention that."

"But I am to ignore it now. Even though you've scandalized London by accepting him in the first place. Now I should toss those letters in the fireplace because you are absolutely sure you don't wish any more to do with him. Donnatella."

She met his eyes.

"You are quite sure that after years of looking for the perfect husband, you don't want the one who offered for you and danced with you such that you actually looked happy."

That made her shake her head. "I am very happy with you and Lord Preston and the life we lead, sir, this family makes me quite happy enough!"

"If you had said simply *happy* instead of *happy enough*, I might have believed you."

Tella looked back out the window.

"Just be sure, Tella," said the Duke in a gentler voice than he'd used in a long, long time. "Chances are rare."

"Chances for what?"

"Chances for what we really want most."

* * *

THERE WERE no servants about when Mr. Storey fished his own key from the pocket of his waistcoat and let himself into his house.

This was both because Mr. Storey did not wish to be observed, and because it was cheaper for Mr. Storey to pay servants to work for him only in the daytime hours, here and there, where it suited him.

He drew a reed from its jar upon the mantlepiece, held it to the banked coals, and used the resulting tiny flame to light a lamp. Then pinched out the reed and replaced it to use again later.

His parlor was also his drawing room, his study, and his office. The low, steady light showed it all to be exactly as it should be. No book had been moved, no paper seen.

At the small desk, he drew out a narrow ledger and turned to a blank page.

And took from an inner pocket the small slip of paper that Lady Winpole had passed to him during one of their exchanges of decks of cards.

Close to requested £ per board ft. When agreement reached, first shipment will be delivered. Change crew and wait.

Mr. Storey had this small desk, and this room, and this house, because he followed instructions exactly. He had begun very early with his mother's injunction never to be poor, and was driven forward by his own revulsion for their ragged house and scanty food. He had continued through a number of positions to the one he occupied now, and which he intended to keep.

Therefore he made very careful note of her ladyship's instructions in the ledger, which bore nothing on it of her name, nor the names of the ships with whom he conducted business on her behalf.

Her ladyship had unique views regarding how to conduct business. Since Mr. Storey had adopted her methods, he had returned her ladyship's investments many times over, and by following her direction with his own money, had transformed himself from struggling to comfortable.

Their relationship did not admit of anything so familiar as gratitude.

Nonetheless, it would never chafe upon Mr. Storey that Lady Winpole did not speak to him or acknowledge him in public. He admired the upper class, and aspired to be a part of it, but only with regard to its most measurable characteristic: money.

As long as her ladyship's ideas made him this much money, he would happily do anything she wished. Stack cards for her? He would have taken a bullet for her.

The columns of numbers made him feel like he was Mr. Storey, regularly washed, regularly fed, wearing a good suit. And for that, he would commit any crime.

Her ladyship seemed close to striking a deal for her illegal American timber, and she wanted him there when first delivery was made. But she also wanted him to lose the current crew.

That would of course include Mr. Burgiss, one of the least pleasant people Mr. Storey had ever had the misfortune to employ. This did not worry him. In Mr. Storey's experience, men hired to do the type of work Mr. Burgiss did, behaved as Mr. Burgiss behaved.

Indeed, it was dispiriting, how seldom they divined how unimportant they were, and how easily they would be disposed of when their work was done.

His bookkeeping done, Mr. Storey allowed himself ten more minutes to remember all the luxuries of the affair he had just attended. The lovely young women in their petal-colored gowns, the drinks that only made one thirstier, the food meant to amuse more than satisfy.

Her ladyship would be ready for her next step soon, which meant Mr. Storey must make ready everything she would need. And prepare to change the crew. The current one would have to go.

It would be preferable in so many ways if that stinking curious writer disappeared before Mr. Storey had to change the crew. Him and that boy in the cape who bothered Burgiss so much.

Mr. Burgiss must finish his tidying job very soon.

* * *

THE BREAKFAST TABLE WAS DIRE. Why did the Gravenshire house not have seed cake?

Perhaps the cook should send for something from a bakery.

Tella hadn't left the house for two nights. She exercised in her basement closet, and she let her arm heal. The Caped Count couldn't be seen right now.

If Lady Winpole were involved—if that Storey fellow had been *in Tella's house*—then the Caped Count could not investigate them anyway. Tella couldn't let the Caped Count be connected to the Gravenshire home.

And she'd sent Fitz away.

Tella would have to do it.

More dangerous. London society did not expect the Duke's dizzy daughter to ask questions.

Less dangerous, in that it kept Fitz out of the path of any large men with muskets. Or anyone's path at all. Fitz clearly didn't care for society, so she wouldn't be running into him again. He'd only come for her.

And she had sent him away.

But he'd be safe.

She stabbed the piece of plain sponge cake straight through.

He'd be safe, she'd be fine, and Julia would be married soon.

Tella glanced at her father's empty chair. The Duke had taken her at her word; since his assistance wasn't needed to find her a husband, he'd gone back to Parliament.

And each morning, her uncle seemed a little more tired. He wouldn't be with them for too terribly much longer.

Tella would be alone, but Fitz would be safe, and she would be fine.

The Duke's dizzy daughter, however, could not begin interrogating the members of London society about Lady Winpole. Or even about Storey.

People would be suspicious of both of them, and news would reach them. But far more importantly, people would be suspicious of *her*.

Lady Donnatella needed a new interest in the people around her, subtle, but new.

"Your post, Lady Donnatella," murmured Percival, bending toward her with a silver tray.

There must be something in these cards she could *use.*

Aha.

Tella opened the note from the Duchess of Talbourne first, and found exactly what she needed.

* * *

"YOUR READERS PURCHASED Bridle's Gazette before there were any stories of the Caped Count, and they will again."

Fitz' knees splayed wide as he slumped in a chair too small for him, in Clement's office.

"How the publishing business works, is that I tell you what my readers will buy, and you write it."

Clement still looked cheerful enough, but Fitz could tell from the set of his jaw that he wasn't joking.

"Look," Clement added when Fitz said nothing, "you and Gerry turned out half a dozen small pieces, and it's all we hear about now. People want more. It might only be the Regent and the mad King who don't want more. Papers run on what the people want. And they want the Caped Count."

Fitz sighed, let his head fall back.

He wanted the Caped Count too, but he wasn't going to write about that.

"Here's the thing, Clement, if the Caped Count doesn't show himself, I can't write about him, can I?"

Clement seemed to chew at his cheek. "Sure you could."

"This paper is supposed to be true reports, not fiction!"

"This paper is teetering on the edge of financial ruin. Do you know how many newspapers London has right now? Do you know how many papers Londoners buy with the sky-high tax on them right now? The Crown doesn't like newspapers, Fitz, or perhaps you didn't notice."

"They won't like them better if they start publishing fiction under the imprint of news."

"As long as it's not about them, they won't care. I'm not proposing you make up incidents whole cloth. Just... just whatever you need to do to get me more stories."

Fitz scrubbed his face with both hands. He couldn't write stories of the things he and Tella had actually done; it would have identified them both. He and Gerry had written the last few pieces by talking to people in that area that the Caped Count had helped. There were plenty.

He could keep doing that. But it was killing him.

All those people had different stories about the person who had saved them. They didn't even remember what the Caped Count really looked like.

But *he* remembered what he looked like, perfectly. He saw that face everywhere. That sharp determined jaw and those beautiful dark eyes and shining hair and smooth skin—he saw his Fred everywhere.

Except beside him.

And it was killing him.

If she wasn't to be his bright, sharp life, he must find something else.

"Fine. We'll find Caped Count stories for you, Clement. But what are the odds that a killer like that stops at one crime? And I've seen him." He and the Caped Count. "Whether or not the caped fellow is seen again, I'm going to find that murderer, and I am going to tell London all about it. And then I'm going after bigger stories that affect even more people. Stories with depth."

"Fine. You have to prove whatever you write. But fine."

Fitz launched himself from the chair and waved his hand on the way out.

He had to prove whatever he wrote about a murderer, but

he could make up stories all day long about the Caped Count.

If Tella didn't want him, he could understand that. He had his faults. But if he weren't at her back, then who was looking after the Caped Count?

He couldn't spend all his days talking about her, writing about her, thinking about her, without wanting so much to be with her that he wanted to march right to that big house in Claremont Square and bang on the door.

If he did that—or when he did that, Fitz thought grimly—he'd better have something good to say.

Or not say. Show.

Julia's voice was still ringing in his ears, and if Tella didn't want him, he'd stay away. But couldn't he show her that he meant what he said about not trapping her in? He didn't expect her to stop being the Caped Count any more than he expected her to stop breathing. And he could give her a home, *with him*, that provided for that.

He had a good start in his pocket. But he needed to know that taking it wouldn't hurt his brothers, absent as they were.

The printing press itself took up most of the space at Bridle's Gazette; typesetters were leaping about with their trays. Few writers came to these offices, which were bare and smelled of ink.

Gerry was one. There he was, sitting at a cramped table by a window so dusty the light barely came through.

"Gerry." The man was bent over a piece of foolscap scratching at it vehemently with his pen, and the tip of his tongue showing out the side of his mouth as he concentrated on writing.

"What?"

Fitz put up both hands to show his peaceful intentions. "You must know where I might find Dan Fox, don't you? I need his help."

CHAPTER NINETEEN

"This is a weapon, surely." Julia prodded the ends of her knitting needles with her fingertips.

For once Julia echoed perfectly Tella's own thoughts.

The thin pointed needles could not cut, nor would they stab well through clothing; but into an attacker's softer parts, yes.

"The Duchess is not a person who stabs," Tella assured her friend as she tried to maneuver one needle around the other and through the yarn in order to make the appropriate loop.

"I see no reason why you would say that." Julia flicked her eyes in the direction of the Duchess. Her Grace sat tall and elegant in her embroidered day gown, the very picture of propriety.

Working hard, Tella thought grimly, to recover her reputation after its public damage, including at Tella's own ball.

"Though you may be right. I believe she would simply arrange to have one quietly murdered far away, if one angered her."

Julia might have a point there, but Tella would not

confirm it in public.

The place was buzzing with gossip, but none about Lady Winpole. Tella had chatted with three different ladies nibbling biscuits like rabbits. Nothing.

And now they were all discussing...

Whoops. They were about to be discussing the Duchess of Talbourne's reputation, and Tella wasn't having that.

Tella wasn't sure how the conversation had swerved from Lord Rawleigh's illness, which was sad but not interesting to Tella, to a veiled insinuation that the Duchess was carrying on an affair.

Not very veiled, either.

One of the ladies managed to make multiple insults out of one comment about the Duke. "Maybe at his age one's energy has run out. Lord Callendar, for instance, is far younger and more energetic. Don't you agree, Your Grace?"

Callendar, he of the longing eyes and satin cuffs; Tella remembered him from her party. Remembered him watching the Duke and Duchess leave.

This was why Tella stuck to knives. The fighting that took place in parlors was far too vicious.

But she was not about to let them tear apart what was left of the Duchess' reputation.

Mercifully, she remembered this woman's name.

"Really, Lady Worringlen, I don't know why you bring up Lord Callendar. He does not sit in the Lords and I hope it may be some time before he does. He is too busy socializing with all of London to attend to any serious business."

It felt odd to use her position for anything but to hide her true intentions. Her set-down stopped Lady Worringlen's barbs immediately.

The Duchess' mother then reappeared—when had she left?—in the door, with the Dowager Duchess, the Duke of Talbourne's mother.

Who dispensed with the question of what Callendar did on his frequent visits, in very few words, then went on her way, uninterested in further discussion.

There was not a woman in the room, perhaps not in all London, who would gainsay the Dowager Duchess of Talbourne.

A Lady Ayles steered the conversation back to the political questions that interested the Duchess, and Tella was able to relax. It would be fine.

"The knitting is complex enough without the politics," Julia muttered softly next to her.

Or the gossip, Tella wanted to add but did not.

She had to find someone before this affair was over who could tell her more about Lady Winpole.

"Or are you here for the politics?"

Tella looked up.

Julia was sitting with her head cocked, looking at Tella. The yarn and needles in her lap were neat, as Julia would never be messy, even if this knitting business defeated her.

"You might as well tell me. You used to tell me everything. We told each *other* everything. I know—" Julia shook her head, stopping whatever Tella was about to say. "You are doing things now that are complicated, or your life is more complicated than mine. But are we so different? If you recall, we used to spend hours discussing what advice of my mother's to take, and what to keep." She smiled one of those smiles with the dimples. "Don't you recall? I decided to take her advice about a hairstyle that would not make my head look bulbous, you decided to take her advice about flat slippers—"

"Well, obviously."

"—and we both decided to ignore her advice about not judging a man by the way he danced. Or at least, I thought we did." She gave Tella a steady look.

The old joke they had always made about that came back

to Tella now but it made her mouth dry. "Lady Shoreton was wrong. You can tell a great deal from the way a man dances."

Julia nodded, her eyes fixed on Tella. "We were right, weren't we? Between us, we have generally been right." Her eyes were searching. "If I am to help you, you have only to tell me what we wish to accomplish."

Wasn't that what Fitz had said? Something to the point that Tella should stop running away from him, and they might accomplish something?

Tella wanted to shout that *she* was not running away. It was time marching on that was her enemy. And it was Julia getting married and going off to be... someone who wasn't her Julia.

But must Tella give up everyone, all at once?

Could she not have even a little help?

"I don't wish to say why, but I must know more about Lady Winpole's background. Her family, and most especially her money."

Julia didn't question. "Aha. Well, she isn't here. That will make it easier to talk about her. Lady Ayles' son is that Lord John you draped yourself over at your party. He's been playing quite a lot of cards with Lady Winpole of late; so I will speak to his mother. And if I have their ages right, Lady Winpole must have debuted in society around the same time as Lady Redbeck. I will speak to her, too."

The rush of feeling for her friend in that moment called for hugging, squeezing *very* hard in fact. Tella restrained herself by saying, "I love you, just as I always have, you know."

Julia patted her arm and smiled again. She knew.

* * *

"Burgiss is a murderer, but Mr. Green Coat tells him what to do," Fitz muttered into his tankard. "You're sure you can't find out Green Coat's name?"

Dan Fox had actually bought him the beer, at the Bottle and Bird, which was very kind of him as Fitz was about flat broke.

Clement was through advancing him money.

"Avoid murderers. It is a business rule of mine." Dan Fox also sipped a beer, slowly. "Let me remind you that I only told you he'd been seen, I didn't even have his description. I get my information second-hand because, and this is worth repeating, I avoid murderers."

A reasonable place to draw a line when one was a thief-taker, Fitz supposed.

For he'd finally gotten to learn a bit more about Dan Fox. The man made his living, such as it was, capturing criminals with complaints sworn against them and bringing them to be arrested. He traded on knowledge. And being a bit faster than his quarry.

"Never mind; it was just a hope." Fitz would look for Mr. Green Coat himself. "I actually looked you up because I need your help for a personal matter."

"What, another one? You just said you need to convince some woman to marry you, and for that you need *cabinetry*. Fine, done. I've already told you what I know about where to get the best; you've already given me your last fivepence."

"And you've thoughtfully returned part of it in the form of a beer, so thanks for that." Fitz lifted his tankard in salute.

"You have plenty of problems."

"This problem is related to the marriage issue *and* the cabinetry."

Understandably, Dan only snorted. "I don't do work on account, and not for priorities like yours."

Fitz persisted. "I *can* get money to pay you, ample money."

"Surely." Dan Fox apparently didn't like to argue. "Just, as I said, I don't do work on account."

An idea struck Fitz, and he hoped it wasn't just the beer talking. "Come with me."

Dan pointed at the tankard. "Finish it. You don't know when you'll get another."

* * *

"No more unwanted visitors, Your Grace?" Tella had maneuvered herself between the rest of the room and the Duchess of Talbourne, to learn if there was any news of her ladies' lounge attacker. "I must take my leave, but I hope you've had no more frights."

"Residing in the heart of London?" Her Grace's smile looked forced. Most people's were, at these things, so Tella paid it little mind. "What chance could there be of that?"

There'd been plenty of chance at Tella's own party, which both of them knew quite well, so Tella took her to mean that there hadn't. "And no news of our mutual unpleasant acquaintance?"

"*I* haven't, and I assure you that if the Duke had, I would be the last to know." The Duchess wasn't happy with the Duke, that much was clear.

Tella leaned a bit closer. "I hope His Grace—or even Lord Callendar—is attending to your safety."

"They can both fall off a cliff for all I care today." The Duchess had a wonderful way of smiling while she sounded as if she meant it.

"I see." Tella didn't. "Keep some friends close, then."

"Always good advice." Her Grace listened for a moment to the murmur of collected voices. "I hope I may count you among them. Didn't you say that we must be friends, Tella?"

Had Tella even meant it when she'd said that? When she

couldn't even explain herself to Julia who was her oldest friend? "Your Grace—Selene—I hope you have many friends better than I could ever be."

* * *

IT WAS hard to say who was more surprised when the door opened to the house Fitz' father had given him, Fitz or the butler.

"My apologies for startling you," said Fitz, stepping in and realizing for the first time that day that he was not wearing a hat. "Lord Ashbury has deeded me the house. This house."

"Of course, Lord Henry."

He and the butler and Dan Fox all stood about looking at each other.

If Fitz ought to just sweep in, that wasn't his style. "And you are?" he pointedly asked the butler.

"I am Mr. Cudjoe Stuart, I am delighted to be of service. I have been in the Ashbury employ for many years." The butler, an imposing man of color, didn't look impressed by Fitz's lack of propriety, but played along with it. He turned to Dan Fox as if they had all just met, perhaps at a party. "And you, sir?"

Which was generous of him. Dan hardly looked like the usual companion of a young gentleman of society.

But Fitz didn't introduce him. The less said about Dan Fox the better, at least until Fitz determined the loyalty of the butler.

"Thank you, Mr. Stuart. I did want you to see this gentleman; if he returns, do admit him. We do know each other."

Mr. Stuart studied Dan carefully. "Of course, sir," he said again, obviously to humor Fitz.

"Will you agree to extend me that *small* line of credit now?" Fitz asked Dan Fox in a very pointed way.

Dan took in the grand house and its grand butler. "Just this once."

Fitz bowed, and when Dan had set off back down the street, Fitz turned back to the butler. "I need to see the closets."

Even allowing for the peculiarities of the gentry, Fitz's stock with Mr. Stuart was plummeting. "Closets, sir?"

"Yes. Any cupboard or small room on the lower floors, if you please. And I'll want to see the basement."

Mr. Stuart held open the door, allowing Fitz to walk into Mercywall House, recently owned by Lord Ashbury.

Now his.

Someone must have used the house, at least occasionally. The wallpaper was recent, a soothing pattern of ducks in gray and blue that Fitz rather liked. It blended harmoniously with the white plaster moulding and wall medallions, the silvery glint of the lamps, and the polished glow of the sideboard table.

"I have been awaiting your arrival, sir," said Mr. Stuart, "as your mother has sent you a parcel, in anticipation of your residence. The basement is this way."

Fitz liked Mr. Stuart already. He'd have to see if he could persuade Mr. Stuart to like *him*, despite his irregular habits with introductions. "Tell me about yourself, Mr. Stuart. I shall follow you."

* * *

TELLA COULD ONLY TAKE up so much time with pacing.

On her fifth day of doing nothing but remaining in the house, she burst into her uncle's sitting room and said without preamble, "Surely we could play chess or *something*."

"You are terrible at chess. All your pieces are lost in a few moves and you get stuck."

Tella sighed long and loud and fell into the chair opposite him. "Should I go to the country?"

"By yourself?"

Her voice was sharp. "How else?"

Lord Preston looked at the way Tella slouched a little in the chair, her legs crossed at the knee and one foot twitching. "If you don't like what you've got, then get something different."

"Please don't… never mind." What she really wanted was his advice on how to learn more about Mr. Storey, and the perplexing Lady Winpole.

But if he knew again what she was doing, he would be troubled again by all that worry. Or, worse, he might simply forget it all again. And imagining that only brought home how soon he, and his memory, would be gone from her entirely.

"Tell me a story about gathering intelligence. A reconnaissance behind enemy lines. Map drawing. Anything." He knew so much more than he'd had time to teach her. And Tella was discovering that finding things out was far more difficult than simply throwing herself and her various implements into a fight.

"Actually, I've been thinking I should write some of my old fireside stories on paper. To share them with people besides my favorite niece."

Tella pointed a finger straight at him, reveling in the chance to be childlike. "That is a *brilliant* plan. Have you a secretary? Should I engage one?"

"I can still write." The look he gave her was splintery. She stuck out her tongue at him.

"I really feel it is a marvellous plan. It is a shame it cannot contain everything you have developed in the manner of training men and preparing them for battle."

Lord Preston looked surprised. "Do you know, I never

thought of that. Why not record some of my thoughts on those matters? The men who come after me may be able to do more than I have done to prepare our soldiers better. If they must fight, then *when* they fight, I would so prefer that they come home."

Tella's head was lolling on the chair, her eyes tracing the patterns of the ceiling. "I imagine they would prefer to come home as well, uncle. That is your innovation. That you always knew that you commanded men, most of whom left behind all they held dear to follow you."

"I wish I had a way to write down what it felt like. They believed in me so I could believe in them."

"Really? I had always thought it the other way around." He'd taught her so much how to think a fight through, not just react. For Tella, he was the fountain of all knowledge, and it was hard to imagine his troops anywhere but down-stream, drinking down all his knowledge so that they could survive.

"No, I don't think it was."

Something about his face, or his voice, made Tella afraid for a moment that he was going to say something else about lost chances. As long as she stayed in the house, Tella could pretend that Fitz was long gone, that she had sent him away ages ago, and that it was all quite, quite over.

She couldn't bear any more lectures about lost chances.

But he didn't. He said, "I reached quite an old age before I looked back and realized all our connections had gone both ways, between my soldiers and me."

"Really?"

"That is the problem with Napoleon, you know. He has that connection to his soldiers, and they to him. What they do, what they want, how they think, where they are. They are all of a set. If we could break that, we could break this French empire."

Tella could not imagine a connection between even a handful of people, much less the tens of thousands in an army. She thought Lord Preston ought to have seen the Duchess' knitting affair. No visible weapons, but more traps than people.

She refused to think of Fitz and how perfectly they'd stayed in formation when following their quarry.

"So complicated, and so dangerous," she said, swinging that twitching foot. "Didn't it ever occur to you that a lone soldier, comfortable behind enemy lines, willing to succeed or die, could do so much more than any company together?"

"No, it did not, and I don't believe that's true," Lord Preston said brusquely. "Thank God that thought never crossed my mind."

Desperately her eyes sought the room for some distraction. "Are you sure you don't wish to try some chess?"

* * *

"Do stay, Mr. Stuart, you must be curious about this parcel." It had been brought by two burly, rough-looking men, Mr. Stuart had said.

The butler stopped at the door. Fitz cut the string that tied up the bundle his mother had sent, peeled back its woolen wrappings.

"I would never wish to intrude, sir," said Mr. Stuart, drawing a few steps closer. He was the perfect British butler, dignified and confident of the proper way to do things, but Fitz would rather have him as a friend.

"Mr. Stuart, I have been through a dozen Spanish towns in the company of hundreds of British soldiers, but now I find myself on a new campaign, alone. I have no wish to impose upon you, but you are the company at hand, and good company at that. And you've brought me something from my mother, whom I have not seen these seven years and more." Fitz' hand paused. "It might make a good story."

Mr. Stuart stood beside him now. "Perhaps that depends upon what is in the box."

Quickly, Fitz' fingers probed the small wooden case's lid, bottom, and sides. "There is a lock here, and it is fastened. But there was no key?"

"Nothing but that parcel, sir."

Fitz thought. Then raised a finger. "Wait here."

Fitz had taken the master's apartments. A door connected his sitting room and that of the lady of the house.

Through there, it was only a few steps to the bedchamber his mother surely occupied whenever she was last in this house.

In a tiny drawer of her dressing table, along with a handkerchief and some dried leaves pressed in a glass locket, he found a tiny key.

Back in his own room, he held it up to show it to Mr. Stuart.

Of course, it fit.

Unlocked, the box's lid opened all the way open. Inside was a letter. And below that, several little packets of folded fabric. Velvet. All velvet.

He picked one up and as he did, a glittering chain fell out, its weight dragging a pendant behind it. Fitz caught it before it hit the floor.

It was a trembling pear-shaped diamond, big as his thumbnail, hanging from a silver link inside a frame of more pear-shaped diamonds. The stones' edges were black when viewed from one angle and fire when viewed from another.

Holding it in one hand, Fitz unfolded the letter with the other.

Henry: I have always had faith that you would exceed me in achieving your dreams. It is all that I still want. You can find your heart's desire with nothing but a penny in your hand, I am sure of it. But I understand that you have found it somewhere rather grand.

I don't believe you need jewels to convince a woman to love you. But if they smooth the way in convincing a woman to marry you, I hope you take them, and use them, they are yours. And if not needed for that, let us consider this gift a celebration. Not just for you, but for your betrothal.

You never hesitated to give hugs and smiles as a child, and I am sure you are the same sweet fountain of love I was astonished to produce all those years ago. Do what I didn't, Henry. Marry someone you love.

Love. No one had said love to him, not in all their conversation of marriage.

Nor had he said it to her.

"Mr. Stuart," Fitz said thickly. "Do you believe that marrying for love is all that it takes to give your life radiance and meaning?" He looked up to the puzzled butler's face.

"That is a very personal question, sir, as my answer is bound to say more about me than you," said Mr. Stuart, drawing himself up. "But I can imagine it could be."

Fitz let the diamond pendant swing from his fingers, observing how its edges cut the light. "I can imagine it could be, too."

* * *

Burgiss had been down this street before.

He walked slowly, determined this time to see and know every detail of it.

The Caped Count wasn't anywhere, and he was hungry to be done with the man.

People were talking about him. Snippets on street

corners. But always something he'd done. Past. That writer had been collecting them.

Burgiss knew he was cleverer than Mr. Storey thought. That writer wasn't just an unlucky witness. He was making the Caped Count bigger every day. People wouldn't fear Burgiss if they thought the Caped Count would come to save them. And fear was Burgiss' business.

People who refused to be frightened were always the biggest obstacle in life. Burgiss had plans for himself, grand plans, and they depended on people fearing him. And most did. The ones who didn't, disappeared.

If that writer disappeared, well, that would draw a very clear line. And clean up half his business to boot. His goal was to erase tracks, not make them; but he could make an exception to make a point.

That Caped Count, though; when he disappeared, it needed to be as quiet as the grave.

Burgiss' influence was expanding through these neighborhoods fast. And he needed to tidy up this business fast, so he could focus on bigger and better things. Some big financial deal was on the way, between Storey and the woman with the plan; and when it happened, Burgiss must be free to move boldly, and quickly, to own these streets. Everything he could see.

There was a foot.

There was a foot thrust out from a doorway, halfway down this street.

A foot that belonged to a drunken old man who, just as Burgiss liked, frightened very easily.

A drunken old man who was always around and likely had seen a lot.

"I need you to tell me about that caped feller," Burgiss told the man as he crouched over him, fitting himself in the doorway too.

The man sobbed and retched and wet himself, all of which Burgiss ignored, as he thought it was simply a prelude to finding out what he needed to know. Where to find the Caped Count.

When he realized the man wasn't going to tell him anything useful, thick burning anger swelled his chest—half from being thwarted, and half because now he was going to have to kill this man, which he hadn't expected to do.

But it would be easy. The man was old, and pathetic. And of course alone.

Burgiss had no last words for the fellow. It was easy to do, crushing his nose and mouth under his hands and blocking his breath, fighting the bony old body's convulsions till he was still.

There was no reason not to leave him in the doorway. Burgiss hadn't got what he wanted, but in its place, what he needed was the man's silence. He walked away and left it behind him.

It was a type of tidy that he liked.

* * *

DAN FOX MADE his living knowing where people were.

He was willing to walk a long way, he did not mind being humble in some circumstances and threatening in others, and he considered money more important than almost anything else.

So it was that his commission, on account, for Henry Fitzwilliam didn't take long at all.

Quite quick, in fact.

When he knocked again on the front door of the Ashbury house off Grosvenor Square, Mr. Stuart the butler admitted him immediately.

And never questioned why someone dressed in an assemblage of rags had the temerity to come to the house's front door.

* * *

"Your oldest brother is living in Lincolnshire."

"What?" Fitz didn't remember any family holdings in that area. "What for?"

"He does math."

"I'm sorry, but… *what?*"

"He does mathematics. He lives on the estate of his patron, and he does mathematics. I don't know more about it. I wish I did." Dan did look rather wistful.

Fitz couldn't wonder right now about Dan's affection for numbers. "And this was easy to learn?"

"Oh yes. He writes to your father's solicitors several times a year."

"Several times a *year?* How long has he been there?"

"Quite some time. Your middle brother hasn't been heard from. I cannot be sure, but he appears lost at sea."

"Oh my—No. My mother would have told me. If he were gone."

Dan looked sympathetic. He clearly had practice in giving bad news. "I do offer my condolences, Lord Henry."

"For the love of God, call me Fitz."

Fitz sank into a chair.

He rang for Mr. Stuart, first for his reassuring company. Though he would also know where Fitz could find some brandy.

This, this was why his father wanted him to take the house and the Duke's daughter. His heirs were missing or gone.

And he hadn't wanted to tell Fitz. Tell Fitz that he was the only remaining heir.

No, that couldn't be right. His oldest brother would still inherit the title, and the entailed properties, if he was alive. And he *was* alive.

Lord Ashbury must not want anything to do with him for some reason. He was pinning his hopes for the family line on Fitz.

Well. He would have to find out more about all this.

But for now one thing was clear. His brothers didn't need this house. His father surely didn't need this house. His mother had no need for this house.

But Fitz needed it.

And he would take it.

It had entirely satisfactory closets.

* * *

MR. STOREY PULLED his collar more closely around his neck. He ought to have an overcoat. It wasn't supposed to be this chilly in the springtime.

He found Burgiss waiting in the usual place.

"You like me waitin' for ya, don't ya," Burgiss said as he straightened, without much heat.

"It is simply the most efficient use of my time. Have you found your quarry?"

Burgiss wouldn't meet his eyes. Just shook his head no.

"I presume, then, that you understand the need to change your course."

"That's an interestin' point." Burgiss returned to leaning against the alley wall. "If you change your course, do you get where you're goin'?"

It was generous of the man to remind Mr. Storey why he'd been hired in the first place. Constancy was an admirable quality.

Constancy to the point of obstinacy, of course, was not.

"Our patron is not looking for a young man in a blue cape. Our patron is attempting to secure a timber deal that will be very profitable for her and through her, for us. If you're arrested for murder, that would interrupt her plans."

In fact, if Burgiss were arrested for murder, he would likely tell everything he knew to anyone who promised to let him out. And that wouldn't do.

Mr. Storey prided himself on taking care of his employers. Bank drafts, ledgers without their names, and if necessary, the disappearance of unsatisfactory employees.

But if Burgiss disappeared now, who would handle the problem of these follow-abouts?

Perhaps this situation called for flattery.

"I know you understand the gravity of the issue. Should the man with all the questions keep asking questions about *us*, he may stumble upon, oh, an aggrieved person with whom we've previously done business. With whom *you* have done business," he tried to drive home the point.

Burgiss seemed to chew this over.

"My thinkin' is along the same road. I'm gonna make a bit of a show of yer writin' man, and he oughta give up his friend afore I'm done. That'll do nicely for all, won't it."

"I think it will," said Mr. Storey.

"I'll need a spot where I can spend some time with th' man and not be heard."

* * *

TELLA WAS JUST ABOUT to enter her uncle's chambers when the butler approached. "Madame, there is a very early caller."

Tella took the card he handed her. *Mister George Cullen* had been crossed out by hand, *Miss Cassandra Cullen* written in and also crossed out, then *Mrs. Oliver Burke* squeezed in at the bottom.

"But I don't know any—"

But she did. Dr. Burke. Who could well be Dr. *Oliver* Burke.

"I will see her in my father's study, Mr. Heath. In fact, never mind; I will come now."

"Very good, madame."

In the entryway, Tella found a tall young lady, only a few inches shorter than herself, in a remarkably plain black gown.

With very large pockets.

The lady was examining the door frame, of all things, and didn't turn when Tella drew near.

Tella waited a moment longer; her visitor was still absorbed in the door frame.

"Mrs. Burke?"

The visitor whirled. And clutched a little at her neck. "If we must be formal, yes. And you are Lady Donnatella Fairchild?"

Tella just nodded. The lady's grey eyes were arresting; Tella thought surely she did not know her. Wouldn't she have remembered her?

"My apologies for such an early call. I have been traveling in carriages for *far* too many days and… if you will forgive me, I needed something to do this morning."

Ought Tella be concerned? "Are you well?"

"Well enough." With a flash of a smile that faded quickly. "Some sadness in the family. Nothing that need concern you."

"Are you not here because I know your family? You are— Aren't you *married* to Dr. Burke?"

Whatever she expected her visitor to say, it wasn't what she said. For the lady sighed deeply, leaned back against the door frame, and just shook her head. "Oh, *no*. Not another lady in love with my husband."

* * *

SENSING that this was not a conversation for the entryway, Tella ushered the guest into her father's study, and waved her offer of a chair.

Tella closed the door. It seemed like this conversation required it.

"I'm sorry, I did not want you to repeat anything terribly personal in the hallway, but… what?"

Again, Mrs. Burke did not respond. She stared at her hands, shaking her head, and chuckled while looking about to cry.

Tella moved closer. "Mrs. Burke—"

"Oh." The lady startled, just a little. "I am quite deaf, I should have mentioned. Do sit nearby. I am sure you don't wish to shout."

"No, I don't." Tella also sat with her hands in her lap, but leaned toward her extraordinary guest. "Though I can assure you I am *not* in love with your husband. I don't think."

He *was* ridiculously beautiful, but… No. Not at all.

She'd discovered she much preferred a shaggier, more long-limbed look.

Her guest breathed deep. "Well, that's a relief. You have no idea what it's like, never knowing when one's travels through London will bring one to the doorstep of yet another woman nursing a *tendresse* for my husband."

Honestly, that did make a kind of sense, if they were speaking of the same Dr. Burke.

"Excuse me, but… Your husband is Dr. Burke, is he not? A physician who became a surgeon for the Army?"

"Oh yes." Mrs. Burke still looked very tired, but smiled a slower smile. "The very fact that you describe him that way makes me think that you do actually know him from his medical practice, rather than socially. Although… you have never been married, I think?"

What an extraordinary conversation. "No."

"Ah well. That explains the lack of social connection."

Visits were not supposed to run amok this way.

"Madame, is there a *reason* you have visited today? Is Dr. Burke quite well? Have you brought me some message from him?"

"Dr. Burke is well enough, thank you."

"Ah. I am glad to hear it. He has been so valuable. In fact, he visited my uncle quite recently, and he looked well. I would hate to hear that anything has changed."

"Things have changed. His father has recently died."

"I'm so sorry to hear it." She *was*. "Is there any way I can help? Is that why you've come? I would be really glad, so glad to do anything I could for Dr. Burke."

"I'm sorry, no." She still watched Tella a little closely, as if suspecting her of secretly being in love with her husband. "I am actually here on my own behalf to conduct some business, if you can believe it."

"*That*, Mrs. Burke, I have no trouble believing," Tella assured her.

* * *

MRS. BURKE KNOCKED on the strange townhouse door with the same confidence with which she'd bundled Tella into a carriage brought her here. And addressed the butler the same way. "Mr. Stuart. I have come to show Lady Donnatella Fairchild the closets."

Tella was not used to trailing after another woman, but Mrs. Burke wasn't deferential. Or perhaps she simply went where she wished so that she would be heard.

The butler seemed to know her; he opened the door wide

for both of them.

The entryway was attractive, cool in feeling and simply decorated, but Mrs. Burke did not delay there. Though it was broad day, the butler lit an Argand lamp, and handed it to the lady.

Feeling that if this was a trap, it was a very odd one, Tella followed her through the main hall, along a side hall, to a small door that Mrs. Burke waved towards as if Tella ought to precede her.

Half-expecting to be pushed down the narrow stairs, Tella found herself in… a basement.

"The kitchen is through there," Mrs. Burke said dismissively, setting the lamp down—was it a stump? Was it a table? —and drawing off her gloves. "There is storage over there for wine and foods that must stay cool."

Before them was an old painted iron latch.

Mrs. Burke lifted it.

Beyond it were shelves—shelves that stretched above them and disappeared from sight. Deep shelves, small shelves, shelves with sliding doors. Tella stood in the small dark space and stared up. This closet—for closet it was— must extend up to the main floor of the house. Perhaps beyond.

"A china cupboard, as you see, but extremely large as a floor above us has collapsed. Some upper shelves are still used, for china. I am tasked with moving that china and refitting this."

"Refitting it for what?"

"For whatever you say."

Tella whirled on the woman.

"I don't understand."

"I was so grateful to get this commission. You cannot imagine what a nightmare it is to travel north quickly, and a sad occasion to make it worse. Though I admit it may be at least partly because I never do make the trip at a sedate pace. And then back at the same rate! A note from Mercywall's owner was on my desk when I returned yesterday. Lucky, I suppose, that it was the first one I opened. Truly lucky, for me."

Apparently when Mrs. Burke let loose the flood of conversation, it all happened quickly.

"Mrs. Burke," Tella said, moving quite close to ensure that she could be heard, "who has engaged you? And to do what, precisely?"

"The owner of the house. Lord Henry Fitzwilliam. It is a singular commission; I am sure you must understand it better than I do. He gave me the direction of your home, and specifically asked that I show you all the closets on the lower floors and ask which one, or ones, might be refitted to be suitable for your use."

"*My* use?" Tella's mind was a whirlwind of questions, and hopes, and terrible fears. *Fitz* wanted her to see this? *Fitz* wanted her to have a *closet?*

No. Fitz wanted the Caped Count to have a closet.

There was no clearer way for him to offer a home, not just for Lady Donnatella, but for the side of her he knew first. And, possibly, best.

"Mrs. Burke, I hope you don't mention to anyone that you—"

"Lady Donnatella, I ought to have introduced myself more thoroughly. I do apologize. I have been overwrought, you cannot imagine what a trial my husband's family is, and then I thought you were yet another lady with designs on my husband. I do try to keep my sense of humor about those, but I *am* tired. What I do—My services are generally required for people who need their home to be different, people who live in a rolling chair, or lack a hand, or leg. One cannot always judge by appearances, but you don't seem to have any needs of that sort; plus, in those cases one might wish to avoid closets."

She looked up, up, into the shadows, where the shelves grew distant and small. "This is extraordinary. I wonder why that floor is gone? I shall investigate. At any rate. I was informed that I should rebuild this closet however *you* see fit. You needn't even explain to me how you wish to use the space. Though if you do, I might be able to make some rather clever adjustments. I do pride myself on being good at such things."

The dark-haired lady looked around the basement floor, with its dust and cobwebs and evidence of mice, with what seemed to be tremendous satisfaction. "The building has a very good foundation and these walls are solid. Though that may not matter to you. I am used to building things that require strength and the ability to support levers and pulleys. I will be interested to hear what you would like. There are two other closets you should see, both on the floor above. In case you prefer one. Also, I understand that your uncle might need an apartment fitted for him? More in my usual line of work?"

"Really?" At that, Tella just started shaking her head and couldn't seem to stop.

Mrs. Burke ignored it. "Apparently he is a bit older, and the house's owner worried that he might need a comfortable apartment without too much walking?"

"The house's owner." She knew, she'd heard Mrs. Burke say it. She wanted to hear his name again, that was all.

"Yes. Lord Henry Fitzwilliam, as I said."

"Yes. You did say."

Tella looked again at the cobwebby empty shelves that stretched up into the shadows. Was that the sound of wings flapping a little, high up there in the dark?

It felt like it could be home.

CHAPTER TWENTY

The rest of the tour was efficient; Mrs. Burke did not waste time. "Though I much prefer to be called Cass, if it isn't too shocking an imposition."

Tella smiled, but did not nod. She did not call people she barely knew by their first name, much less a shortened version of it. Mrs. Burke seemed quite new to the name Mrs. Burke.

They finally ventured to the upper floors. Parlors, drawing rooms, and then on the next floor above, private chambers.

"I'll be right back; I thought this wall bore much of the building's weight, but it doesn't seem to extend to the top story. I must go all the way up."

She left Tella in the receiving room of some suite, perhaps for a great lord. The furniture was as large and heavy as that in her father's house, polished and carved in designs that reminded her of the Tudor kings of old.

Tella slowly trailed into the inner chamber, and stood, transfixed. The room seemed filled with the frame of a huge bed, clearly so heavy and massive that it would never be moved.

A bed that seemed very much appropriate for a house that belonged to Fitz: large, sturdy, not to be moved.

It had mattresses upon its frame, and someone had tossed a rough blanket upon it.

One of the chairs, too, had its dust coverings removed, and the curtains drawn back around it were free of dust as well. The house was clearly well kept, if seldom used.

What kind of lives had people lived here?

What kind of life might yet be lived?

Not for her, nothing for her. But she could still imagine.

Tella heard someone behind her, and turned.

* * *

FITZ KNEW Mrs. Burke had brought Tella here. He hadn't intended to force himself upon her presence.

He'd just wanted her to see what could be a home if she were in it.

As she and Mrs. Burke made their way through the corridors, he'd heard her voice. Tella spoke rather more loudly than usual.

The sound made Fitz give up the idea that they could just talk about locating the man in the green coat, or the lady who gave him orders.

All he wanted was to see her; and he wanted to touch her even more.

He hadn't expected Mrs. Burke, lost in thought, to drift right past him in the hallway, never seeing him.

Once he knew Tella was alone in the master's chambers, there was no going back.

* * *

FITZ WAS STANDING in the doorway, disheveled hair glinting gold in an unexpected beam of sunlight. Why did he never wear a hat?

She had never, anywhere, seen such a beautiful man in her life.

Slowly he closed the door.

For once he didn't say anything. No quick remarks, no jokes, no words at all.

Just looked right at *her*.

Tella took a step towards him, stopped herself. Tried to start again. Her hands, her feet, her whole body wanted to be near him more than she wanted to stay still. But she stayed where she was through sheer force of will.

"Go ahead, fly at me. If you remember, I quite like it," he said softly.

She mustn't. She took a step toward him again, then another. And stopped again.

Still looking right at her, Fitz said, "You can. I'll catch you. I will always catch you."

Tella could feel her blood pumping, her muscles singing. Like the prelude to a fight.

She didn't want to fight.

She did throw herself into his arms.

And he did catch her.

* * *

SHE FLUNG her arms around his neck rather as she might do in a brawl, but as soon as she was safe in his arms, she stretched up on her tiptoes, and kissed him.

Fitz had never been so lost in close combat as he was now in Tella's arms.

They *had* to talk. He had so many things to tell her, even if she would tell him nothing.

Her hands tugged at his hair, tangled in his coat, pulling him closer. She might have muttered *"ridiculous"* under her breath, but that was all.

With Tella, Fitz thought, talking might be overrated. But only with Tella.

He crushed her in his arms, loving the noise she made as he pulled her tight against him. His eyes closed. There must be a way to hold her tighter.

She let her head fall back, let him kiss all the bare, taut skin of her throat and down to the hollows of her collarbone, perfect little shadows in the light.

"Do you know how to do this?" Her voice was right in his ear, as impatient as ever.

"Do what? Kiss you? I'm dying to kiss you, Fred, but I'm worried if I do you'll run off again. That *is* what you usually do."

The noise she made then was half a growl, half an exasperated grunt.

Fitz started to pull away, but Tella's arms tightened around his neck. She only let him far enough away to look into her eyes.

"If you'd stop moving about so much," she whispered to him, "we might accomplish something."

* * *

"What do you—"

"Everything."

"Now? Here?" Fitz looked confused. Her Fitz, her smiling towering man, confused and drunk on her kisses.

She had looked into many men's eyes and she'd never seen this look before. She would never forget it.

Tella squeezed again, and dove in for another kiss.

When they parted again, Fitz's eyes followed her lips. He didn't look drunk. He looked hungry.

Reluctant to let him go even for a moment, Tella ripped off her shawl, her hat, and finally her gloves, heedless of any damage she might do to them.

She had so longed to see him again, and he was *here.*

As soon as she dropped her last glove, she slammed full-length against him again. He could likely feel her stays under her gown, they were pressed so close.

"You still want to kiss me, dressed like this?" She nosed along his jaw to bite him a little on his chin.

"It is novel for us, I will admit," he rasped, pulling her hips closer.

The slightly salty taste of him just made her hungrier. He smelled of wood smoke and the water's edge and a warm sweetness that she suspected was just Fitz. He smelled *delicious.*

She could feel him, too, underneath his clothes, the length and hardness of him surprising her both for its strangeness and its rightness.

That was for her. Because of her. That was *hers.*

She had no longer-term, strategic goals in mind. He was here, she wanted him, and she wanted all of him.

The same part of her mind that made quick decisions in a fight made her slide her hands behind Fitz to feel at the door.

There was a key in the lock.

She turned it.

* * *

WHEN THE BOLT in the door shot home, Fitz heard it.

He raised his head a little.

He hadn't even planned to speak to her. This was not the way to persuade her.

But then again, it very much was.

He wanted to speak to her of the danger of what they were doing. The impropriety, apparently, didn't interest her.

He wanted to speak to her of his heart, and that she ought to be serious with it, as it was very serious about her.

But he never, ever wanted to ask her if she was sure.

She moved as deliberately as when she danced, or when she parried a weapon. Fitz would never want her to stop.

But he did hesitate.

His hands, all on their own, had undone the buttons that held up the front of her dress, and found the bodice lacings, the thin linen below them, the silky skin below that.

Her hands had unbuttoned his high collar and done away with his cravat, which now lay crumpled and collapsed on the floor.

Tella wrapped the front of his shirt around her hand as if to interrogate him.

"Are you with me?"

* * *

She didn't know what she was saying. She did know what she was doing: something she needed very much.

Past and future were gone. All she had was right now, and right now Fitz was here. With her. And if he was with her, they could do this.

"Always," said Fitz in a voice of eternal certainty.

And despite her hand in his shirtfront, he bent her back again, this time his mouth traveling beyond the hollows of her collarbone to the valley of her breastbone, and lower.

When his lips found the peak they were searching for, straining against the fabric, he bit lightly at her; she made a little cry and pulled his head even closer.

"Can we do this standing here?"

Fitz' eyes flicked toward the bed. But Tella didn't want that. Even two steps would be too long, and she wouldn't risk changing her mind.

She wanted him now, right here, in a way that made him utterly hers.

"I can do anything you wish," said Fitz, nuzzling her shoulder where her gown had fallen away.

Tella had never heard a lie so lovely.

HE FELT her hands scrabbling at his waist. When he pulled back even an inch, Tella made a noise of irritation.

There would be no time to take his shirt entirely off, he could tell. He barely had time to unbutton his waistcoat. Tella's hands had pulled his shirt from his trousers and her fingers struggled with the buttons at his waist.

"There are eight million buttons here," she muttered, tugging till Fitz was afraid she might simply pull them off.

"Wait, wait," he tried to soothe her as he took her hands in his. "I'm not going anywhere. We have time."

Opposite his intention, his words made her lips part and tremble, and those sparkling dark eyes filled with unshed tears.

"We never know that."

Yes, there went a button, flying off into somewhere. Fitz ignored it.

Was her urgency all the same as his? *Should* they stop? "Tella. This is dangerous."

"I do dangerous very well."

* * *

Time? Time was the one thing they didn't have. She'd never get to have this again, and she was desperate to get all of him she could before it was over.

She wanted to spend hours feeling him, wrapping the feel and scent and taste of him around her till she could never be lost, never feel alone.

She also could not wait another minute.

Her body was hungry for him, hollow without him. She'd never felt the sensation before but she knew it. She had to have him inside her. She wouldn't be satisfied without it.

"Can you hold me up?"

Again his eyes flicked questioningly at the bed just a few yards away.

"I don't want to go that far."

In immediate surrender, Fitz slid down against the door, not coincidentally holding it shut with his body, for which she silently applauded him. "Then let us try the floor."

He managed to lower himself with his breeches around his legs, which was another excellent maneuver. They were tight; that couldn't be comfortable.

She ought to take off his shoes, stockings, everything. But she couldn't wait.

Some part of Tella egged her on, whispering that she could have this moment, take it, not to think about an hour or a day from now. Only now.

He pushed her skirts higher, and she pulled them up farther, baring her legs to the cool spring air.

She knew she wanted that part of him that stood seeking her, and his hands against her hips pulled her down to find him.

"You can—"

But they could skip whatever he'd tried to say. She already had.

They fit together so perfectly. The small gasping cry she made against his lips was one of surprise at the perfection.

* * *

HIS HEART WAS full of endearments but he couldn't put them into words.

Tella had him surrounded.

He had the evidence of her body that her urgency had matched his, or more. The liquid heat of her forced a groan out of him; he tried to smother it.

Fitz' eyes closed; his head thumped back against the door as she began to move.

"Will anyone hear it?" There was Tella's habit of ensuring that she was being sufficiently stealthy.

"Not even if I scream." He was only telling her the truth.

"*Will* you scream?"

Her words, quiet, gasping, so innocently wicked in their own way as her body held and grasped him, her moving against him with a sweet urgency that made him feel more wanted than he had ever been, nearly pushed him over the too-close edge.

"I might," he whispered back, wrapping his arms around her and doing his best from his awkward position to plunge as deeply into her as he could.

* * *

TELLA KNEW HE WAS RIGHT. She might too.

Their movements grew even more frantic, Tella bracing one arm against the door to lever herself forward so he could suck at the spot on her neck that she now knew she adored. Fitz' muscles bulged and strained to move them both faster.

His hands on her hips helped her thrust just as hard as he did.

"I don't think I can finish in this position." His breath was warm against her ear, both of them with skin growing slick from exertion. "I hope you will."

"How do we finish?" She was gasping, her body moving faster and faster. The hard length of him was exactly where she wanted it, pressing and rubbing at her core with every movement of them both, and she felt herself tightening around him, which only made every movement even better.

Something was gathering inside, something astonishing.

"Oh my darling," and Tella could tell Fitz meant every word, "I believe you are finding out."

He was right. The gathering, tightening, rushing feeling just kept growing and growing, until Tella knew something was about to fall over the edge.

And then she did.

Her breath was frozen in her, too immobile to scream. Everything in her drove against him with all she had, the shattering, shuddering waves of pleasure breaking through her and through her till she feared she might faint.

Then some part of her realized, dimly, that if she fainted she would be fine; he would catch her.

When the pleasure finally released her, Tella fell limp against Fitz' chest, desperately trying to get air, clinging to him with trembling arms.

"Oh."

* * *

FITZ CHUCKLED INTO HER HAIR. She never, ever failed to amaze him. "Yes, oh," he murmured against the shell of her ear. She shivered.

Perhaps he *could* finish in this position.

"Shall I come with you? It might—" It might get her with child; he wasn't sure she knew that. Oddly, it was the very urgency he felt to bury himself deeper within her that made some part of him wake up to that particular danger.

"Yes, come with me," she murmured, kissing his temple, brushing droplets of sweat into his hair, and he didn't have a choice. Tella clung to him, whispering things he couldn't hear over the roaring in his ears, and he did.

When he came back to earth, he was still in her arms—indeed, he'd never left.

And while he fought to catch his breath just as she had, he kissed where her eyelashes fell against her cheeks, and felt tears.

"Why are you crying?" If only Fitz could fold her up inside his heart and keep her safe.

"Surely everyone does, after that," she half-laughed, half-sobbed.

"I don't think that's ever happened to anyone ever before," he told her, one of his thumbs wiping the worrisome tear away.

* * *

Tella had not guessed that sating her body's desperation would start her mind racing again.

At least somewhat sated; she could still feel him, inside, and squeezed to see what would happen.

Fitz moaned, and slid from inside her, and she hated that.

"May I...?" She reached for the handkerchief in the breast pocket of the coat he was still wearing.

"Of course."

That gave her something to clean him, a little, tuck him back into the smallclothes from which she'd practically ripped him, and let him pull his trousers back on to a more comfortable position. And clean herself, to the point she could rest back on his lap. She dropped it on the floor. "You can burn that."

"I am going to frame that." He sounded tired, his head lolling against the floor, and his blue eyes a little sleepy, but glowing.

Tella laid her head on his chest. Her dress would be unforgivably crushed, but who would know? Perhaps the wrinkles would fall out before she reached home.

"If that were only to happen to me once in my life, I am glad it was with you," she said softly into Fitz' shirtfront.

His arms came around her shoulders. "Why should that only happen once?"

She closed her eyes tightly. "It would be as dangerous to… to do that often, as any other sort of contact. The people I am following, or who follow me, will not have mercy for our… our indulgences."

His hands stopped stroking her back. "That was an indulgence?"

That had been as necessary as breathing.

That didn't mean she could have it again.

"We did indulge ourselves. Isn't that the right way to call it? Out of our heads with…." With passion, with need. With *hunger.*

That wasn't how they said it.

It didn't matter. If he was this close, he was in danger from being too close to her.

It was all she wanted and nothing she could have.

* * *

"Out of our heads with *what*, Tella?"

A cold, sick feeling was creeping up inside Fitz, the kind

280

that happened on the battlefield, the kind where someone's life ended.

"With… that! That urge."

That urge? That had not been an *urge.* That had been fire. That had been a conflagration.

"My urge is to be with you. I want to marry you, Tella. You can do anything you like. I put this house in your hands. I would *deed* it to you, if you could own property without a husband. And I very much want to be that husband."

He gathered her up in both his arms.

Tella just closed her eyes, laid her head on his shoulder.

That wasn't panic rising in him. It wasn't. "What husband would you *have*, if not me?"

"I cannot, Fitz, I told you I cannot! It isn't a matter of your place in society or your house—your beautiful house." Her eyes opened and she looked at that bed. "I cannot lose one more person dear to me. I cannot."

"If I fought a *war* and still came home—"

"Wars have battles. Cities have thieves. All it takes is a sneak with a cudgel and life can be lost in a minute. I know."

"Tella, you are going to have to trust me."

Her hands snuck around his waist. "I do trust you. It is everyone else in London I suspect."

* * *

WHY MUST he make this harder? Wasn't it obvious that she had been overcome, seeing him there, so close? Her weakness changed nothing.

Except perhaps to make clear that her weakness was their weakness.

That was not better.

His breeches were still unbuttoned, and his waistcoat; the neck of his shirt was twisted where she had grabbed him. It felt alarming, the evidence of how much she had wanted him.

She still did.

And now Fitz was angry.

She'd never seen him angry, and she didn't see it now, because his arms, his hands were still holding her and she was leaning on him. How could he *be* like this?

"Then you intend to walk out that door, never return to this house, never come back to me. To this."

"Yes. I must."

Tella, too, moved; she moved away.

Smoothing her skirt hopelessly, buttoning up the front of her walking dress, she did not meet his eyes.

"Tella." Fitz levered himself to his feet, fast, and stood before her, ignoring his unbuttoned and disheveled clothing. "Tella, is it that you don't wish to marry me, or… that you don't wish to love me?"

Finally she had to look up.

And those eyes… it hurt more than a knife between her ribs to see the pain she had caused him.

She had to make him understand.

"When I was little, after my mother was gone. As soon as I closed my eyes at night, I saw her hand, reaching in front me. I *had* seen it, just like that. She was trying to protect me, in her last moments. She was worrying about *me*, when it was she who was hurt—someone threw her down, her head hit a paving stone, and she did not wake up. For a long while I thought it was the blood that killed her—it seemed as though there were rivers of blood—but I when I asked my uncle, he said no. It was the way her head hit."

She closed her eyes and swallowed. She couldn't look at him.

"I wasn't the reason she left the house. I wasn't the reason she was there. But she was trying to protect me, *because I was there*. The exact way she was standing, the exact way she fell —it was all exactly right to kill her. Because of me. It was because I was there, Fitz. Because she was near me."

He moved as if to take her in his arms again.

Tella just held up a hand, *stop*.

"I can lose my uncle. I can lose Julia. I don't know if I could bear to lose you." She stood shaking her head, looking at the floor, or into the past. "But I could not bear to lose you because you were near me."

Slowly she drew on first one glove, and then the other. She bent and picked up her shawl, and her hat.

She stood there for several moments, trying to think of something else to say.

All she could think of to say was that she loved him, and that she wouldn't say.

"I shall not marry, but if I were to accept anyone," she said, finally looking up into his anguished blue eyes, "it would be you."

And then she was gone.

CHAPTER TWENTY-ONE

She found Mrs. Burke wandering around the attic, drawing things on a folded up sheet of foolscap.

The woman didn't seem to notice how long ago she'd wandered away.

Tella declined to be shown around the rest of the house. She had things to attend to at home, she said.

Lying had become so easy.

At least she'd never lied to Fitz.

Mrs. Burke spent the ride back to the Gravenshire house poring over her notes and making more, tiny pencil gripped tightly in her fingers.

She seemed quite used to not conversing in carriages. Perhaps it was not an easy place for her to hear.

"Of course you will let me know if the china cabinet won't do," she said at one point, barely looking up, saving Tella the need to pretend to answer.

Tella would not be letting her know if the china cabinet wouldn't do. It would do, but she would not be using it. She would not be the lady of that house and she must learn to do without the deep, passionate, and abiding love she had accidentally, unfortunately, found.

* * *

HER MIND HAD TRAVELED SO FAR AWAY that she didn't notice where she was going until she arrived at her uncle's door.

He answered when she knocked.

Which was, for some reason, such a relief that she almost cried again.

Lady Donnatella, the Duke of Gravenshire's only, beloved daughter, swept in and gave Lord Preston a wide smile.

He, resplendent in a blue and coral banyan robe bursting with printed chrysanthemums and lilies, had not yet finished dressing.

But he had moved to his little Eastern tiled table, with a writing desk upon it, in the light.

"My very favorite uncle." Tella meant it more each time she said it.

She sailed over and perched in the chair opposite him. "Let us do something today, something together, something pleasant."

"You know you are also my favorite, and only, niece," said Lord Preston a little absently, "but it has so revived me, to think of how to write about my campaigns, I have been thinking of nothing else for days. And I've just had the first idea on how to begin."

"Did you?" He was so straight and tall, he quite reminded her of Fitz—how had Tella never noticed that before? Though with his white hair brushed back from his face, he was a good deal more groomed. And his hand, as he moved it to lay down the pen he was holding, shook a little.

Her eyes filled with tears. Would that keep happening now? It was too unfortunate. And always at inopportune moments. "I so would like to spend some time with you today, Uncle Albert."

He was a slightly fainter version of himself: a little smudged around the edges, but still her great-uncle. His eyes were keen enough. "Something's upset you. What?"

"I want to sit in the garden and watch you drink tea, darling. And I want to read to you, and perhaps knit you socks. Did you know that the Duchess of Talbourne taught me to knit?"

Lord Preston sat back. "No, nor can I imagine you knitting."

"I wonder if socks are difficult. I must send her a note."

Tella's elbow met the table; her head slumped on to her hand. She hoped she did not look as exhausted as she felt.

"And why the sudden interest in these domestic pleasures, my favorite niece?"

His voice was so kind. And he knew things. He did know her.

He no longer even remembered how much she'd learned from him, everything she'd done with it. But he was here, and she was glad.

"I'm tired, more tired than I thought this morning. I need a rest, perhaps." Then her jaw snapped shut. She ought to take him out to the country, to rest and recuperate during the summer months.

But she couldn't leave London with a killer on the loose.

Then she snorted. Whom did she think she was fooling? Burgiss was the murderer, Storey employed him, and she hadn't been on the street in days, hoping her research among her social set would give her proof against them or the woman who'd sent them both in motion. Three outlaws, *traitors*, just waiting to see if she could do anything besides frighten away pickpockets.

It was Fitz she didn't want to leave.

She sighed.

Then she stood, and knelt at her uncle's feet, her head on his knee like she used to do when she was little.

Lord Preston's hand rested briefly on her hair.

"Your mother always tired of society this time of year too. She said it was the time to get out of London and breathe fresh air, if one was lucky enough to do so."

So like what Tella herself had just been thinking.

She rested her temple against his knee. "Why don't you talk about Mother more, Uncle Albert? I would like it."

"Would you?"

Her uncle sat for so long without saying more that Tella wondered if perhaps he had fallen asleep. Her eyes were drooping; she might fall asleep too.

But then he said, "I never liked talking about your mother because I failed her so badly. But perhaps I should speak of her more often, and find a way not to fail with you."

That woke Tella right up.

"Never tell me so! There is no better uncle in all of London, in all of Britain, no, in all the world. What a false-hood, sir, so false!"

She'd turned to grab his hand in hers and look at his face.

Lord Preston only nodded. "Yes, a failure. My wife and I never wanted your mother to be afraid. It's common for children who have lost their parents to be afraid, and we wanted her to be brave. And she was. She didn't learn that from us. She simply was brave, every day of her life. What we didn't teach her was to be cautious."

He patted her cheek. "So when I had the chance to try again with you, I erred too far the other direction. You are too cautious, my child, far too cautious, to the point where I fear it is hurting you."

"Cautious!" Tella stood on her knees. "Why, every night you are—"

She stopped herself just before she spilled everything. He didn't remember it but he had cautioned her *every night*. Always asking where she intended to go, always reminding her to check all her supplies, to look behind her, to *be careful*.

Lord Preston seemed to be waiting for her to go on. When she didn't, he just said, "I'm glad you are cautious, child. Just don't look behind you so much, you miss what's in front of you."

Like Lady Winpole? How could a member of her father's set be arranging arson, at the very least, right in front of Tella's nose? How could she be cheating at *cards*?

"Do you know, Uncle, I think I've found out that Lady Winpole cheats at cards? I am astonished."

And she was astonished again when her uncle shook his head. "I don't mean that you miss the bad, Donnatella. I worry that you might miss the good."

It was so near what her father had said, that for a moment Tella thought of accusing them of conspiring.

But in the next moment it washed over her that she was walking away from happiness *right now*, and if he knew all the details, her uncle wouldn't approve.

Not only because she wasn't marrying the man she'd… well, frankly, that she'd ravished; but because she was missing her chance.

"It might be that keeping the ones we love safe is more important than our own happiness," she said, carefully weighing out each word.

"Hm." His head tilted a little. "An interesting question. As if we have all the choices. If I could have laid down my life to save my wife, I would have. I did not have that choice. Her illness killed her, nothing I could control. If I had put her aside out of fear of the end of her life, I would have missed our entire life together."

He was still her darling Uncle Albert. He was far more knowledgeable than she about oh, so many things.

But only Tella could judge her own breaking point.

"So shall I measure you for socks, or would you prefer to bring your writing into the garden?"

Lord Preston glanced at the window. "It is raining, you know."

She didn't know.

"Socks it is, then, darling."

* * *

THE DUKE OF GRAVENSHIRE'S outthrust chin identified him, even in silhouette.

He was walking along the front of the Lesser Hall where the House of Lords met, his carriage and two must have just delivered him to the spot near the Palace Yard.

A small black dog ran across his path and caused him to look up.

Fitz stood there. The Duke frowned.

His greeting was equally unwelcoming. "This is most irregular, sir."

"My apologies. I have called upon you at home these last two days and was told both times that you were here. I thought this might be easier."

"You were at my residence? Looking for me?"

"Yes, sir."

"For what possible purpose?"

"To—to assuage my guilt, I suppose."

The Duke drew himself up. "Guilt for *what?*"

"Your criticism of me has been correct from the beginning; I should not have importuned your daughter in so public a place, or pressed my suit where all could hear so that

—" Here Fitz swallowed, and looked up for a moment before he could go on, "so that she would be too inclined to accept."

"So she means her refusal, then."

"Oh yes." Here Fitz met the Duke's eyes quite squarely. "She has been very clear on that."

His Grace nodded slightly. "I won't say my daughter is terribly constant, but when she is set on something, she is set." He looked Fitz up and down, saw the same slightly scuffed young man without a hat he had first seen dancing with his daughter. "I don't know you, sir, so I cannot say I am sorry that she has refused you; but for your sake, I suppose I can offer condolences."

A small ghost of a smile came and went at the corner of Fitz' mouth. "Kind of you, sir, and more than I deserve. My interest has always been entirely in Lady Donnatella; but yours would have been a congenial family to join, it appears."

"Yours cannot be terribly congenial."

"Ah, do you know my father?"

"Not well. Enough."

"Yes. Enough."

"So what will you do with the money and house that he wrote me he deeded to you on the promise of your excellent marriage?"

It was a very personal question, but since Fitz had practically tried to carry the man's daughter off right beneath his nose, he supposed His Grace ought to be allowed a few personal questions.

"I don't know," Fitz replied quite honestly. "I had not seen my father for some years; then, this, all unasked. I engaged someone to look into my family, as I have not seen many of them for a long while. It appears that neither of my brothers is on speaking terms with Lord Ashbury; one hasn't been heard from at all for some time. So I'm not quite sure what my father was thinking."

"But you have not asked him."

"Nor do I expect to any time soon." Fitz' smile was real, and lasted longer, on that point.

Then his smile faded away. "I wanted… I had thought Lady Donnatella would like the house." His shoulders slumped a little. "I don't suppose… there's no way to pass it on to her."

"She cannot own property in her own name, as you know."

"I wish she had…" Fitz remembered that he wanted to make amends. To Tella, but since she would not let him, to her father if he could. "I wish she'd wanted it. Or anything I'd hoped to give. I had… my mother sent her some jewels of her own, to celebrate."

The Duke just nodded. In a family as distant as Fitz' was, it was more than a kind gesture.

"What will you do?"

* * *

FITZ LOOKED out over the broad expanse of the carriage yard. His smile came back. "I will look for a way to live a bright, sharp life without her."

The Duke's face invited further comment, but Fitz found that after all, that was all he had to say. "Good day, sir," he said with a bow, and left.

* * *

FITZ STOOD in the street and stared up at Mercywall House. His house, in fact.

He had no idea what he should do with it, because he had no idea what he should do with himself.

Among the true things Lord Halworth had said, was that

fighting the war had been vivid, and scarring, but unforgettable. The worst and most sorrowful part of his life, and he would never want to go back.

But it had honed him and made him more than just impatient with British society. It had made him impatient with time. There was no time to waste by doing nothing for others. No time at all.

Meanwhile, his door—*his* door—was being held open for him.

Because Mr. Stuart was holding it.

"Mr. Stuart." Belatedly Fitz realized he ought to be wearing a hat he could now take off.

"Lord Henry. What time would you like to dine, sir?"

Time spent dining would be time that made Fitz impatient.

At least, if he dined alone.

He looked at the butler, from the shining tips of his shoes to the faultless folds of his cravat. He'd asked before but hadn't pressed; he ought to ask again.

"Mr. Stuart. I am a poor excuse for a nobleman, and I have no idea how long I may be here or under what circumstances I may leave. I know it is an imposition upon your time and your station to ask you this. Sadly I have but one constant in my life, carried from my time in military service to my current vocation, and it is to hear the stories of others and perhaps make something of them."

He inclined his head toward Mr. Stuart. "I don't know you well, and I would like to. Will you seize the moment and dine with me? Or if not, just… please, tell me anything you are willing I should know. I would like to know."

* * *

"Julia, please do tell me about the Isle of Wight." Tella flung herself into the chair nearest where Julia sat pinning some leaves on paper, for some reason.

"You are not interested in the Isle of Wight." Julia didn't even look up.

"I am interested in your wedding, and your wedding trip." Tella was determined to be brave about this. This was a happy loss, not a sad one; and as Julia said, she would be returning, though Tella's world would not be the same.

Julia put down the paper in a very deliberate way that made Tella think she was about to be lectured.

She was right.

"I've made several social calls since the Duchess' knitting affair. Lady Shoreton went with me, of course. I'm sure she wonders why I am so interested in Lady Winpole all of a sudden, but she has been politic enough not to ask."

Tella nodded. It was reasonable. Unless it had to do with the acquisition of husbands or the etiquette around same, Lady Shoreton was unlikely to have much opinion.

"You may recall that Lady Winpole's husband died some time ago. Almost ten years, I think. Lady Redbeck does not recall her being a particularly gay person even when she had her first social season. She has always been serious and quiet, no scandals, no gossip."

"I wonder why she didn't attend the Duchess' affair, then," mused Tella.

"That is no mystery; she has no husband to vote."

Tella inclined her head; that point was obvious, given the Duchess' interests and the topics of conversation.

"Does she have funds?"

"No one knows. One presumes her husband left her property and money, and she still resides in the house they occupied in London; his heir has stayed in the country and does not take his seat in the Lords. She does not live extravagantly in any way, so who can know what her money is?"

Tella nodded again. "She spends little money on clothes and entertainments, and she must have won a hundred pounds at the whist game at my party."

"*Did* she?" Now Julia looked surprised. "What an extraordinary sum. One would not have thought it to look at her."

Tella didn't mention Lady Winpole's debt to Tella herself, but she agreed. "Not at all. Now that I think on it, I wonder how many nights in a season she has a windfall like that."

It wouldn't do to imply that Lady Winpole was a cheater at cards.

Tella would so much rather think about this problem than anything to do with Fitz.

Julia was still taken aback by the money. "It must be rare, surely."

"Must it? She was playing whist at the Woolacre ball as well. And a few nights before. You know, that night I met the young Lord Harriman. No, that isn't right. Lord John Harman, that was it. One of Lady Ayles' sons."

"Why, Tella. You remembered his name!"

"He was a good dancer."

"Not that good." Julia settled herself back into the arms of the heavy upholstered chair. "Well. I suppose whatever is going on with you is for the best, if it makes you actually notice the attractive young men who are *trying* to gain your attention."

Tella winced a little. She'd noticed Fitz, and that hadn't been for the best, not at all.

She missed him every minute of the day and night, and hated herself besides.

"Never you mind about me. I will be still waiting for that deep, abiding, *passionate* love, long after you are married, with handsome children, with a long line of friends ahead of me at your door."

Julia was watching her with those eyes that saw a great deal. "I don't think you will be at all."

That made Tella sit up straight. "Why on earth not?"

"Because I don't think you are looking for it at all. I think you found it, and for some reason, you've thrown it away."

To that, Tella couldn't say anything at all.

After a moment, Julia leaned in. "I saw you behave differently around Lord Henry. Like someone I don't know. And when I ask you about that person, you didn't tell me the true story. I know you didn't. I am not stupid."

"No. You have *never* been stupid."

"I don't know anything about Lord Henry. I don't know his family, I don't know what type of life he offered you, I don't know how many pounds he has a year or whether he has employment. I do know that he touched something in you, more than anyone else ever has, and he made something come over you. Some sort of gentleness. Perhaps it was peace." That made Tella look up; Julia went on. "And if you sent that away, you sent *him* away, I don't imagine there is anyone else who will ever truly be the man you are seeking."

Julia folded her hands tightly before she went on, pressing them into the front of her dotted linen day dress. "I find myself wondering what you said to him before he touched you that way. Before, as you say, you kissed him. I find myself wondering what you said afterwards. And I am sorry to say it, but I find myself wondering how much of it was the truth. And then..." She looked back at Tella. "I find myself wondering how much of what you have told *me* was the truth."

Tella wanted to leap up and say *everything, everything*, but she knew she could not. And so did Julia.

"And then? Then I find myself thinking that if my closest

friend cannot tell me the truth… then she is not really my closest friend."

Tella felt those words like a blow to the chest. She knew she was losing her friend Julia; she had not expected to lose her like this.

But Julia was full of words today. "So I have given you what I know of Lady Winpole. No husband, no children, no news of her money, no extravagances, and very good luck at cards." With a cutting look. "Unless you care to elaborate."

"Lady Winpole is of no serious importance, Julia, not compared to you being angry with me—"

"I am angry, a little. But I am mostly surprised. Disappointed, I think. Yes, disappointed and surprised. And angry," Julia admitted. "I cannot keep claiming to be your friend, Tella, until you feel the same. And until then—" She looked around a bit as if she surprised even herself. "—until then, good day, I suppose!"

* * *

"I AM HOPING to God that you are not serious, but I know you are." Fitz was poleaxed with horror.

Mr. Stuart was a broad man, with muscled legs. He had unbuttoned his coat and loosened his neckcloth.

They had been talking a long, long while.

Mr. Stuart's eyes flicked back over towards the door he had locked himself.

Fitz understood. The other servants would be appalled, perhaps even angry, to see Mr. Stuart and Fitz speaking as equals like this.

But they were not equals. Mr. Stuart was a better man than Fitz in every regard, and yet was labeled less.

Fitz went on. "I cannot imagine being a child in the circumstances you describe. I ought to have known more of the prisoners of war Britain has had. But to go from there into service among the very people who kept you imprisoned; to be considered a slave—" Fitz had studied the man's face for hours now. Mr. Stuart had given up the last traces of formality and distance. He looked exactly like what he was: the patriarch of a family, an avid reader of both books and periodicals, a man with a weakness for pastries.

Fitz would never have guessed that he was also not free.

Not a slave, but not free. Because he had been brought to this country as a prisoner of war and no one had ever documented him as otherwise. Because a man of color had to prove his freedom.

Because of Fitz' father, who had raised disinterest to the level of cruelty.

The people of Britain needed to know how the wars reverberated on and on.

Mr. Stuart poured himself some more claret. They'd been talking for quite a while. "I spoke to your father about it once. Only once. When he came into possession of this house. I told him, as clearly as I could, that I would be grateful for something written down on paper that clarified that I was a free man."

"And he wouldn't." Fitz had thought he despised his father before. There was farther to go.

"I wish I could say why he wouldn't. I have had years to think about it." Mr. Stuart sipped thoughtfully from his glass. "I finally realized that I do not have to understand it. It is humiliating enough that I had to ask."

"I did not know."

Mr. Stuart regarded him over the glass. "How would you have known, sir?"

Fitz felt sick. Would he have known if he had studied that thick sheet of paper more closely? If he had consulted with the solicitor who provided the information? If he had cared to find out what his own life was before criticizing the lives led by others?

"I have to thank you. I believe you've given me vivid purpose I sorely needed. But I would not have had you suffer what you have suffered for anything. You have been very forthcoming with your history, sir, and I consider it an honor."

Mr. Stuart saluted with his glass. "You have told me some of yours, sir, and I am glad to know it."

"If I do nothing else with this house or the situation of owning it, I will get you a paper that says that you are free. And I will thank you until the end of my days, as you have reminded me what drove me before I..." Fitz faltered, but went on, "before my heart was lost, and I will find my way back to it again. I promise you."

Then immediately Fitz shook his head. "My family owes you for years of pain and doubt, and you give me a gift. Nothing I do will truly repay you for it."

A slight touch of a smile, without much humor, reached the corners of Mr. Stuart's eyes. "I will be interested, very interested, to see if that is true, sir."

That impressed Fitz entirely, as the stories Mr. Stuart had just shared convinced Fitz he didn't deserve Mr. Stuart's interest. His family certainly didn't.

Along with his other qualities, Mr. Stuart had more faith in humanity, and optimism, than Fitz had.

Fitz just raised his own glass. He'd found something in himself he'd thought was gone. He didn't feel whole, but he felt good to have it back.

* * *

Tella had no parties tonight.

She dined alone; her father was in Parliament for the evening, and Lord Preston had fallen asleep.

"Would you care for more fish, madame?"

She looked up at Percival, and noticed for the first time that he was kind, far kinder than she deserved given that this was the first time she had noticed it.

"No thank you, Percival, I believe I'll retire."

The rest of the staff all made appropriate murmurs and Tella rose from her chair and left the dining room and its glittering silver and candles knowing they felt sorry for her, and feeling very, very alone.

This was how she always knew things would be.

She wandered aimlessly into her father's study, then shut the door behind her.

She sat in a large leather armchair in this masculine room, heavy with carved wood panels and the smoke of past tobacco, and looked into the dark.

When she exercised, and dressed, and ventured out into the streets, she had always been alone.

But she had not felt lonely till now.

For many hours, Tella sat there in the dark and thought about the difference.

* * *

BURGISS CAME out of the shadows in the alley just as the Covent Garden nun, as the name went, slipped out the side door of her establishment.

He liked to make women jump.

When her startlement was over, she groaned at him. "You again. Push *off!* One shout from me and there'll be pistols out here in yer face."

"It's part of my job knowing who to tell to be quiet and

getting 'em to listen." He wiggled his hands in front of her face.

She recoiled. What was *that* for? Sure, his fingernails were ragged, but his hands were clean.

"I'm lookin' fer that tall gob, the one who asks everybody all the questions."

"What for? He ain't askin' about you."

Burgiss stepped closer. He liked the way she leaned back. He nodded.

"That's right. You have the idea. Life is knowin' who's on top and who's at the bottom. Yer at the bottom, and I'm gettin' closer to the top ev'ry day. You need to listen to me."

She paled a little.

He nodded again. Looking certain made a difference, and he *was* certain. "One grip of my hand and you'll never scream again, you know." He looked at his own hand. "It's easier'n you'd think."

"You're not gonna hurt 'im, are ya?"

"Awww, what a big heart. I tol' ya, he just needs ta listen."

He watched her convince herself that he was telling the truth.

"You must be trippin' over his trail. You know he likes the streets around here, and of an evenin', he don't come here. Or anyplace like it. Pity."

"Come on, little thing." Burgiss wiggled his fingertips, pulling the words out of her. "Where *does* he go?"

"Oh, everyone finds him at—at t' Bottle and Bird." She swallowed, and immediately became defensive. "You coulda found that out from anyone, not just me!"

"But it was from you," said Burgiss, not thanking her, and passing close as he left her standing alone in the alley.

* * *

"CLEMENT, you have to believe that I can write a story about prisoners of war in this country that will keep the readers of Bridle's Gazette riveted."

"I don't have to do a god-damned thing, Fitz." Clement wasn't indulgent this time; he was genuinely angry, chewing on the end of a burnt-down cigar and glaring. "My readers don't want weepy politics and my sovereign doesn't want me printing it. What are you about, getting me arrested?"

"Clement." Fitz stood from his chair, came around it to lean over Clement's desk. "I am *promising* you. These won't be tear-soaked and they won't be dry either. It's people's *lives*, not abroad, right here on English soil. Who can argue?"

"Politicians can argue, Fitz, it's practically the only skill they have. To say anything about it is to take a side and bring the opposite side down on my head—*my* head, mind you— and take my paper down with it. Do you think the taxes on newspapers are so high because the Crown *enjoys* criticism of the way things have been done?"

"Clement, I am promising you. Not criticism. Facts."

"Facts can be taken as criticism."

"Not by anyone I'd shake hands with. Nor you either, Clement, and I already know it. You read what I wrote at the front, hell, you published some of it. You knew what you were getting. And you asked me to write for you."

"Because you're good at it. Dammit. Dammit all. Fitz..."

Fitz just spread his hands, waiting.

"You can have a story about prisoners of war for every story you give me about the Caped Count and that is where my bargaining stops. So take it," Clement said in a rush.

"I do take it, sir," said Fitz with a smile that was close to his old smiles, and swung himself towards the door to leave before Clement could change his mind.

CHAPTER TWENTY-TWO

"*A*n' then, he ups and throws a knife—amazing little knife all in one piece, somehow—and it goes *smash* right into th' tankard knockin' it out of his hand and into the wood of the wall!"

The gentleman telling Fitz this story clearly found this the best part; he slapped the wall next to him with his own hand. "Into the wall! Clear into it!"

"And the man then, y'know, the one who'd been threatenin' to beat my head clean off my shoulders, he just looked —shocked, wasn't it, Ewan?"

"Shocked, he looked shocked," Ewan confirmed.

"And then the shocked fellow just gets up, tryin' to make like he just remembered he oughta be somewhere, maybe? Just stands up, all dripping with ale like he was, gets up as polite as you please and just leaves!"

The man telling the story, Bart, clearly adored this. He slapped his thighs and rocked back and forth with laughter.

His friend just shook his head in disbelief. "We couldn't believe it. I tell you, we couldn't. And I offered to buy the lad an ale, and of course Bart does the same, and he just says something like you ought to be able to live in peace and then he swirls out of here too, very superior—" Ewan enjoyed rolling this word out, he really relished making several stops out of *superior*, "—bang, he was gone, before we could even get a good look at him under that hat."

"Aye, full o' coin, obviously.

"Oh yeah, obviously."

"With that blue velvet cloak," and here Bart moved his hand up and down as if he was stroking the fabric that said his savior had plenty of coin. "But a good lad."

"A very good lad. Saved you from gettin' your head bashed in and that's a fact."

"That's a fact," Bart agreed with Ewan very amiably as he downed most of the rest of his ale.

Yet another story of a good deed done by the Caped Count. These people around here didn't want to read stories about the Count to liven up dull parlor conversation; these people *knew* the Count, and they liked telling those stories because they were grateful to him.

Even though they never knew his name.

These were people, Fitz realized, grateful for Fitz' writing about the Caped Count if only because it gave him a name. Now they could all talk about someone they all knew, even if only by reputation.

What Fitz really hoped to hear was that someone had spotted the Caped Count lately.

And he already knew Bart's and Ewan's answer: not lately, sir.

It did not matter. This would be another good story for Bridle's Gazette, the sort of tale its readers liked; it was funny, another story about the legendary knife-throwing skills of the Caped Count, and it was easy to tell to others.

Fitz was already composing in his head the story he would print about prisoners of war; he intended to start with the people of color imprisoned for years and then turned out into southern England with no assistance of any sort, to live or die. He had an impeccable source of information whom he intended to quote anonymously.

When a shadow fell over his tankard, his mind came back from the place he put together all those words.

"Mr. Fitzwilliam," said Burgiss.

His two musketmen were behind him.

Fitz' first thoughts were of Tella. How much he wished he could see her one more time, yet was so glad she was not here.

* * *

TELLA SAT knitting next to Lord Preston's bed as he slept and wondered how long it would take her to become an entirely different person.

Because the solitude was eating away at her, and it had only been a few days.

For the first time in her life she understood how it was that women had affairs. It must be partly to break up the monotony of days that were always exactly the same, and nights that were the same and somehow worse.

Would her father let her take her uncle into the country?

No, she wouldn't ask. Her entire life had one purpose: to be on the streets of London. To protect the unwary.

No one ought ever to be afraid.

That was why she was so restless: because she wasn't doing what she wanted, what she needed to do. She'd gotten no nearer her targets, and in return for her restraint she was about to crawl out of her own skin.

Looking at Lord Preston's face, his skin a little thinner in the candlelight, a little more marked by age, Tella admitted inside that lying to herself did not work. She was restless because she missed Fitz.

She ached for everything about him. She wanted his hands and his laugh and his constant words. She wanted his steadfast strength.

She wanted him with her, every day and all night.

She would find a way to adjust. Like the cinch strap of a leather saddle, she needed to stretch a little, to fit her new situation. She'd been pulled through a buckle, that was what it was. She'd soon fit her new life.

But she wouldn't adjust in here.

Standing, she pinched the candle out.

* * *

"Meg, did you bring my friends a round of ale?"

The serving maid approached the table warily; the others Fitz had talked to, Bart and Ewan of the Caped Count tale, had disappeared.

"We don't drink much," Burgiss told him.

"I do," one of the musketmen said.

Burgiss just turned and fixed the man with a look.

He fell silent.

"We are working men, not such fine stuff as yourself, and we still have tasks of an evening. Many tasks." Burgiss seemed to be enjoying being mysterious.

"Bring them some ale anyway, Meg; your ale is too good to waste. And Meg." Fitz turned over his shoulder and looked the maid straight in the eye so she would see and remember him. "I need some paper, Meg, and pen and ink. More than anything. You can find those for me, can't you?"

"It's a tavern, Fitz, I don't—" Her soft brown eyes searched his face. "Let me see what I can find."

"I said, we ain't goin' ta drink yer ale." Burgiss was clearly annoyed.

"No worries then, gentlemen, I will drink yours for you."

Fitz stretched his legs under the table.

How had Burgiss found him? He strongly doubted Mr. Burgiss often took Bridle's Gazette. Had his employer read Fitz' stories? Possibly, but Fitz suspected Burgiss had found Fitz' trail exactly as Fitz and Tella found his: he'd asked around on the street.

There were some disadvantages to being tall.

It was funny, but Fitz had always thought the dangers of being tall had stayed on the battlefield where he'd presented an unduly large target.

If his life were to end tonight, he had many, many regrets. There were many things he ought to have said to Tella, his Caped Count, the love of his life. It was a shame he would have no chance to say them.

He desperately hoped Meg could find him that pen and paper.

* * *

TELLA HAD GONE through her armoire, down the stairs, and into her locked basement closet before she'd really stopped to think. As if something had pulled her here.

Now, at the bottom, she found herself looking up. Thinking how tall the closet had been in Mercywall House.

Would Fitz continue to live there? Would he marry? It would be a lovely place for him to have a family, if he wanted one, she supposed.

What other ladies would he dance with?

Of course, it would also be a lovely place for the Caped Count to have a truly magnificent hideaway. She had every faith that Mrs. Burke could outfit the place with anything she might need.

The wall on one side should pivot, for instance, so that she could hide away all the ropes and chains, even whips she kept coiled on hooks. Her whips were custom made to her requirements, and some were small, even dainty; a cabinet from Mrs. Burke would keep them ready.

Drawers could be fitted with boxes for small things like marbles. Her Huntsman knives and hooks should be stored in oiled canvas, to keep from rusting.

She did not care for pistols, which also avoided the problem of storing powder and shot.

But she had many leather things, like her beloved gloves, that must not be subjected to mold.

It was interesting to imagine and kept her busy all through the process of checking her belongings, ensuring they were securely hidden around her person, preparing to go out again without ever really deciding to go out. And she comfortably forgot that she would likely never have a reason to go back to Mercywall House.

* * *

"YER IN LUCK, Fitz, Charlie was willing to tear you a page out of his ledger and I've got a pen and some ink if ya want."

"I do want, Meg," and Fitz's easy, wide smile wouldn't be all the thanks he'd leave. He'd leave all the coins in his pocket if he could before he went.

But before he went, he had to write just one thing down.

"You don't think I'm gonna let you write down who we are or where we're going," Burgiss told him. Too smart to draw attention to himself by looking threatening, he was sitting sipping his ale, calm as you please, only occasionally looking at Fitz with those eyes as vicious as a rabid animal's teeth.

"I'll be happy to let you read it, sirs, when I am through."

Burgiss just snorted.

Fitz dipped the pen, uncaring if it dripped on the table.

* * *

Claremont Square was so quiet Tella began to wonder if there was a cutpurses' holiday. Was she simply out of rhythm with the street?

She checked her usual spots for no other reason than that it felt good. She had this, after all; this made up her life.

Tella hadn't found out much more about Storey or Lady Winpole, not yet. But she wouldn't give up.

Her third visiting spot was awry. Tommy was missing.

She knocked on the door in the doorway where he usually slept. Mrs. Somethingorother, she never remembered the name, was a pleasant lady who lived with two of her sisters and didn't mind Tommy; she often saved a bit of bread for him.

Mrs. Somethingorother practically jumped back in horror at the sight of Tella in her evening guise.

And then burst into tears.

CHAPTER TWENTY-THREE

"It's awful, I know! So awful! I knew you'd come, it's been days but I knew I'd see you, I just knew it!"

"What?" That was all Tella could think. *What?*

"Died right there, he did, right where you're standing, and I can't stop wondering why I didn't hear a thing! He must not have fought. Of course not, how could he fight? The drink took it right out of him. But I wish I'd heard."

Someone had *killed* Tommy? Right here on her streets?

"Why didn't I see it in the papers?" Tella asked before she could stop herself.

The lady put a hand to her cheek. "None of them would write about poor old Tommy."

No. No one paid attention to Tommy. That was why Tella did this, why she was here.

Of course, Fitz would have paid attention.

Something in the back of her head was trying to come to the front. Too many little things that wanted to string together. Who would have killed Tommy, but the murderer she already knew?

Why would anyone kill Tommy, unless they thought it might lead to her, the one most often seen in these streets?

Or to Fitz?

"Thank you, ma'am," Tella said, tipping her hat, "I must go."

* * *

As she passed the spot, Tella had an inexplicable urge to stop where her mother had died.

But there wasn't time right now for all the people she'd failed, starting with her mother and ending with Tommy.

It wasn't wish fulfillment, she'd never wish that Fitz was in danger. It was all the little instincts she tried to hear before it was too late.

* * *

"Satisfied?"

Burgiss just shook his head—was that actually a chuckle? —and handed the paper back to Fitz.

Fitz took it carefully; it was a little smudged. Still readable. He ought to have made sure it was dry before he'd handed it to Burgiss. But he was in a hurry.

"Hey, Fitz, what you doing here? I thought we agreed to look more southerly for summat more about tha' Caped Count."

Fitz closed his eyes.

No, there was no wishing it away.

That was Gerry, standing right next to his table.

* * *

"Gerry, you don't know Mr. Withers here. I'm writing an item about his business. He trains cats. Mr. Withers, Gerry Frost."

Silently Fitz thanked all the holy things at once that neither gentleman was stupid enough to correct his name.

"You don't say." Gerry had been about to sit down; then catching a closer look at Fitz' companions, decided to stay standing. "I have the night wrong, then, when you and I had an appointment, don't I?"

"You do, old fellow, I'm sorry to say that you do." Fitz folded the paper in his hand and gave it to Gerry, looking him in the eyes to hold his attention. "For the sake of your washerwoman, take this to that house we saw, would you?"

He ought to have done the thing right, legally, but he was out of time.

Gerry thought hard but, thank God, he didn't look round. Fitz didn't know what Burgiss would do if Gerry took an interest in him, or made note of his appearance, or that of his henchmen.

"Where you asked questions of that colleague of mine?"

"That's the one."

Burgiss, surprisingly, spoke up. "I'd think you'd ask questions about every house, Fitzwilliam, if you asked questions at all."

"You'd think. But no, I reserve my interest for stories I think my readers will read. Mr. Frost, if you would just take care of that now?"

Gerry's eyes were searching his, for a hint of what he should do. Fitz just nodded. "I'm sorry I can't keep our appointment, but these gentlemen have a prior arrangement with me."

"It's no worry, Fizzie, I'll take it." Gerry seemed to shove the paper into his pocket carelessly, but Fitz had faith in him. Faith that Gerry would take that paper where it needed to be, and faith that Gerry would get out of here without doing something very foolish, because he loved his wife and he wanted to go home to her every night.

Fitz was deeply, burningly jealous of the man.

"Later, Frost," and Fitz nodded toward the door. He should go.

Gerry just saluted with two fingers and disappeared.

* * *

TELLA HAD PACED ALL the side streets round Claremont Square like a panther with sore paws, circling and circling and hating it more each time.

No one would say if they'd seen Burgiss lately, and a few of her usual informants wouldn't even speak.

Someone had frightened them. Someone with reach, and the ability to convince others that he was happy to hurt them.

Someone, Tella suspected, with mean, mean eyes.

And the spot between her shoulderblades itched as if someone had a pistol aimed at her back. Her father and uncle were safe, undoubtedly Julia, curtailed in her travel as she was, was fine too.

She wished she could be sure that Fitz was safe as well.

* * *

FITZ WATCHED Gerry go with gladness.

He liked Gerry a bit these days. And he liked Mrs. Hirst.

"I think that you've put on as much of a show as any opera house," said Burgiss, still pretending to be quite calm, with anger simmering just below the surface.

"I've been terribly accommodating, gentlemen." Fitz was

happy to take a last look around as he followed Burgiss out, the musketmen behind him forming a tight knot.

He loved people. And these were good people.

He was glad they would be the last good people he would see.

CHAPTER TWENTY-FOUR

*B*urgiss prided himself on being a man of business, not some childish bully.

He was angry that he'd been so excited to see Fitz that he'd accosted the man in public. It had limited what he could do.

And Fitz had kept his head enough to use the public location to do… whatever that had been.

But the paper didn't interfere with any business of Burgiss', and he couldn't spare anyone to follow the man who took it. It was neither valuable nor useful for frightening people, so he let it go.

He'd attached himself to important people, and when this was all cleaned up, he expected to replace Storey in the ranks of their little business.

Everyone needed a man who knew what to keep and who to frighten.

"Going to march me to… wherever it is?" Fitzwilliam looked down at him with some sort of cheerful calm.

"You're an odd duck." Walking him all the way would give

him too much time to do something. Larger carriages, however, weren't to be had for hire on this small a street.

Burgiss really did pride himself on an ability to solve problems.

He quickly stopped a cab, tossed its driver a half guinea. The lad opened his eyes wide and settled his horse to wait as long as Burgiss wanted.

Then Burgiss pulled a piece of rope from where he'd tucked it again at his hip. "Getty, if he moves wrong, shoot him."

Getty, one of his musketmen, planted himself just out of the way of the cab's rocking wheels, and opened his coat to show Fitz his hand upon the butt of a pistol.

Fitz put his hands up placatingly.

"Very nice," said Burgiss, and tied Fitz' hands together, then his feet.

Between them, Getty, Burgiss, and the other man with them mostly blocked the view of passersby.

Trussed like a calf, Fitz followed Burgiss' hand waves and scooted backward into the cab.

And Burgiss climbed in after him.

* * *

"DON'T you know this is the wrong place to try thieving?"

Gerry stiffened as a rasping voice came out of the shadows under the trees.

And what felt like the point of a knife pricked him through all his layers of clothing. In the back, right against his ribs.

* * *

Gerry had only been standing there, looking up at the largest house that took up one whole side of Claremont Square. He'd wondered if he had the house Fitz meant, and thought it must be because it was the biggest.

But then, it must be wrong, because why would Fitz want him to bring this note here, now? The knife in his back also made him think he was in the wrong place.

"M'not a thief." Gerry felt short of breath.

"You are acting like one." The knife point poked. "Or a murderer, perhaps?"

"Until you see me go in a place that isn't my own and take something out, I'll thank you to keep your name-calling to yourself." Gerry wouldn't even dignify the murderer bit by noticing it.

"Let me see your hands."

Gerry showed his hands, fingers spread wide. "I don't even have a damn weapon."

"Then who are you, and what are you doing here?"

The knife went away; Gerry turned.

The fellow came out of the shadows a little. A tricorn hat, covered by a cape's hood. When it was a fairly clear night with only a wisp of fog.

A blue velvet cape.

Gerry looked at the young man's sharp jaw and fell back a step. "You don't… you don't know who lives here, do you?"

"I know a lot of things."

"I was just… A friend of mine told me to bring this here and I don't mind saying, I'm not sure why or even how. It's the middle of the night and if I knock at the door…"

"Bring something here? To *this* house?" A leather glove, heavy, came out of the folds of the cape. "Give it to me."

"My friend told me to deliver it to this house."

"And here you are, at this house. Hand it over."

"Look. I don't feel good about what I just did. Fizzie's a

good man and he looked in a tight spot, and I just walked away and left him. So don't push me to put the letter he gave me in a place he didn't tell me to put it. I've got to do this for him." Gerry shook his head, looking up at the skies. "God help me, I hope I didn't just leave him to die."

The change that came over the Caped Count was almost too fast to see.

He grabbed Gerry by one wrist, turning him and twisting the hand till Gerry bent over from pain; then let Gerry's weight take him to the ground.

And knelt on him as he searched all of Gerry's pockets.

His coat pocket tore a little as the heavy gloved hand wrenched it wide to take out the folded piece of paper.

"Be careful of that paper, you sewer-clod. A man may have just died for it."

* * *

Fitz' legs did not really fit within the cab.

"My legs don't fit," he said, and as Burgiss sat next to him, a knife point in Fitz' ribs, Fitz lifted his knee nearly to his ear and stuck his foot out the window.

"Stop that!" Burgiss' fist was fast, and might have done some damage to Fitz' ear, he'd hit so hard.

But Fitz kept squirming. "I do not *fit* in this *cab!*"

"Well I couldn't cut yer *legs* off before I put you *in* it!"

Fair point, thought Fitz, and stuck a hand out of the window next to his leg.

Surely someone would notice that.

Just who, he didn't know. But though all his affairs were in order, as in battle, he found he wasn't ready to die.

* * *

TELLA'S HANDS were shaking as she unfolded the paper. And it wasn't because the thick gloves made it difficult.

Her eyes couldn't focus.

Finally she made out the words in the dim light of the stars.

I, Lord Henry Fitzwilliam, owner of Mercywall House on Grosvenor Square, London, write this to document that Mr. Cudjoe Stuart, employed as a butler there, is a free man, owned by no one and indentured in no way, and moreover that he has always been a free man.

Signed,

And Fitz' signature was as large and sweeping as the rest of him.

"Where is he?" Her voice rasped with no effort at all.

"He was at th' Bottle an' Bird. They left. Them fellas he was with, they all left together."

"Where did they go?"

"I don't *know!* I'm *here,* ain't I? Instead o' there. I oughta be there."

* * *

TELLA OUGHT TO BE THERE.

Fitz was in trouble, and she ought to be where he was.

Carefully, deliberately, she folded the paper that Fitz had entrusted to her, slid it into the waterproof leather case she used for documents, and slid it into a deep, hidden pocket in her cloak. She'd protect that document with her life, as Fitz had known she would.

"Do you have children?"

"What?" Gerry squirmed under her knee. "Yeah, but they're grown."

"Do you have a wife?"

He stopped squirming. "Yeah. Yeah."

"Does she love you?"

"More than I deserve."

When Tella levered herself back on her toes and stood, Gerry managed to struggle to his feet. He brushed at the dirt on his trousers, the front of his coat.

It had a neatly mended tear on the cuff, Tella saw.

Yes, he had a wife, and yes, she loved him.

"Go home."

"I won't."

* * *

As the Caped Count shifted his weight, his cape swinging, there was a rustling, clacking noise behind Gerry.

Already tense, he whirled.

At first he could see nothing; but when he bent to look, he saw a small… something, resting on the ground. A little piece of leather wound on a springy twist of raw wool, strung between the legs of a split stick.

He picked it up. The wool had untwisted, slapping the leather against the ground several times, when it hit.

That was all there was.

Someone had thrown it. To make noise and distract him.

Likely the Caped Count.

Who of course, when Gerry looked, had disappeared.

CHAPTER TWENTY-FIVE

This was different from war, Fitz realized as he tried to collect his thoughts after yet another hit to his face.

His had never been a beautiful face, and it certainly wouldn't be now.

Fitz thought of the wound he had taken in battle, the weeks of healing, the fevers and the pain. The wise surgeon who knew how to bandage it and let it heal. The work of loosening the skin and muscle before they knit together, keeping his arm working as he had.

Slow pain.

This was different. This was a very fast pain, he thought as Burgiss hit him again in the ribs.

Something cracked inside, and it was a terrifying sensation.

But after all, Fitz could separate some of his mind from the terror. He was going to die, and it would be painful, but he had known this was coming from the moment he saw these men in the Bottle and Bird.

Just what Tella had been afraid of.

Except not. What truly frightened her had been that she would see it. That it would be because of her.

This wasn't. This was because Fitz had run straight into a street fight without a second thought and, without knowing, had gotten far too close to a murder.

He hoped Tella knew, hoped she would know, that this was not because of her.

"I need ta find your friend in blue."

Fitz spit out some blood. When he opened the eye that still opened, he saw dark rich wood, crystal, finely patterned wallpaper in many colors. This was someone's very fine house. Someone on whose no doubt very fine carpet Fitz was now bleeding.

The part of his mind that asked questions of everyone he met still worked. "Does this house's owner know you plan to kill me here?"

* * *

Burgiss just shrugged. He couldn't hide his annoyance. Fitz had answered no questions and kept asking them.

Not that Burgiss was foolish enough to answer, though yes, Fitz would soon be dead. But Burgiss wouldn't kill Fitz till the Caped Count was in his hands, and that might take a while. This could last for days, if need be.

Fitz didn't know that. Burgiss needed to give him a prod. "If y' don't start answerin' questions soon, I'm goin' to get my knife out and start cutting off parts till y' do."

"More blood on the carpet." Fitz looked dizzy, the eye that was open a bit muzzy. Surely he would answer Burgiss' questions soon. Tell him where to find the blue caped bastard.

Burgiss bent over to look into Fitz' face, pulling his head upright by his hair. Fitz started to yell, smothered it. They both understood the rules. If Fitz yelled loud enough for anyone to hear him, Burgiss would simply kill him now.

Fitzwilliam even seemed to understand that he wasn't getting out of this alive no matter what. Which, actually, didn't help.

"Th' house's owner's away, an' too cheap to keep servants on. He has a watchman. I pay the watchman. When th' owner comes back, oh, say sometime this winter, he could squawk because he's missin' a very expensive carpet. He'll never know it's in th' Thames with you inside. You belong to me now; I'm the one who decides if I keep ya or kill ya. You're livin' because that's what I want, right now. So stop askin' questions. And answer. What d'you know that you didn't print, and where's your mate?"

* * *

Fitz' breath heaved in his chest. He wasn't going to answer any questions, and he would stop asking them when his last breath was gone.

"Why would I tell you anything?" was the only question he really had in mind.

* * *

"Because I'm a businessman, and I'll do whatever I have to real slow, if I have to."

* * *

Tella did not go lightly through the Bottle and Bird.

She tore in like a whirlwind, checking the few corners and behind the bar, ending by grabbing Charlie the barkeep by the front of his shirt.

"Where did they go?"

Charlie, smart man that he was, didn't have to guess hard. "If y' mean Fitz, those big brutes went out the front wi' 'at mean-looking fellah, an that's what I know. Honestly, I'd tell ya more if I knew it. Don't like those types."

She crashed out the door, back into the street.

Standing in the middle of the street's hard-pounded clay, Tella turned in a circle.

She was alone in a crowd.

Shopfronts and dwellings with all kinds of lights surrounded her; the street was full of people. The sun was down, it was dark, but the night was young, and people were everywhere.

Hundreds of buildings, thousands of people. All of London's streets.

And she had no idea, none, where to look for Fitz.

She fell to her knees.

Why had she thought that watching him die would be the worst thing she could imagine?

He'd written that letter as his last act. No, he'd sent someone with it to her house as his last act. Clearly a duty he wanted to discharge before he died.

Rocking back and forth on her knees, shoving her gloved hands into the bones above her eyes, Tella pulled her arms into her body tight, and she *screamed*.

Over and over her brain kept running through the same thoughts—Fitz dying alone, now, without her, her mother's blood running between the cobblestones in that small street, the lights and doorways and vast nothingness of a London *full* of people but no Fitz.

How long had it been since they'd taken him?

How long did he have left?

"Child, you'll hurt yourself."

Dimly, Tella realized that the voice was talking to her.

She opened her eyes.

There was an old woman standing in front of her, tugging on her arm. Tella hadn't felt a thing.

"Stop crying now, tell me what's wrong."

Coming back to herself, Tella looked again. The street was quieter, because everyone was looking at her.

Several were coming her way.

A group of women from the bawdy house. And from the Bottle and Bird. And from the alleys where apartments sat over the closed-up shops.

Nearly all women. A few half-grown boys.

Coming to her.

"No, don't—" Don't what? She was the one who'd stood in the street and made herself a spectacle. "Go on, go home."

"Never mind, lad, tell us what's wrong." The old woman now had half a dozen younger ones at her elbows. And they all nodded.

Looking at them, Tella thought… she thought some of their faces were familiar.

The old woman clicked her tongue. "You've helped enough of us here, child, you ought to know we'd do you a good turn if we could. What is it? What do you need?"

Tella's throat was raw and dry; perhaps the scream had lasted.

"You saw me help you?"

"Witless, he's gone witless." The old woman rested a hand on Tella's shoulder, patted it.

The faces swarming around her were young and old, frightened and determined, and she couldn't believe it. Couldn't believe they were there.

She'd always thought they'd forgotten her the second she was out of sight.

"I never…"

A little honesty might be her last chance.

She said, "Can any of you fight?"

* * *

A MURMUR RAN through the little crowd gathered around Tella.

The old woman waved at them in a *shushing* slash of her hand. "Poor lad. Used to be so clever, too. Here, you, help him up."

He. They still saw only the Caped Count. That was good. Safer for her.

Not so safe for them.

"*Can* any of you fight? I need hands."

But she couldn't endanger them unawares. They'd all been through that before. That was how they'd met her.

"I need some hands for a fight with the men who..." She choked a little. "The men who took my friend away. Fitz. You've all seen him around. I know you've seen him in the Bottle and Bird. The tall man. No hat."

"A fight?" one asked. "Like a brawl, you mean?"

The milling figures of the little crowd hemmed and hawed and looked about. A boy barely in his teen years raised his fist. "You bet I can." The lads with him cheered. "We'll go with ya!"

But most of the crowd were women.

After some shuffling among them, one woman, squarely built, stepped forward. Even her jaw looked muscular.

"I can use my fists, I can take a hit."

Tella nodded. "I believe it." She looked like she boxed at Gentleman Jackson's club on the week-ends. "You work in a grain mill?"

The woman cracked her knuckles. "Butter maid."

"Your name?"

"Ellen."

Ellen the butter maid had clearly seen some things.

"Glad to have you, Ellen. But I need a few more hands. I can pay. I know your time is your money. Do you know of anyone else who could help?"

Two of the women from the bawdy house stepped forward. Tella examined them closely. They certainly didn't have the raw power of the butter maid. "Have you any weapons?"

Looking from right to left first, both women then reached down to grasp their hems—and completely raised their skirts.

Baring all their birthright gifts to the world, and the garters at the tops of their stockings that featured daggers, one on each thigh.

"Plus I've this," said one, producing a cudgel from somewhere.

"Oh, we've all got those," scoffed one of the other light ladies, waving her own cudgel, and there were murmurs of assent throughout.

Tella felt a tiny spark of hope.

"Ladies, we must find out where those men went. If you spread out and ask everywhere you see, we should find the direction in which they departed, and follow them. But it must be quickly."

* * *

Fitz did lose consciousness.

When it came creeping back, he still had enough wits about him not to show it.

"Mr. Burgiss, you have made a tragedy out of a predicament."

Fitz didn't open his eyes. It wasn't hard to keep his

breathing shallow; the sharp pain in his ribs every time he took a breath made it too easy, in fact.

But didn't he know that voice?

That was their man in the green coat.

And then someone else spoke. *A woman.*

"A tragedy, Mr. Storey, is when people act as they must due to their natures, and suffer the consequences. This is dangerously close to farce."

"My apologies, madame. I'm afraid this is Mr. Burgiss acting as it is his nature to act. It is my mistake to have hired him; he cannot act in any other way."

"I'm standin' *right here*," Fitz heard Burgiss snarl.

"As long as we are sharing our faults," said the woman, "mine is that I thought you could be trusted with difficult work, Mr. Storey, including hiring people to do whatever must be done. It turns out you're just a shopkeeper after all."

That seemed to pain Storey. "Madame, a mere shopkeeper cannot arrange for fire brigades to look the other way. Nor can a mere shopkeeper find buyers for the illegal timber you have brought to Britain, not even when your competitors' lumber mysteriously burns."

"Have I insulted you? My apologies. I suppose no shopkeeper likes the truth."

"This ain't keepin' shop." Burgiss clearly did not like conversation going around him. "Neither of you has the sack to do what's got to happen, and that's why you need me."

"Do I?"

At the lady's dry question, Mr. Storey rushed to fill the crackling silence. "Let us not break the fragile ties that hold us all together now, when we are so close to our goal."

"Only one of my goals, and far from the most important. And I do not wish to be tied to you, or your poorly trained dog. I want no ties at all. I was foolish to give you the direction of this house without knowing what you intended to do. Clean it up, Mr. Storey. Clean it all up."

The sound of a lady's shoes walking, and skirts rustling, disappeared into the distance. Fitz thought he heard a door somewhere close.

But he made sure to hold still. For the tension here was thick.

"If ye're thinkin' to clean me up," said Burgiss, with a furious hiss, "know my gunmen belong to me."

"Mr. Burgiss," and Storey sounded as cold and hard as Fitz had yet heard him, "I *pay* them."

After a few long, long moments more, whatever contest of wills held them silent was broken. Storey spoke again. "Clean up your mess, with no more mistakes, and you may be back in my good graces, and our employer's. But I won't take your word for anything, you must know. I'm watching you."

Burgiss snorted. "You're goin' ta watch me pull his fingers off?"

The fear his words caused in Fitz were followed by a warmth, a calm, deep down inside. Yes, he had regrets, but he'd had his bright sharp life. It had been enough. And on top of that, he was the luckiest man in the world.

He'd loved Tella.

* * *

IT WAS DARK NIGHT BUT, travelling in her pack of companions, Tella felt exposed as if in sunshine. People could see her, on all sides; an attack could come from anywhere. Her skin was crawling.

But it couldn't be helped, and the pack was making very good progress.

None of the women were shy, and Tella was taken aback at their willingness to open doors and shout inside.

They just opened their mouth and let *anything* out. Tella had never been in such frank company. She found herself wishing she had talked more, to all of them.

But they apparently knew her well enough to help her. Once she'd asked.

They also didn't hesitate to accost strangers on the street, and they wouldn't be pushed aside. Tella had never marshalled a personal mob before. She'd have to keep an eye out for night watchmen. They would all be taken up for rowdy behavior if they weren't lucky.

Very quickly, they had answers.

Along the trail where the three men had taken Fitz, bystanders had noticed. Not respectable passers-by, or shop customers. But people who lived here.

Some of them knew Fitz, and all of them had wondered at the sight of a tall man being escorted away by such evil looking characters. Without his hat.

And many of them, quite a few, knew the mean-eyed man all too well.

Burgiss had put Fitz in a cab. Tied him up.

"Up that crossroad, they went right," said one of the fastest-moving interrogators, a maid from the tavern apparently named Meg.

Perhaps the one Fitz had tried to lure onto his knee that first night they'd been there looking for information. She seemed quite committed to finding Fitz.

Well, all right, Tella thought to herself.

* * *

DAN HEARD the commotion heading up his street and turned his lamp down to see out. There was little fog; it had been colder than usual.

The tumble of voices was followed by a crowd of people—he could just see them. Mostly women.

Shouting and charging up the road like they were out to do someone dirt.

Quickly, Dan slipped down his stairs.

* * *

ONE OF THE knife-wearing women trotted back to Tella in the center of the group. "How about a cab with a foot and a hand sticking out? Sounds like our fellow, maybe?"

If Fitz had been taken against his will, he'd leave any kind of sign he could.

And truly, Tella had never seen a cab with a foot *and* a hand out the window at the same time.

"Sounds like our lad."

Without another word from her, the little band surged in that direction.

What were they doing? What was she doing *with* them? She should be doing this by herself. Safer for everyone.

But she couldn't have done this by herself.

They couldn't know that they were saving her life in return. Trying to, anyway.

But Tella knew. The flood of gratitude she felt at every step would have overwhelmed her, had she not needed to stay on her feet to find Fitz.

* * *

COMING UP ON THE REAR, Dan tapped the shoulder of someone he knew.

"Ruth, what's going on?"

That lady whirled, both fists up and looking for a fight, but dropped them when she saw it was only Dan Fox. "We're helping 'at caped fellow find his friend."

"What friend?"

"Eh, 'at fellow what writes 'e stories. You know 'im."

That fellow? Dan *did* know him. Likely was the only one here who knew the man's name and where he lived. "He's not at home, then?"

She snorted. Then ran; their little band was moving quickly, and she intended to keep up.

Dan sprinted after her.

"'At bastard what's been tryin' to steal us away stole *'im*, right out o' Bottle an' Bird. Tonight!"

"And what are you lot going to do?" Dan looked around. Aside from a couple of half-grown lads and the Caped Count himself, who wasn't much burlier, it was women from the neighborhood, women from the streets where they sloped down to the river.

"We're goin' t' get 'im *back!*"

Dan went to grab Ruth's wrist; she shrugged him off. "You see," he hissed, "this is why I didn't want to get you those knives. They give you a false sense of security. You were supposed to use them only in a catastrophe."

Ruth tossed her reddened hair and gave him a pitying look. "And where would any of us be without t' fellow in t' blue cape? If we don't look out for each other? Wake up, Danny, it's a cata-stafa."

Dammit.

"You didn't tell him you had a knife?"

"I *showed* him. Glory did too."

"Dog's balls." Ruth gave an exaggerated gasp. Dan rolled his eyes. "Sorry." They'd lost their marbles, all of them.

Dan didn't like to run towards danger. And he had his own reasons for wanting to stay alive.

But he'd better join in.

* * *

"That's it."

Ellen bumped Tella with her shoulder, and pointed at the house.

"The cab went there. Stopped and seemed to take a while letting folks out. They went in a group, slow. Like Fitz was tied up, maybe?"

The rough and tumble little crowd of people came to a quiet stop, of their own accord.

And looked at the Caped Count.

Without conscious thought, Tella flattened herself to the wall, as invisible as possible, and waved the rest of the little band behind her, to hide around the corner.

They shuffled and murmured and went where she pointed.

Surveying the length and width of the house, one part of Tella's mind captured every detail of its hulk and the surrounding space. The height of the floors, the closed and darkened windows, the locked gate that edged the road and led down to the kitchens.

"Wait for me here."

There was a burst of whispering dissent behind her. "We're comin' wit you!" "Nah!" "What're ya thinkin'?" "Never say so!"

"I can move faster by myself."

The butter maid, Ellen, just shook her head. "But not stronger."

Tella looked over all their faces. They all nodded.

She couldn't say they didn't know what danger was; they did, every one of them.

Would it be rude to tell them bluntly that she hadn't saved them before to get them killed now?

Or that just because she'd saved some of them, didn't mean they owed her?

Fitz' voice came back to her, along with that keenly piercing look he gave her right before he laughed. *Everyone here has a story, Fred; you just don't know what it is.*

Tella had thought their story was what they told him.

Fitz had known their story was the choices they made.

Somewhere inside she'd known that already, known he was right.

It wasn't the streets she loved, with their fog and refuse and everlasting stones. It was the people. These people. They deserved to live out their whole lives, as her mother hadn't. She wanted that for them.

And God above, they seemed to want that for her. And Fitz.

She couldn't make them leave her alone; she couldn't *make* them do anything. She could only do what she could do.

"Anyone who wants, go on home now. I'd rather you did."

Not one of them left.

Tella wished her uncle were here. She was in possession of a small untrained force, and needed to capture a fortress that was weak but manned. She wished for his experience and his training.

But then, as she thought of him, and thought of *training*, all the hours and days and months of his voice telling his every story over and over again came back to her.

She had the training. In a way, she had him here right now.

It was Lord Preston's voice in her head that said *You are*

not capturing a fortress. You need not take the building; you only need your man back. You need to find him, retrieve him, and retreat. There are many entrances and many exits; the enemy may use them all, and so may you. What do you do?

Fitz had been walking when they had taken him. He could easily be on any floor. She had to find him.

Hopefully he could walk out.

Tella remembered something her father had said. *The night watch are mainly there to keep things quiet. The rich of London don't want their sleep disturbed.*

If they made much noise, they'd rouse not only Fitz' captors but the rest of the street. The night watch, if they came, would not be friendly to her motley band. A three-sided brawl was to be avoided.

But could they be used?

When she looked back again over her shoulder at her people, again their whispers died out. They were watching her. Waiting to see what she would do, her signal telling them what to do.

And Tella heard her mother's voice.

Let's not stay here, Donnatella. Come with me. You don't have to be afraid.

Pressing her back into the stones, Tella squeezed her eyes shut. If she couldn't keep her mother safe, what could she do for Fitz? What stood between one loss and another?

She didn't know.

But Julia had. *You do have friends, you know.*

"All right, listen very carefully." Her voice was raw from her screams earlier and the thick night air; she had no trouble sounding like the Caped Count should.

They listened.

"When we are through with this, you scatter. So I'll tell you now. I already owe you a debt I can never repay. If you need anything, ever, you leave me a note at the Bottle and

Bird with Charlie and I will help. Anything. No matter what happens. Got that?"

There was a round of fast rustling nods.

They looked committed. She would take their commitment.

There could be servants in there that didn't deserve to wake up inside a pitched battle. She heard her uncle warning her that it was dangerous to juggle fighters and spectators. She'd get them out if she could. Burgiss and Storey's men were another matter. By forcing this confrontation, they'd actually simplified her problems.

It would be a tremendous effort to keep Fitz, and any servants, safe, *and* avoid killing any of Fitz' captors.

Tella was not going to make that effort.

"You can attack anyone besides me and Fitz. Meg, you come with me and we'll try to get any servants out. All of you, chase out anyone you can but don't get hurt. You don't *have* to kill anyone but don't worry about their safety, worry about yours. I expect every one of you to come out of that house. You can use anything you find for a weapon."

"Got it," said Ellen, cracking her knuckles.

Tella would send her through the kitchen. She'd be hell with an iron kettle.

"There are four doors." She carefully pointed them out. "Let people leave, but not with Fitz. Don't let him walk past us or—or be carried out. Got that?"

They all nodded again.

She needed time. Time to explain how to enter together, how to communicate silently, how to meet again at a specific point.

There wasn't time.

"Check rooms before you go in, and if Fitz is in there, don't go in, find *me*. Stay silent, keep moving. *Don't* get hurt.

Watch out for each other. And when I start the big noise, well, you make noise too. Everyone understand?"

They all nodded.

"All right. Can you all count to a hundred?"

Mostly nods.

Tella pointed at the black-haired man. "You—what's your name?"

"Dan."

She nodded. "And you ladies with knives?"

"Ruthie," supplied one of the armed ladies, "and Glory, that's 'er.'"

Quickly, Tella made them all say their names.

She'd by God remember these names and faces.

"Dan, I don't suppose you know how to pick a lock and have anything for that with you?"

The man's nod was an encouraging surprise. "Yes, and yes."

"Brilliant. Take the back. You, Ruth, go with him, count to three hundred while he opens the door. Once you've reached the number, go in. Wait to reach the number. Ellen, I'll let you and Glory in through the kitchen. I'll unlock the door first, you count to a hundred fifty, then go in. Meg and I will take the front."

Then she turned an eye to the half-grown lads. Yes, one was the boy she'd rescued the night she'd first met the mean-eyed man. He couldn't have more than fourteen years on him. She pointed a finger at his nose. "I have a job for you. You stay right on this corner and you keep watch. I mean you grow eyes in the back of your head and watch both ways on this street. If the night watch or anyone else looks about to go in that building, you make all the noise on earth. Once you hear *our* noise, same business. *Noise.* Till the sky falls, if necessary. A ruckus to bring all London running. Do you understand?"

The boy went from ready to argue hotly to grinning. "Aye. We will." And his two new friends agreed.

"Please. My friends." They'd never know how much she meant by that. "Please, Mr. Fitzwilliam and I are both forever grateful for your help. We're both begging you. Don't get hurt."

She had so much more she wanted to say to them and they had to hurry.

"You've got it, right? If someone runs, let them run. Let's see if we can give them a few reasons to run."

CHAPTER TWENTY-SIX

She took Meg with her round the back, the east side, to get the lay of the building there, see Dan's door.

She noted the two-story windows on the north side; a room there extended the whole way.

She thought she saw a faint glow in those windows, but she could have been wishing. Nothing moved.

Trusting Dan could do what he claimed, she left him and Ruthie to it and slipped around the south wall to the locked western gate in front.

From the depths of her cloak she slid the thin bits of Huntsman steel she kept for manipulating the mechanisms of locks. They were almost too delicate for the thick lock built into the iron gate.

A few short moments later she vanquished the kitchen door lock too, then left Ellen and Glory there and swept back up to the front door itself. Her cloak and dark hat kept her mostly hidden.

Meg, beside her, wore a thin cloak too, and clutched her hood tight around her head. Her face was set.

A guard ought to be watching inside the foyer. She

opened the door wide enough that both she and Meg could be seen.

Yes, there he was, lounging against a sideboard table. It held a vase full of early lilacs. He held a musket.

Just as Tella had prompted, Meg flounced in and walked right around him. "Hel-*lo*," she said with her widest smile.

And as the man gaped at inviting Meg, he quietly collapsed. In a shower of porcelain fragments.

Tella was pleased. Her uncle's lectures on where to hit heads to make men collapse had always been academic.

* * *

ELLEN AND GLORY picked their way through the dark of the kitchen; there was no light but a slight glow from the banked hearth.

They woke the kitchen boys, shushing them fast and whispering they'd be safe if they ran outside quietly, quietly, and down to the next street.

Why they should run wasn't mentioned, but, confused, the boys did as they were told.

Ellen did indeed find herself an iron kettle, one with three stubby legs for the coals and a good worn comfortable handle.

Silently, she offered it to Glory, who just shook her head and waved her knife.

Not put off, Ellen snatched up the kitchen's cleaver. It had the size and shape of a battle-ax.

Glory, eyes wide, waved her own knife harder. She'd stick with that.

Slowly, silently, they stole closer and closer to the indoor stairs. Putting their faces close before they set foot on them, they found a man there in the gloom, sleeping, cuddling a musket in his arms like a baby.

Ellen just looked at Glory and shrugged. She raised the kettle.

Glory made a *stop* motion with her hand. This one was hers.

She leaned over the man and said in a professionally seductive voice, "Let this go, big man, we can't have any fun till you put that gun down."

Smiling in his sleep, he surrendered his weapon.

It confused him, moments later, when Ellen grabbed his collar and shook him awake.

"You want to fight, or run?"

Later, Ellen wanted to believe he ran because she was threatening him with the kettle, but she had to admit it was probably because Glory was pointing the gun at him as if she knew how to use it.

* * *

DAN HAD his own reasons for being good at sneaking quietly into houses, and Ruth had a few too.

None did much good; they met a guard right inside their door.

He looked tired as hell, which might have been why he made the mistake of grabbing Dan around the neck as if he were harmless.

And apparently thinking Ruth was harmless too.

As Dan wrestled the man along the wall, he turned the man's back to Ruth.

And Ruth grabbed his hair and stuck the point of her knife into his back.

"I'd be happy to try killing a man," Ruth said, really quite cheerfully as the man froze, practically holding his breath.

"No no, no no no, no no." He wasn't fighting *now*.

Dan watched his every move as slowly, slowly, the man lowered his arms.

So when the man lurched, swinging his fist behind to try to meet Ruth's head, Dan charged forward, slamming his own head into the man's gut.

As he lay choking and rolling on the floor, trying to catch his breath from the deep, hard blow, Dan hissed to Ruth, "Got anything I can use to tie him up?"

Ruth flipped the man over on his stomach, still trying to breathe, pulled his hands behind his back, and knelt on them. "Surely we can find something."

* * *

EVERY STEP NEEDED Tella to stretch all her senses as far as they would go. She was looking, listening, feeling, smelling all around her, desperate to find others before they found her.

Her whole little band must be in the house by now. It would be lucky if they'd dispatched all the guards. They'd had surprise on their side and Tella had some hope. She was due for some luck.

She heard a footstep. Tella crouched down, Meg beside her. Luck was fickle.

It was Ellen, and Glory.

Tella waved them to her right; she'd go left, to those two-story windows. She thought Fitz likely to be there; she was *certain* someone there was still awake.

Still, she checked the rooms off the entryway as she went —a library, a ballroom—with Meg following close behind her.

As they got closer to the door at the hallway's end, Tella heard voices.

She and Meg stopped together at the foot of a servants'

staircase.

Tella turned and looked back. Ellen was out of sight, but she just make out Glory.

Tella waved in a way she hoped conveyed that people were in this room, and to *stay back.*

Glory waved as if she understood, and disappeared from sight.

Quietly, quietly, Tella breathed, "Can check for servants? All the way up, check every room? Don't get into a fight. Just get people out."

Meg nodded.

Brave Meg, with no weapon. And Tella was sending her up there alone.

Tella reached into her cloak, pulled out one of her knives, meant for throwing. It was one dense piece of perfectly sharp metal.

Meg nodded, eagerly, and took it. Disappeared up the stairs.

Tella gave her enough time to reach the next floor, even though every muscle in Tella's body pulled her forward.

There were voices in that room.

She needed to see inside.

But she'd be damned if she'd go in at their level.

* * *

DAN CONSULTED Ruth in whispers when they found the main hallway. "Keep going up?" A grand stairway swept up before them.

Ruth just shook her head *no* and pointed. They were just yards from Ellen and Glory.

"The caped man found Fitz. Down there." Glory waved down the hallway, then stopped as if her waving hand might draw attention.

"Then where is the bastard?" hissed Dan. Because the door to which Glory pointed was very closed.

"Up the servants' staircase, a few seconds behind Meg. I think he wants us to stay here." Glory jerked her head toward an archway. "Maybe a little outta sight?"

"I suppose. Until there's a big noise."

"I'm lookin' forward to the big noise," Ellen said very quietly.

* * *

THE STAIRS SHOULD HAVE lead to *something* that would let Tella into that great room.

They didn't. There was only a smooth wall.

When she put her ear to it, she heard very faint voices.

She didn't have to think about it, she trusted her senses. That room was two floors. The upper level was right in front of her. There was likely a way in.

She trusted what she knew like she trusted that voice of her darling uncle's in her head.

Like she should have trusted her senses every time she'd seen Fitz.

Moving to her right with careful slowness, defeating any creaking telltale floorboards, Tella found it. A little nook, holding a modest door that led left. That had to be it. A balcony? A gallery?

Then held her breath. Footsteps came down the stairs.

It was Meg, leading an old man in only a night shirt, his hair topsy-turvy as if he might have been gagged.

She nodded to Tella, who nodded back.

He and Meg disappeared down the stairs.

Tella backed against the wall. The door before her was now the whole world.

Surely that was the smallest flicker of light she saw at the base of the door.

So close. She was so close, now. She couldn't be too late.

Her past was past, but her future was right in front of her.

* * *

FAST AND PRECISE, Tella picked tiny bundles from hidden pockets. Bundles wrapped in parchment.

Three gritty cigars, with fuses embedded in their tips. A shallow tin held a marching row of tiny twisted papers, like musket cartridges, but with cotton stuffed in between. Very carefully, she set it down.

A second tin held slivers of wood tipped with gum.

Gingerly, delicately, she produced a flat round canister and opened it. It smelled like the fires of hell. Hopefully it wouldn't give her away because she planned to do that herself. Inside, a woolen pad obviously held sulfur.

When Tella held the gum end of a small wooden splint against the sulfur pad, it burst into flame.

Briefly she considered setting fire to the house. If she must, to get to Fitz, she would. But fire in London was the definition of a double-edged sword.

She shouldn't have to do that.

But she could make them think she had.

Holding the burning Chancel igniter to the three fuse ends, she lit all three gritty cigars at once. Three small bombs that made only smoke, though smoke of an eerie green which she found particularly effective at persuading people something very bad indeed had happened.

Then she ground the igniter out with her heel—it would not identify her—as her tins disappeared into pockets. One hand cradled tiny paper cartridges, the other the smoke bombs.

Slipping down the hall, she peered down the main staircase, saw Glory peering up. Gave her a nod to indicate all was well. And dropped a smoke bomb through the railing.

* * *

BACK IN THE NOOK, Tella slowly, slowly opened that door.

She tried to grow eyes on stalks and look around corners. That was a wish that didn't work, so she lay on her belly and peeked in with eyes just inches from the floor.

It was a gallery, its inlaid floor and railing faintly lit from a candle below.

Tella inched in, her cape making her a featureless lump of shadows heaving slowly inside. She left a smoke bomb behind on the floor, about to billow.

Billiards. She could see the polished edges of the table.

Next to one billiard table a man sat tied into a chair. His back was to her. She knew that shaggy hair.

His head lolled to one side.

She would not take time to panic.

One of the musketmen was down there. She thought he might be one of the men who'd chased her from the ship, but she wasn't sure; she'd barely seen their faces.

In front of Fitz, hand raised to strike again, was Burgiss.

Holding her breath, Tella settled her elbows, then the rest of her against the floor. Staying flat, she slid her last smoke bomb through the railing to fall to the floor below.

It made a soft *thud* as it hit but that didn't bother Tella. The point of it was to do what it did: billow frightening green smoke, and make Burgiss shout for someone to find out what was happening.

Behind her, smoke swelled into the gallery and rose toward the ceiling. As it joined with the cloud coming from below, Tella dropped the paper cartridges she held in her hand.

They hit the floor and, even on the softness of the carpet, they exploded.

Their payloads, tiny spoonfuls of sand and gravel, weren't enough to do damage. They were meant to distract. And they did.

Both men down there were peering into the cloud where they'd heard little explosions. The musket man leapt from billiards rack to billiards rack, looking for Tella behind the game cues as Burgiss shouted.

"What the—"

Above, Tella rose out of the shadows and smoke, and drew a knife.

Burgiss was looking and shouting in every direction but up. From here, he was a perfect target.

Then she heard the creak of someone cocking a musket.

* * *

SHE HADN'T WATCHED her left.

The other musketman. On the balcony, with her. Barely five feet away.

One of her beautiful little throwing knives was ready in her hand. But the bore of his weapon pointed straight at her heart.

Tella did not think, she did not calculate or second-guess. The part of her that was trained knew what to do.

Her left hand, by her waist, found by touch the handle of the little snake-whip wound around her belt.

A snake-whip shorter than the span of her arms, and easy to slide free.

She said, "You know,—"

She leaned forward with the words, so he looked at her face and not her hands, and before the gunman realized what she was about, *crack!*

Her left hand lashed and the whip's end grabbed the musket.

Tella yanked with everything she had.

She looked down. Burgiss looked up.

Tella *threw that knife.*

She had the musket, she was in the air, vaulting over the railing before the musketman grasped where his weapon had gone. Dropped and rolled, pointing the musket away in case it misfired.

All in the same moment the hilt of her knife appeared in Burgiss' chest, just to one side of the breastbone.

And she was *screaming.* All silence broken, she screamed as she ran for Fitz, words and sounds she couldn't later remember. Anything to add to the confusion.

Burgiss fell to his knees, clutching the blade. His face was still red with anger, a man who hadn't yet realized he was dead.

The knife in Burgiss' chest, or her screaming and waving a musket, unnerved the man in the billiard racks. He ran.

And tripped over her compatriots who charged in, against all orders, to block his way.

They all shouted too, howling, unholy noises, and echoed by other voices in the street.

Tella had Fitz. He was here. She wasn't frightened; what could go wrong now? She knelt before him, fingers ripping and sliding at the ropes around his chest. But he didn't wake. He was limp and silent. She *was* scared, too scared to feel for a breath; his eyes were closed.

"Fitz." She threaded her arms through his bound ones, her chest to his chest. She couldn't carry him that way. And it wouldn't be good. She knew the crushed look of broken ribs.

Her head pressed his, her hands clutched his hair. She had to get him *out* of here.

Something flew past and thumped into Ellen. Still half-cradling Fitz, Tella looked up. The other musketman was still on the gallery, shouting and throwing all he had left: books. Ellen roared at him, brandishing her kettle.

From outside the howling was now punctuated by the smashing of glass. Someone screamed as if they'd been killed.

The disarmed musketman gave up his book attack, and ran.

Tella checked. Down here the other struggled, with three of her friends—yes, friends—on top of him. Ellen turned to him and swung her kettle. Tella wasn't sure the fellow would make it.

Burgiss had long ago finished falling to the carpet and no longer moved.

She came up on her knees. "Fitz, you *are* smart, so smart not to fight against these and make the knots tighter."

She was breathless, panting, trying to stay calm.

With all the scuffling, she couldn't listen for his heartbeat. But didn't she feel it? Wasn't that flutter under her fingertips his heart? She'd never had to look while her hands were shaking like this.

"Fitz. I'm saying nice things about you. Wake up." Without a glance at Burgiss' face she pulled the knife from his chest and cut away the ropes around Fitz. Her touch said his arms weren't broken.

She held his head, his dear, shaggy head, her mouth close to his ear.

"Henry. Henry, darling. Please wake up. I need you to wake up, we must go. Please."

Pressed her cheek against his.

"Fitz, please. I'm flying at you. I need you to catch me."

And her heart started beating again as his eyes fluttered open.

And looked right into hers.

"Of course, Fred," Fitz said in a broken, battered voice.

CHAPTER TWENTY-SEVEN

Glory's leg was cut.

The second gunman did not get up. Tella assumed he was dead.

But he'd had a knife, which no one knew until he sliced into Glory.

Had he hit her higher up, she would have bled to death in seconds.

As it was, she lay with her fists clenched in the fabric of her skirts, which she'd pulled away from the pain, baring her leg. A leg too small for all the blood that poured from it, just feet from where Burgiss' pooled as well. Glory rolled her face into the carpet, trying not to scream or cry.

Tella had to leave Fitz' side. "She'll be all right. Give me a petticoat. A shirt." Now that Fitz was awake, all Tella wanted was to get him out of here.

But she'd be damned if she left one of her soldiers behind, and she knew Fitz was the same way.

She wrapped the wound, tied it tightly, the great flapping ends of the petticoat Ruth had handed her hanging out from the bundle she'd made of the leg.

Glory was weeping, a few moans escaping her now and then, and she looked frightened. But—"You're doing justice to your name," Tella told her.

Glory managed a small wobbling smile.

Outside, servants from neighboring houses were yelling at their boys in the street to go *away*.

The night watchmen would come soon.

They had to go.

She pulled Fitz' arm around her shoulders, held him like glass, leaned in close.

"I think I know where to take everyone," she murmured. "Have you got any money for a cab?"

She instantly regretted making Fitz laugh, even a little, as he choked and winced.

Inside, she swore to herself that he'd heal, and she'd make him laugh over and over again, for as long as they both should live.

* * *

FOUR HANSOM CABS *clop-clopped* up to the doors of the Shoreton house, in the very darkest hours of the night, before dawn.

One of the young boys, the one who looked almost reputable, burst from a tight crush with three other people.

When the night footman, astonished, answered his knock at the door, the boy, as instructed, said all in a rush before he could be stopped, "I've an urgent message for Lady Julia from Lord Wendover."

Watching from her own cab with her arms still around Fitz and letting his feet hang out the door, Tella thought it took years for the door to open again.

But as she'd expected, there was Julia, a shawl wrapped

around her night rail, eyes as wide as if she'd responded to the shout of *fire*.

Instead of a fire, or Lord Wendover, she found a young man easing a battered and bloody Fitz out of a cab.

The variety of noises she made did not resemble words.

"Wh—fi—I—"

A young man in a billowing cape, whom she did not know.

"Julia."

Julia stopped sputtering her horror and confusion, and looked the young man in the eyes. And saw her friend.

"Lady Julia," Tella said more formally, "Lord Henry has been badly hurt, as well as another friend of ours. I apologize more than you will ever know for imposing, but I need a safe place for both of them that will not draw attention."

With her eyes, she tried to say the rest.

"I see."

Tella was imposing horribly by coming here, and in such dire straits, and with others. And these sorts of others.

She was either a heartless user of people's kindness, or considered Julia a very great friend.

It was up to Julia to decide which.

Julia decided immediately.

"Clarence, fetch some of the other footmen, would you? They needn't wear livery at this time of night. Then tell Mrs. Jones I need clean rags and water in the servants' quarters. We'll take the wounded gentleman and his friend—" She paused at the sight of Glory, limping towards her front door with Ruth on one side and Ellen on the other, "—both his friends to the servants' quarters on the north side, please, away from the street where it will be quieter. And wake Phillip, I need him to go for a surgeon immediately. Lord Henry—"

"Both of them," Tella put in softly.

"—both our ill guests will require a surgeon."

"Wait. Not you—" to Clarence, "—you go, but Lady Julia —" Tella gave Fitz' arm to Ellen, well capable of supporting a wounded person on each side.

And rooted around in the myriad pockets of her cape.

"I have a card—the direction of Dr. Burke's home."

"Good." Julia took the card from Tella's bruised, scraped hand. She stopped, and looked at it.

Took it, and very gently squeezed it.

But she didn't stare into Tella's face. "I'll give this to Phillip myself, ask Dr. Burke to come here. You," she unceremoniously hailed one of the cab men, "Yes, thank you, you *are* already here, may I engage you to take another trip for me, please?"

Tella ungallantly and inappropriately let Julia arrange the cabs—including telling them to wait, please, and she would gladly pay them—to repossess Fitz' arm instead and start helping him to the stairs.

And towards their allotted beds in the servants' quarters. Because, of course, she knew the Shoreton house perfectly well.

* * *

BY THE TIME Julia came in, Tella had Fitz on the bed, slightly propped on pillows to help him breathe, his blood-stained coat, waistcoat, and shirt thrown to the floor. He had no neckcloth any more.

Fitz' bare chest was exposed for Julia's view. And Tella's.

Julia did not comment.

"Keep him covered. He must stay warm."

"Yes, you're right."

Julia had brought a maid, who peered over her shoulder, trying to see. "Clara has done some nursing—your other friend is settled right in the next room. Clara will keep an eye on both of them."

Tella knew that meant that Julia was asking her to leave Fitz' side.

She looked up, knowing Julia knew exactly who she was. "I can't."

But Fitz' hand came up and rested over hers, where it lay, so lightly, across his stomach.

"We have imposed horribly on our hostess, you must oblige her," he whispered.

No. Tella didn't want to leave him again. Not for a moment.

"And you must tell her how grateful you are. And that you do not pay your own cab fare."

This time Tella chuckled, only for a second.

* * *

JULIA WALKED Tella down to her own room. A room Tella had been in hundreds of times.

Though never dressed quite like this.

"I have many questions," Julia said, folding her arms over her chest. "I don't even know where to begin."

"I do. I'm sorry. I'm sorry I never told you anything. I— had reasons but not excuses. Forgive me. Or you need not, I will still be forever grateful. Thank you for this."

The door started to swing open.

Acting without thought once more, Tella slid behind it.

"Julia! What on earth is the meaning of all this hubbub in the middle of the night? Not even, for it is surely near dawn. Have you taken ill?"

"Yes, madame, I feel unwell. I've called a surgeon, in fact."

"A *surgeon*!" Lady Shoreton, her hair neatly capped, pulled her sturdy night rail about herself more tightly. "Is this a barnyard, that we must stoop to people who pull teeth? We will consult a physician, there is a reputable one used by Lady Redbeck—"

"I have it completely under control, Mother."

Tella closed her eyes. She had never heard Julia take that tone with anyone, much less Lady Shoreton.

When she opened them again, and peeked around the edge of the door behind which she was hiding, Lady Shoreton still stood there, motionless, an unyielding Julia before her.

"As I will soon be mistress of my own house, you may rest assured that all your instruction has born its necessary fruit," Julia said quite calmly. "It is only a small crisis, and a few servants are assisting me, so there is no need for your alarm. Is there, Clarence?"

Clarence stood in the hall, awaiting an opportune moment to interrupt. No doubt with an update on the messenger sent to Dr. Burke's home, or the settlement of two bloodied strangers in the servants' quarters upstairs.

He looked back and forth between the imposing, stalwart Lady Shoreton, and soft, sweet Julia. Who, with set jaw, asked him to lie to the lady of the house.

"No need for alarm at all, Lady Julia," Clarence said. "I will return to my post."

"Thank you. I do apologize for the disturbance to your sleep, madame."

Perhaps Lady Shoreton noticed, as Tella noticed, that Julia did not say it wouldn't happen again.

Clearly *something* of import had happened. But Julia said nothing. And gave no inch to her mother's pressure.

Having raised her daughter to be, of course, her daughter, Lady Shoreton had little option but to accept her at her word.

"Of course. I will leave you, then. I hope you feel well

tomorrow. You intended to see Lord Wendover before the evening outing, I am sure you recall."

"I do indeed. Thank you. Good night."

And Lady Shoreton, amazingly, retreated.

* * *

DR. BURKE CAME at a run from the carriage.

After what seemed a decade in Glory's room, he finally appeared in Fitz', where Tella again held Fitz' hand.

"Is that your dressing on the lady's knife wound? It looks good." He was looking at Fitz but talking to Tella.

Fitz couldn't even ask Dr. Burke a question.

Nor did Dr. Burke interrogate his patient. He examined straightaway every part of Fitz he could find, not bothering to tell Tella to leave the room when it came time to roll the patient over and gently remove his breeches.

Dr. Burke was another friend, Tella realized, who wouldn't disappear.

Neither did Fitz protest being stripped, and Tella was soon glad the doctor was so thorough. Beyond the wounds to his body and face, a horrific bruise was purpling near one knee. Dr. Burke examined it carefully to see if it was broken.

Fitz had fallen asleep when the physician tucked the quilts back around him.

In the hall, he kept his voice low. "I've stitched that knife wound on the lady next door, and it will heal beautifully. She's lost a lot of blood; I want her drinking clean boiled water and a little sugar, somewhere she can be cared for, and I want to see how it heals."

"Thank you." She was being polite, she was. But her eyes gave away what news she really wanted, wandering back to Fitz' closed door.

"He's not—" He began again, perhaps realizing that he

355

was not talking to the fighter he knew, but someone young and very attached to that young man. "He's breathing, but he's very injured. I've seen men with broken ribs die for no reason I could discern. You need to keep him from moving if at all possible. I will bandage him, and I would recommend tucking the quilts tightly enough all around him and the mattress that it will hold him motionless."

"Dr. Burke. Please just say that he will live."

"Even if it is a lie? I can't know that yet." He looked haunted.

"*Sir.*" Surely he could tell she was closer to despair than the day she'd come to him with her own ribs sliced open.

"I can only tell you the truth. He has a good chance of living; he has a fair chance of dying. Let us do the best we can. No one's body can take fearful abuse and not risk losing the life within."

"I know. Thank you."

"Are you any good at nursing?"

"I will be now."

* * *

LONG AFTER DAWN, when Julia next slipped into the room and closed the door, Tella woke.

She'd fallen asleep sitting on the floor, her head leaning on the edge of Fitz' mattress, his hand in hers.

Julia, dressed now, put her finger to her lips to tell Tella to stay silent, and put out a hand to help her up.

Julia was, thought Tella, the most beautiful woman in Britain.

Julia drew her into the corner.

"Can you go home?"

"No, of course not." Tella squeezed her hand. It was so

good to be here with her again; she'd missed Julia's face, whether it was frowning or dimpling with a smile.

Right now, Julia's face was sober. "I shall send your father a message that you are visiting me. He won't worry. You must bathe, you know. And I will find a gown we can pretend will fit you."

Tella just raised her eyebrows. They did not share gowns, both because of length and because of measurements of the chest.

"I will find something I can tie back. Something. You must rest, too, you know. If you don't, you will be ill too."

"Honestly, Julia darling, I have never felt stronger in my life." She clasped her other hand over Julia's as well. "Thank you. I can never repay your kindness, your generosity."

Julia looked back at Fitz sleeping in the bed. "You and I have been friends forever, dear. How else could I treat you, *or* the passionate, abiding love of your life?"

"How else *could* you? Many ways. But you are too kind to me, and always have been. Far, far too good for your Lord Wendover."

"Just good enough for him, I promise you. We needn't be good to have love, fortunately for us."

Tella nodded, trying not to let the tears that came to her eyes fall. "I shall always listen to you in future, truly. Always."

"No you won't," Julia said with a mock pout. Well, it was only the truth.

They hugged each other, hard, Tella asking forgiveness with the tight squeeze of her arms and Julia giving it with hers.

CHAPTER TWENTY-EIGHT

When Fitz awoke, Tella was asleep in a chair by his bed. Her hair was down and brushed and gleaming, tied over one shoulder, and she wore a dotted walking dress, but her slippered feet were propped on the edge of his bed as if she still wore the Caped Count's boots.

When he reached out and squeezed her toes in their slippers, she came awake instantly.

"Stay still," she ordered softly. "The best physician I know says you mustn't move too much."

Fitz just nodded. Even if he hadn't trusted her judgment in physicians, *not* moving right now was his favorite plan.

But when her fingers slipped between his, he managed a smile. "I'm so glad you're here."

"I am so, so sorry." Tella was leaning over him, his hand gripped tightly in both of hers.

Fitz just shook his head.

She kept saying it. "I am, so sorry, and I will forever be sorry. I was so selfish. Just at the moment when I should have been brave, I wasn't."

"Sorry? For what? Coming after me? Saving my life?

Never paying cab fare?" Fitz said, squeezing her hand. His voice grew more serious. "You are always brave, Donnatella."

"It isn't enough to be brave for oneself. It's never enough. You were right there, you were with me all along, and I needed to be brave for both of us together." She rested her forehead on her hands holding his. "You always knew it. And I'd heard my uncle's training lectures all my life. I heard it, but I didn't understand. And right at the moment I most needed to be, I wasn't. I should have been. I was so wrong, so wrong, to send you away when I loved you so, and I knew you loved me."

"Everyone's life is their own." He tugged a little, and pulled one of her hands closer to lay his lips against her knuckles. "I wasn't ready to die in Spain. I'm ready now. I had to figure out what I was searching for, and I found it. A bright sharp life, and being lucky enough not to die alone. And I love you."

"Don't—don't speak of dying, Fitz, you know you simply cannot."

He smiled a little, but only a little, since his lip was split. No, nothing dramatic about his Donnatella.

"Well, I would prefer not to," he said, sighing a little.

Her free hand caressed the side of his head. He must need a bath, and a shave. But Tella looked at him as if he were the most dashing young man in Britain.

Which made him feel, he could admit, like he was.

"I got your letter. I would have guarded it with my life—"

"I know."

"—and really, I wanted you to be able to deliver it. I delivered it myself. I thought you would want me to. It was so important, I didn't want you to think I didn't know how much you wanted it delivered. But you must still get just *as well* as if you had to deliver it yourself. I mean—do you follow? Pretend you need to deliver that letter. I didn't deliver it so that you could loll about thinking you had nothing important to do. The things you do are so extraordinary—"

Was she crying?

He tried to reach up to wipe tears from her face. And winced. The bed was still sheeted tightly to hold him in place.

Instantly she leaned over the bed. Took his hand and put it on her cheek.

His thumb stroked her cheek, a tiny motion. "I missed you so much." His voice was almost too soft to hear. "I had so many things I wanted to tell you. Every day. But then, it was almost as if I could tell you. As if you were still with me. As if I could never lose you. Do you know what I mean?"

"I do, darling. I can honestly say that I truly do know exactly what you mean."

* * *

THE BENEFIT of Tella's small family was that it was easy for Tella to walk the half-mile to the Gravenshire house each day, check on her uncle, wave at the chair where her father wasn't, then return immediately to the Shoreton house.

Lady Shoreton hadn't expected an extended visit from Tella so close to Julia's wedding, but Lady Shoreton had stopped telling Julia and Tella what to do every moment of the day.

Tella was still deciding whether that was welcome, or unnerving.

As Tella had a slightly twisted ankle—a reasonable price to pay for jumping from a balcony—there was every reason for Dr. Burke to pay regular visits.

And while in other circumstances Lady Shoreton would have expected to chaperone Tella during the physician's visits, Julia took that over too as though she had already assumed her coming house and name.

Dr. Burke's furrowed forehead eased a little, day by day, until it was nearly smooth.

"It is a good sign that he hasn't—" Despite his familiarity with Tella, the doctor tended to cut his own sentences short.

"Hasn't died. Yes."

"You're going to need to keep him still for another month. I think, though, if we keep his ribs bound, he can turn a little. It's safe to move him, if there's another bed. I don't suppose there's another bed?"

For Fitz' feet hung off the end.

Julia's answer was prompt. "Yes. I will take care of it."

Julia would find a way to explain the acquisition of a larger bed to her mother. Tella wouldn't worry about. That was why she had friends.

"Good." He nodded to Tella. "We will add this to the list of things we shall not discuss, yes?"

"I thought that went without saying, sir."

The physician sighed, a slow sigh, and then Tella remembered what his wife said, that his father had passed away. "Nothing goes without saying."

"I know, Dr. Burke, you are right," and Tella did.

* * *

WHEN SHE WENT BACK INTO FITZ' room, where she spent most of her days, his eyes came straight to hers.

It was disconcerting, being so *seen*, and so often. But Tella was getting better with practice.

She'd given Julia some of the history of the Caped Count, and Julia was still deciding how she felt about her friend taking to the streets at night to thwart those who preyed on the London weak.

But Julia had not changed her mind about being Tella's friend, and that was most important.

The rest of Tella's raiding party, as she thought of them, dispersed. Only Ruth returned once, to check on Glory; Dan Fox brought her to the house. As much as Tella wanted to thank them again, she stayed hidden. It wouldn't do them, or her, any good to know that Lady Donnatella and the Caped Count were one and the same.

Tella couldn't go around being seen by *everybody*.

"Dr. Burke says that nothing goes without saying," Tella told Fitz when she came back to his side.

"You aren't going to spend the rest of the day sitting there again." They both knew, now, that he would recover; and it changed the air between them. Fitz sounded as if that made this different.

"Yes." Funnily enough, unlike those days spent looking for some amusement in her father's house, Tella didn't find sitting by Fitz' bed difficult at all.

And Julia had loaned her some knitting.

Fitz' eyes loved roaming all over her, and Tella was still trying to understand how just a look could be so inappropriate. Because it certainly was.

"Tella, don't torture me," Fitz finally said, softly. He still did not breathe deeply, and likely didn't want anyone to hear.

"Never." She took up one of his hands and threaded her fingers through his. "*That* goes without saying."

"If you are going to send me away again once I'm well, tell me now."

She leaned over him to kiss his forehead, still bruised and pale, the tip of his magnificent nose, then his lips.

"Lord Henry," she whispered, "do you know that you have never actually proposed to me?"

His eyes widened. His shoulders came off the bed as if he

meant to get up; she pressed them back down before resuming her seat.

She couldn't read all of his expression—to her he looked hopeful, and wary too.

* * *

"LADY DONNATELLA," he said, breathing a little quickly, "I have little to offer of my own to give you a comfortable life."

She kept tight hold of his hand in one of hers but pressed her other fingers to his lips. "Shh. Shh, Fitz, I don't wish you to speak badly of yourself now or ever."

He waved his free hand, trying to get her to stop shushing. Instantly she leaned across him to press it, too, to the mattress. "You must keep still!"

"If *you* would stop moving around for a moment, we might accomplish something."

Eyes wide, mouth falling open, she settled back into her chair.

"I can really only offer you myself. Plenty of faults, some good qualities as you may know. Chiefly that I love you, and I wish to do everything in my power to make you happy. Always."

He felt her tears fall on his fingers.

Then Fitz grinned. He'd never had a question he wanted to ask so much. "Will you marry me?"

"Yes. Of course I will, Fitz, thank you—thank you for asking."

Very gently she leaned over him again, this time to press a light kiss to his swollen lips.

"Please get better," she whispered against them. "I have never been the same since I met you and I don't wish to do without you ever again."

"I will do my best."

This time when she leaned back she had a wide, happy smile across her entire face. He'd never seen her smile like that.

It would be a goal, to keep her smiling like that.

* * *

"OH BUT FITZ, do you want to live in the Gravenshire house with my uncle? I don't know if—if you want to be newlyweds there, but the house is so large. My great-grandfather had eight children, and you know they were often all there. There are so many rooms."

"*Eight* children." Fitz felt tired, and he hurt all over, but that also seemed quite a goal. "We must discuss this." He had a feeling he would *love* to herd eight children around, to teach them to march in formation, and do unit maneuvers.

He had a feeling Tella would like it even better.

"Or did you wish to outfit Mercywall House? Mrs. Burke has sent some sketches, but I haven't even bothered to look."

"I don't care." He didn't. "We can live where you like. I suppose I ought to be too proud to take the income my father has given me, as well as the house, but—"

"—but if you use it to finance your work learning about Londoners' lives, and writing about them, it will be worth it."

"Yes. I thought that, a little. You said it better than I thought it. Yes."

"I did understand what you were telling me. That you wouldn't ask me to stop doing what I do. You never have. You never would."

"No. Though I would prefer you had someone to watch your back."

She leaned her elbows on the edge of his mattress. "As I've learned, I always have. I have stories to tell you when you get well. Several very interesting stories that you can never write."

"I will *love* to hear them." He brought her hand to his lips and kissed it, just lightly, again. The pressure on the bruises there stung him a little, but he couldn't wait till he was entirely healed to touch her.

"You really must stop moving."

Fitz frowned. "But the Caped Count's great problem has not been resolved. Burgiss..."

"Burgiss, since you are now well enough for us to discuss this, is extremely dead. And I don't just want Mr. Storey captured. I want Lady Winpole brought to justice."

"I admire your goals, my lady, and I do support them. I will get strong enough to accompany you from time to time—"

"You are too big and slow!"

"—or discuss how to improve your chances when very unscrupulous people are looking for you. They will still be looking for you."

"Oh, I know," said Tella grimly. "But I know who they are. And Lady Winpole cannot be allowed to believe that she is above the law. Not in my Britain. Not in my *London*. I have weapons she'll never have. Not just the stuff in my cape. I have friends."

* * *

GLORY OPENED THE DOOR, took one look at the polished floor and balustrade outside, and shut it.

"I can't just march out there!"

"Not only can you, you must." Julia was wrapping bandages into a shawl for Glory to take with her. "Surely you don't wish to wait till the middle of the night and be hustled out in secret as you were brought in."

"That seems fine."

"Miss Glory, I am more grateful to you than I can ever say. If you are ever in need, I hope you'll come here."

At that, Glory just smiled and shook her head. "I won't, my lady."

They understood one another's looks. Glory would never, under any circumstances, give anyone the impression that her hostess had befriended a night woman. But Julia was grateful.

"Ah, but you must. If you don't wish to stay—"

"This isn't my life, my lady, not interested in it," Glory said quickly.

"So you said. Then you must let me know you are all right. You'll keep your wound clean, won't you?"

"You know I will."

"And—the Caped Count—"

"Shh!" Glory waved her hands to quiet Julia.

"Just between us. He is grateful too, owes you more than he can ever repay. He hopes you'll be well, and that you understand why he hasn't been to visit. But he doesn't wish to cause any more trouble to you, or me, through association."

"Oh, I understand it right enough, never you worry. I'm proud, proud to know him."

Julia nodded. "And he is proud to know you, too. I can tell you so for him."

"I'll slip myself down and not trouble you again."

Julia took Glory's hand. "I will see you down to the cab I've engaged for you, Glory, and tell you again, and forever, thank you."

* * *

"GLORY DIDN'T EVEN SEE ME."

Julia pulled the door of the drawing room shut. Tella lounged a little in the corner of the settee, one foot swinging under the checked lawn of her walking dress.

"She likely saw a fine lady sitting in the room as she passed, and never looked twice, because what has that to do with her?"

"I need to repay them, Julia, I need to find ways of repaying all of them."

"I imagine that they will be visited from time to time." Julia didn't specify by whom.

Now that Julia had met the Caped Count, Tella couldn't have her un-meet him. But they'd discussed it and agreed that their friends in the Bottle and Bird shouldn't know about the Duke's daughter.

"Besides," Julia picked up some fancy stitching work, "I'm not sure that paying this for that is how friendship works."

"Bollocks," said Tella in a way that was reminiscent of her blue velvet cape. "Of course, I'm still working on these things. But I don't think friendship absolves one of the need to repay great kindness. And can we truly be friends, if they don't know all of me? You certainly objected."

"I have known you since you were yea-high, and we've been practically family all our lives. There may be a difference."

"Perhaps." Tella watched her friend's needle. Repairing her friendship with Julia had repaired a great hole in her heart, she knew that.

Though if it came to another broad-scale street fight, she was going to look up Ellen the butter maid.

CHAPTER TWENTY-NINE

The Shoreton social affair was a great success, of course, not only because Lady Julia had planned it, but because Lady Shoreton seemed to have crossed some threshold and no longer fretted that some unforeseen fun could overthrow Lady Julia's impending wedding.

The Duke of Gravenshire's daughter, briefly absent from the social scene, was the same dizzy dancer as always. She danced constantly, in a dress of light and dark blue stripes that everyone agreed had the unfortunate effect of making her look even taller.

No one noticed she'd gotten rather better at remembering faces, and names.

The furor of gossip over her betrothal to a third son, however, was dying down, for several simple reasons: the man was undeniably of noble birth, neither his father nor hers objected, and obviously, he was tall enough to marry her.

And the diamond pendant she wore, her betrothal gift, was a sufficient badge for those who needed to see it that Lord Henry was the right sort of man to marry a duke's daughter. Even though he hadn't attended a social function in weeks.

"Lady Julia, I can never think of such pleasant entertainments," she told her friend as the charades drew to a close with all players laughing.

Tella was sure that if she had to come up with games for guests to play at a ball, they would end with everyone crying, and at some point, weapons would be drawn.

"I am having *such* fun, Lady Donnatella, and half of it is the delight of this ensemble your draper has put together for me." Julia looked absolutely beautiful, her dimples appearing and disappearing all night, and the fetching coral-and-gold gown was only part of it.

"Will the Duchess of Talbourne be attending tonight?" Tella added, as an afterthought, because it wasn't half as interesting to her, "Or of course the Duke?"

"I believe so. It is so exciting! Though of course your own father's attendance is always a great honor."

Tella glanced at the dance floor. The Duke of Gravenshire was dancing, and he seemed to be enjoying it. Perhaps she had underestimated the stress on him of wondering if his only daughter would find happiness.

Now that she had it, he seemed fine.

"You must join me, darling, in encouraging my father to attend more of these things. Soon Parliament will adjourn for the season and he will have no excuse."

"When Parliament adjourns, half these people will retire to the country, of course."

"The more fools they. We will have to entertain ourselves with people who stay in London."

Julia's eyes moved toward the whist tables, though she didn't turn her head. "It is interesting, who decides to stay in London."

"Isn't it?" Tella had told Julia everything. It somehow

made her feel better inside just to *talk* about it. And Julia had proven her worth to Tella's causes time and again.

Tella was through refusing help from the people who loved her.

"I might play a few games of cards myself," Tella said, rising from her chair and fanning herself a little. It was getting warmer, as the days were getting longer.

"I wish Lord Henry were well enough to play." Julia was *not*, however, good at hiding her feelings. And it was clear that if Tella were going to talk to Lady Winpole, Julia wished her to have some sort of military support.

"I can still play games by myself, darling."

* * *

"DO YOU PLAY CHESS, LADY WINPOLE?"

Tella had taken the seat next to Lady Winpole. She had no intention of being the lady's partner.

No one else had joined; perhaps everyone was a bit tired of losing to Lady Winpole.

Tella's question about chess could not seem anything but appropriate to the moment.

"I don't play chess, no." The lady continued to shuffle the cards. "People love to talk about its complexities, but the play itself is not true to life."

"No?" Tella felt a chill go up her spine and had to make a conscious effort to keep her fan swinging carelessly from her fingers. "Whatever do you mean?"

Lady Winpole's eyes only glanced up for a moment, then returned to the cards. "If one has troops, one moves them together, not the artificial restriction of moving only one warrior at a time. Or one does not move at all. A protective concentration would be far more useful in repelling an attack."

"Really? I do not understand the game, I confess it. There are protections and attacks, though, surely, in a game full of knights and kings."

Lady Winpole looked up then. Her eyes were not notable for their color, and yet there was something in her look that challenged one to forget her. Her chin was as firm and resolute as any monarch's. "Knights and kings? Watch the queen's play, Lady Donnatella. She can move the farthest and the fastest. If she were not constrained by the game to benefit the king, she could do far, far more for herself."

Tella nodded, slowly. "As queens must, I suppose."

"As they all too often must. No one protects a queen, no matter what the old knights' tales say. They captured queens as often as they served them. If all the other pieces served the queen… well. As the game is played, the queen is always expendable in the service of the king."

Lady Winpole seemed to have the tiniest, tiniest curve of a smile just faintly catching one corner of her mouth. "If the queen served no one but herself, she would be unstoppable."

"What an interesting idea." Tella could not tear her eyes away from Lady Winpole's face.

She was seeing Lady Winpole, really seeing her, possibly for the first time in her life.

"How frustrating that must be, for a player of your skill," Tella said, slowly and deliberately. "However do you stand it?"

"As I said, I don't. If I were forced to play the game..." Lady Winpole put the deck of cards down, and cut it.

She turned the cut over to show the queen of diamonds.

And smiled before she replaced the cut, putting the cards right back into the order into which she'd shuffled them. "If I were forced to play the game, I would change the rules."

* * *

WHEN MR. STUART answered the knock at the door, he found Lord Henry Fitzwilliam hanging his upper half over the edge of the iron railing to the steps.

"Mr. Stuart!" Fitz righted himself and greeted the butler with genuine joy. "I've come to foist my inappropriate company upon you again, and I bring reinforcements."

"I am glad to hear it, sir. I had wondered at your absence." He did not mention the letter, but his smile went all the way to his eyes.

Fitz did not mention it either; the shame of its necessity was all on his family, after all. "Oh, I generally turn up once people are no longer expecting me. We need to get this plaque that says Ashbury off the front, I think."

Mr. Stuart stepped out to survey the stone tablet set into the front of the house. "It appears set into the original construction, sir."

"I'll chip it out myself if I have to, but I suspect someone better will do it for money. Ah, here is my intended, and her uncle. Lady Donnatella, and Lord Preston, Mr. Stuart."

Tella was walking down the street on her uncle's arm, and examining the building closely, likely for entries and exits.

She, too, as she came up the stairs, greeted the butler. "Mr. Stuart. It is good to see you again. I have brought my uncle to see if he would like to join us here once we are in residence."

"When have you met before? Mr. Stuart." Lord Preston nodded. "It's a house. How much difference does it make?"

"You can't see it from the *stairs*." Tella tugged on his arm.

"It's a house. Your house. You don't want an old uncle cluttering up the place."

"No, I don't, but I would be happy to have *you*. Come see, uncle."

Lord Preston surveyed the carved stone and window-frames that stretched up several stories. "It doesn't have a garden."

"Now how can you tell that from outside?"

Mr. Stuart cleared his throat. "His Lordship is of course correct, there is no garden. The fourth story is narrower than the third, however, and a previous owner of the house did consider building a conservatory there."

"A conservatory in the city! Brilliant." Tella tugged again.

Lord Preston still wasn't moving.

Fitz stepped into the open door and looked round at the old colonel. "We would both be delighted to have you here, sir, if you can bring yourself to leave the splendor of the Gravenshire house. It needn't be all of the year. Please, do come see."

* * *

MOMENTS of peaceful joy like this were worth everything, Tella thought as she watched both precious men disappear into the house together. They came and went, like everything in life, but they were worth it.

She turned to Mr. Stuart. "Whether or not my uncle decides to join us, Mr. Stuart, we expect to take up residence directly after the wedding."

Mr. Stuart acknowledged this with a grave nod. "I'll have the kitchens prepared, Lady Donnatella."

"Thank you. You needn't lay in much. Lord Henry and I intend for the staff to have a holiday, with pay, for two weeks from the wedding day on. We will only be here briefly, and then we will make our wedding trip. A short visit to the Isle of Wight, like my friend Lady Wendover. Ah, and here she is now!" A carriage stopped and swayed just in front of Mercy-wall House. "Lady Wendover can speak for me on any occasion, Mr. Stuart. Please know that I would like her to have anything she wishes."

"Of course." Mr. Stuart watched Lady Shoreton follow her daughter out of the carriage. "And the lady's mother?"

"Slightly less, I think. Lady Shoreton! You are so kind to accompany Lady Wendover. We intend to reside here at least part of the time, and I would so value your insight."

"Whatever Lady Wendover thinks will be fine, I'm sure," said Lady Shoreton, with the kind of careless wave Tella had never seen her make in her life.

"If her ladyship would care to step inside, there is refreshment." Mr. Stuart opened the door wide.

"Yes, I think I'd like that. It is so calming, having one's daughter married, and I shall be twice as happy once you are too, Lady Donnatella. Your mother would be so happy. It must be my duty to feel some of that on her behalf."

Tella curtsied; Lady Shoreton wouldn't welcome a hug on the street no matter how many young ladies around her were married. "Your duty and your right, madam, as your care has been a great deal to me."

"Too little, I'm sure. I wish I could have done more. Your mother would be so proud. Let us all go in."

Julia took Tella's arm. "An entire house to decorate? I cannot wait. Yours may be the fashion sense, but I flatter myself I'm rather good at houses."

"Whatever Lady Wendover says." The words trailed back over Lady Shoreton's shoulder as she went inside. She was practicing them so often, it seemed that she had been waiting to say them for years.

* * *

FITZ FIT in the Gravenshire basement closet. Only just.

But he wouldn't fit up the stairs.

Tella, in her night-time clothes, grinned madly, falling against his chest and gripping him about the waist.

Which he liked very, very much.

But he pretended to grouse a little as he looked up the tiny twisting hidden stairs. "I cannot sneak into your room *this* way."

"Well, you cannot simply march up the stairs."

The wedding was only a few days away. Tella had wanted to set the date as soon as it was clear that Fitz would survive. But Fitz wanted to walk without hobbling at his own wedding.

It had been a very long time. For both of them.

"You are *my* betrothed. It's absurd that I cannot simply go up the stairs."

"Oh yes, that would work *so* well. I can picture Lord Preston meeting you at the top with a saber."

"Why should he be so protective of you *now*?"

Lord Preston not only knew the wedding was in a few days, he had let her jaunt all over London as the Caped Count. He no longer recalled that, and Tella had decided not to tell him again. But he *had* known, and he had let her be exactly who she was. And Fitz knew it, because Tella had told him.

Tella was becoming just a fountain of information, though in select company.

"I think more than anything it is just habit with him, truly," Tella admitted.

"This is an argument for moving to Mercywall House."

"*Your* house."

"As you say. It will be *our* house."

"Mrs. Burke should refit it, regardless. Julia is dying to decorate as well." Tella looked up the tiny staircase thoughtfully. "It would be wise to have a second retreat prepared, would it not?"

"One where I can get up the stairs," Fitz grumped.

"You know," Tella took the lamp from him and set it down carefully, "I know every inch of this room by touch."

"The whole room?" Fitz smiled down into her eyes. "And everything in it?"

"Not yet every single thing in it. There is always a danger, when I bring in something new. Part of the reason I try not to do it."

"I want you so badly I can think of nothing else." Fitz couldn't help that his voice had become rougher. "I thought it might be a nice change to be comfortable, for both of us, while we make love."

"Such leisure. And here I thought you a soldier. A third son can't be so careless either. Surely you'd rather have the contracts signed first? What if I get away?" Her raised eyebrow reminded him that she could, even though she wouldn't, escape. Then she remembered she had no idea if the contracts were signed yet, and dropped her teasing. "*Are the contracts signed?*"

"The wedding is only papers. I already know that you are mine, and I am yours."

* * *

SHE *LOVED* Fitz saying what he felt. She loved the *way* he said them, right out loud. He was having a very positive effect on her, leading by example.

And she *was* dying to touch him. Everywhere. She wanted to explore every inch of him, all the ways she hadn't that first disastrous time. She wanted slow. To convince him, and herself, that he would be there with her, as long as they lived.

And that even if they were separated, she would never be alone.

"And yet," she said, her hands sneaking up to encircle his

neck and pull him down for a kiss, "you've been very skillful in far more dire circumstances."

"My lady, that is slander. That was *not* skillful. The very fact you say so proves how little we know of lovemaking together."

He was right. It hadn't been skillful. It had been desperate.

Here, in the little closet that fit both of them, if a bit awkwardly, it would be a very great effort to make love again, with time for both of them to touch, and taste, and feel, and explore.

Tella was willing to go to that effort.

"In a dire situation, one does what one must, and what one can," she told him.

And kept her eyes on his as she slowly unbuttoned the first of all the buttons on his breeches.

"I prefer we be together, if it is a dire situation," said Fitz, sweeping his arms around her and pulling her against him to lean against the wall.

"Ow," he said without heat, as a small hook full of neatly coiled rope poked him in the back.

"We will make all the necessary adjustments as we go," Tella assured him, and moved him a few inches to one side.

And then joined him in their kiss.

EPILOGUE

The minister mumbled something about *secrets* and Tella nearly panicked.

But no. Her secrets had settled into new configurations. Better ones. Perhaps the right ones. And she had no secrets from Fitz, beside her now.

Beside her smiling. She must have missed a bit, because Fitz reached out for her hand. She gave it.

He whispered in her ear. "You with me in this, Fred?"

Yes. She was. For good and ever. "Yes, always yes."

"Say the words then."

She looked back at the minister. He looked familiar. And a bit puffy. Good heavens, was that the Bishop?

Whoever he was, he wasn't amused. He was impatient, and only repeated the last part. "As long as you both shall live?"

"Yes. I will. I do, I shall. Certainly. Yes."

As the Bishop droned on, Fitz pulled her to fit against him, and again whispered, like a particularly doting bridegroom, "Your reputation as dizzy is secure."

"Hush. I was thinking. And this is going on forever."

Out of the corner of her eye she saw him look at the floor to hide his smile.

Their hands kept hold of each other, and Tella felt that ought to be enough.

* * *

THE FLOOR-TO-CEILING WINDOWS of Talbourne House glittered with morning sun, making everything inside glitter too. Including Tella, whose draper had fashioned a Grecian-inspired gown dripping with crystal beads, their edges sharp and shiny as tiny knives.

It was hard to concentrate on all the sparkle, especially as Fitz was clean, wore new clothes, smelled delicious, and kept smiling at her with those eyes that said he couldn't believe his luck.

Indeed, Tella had a hard time tearing her eyes away. But when the Duke and Duchess approached, she managed. The slight rustle of the Duchess' skirts reminded Tella to curtsey.

"Your Grace. How kind you are to host our wedding and breakfast. Far better friends than I—than *we*—deserve." She *was* incredibly grateful. Their kindness meant that she'd had little hand in planning this affair. Which was fortunate, as Julia had been away on her wedding trip for what had seemed like ages.

"Lady Donnatella! Our friendship was inevitable as we keep exchanging favors. I have not forgotten your kindness at my knitting affair, and I hope this is but one of many thanks I shall give you in return." The Duchess smiled. She had a dimple that came and went when she smiled, as did Julia. "It is a favor for me to host a nice wedding. My own was horrific. We must have at least two more good ones, or the place will be cursed. I only wish I had a pineapple ripe enough to make a gift."

Tella grasped the Duchess' hand for a moment. It was small, but strong. "Surely friends made in dire circumstances in a ladies' lounge are the firmest sort of friends."

At the reference to *that* night, the Duke's hand went round his wife's waist. Tella was glad she'd been right about him. Even when he didn't seem to talk much.

The Duchess squeezed her hand and drew her in close to say, "Bruises heal quickly, and you have saved my pride from much worse damage."

"Though your attacker was finally disposed of with no help from me."

The Duchess only said, "An affair that had nothing to do with you, as I said. You mustn't feel responsible for every misdeed in London."

Tella did; in fact, she needed to expand her territory. "Then, Your Grace, I wonder if you might be willing to take a walk with me?"

"It would be delightfully irregular. We mustn't host *boring* weddings. Your Grace, will you introduce Mr. Fitzwilliam to the Bishop?"

The Duke made a short noise of agreement, and Tella half-wanted to stay and watch Fitz try to get the Duke to answer questions.

But the Duchess released Tella's hand to take her arm. A footman handed her a long walking stick. "The Queen Anne's garden is lovely, empty, and short enough that you can see if anyone is close enough to hear." She smiled that little smile again. "That should suit you, wouldn't it, Lady Donnatella?"

* * *

"My husband deplores our current system of justice," the Duchess said as the two of them strolled through the hedges in strict shapes. "Rank determines what one can do, as well as money."

Tella had given her an outline of a problem beyond her experience: what could they do about Lady Winpole?

The Duchess' questions, as Tella told her more and more details, had a sense of fascinated restraint. She *did* suit Tella, who wished to develop new habits of talking to her friends, but not *too* much. The outline of what had occurred was enough, minus any details about caped counts, kissing, or closets. In fact, anything that might paint Tella in too unflattering a light.

Tella felt that they were running out of time. "Lady Winpole hasn't much precedence among British peers. But she may have quite a bit of money. She needs only one friend like Mr. Storey to spirit her away from Britain if I cannot hold her tight."

The Duchess was using her walking stick to feel the edge of the walkway before she moved. It was a slow amble, but that was fine. Tella wanted five more minutes to feel like herself before she returned to the party. Parties in her honor were generally the worst.

Though this one got her Fitz, which was by far the most she had ever won at a party before.

The Duchess was as frank as ever. "If we are to accuse her of crimes, we must have evidence too strong to ignore. The House of Lords prefers to acquit anyone of title simply on principle." She tapped her walking stick. "Not *my* principle."

"She is very clever, Your Grace. It pains me to say, but more clever than I am."

"Oh, never say so! And you have a better type of cleverness, the type that enrolls allies. Like me. You can call me Selene, you know, as my other friends do."

The noise Tella made was somewhere between agreement

and a grunt of surprise. Making new friends was suspiciously easy.

She must find a way to introduce the Duchess to Ellen the butter maid. And Glory and Ruth and Dan. And Meg.

Maybe not Meg.

"I can imagine several ways to find out what we need to know." The Duchess was rubbing her thumb over her fingers, her hand bunched in the crook of Tella's elbow. "But it will take time. And money. And fortitude."

"I have money and fortitude. I'm not good at waiting."

"None of us are, surely." The Duchess shrugged one shoulder in her exquisitely embroidered gown. "It is a skill that one can practice, like any other."

Tella had to grit her teeth to keep from growling. "But what of that timber? She may sell it at any moment."

The Duchess seemed unconcerned. "You have no idea how much one well-placed letter may accomplish."

"Actually, I do."

"So then. You could solve that today. The larger puzzle of justice for Lady Winpole needs a larger solution. It may take time to discover."

Tella must have made some sort of noise aloud, for the Duchess laughed and bumped her with a shoulder. "We will make good allies, you and I. For you don't much care for longer games, do you? Whereas I adore them."

"As does Lady Winpole." That Tella had to admit.

"Exactly. And you will see, time will fly." Then, playfully, "Tella! Should I not return you to your husband?"

Rather than discuss how delightful Tella found that word, Tella said, "You are married, what, a month now? Two? I expect you will want to give me newlywed advice?"

"If you'd like. I doubt you'll need it. Come out to one of the evenings we host; bring your husband. You play cards, do you not?"

* * *

"Mr. Wharton!"

The Secretary to the Treasury was not accustomed to being interrupted at breakfast.

Nor was he accustomed to foreign gentlemen barging into his breakfast room, but here was the Swedish ambassador doing exactly that.

"Mr. Sahlgren. I won't ask you to sit; surely we can discuss whatever the problem is at a more convenient time." Mr. Wharton wanted his smoked kippers.

The gentleman, however, did not go. "Mr. Wharton, I have a letter here that demands immediate action. Your action."

"Nothing demands action at my breakfast table, sir."

"Not an illegal shipment of American timber that is about to be sold in London itself?"

Mr. Wharton's mouth closed.

The Swedish ambassador tossed a scrap of paper on the table. Mr. Wharton had to put down his fork to pick up the paper.

He frowned. "This looks mad. Every few letters written by a different hand? Who would go to this effort?"

"*That* is your answer? What about its *contents*? Sweden will bring consequences upon Britain if our treaty is not honored!"

"Of course, sir. Sweden is a valued ally in the war against the French Empire, you know that." Inwardly, Mr. Wharton bid his kipper a sad goodbye. "I can assure you that I will get to the bottom of this."

"I will require additional assurances, sir, that this sale does not happen, and won't happen in future!"

"As will I," said Mr. Wharton in perfect sincerity.

* * *

Dan Fox was deep into a column of numbers when a voice behind him rasped, "Whose ledgers do you keep?"

He slammed the book shut and picked it up in one motion, brandishing it before him like a weapon.

Oh.

Dan started to put the book down, then thought better of it. He did this two more times before he said, "Should I be frightened or not?"

The Caped Count just grinned. "Have you done something wrong?"

"Everyone's done *something* wrong."

"Fair point." He tilted his head, as always in his tricorn hat, towards the scuffed door of Dan's bare little room. "How do you feel about a drink?"

"I think that Fitzwilliam fellow owes me one."

The Caped Count pointed a finger at Dan. "It's funny that's the man who comes to mind."

* * *

Fitz was waiting at the bottom of the stairs, feet planted, arms folded across his chest.

"I don't have anything more on your brothers." More and more, Dan felt that he was walking into some sort of trap, and he didn't like it. Oh, the Caped Count was a decent fellow, and Dan was glad Fitz wasn't dead. But that didn't mean he was available for more invasions of London houses.

"My brothers must wait, Mr. Fox," said Fitz, sweeping an arm down the street. "The Bottle and Bird should have room for us, and our colleague here can explain how we think you might help us foil a villain."

The Caped Count's head tilted a bit up toward Fitz, and

though Dan couldn't see it, something about his look put a funny little smile on Fitz' face. "Well," said Fitz, without looking at Dan, "I'll likely do most of the talking."

* * *

*W*ANT MORE *of Tella and Fitz? Sign up for my newsletter now and receive a Bonus Scene of their honeymoon trip, free!*

*T*HE *D*UCHESS OF *T*ALBOURNE *has her own love story in* What a Duchess Does, *where you will see that party from quite a different point of view.*

*A*ND STAY TUNED *as Dan Fox takes up pursuit of our villains in* The Clandestine Countess. *No one but Fitz could convince Dan to look up the girl he left behind...*

Just a few steps through the courtyard and she'd be back among the players, hot and laughing. Scattering for the rest of the night.

But the second she opened the door, she froze.

Blue lightning in the sky did nothing to illuminate the dark shape in front of her. His hand reached toward her.

No thought. Only reaction.

With the tiny, focused strength of a *ballerina* she grabbed that hand and pulled it closer to pinch in a very particular place above the elbow.

When it bent with inescapable pain, she lifted it backwards and drove a hard knuckle, just as precisely aimed, into the pit below his arm; then as he fell back, once more, over his liver.

It was all so quick and smooth that an observer might have thought the shadowy man had simply groaned and collapsed at her feet. If anything, she might have appeared to help him down amidst terrible pain.

He *was* in pain. Now. For her touches were terribly painful.

"Hello, Bess," he managed to say, with an all-too-familiar, teeth-gritting acceptance of pain. Rolled on the flagstones at her feet till she could see his face.

It was the face she'd been missing. Every happy memory she had, and all her saddest ones, were cut through with shadows of that face.

Tears, hot blood, *something* flooded through her, remnants of all the times in five years she'd turned to tell him something, and he wasn't there.

He'd been alive all this time? While she'd wondered night after night where he'd gone, what she'd done? Wondered what could possibly have taken him away from her side when he'd been there every single moment of her life?

How could he have been gone so long and still be whole, alive, here, now, simply appearing at her theater door?

She'd kill him herself.

No performances for Dan. He'd get the real Bess, the one he'd made. The one underneath all the bits and pieces from which she built her performances. The one that was pure ice.

"Dan," said Bess. "Whatever it is, I don't care."

* * *

Follow Dan and Bess as they join the fight against the evil Lady Winpole in The Clandestine Countess*!*

AFTERWORD

My readers have come to expect an author's note giving them some of the research that went into the book, and I have much to say about prisoners of war, smoke bombs, and matches.

But first, a word about words.

Many everyday words were "invented" long after 1813, especially in the explosion of slang that happened in English between about 1880 and the 1930s. We sometimes think of those words as "archaic" but they are far too new for this time period.

"People of color," however, has a long history in English, especially in the United States, where I'm from, and which has always been deeply invested in enforcing divisions of race. I shared some of my research on this term on social media, so I won't reproduce it all here, but suffice to say it dates at least to 1803 in the United States, and I feel perfectly justified in using it in a book set in London in 1813; all the more so because my readers will be familiar with it.

Researcher Abigail Coppins has been uncovering the history of 2,000 Black prisoners of war (and 99 women and children) from the French Caribbean, who were incarcerated in Great Britain, in Portchester Castle, in 1796. Eventually they were just released, without support, in the country they had been fighting, and in which slavery was still legal. Curious readers will be interested in Mark Brown's article "Hidden story of 2,000 African-Caribbean PoWs in a medieval castle" in *The Guardian* on July 18, 2017.

In fact, I did not know prior to writing this book that Napoleon invented the method of keeping prisoners of war, so that the soldiers would not return to fight his soldiers again. Gavin Daly's "Napoleon's Lost Legions: French Prisoners of War in Britain, 1803–1814", in *History*, Vol. 89, No. 3 (295) in July 2004 (pp. 361-380) educated me, and has inspired a few more story ideas for me. (Alert readers may have noticed a mention of this in book 4 of my Lords and Undefeated Ladies series, *Crown of Hearts*.)

(And speaking of things that might seem ahistorical: we associate gas lamps with the Victorian streets of London, and rightly so. But everything has a beginning, and their invention in the 18th century is a series of widely agreed-upon dates reported by many different sources. A full London street, Pall Mall, was lit by gas lamps in June of 1807 to celebrate the King's birthday; and Parliament granted the charter for the London and Westminster Gas Light and Coke Company in 1812.)

The more I research the Regency period, the more I am fascinated at the explosion of creativity in this wartime period, born either of necessity or from the international sharing of knowledge that flourished before the wars cut off so much conversation. Aeronauts! Bicycles! (Appearing in future books!) And Huntsman steel, which is very real—a hardened steel, excellent, one might say, for a one-piece throwing knife with no handle. Huntsman steel may have been the finest in the world, and the company that made it had nowhere to sell it because of the world wars in which Britain was enmeshed at the time. So it was. Tella, of course, must have the finest.

The rope industry, on the other hand, flourished in a world that constantly needed to supply ships, and Tella's favorite sinew rope was definitely made in the United Kingdom at the time too.

I also shared on social media my fascination with the whole industry of producing porcelain marbles at the time, before they were supplanted by easy-to-make glass. One could certainly buy them in beautiful painted colors; but Tella, of course, needs the unglazed kind that reflect less light.

I particularly enjoyed following the history of matches. Tella very obviously needs matches. (Who doesn't?) Strike matches were invented in 1843, the Internet says, but how did people create fire before then?

In a number of fascinating ways, including matches that ignite not from friction, but from chemical action. A fellow named Jean Chancel created just such matches in 1805, using bits of wood with a gum paste on the end mixed with sugar and potassium chlorate. (Sugar is surprisingly flammable—it's also in the smoke bombs!) This match was lit by dipping it in sulfuric acid, and I'm amazed Tella hasn't had more injuries carrying such things around in her cape. Of course, we don't know the provenance of all her scars.

While I in no way endorse putting it to any practical use, I did find the book *Explosives* published in 1919 and written by E. de Barry Barnett and Samuel Rideal very detailed in their explanation of the Chancel matches.

And though chemistry was not a major interest of mine in school, I was riveted by the story of Edward Charles Howard, a late 18th century chemist who discovered many different salts in a planned, methodical investigation of such materials, including the highly explosive fulminates like silver fulminate which, as it turns out, is used in those little paper-twist toys filled with sand that I used to get as a child and throw on the ground to make little explosions. Irresistible. Tella got some of those too.

I might have been more interested in chemistry as a kid had my chemistry teacher demonstrated how easy it is to make smoke bombs. But then again, I can see why they didn't. Smoke bombs are easy to make today and would have been easy to make then, of moldable paste with long fuses. My primary worry was whether or not the chemicals to make the smoke green would have been available at the time. They were! Happiness.

All this research of course led me to the question of where Tella gets these marvelous devices, and I very much hope to tell the story of her chemist one day. Though Tella lives quite near Parliament (Claremont Square is fictional and in no way resembles St. James's Square), her chemist lives far outside London, as you can well imagine, where the odd explosion wouldn't be noticed.

No, it is more important that we pursue Lady Winpole and the dastardly accountant Mr. Storey, and for that, we have *The Clandestine Countess* coming up. I hope to see you then!

ACKNOWLEDGMENTS

An enormous thank you to Susannah Erwin, whose input made this book better (and made me smarter).

Always thank you to my baby brother Dave (Daaaave!), *professeur de jiu jitsu* and fight coordinator to the stars. All the good ideas in fight scenes are his and any blemishes are on me.

Thank you to Anne who read the first draft and told me my eyes were limpid pools, and Karl who inspired me to buckle down and finish it largely on schedule.

A huge shout-out to Laura Givens, who did a *beautiful* and exciting original cover for my Caped Countess; and to Barbara at Forever After Romance Designs for her creative and exciting redesign.

Thank you to every reader of the Lords and Undefeated Ladies series who said "Sure, I'd read action/adventure Regency from you!"

And first, foremost, and always, my beloved. When I told him, "I have this new idea for a book and a whole new series," he's the one who said "Write it!" Thank you, my love.

ABOUT THE AUTHOR

Judith Lynne writes rule-breaking romances with love around every corner. Her characters tend to have deep convictions, electric pleasures, and, sometimes, weaponry.

She loves to write stories where characters are shaken by life, shaken down to their core, put out their hand…and love is there.

A history nerd with too many degrees, Judith Lynne lives in that other paradise, Ohio, with a truly adorable spouse, an apartment-sized domestic jungle, and a misgendered turtle. A past writer of SF and screenplays, she pens Regency romances of love you can believe in, with a rich sense of place and time.

If you enjoyed this book, help keep them coming - share a review at your favorite bookstore, Bookbub, or Goodreads!

Sign up for the author's newsletter, including exclusive book news and sneak peeks, at judithlynne.com.

ALSO BY JUDITH LYNNE

Lords and Undefeated Ladies

Not Like a Lady

The Countess Invention

What a Duchess Does

Crown of Hearts

He Stole the Lady

No Titled Lady *Series prequel*

Maids Done Waiting

The Lord Trap

The Lady Escape *Forthcoming*

Cloaks and Countesses

The Caped Countess

The Clandestine Countess

The Castaway Countess *Forthcoming*

Ladies' Own Bakery

Ladies' Own Bakery Season One: The Collected Episodes

Ladies' Own Bakery Season Two: The Collected Episodes